CONTENTS

Kerri Mountain grew up surrounded by books and storytellers, writing stories of her own since elementary school. But she never thought of writing books until searching for a degree in children's literature. What she found instead was a master's degree program in writing popular fiction. With strong support of family and faculty, she learned to develop the seed of a story into a novel.

Kerri lives in rural western Pennsylvania with her parents on their small family farm, but enjoys traveling at every opportunity. She especially enjoys the mountains of Wyoming and visiting the national parks. She is blessed by the quiet lifestyle of country living, and by spending time spoiling her nieces and nephews on a regular basis.

Books by Kerri Mountain

Love Inspired Historical

The Parson's Christmas Gift
Wyoming Promises

THE PARSON'S CHRISTMAS GIFT

Kerri Mountain

This is what the Lord says:
Stand at the crossroads and look, ask for the
ancient paths, ask where the good way is,
and walk in it, and you will find rest for your souls.
—*Jeremiah 6:16*

To Mom and Dad—there aren't enough words to say thanks for all the love and support you've given in any adventure God allows. Love you both!

And a big thank-you to all the critique partners, mentors, friends and family who have helped develop and improve this story far beyond anything I might have imagined it could be. I praise God for putting each of you in my path at just the right time.

Chapter One

She'd pay ten dollars for a hot bath if she had it.

Journey wiped the grit from her eyes and slid from her horse. She felt as if she'd been born in the saddle—and spent all of her twenty years there.

She checked her saddlebags. Eight dollars and some hairpins.

She scanned the town as it started to wake. Slowly the sun stretched over buildings, quiet and fresh as the barren peaks surrounding the settlement. Nothing like Savannah, still fighting to recover from the destruction of the War Between the States some five years past. Nothing like Independence, always bustling with folks coming from and going to parts unknown.

"It looks like we may be in luck, Gypsy," she whispered to her horse.

The shop she was looking for sat near the end of the street—one with a plain, honest front, a quaint little porch and a worn sign proclaiming General Store in faded blue letters. Underneath, smaller letters spelled out a wide variety of items.

Journey slipped along the shadowed side of the building and pulled a small silver mirror from her satchel. Dust muted the freckles over her round cheeks, and she debated as to which was the worse. Her skin had darkened over the miles, despite the broad-brimmed hat she wore. But no amount of color hid the exhaustion from her dark brown eyes. Pulling the hat from her head, she ran strong fingers through the curls that coiled around each other until she could feel the tangles before she touched them. She remembered the brilliant red of her mother's silky waves and wondered what had happened that it had translated to her as a dingy auburn, uncontrollable mass.

She tugged none too gently at her tight locks and poked hairpins in strategically. "If they catch me talking to you, Gyp, I guess it won't matter how civilized I look." She tugged the horse toward the front of the store.

Her dress barely showed its original flowered print and she didn't know how much shorter she could cut her petticoats to reinforce the material. But she brushed the dust off as best she could and looped the horse's reins around a post. With a deep breath she pulled on her shapeless hat and mounted the steps to the open door.

A cloud of grime swept over her worn skirt.

"Sorry, ma'am! I didn't see you there."

She drew her lips up in a gracious smile. So much for looking civilized.

The man stopped sweeping and leaned against the broom, nodding her through the doorway on his way out. "My wife'll be with you in a little bit, ma'am. Take a look around." Journey watched a grin peek from below his full mustache.

Whitened walls gave the store an open feel, much as the landscape did for the little town. An inviting stove glowed in the center near the back. Canned peaches, harness fittings and an odd conglomeration of pans and kettles rested on shelves and pegs behind the counters on either side. Barrels marked Flour and Sugar sat in front.

She tried not to notice the curious stares following her as she browsed her way along the bolts of yard goods, but still started when a young woman asked her, "Anything I can help you with?"

Pulling a bolt of navy broadcloth from the wall, she responded with a flash of smile, determined to be calm. "I'd like a dress length of this, please." It would cut into her meager funds, but a purchase always made an impression when she needed information. She'd need a new dress before winter anyway. Tattered hems made only wrong impressions.

She stepped toward the counter. Though she'd always been short of stature, the shopkeeper's wife dwarfed her by a good eight or nine inches. The woman must've been about her own age, judging from the smooth skin and bright green eyes. Honey-blond hair hung in a low tail down her back.

"I haven't seen you around here before," the lady said as she measured the cloth. Journey nodded when the woman glanced up. "I'm Abigail Norwood—Abby to most. Have you met my husband, Sam?"

"Yes, she did, I'm afraid," the low voice called from the porch. He wedged through the door and made a show of putting the broom in its corner space. "I gave her a right unfriendly greeting, though."

The woman shook her head in mock despair. "The one time I get him to sweep up in here." A sheepish grin drew across her lips. "Anyway, it's always nice to see a new face in town."

"Thanks," Journey said. She hoped her smile didn't waver.

"You visiting family?"

She shook her head, making a show of fumbling with the latches on her saddlebag.

"Just passing through, then?"

Sam Norwood stepped back into the room from what Journey guessed was a storage area. He smiled under his thick mustache again, and his eyes twinkled at his wife. "You'll have to forgive her," he said. "She has a soft spot for the curious cat."

A blush lit Abby's cheeks. "I didn't mean to pry. I just like to meet new folks. My apologies if I've overstepped, Miss…?"

"Smith…Journey Smith. Actually, someone with a little curiosity could be exactly the person to help me." She breathed deeply, gathering any poise and confidence she could muster. "I wondered if you know where I might find work around here."

"So you're planning on staying? Most folks pass through on their way to Virginia City. What type of work are you looking for?"

"I've done a little bit of a lot of things. Tended children, waited tables—"

"Ever done housekeeping?"

"My own."

Journey stood steadily under Abby's gaze. She

thought if she held her breath she could probably hear the gears whirring in the woman's brain.

Abby turned to her husband then, looking down slightly to meet his eyes. "What about Miss Rose? She's been hoping to find someone to help out around her house. I'm not sure what arrangements she's thinking on, but I could take you out there if you're interested."

"I'm not sure how long I'll be in town. I was thinking—"

"Nonsense. Miss Rose is a fine woman. Once you meet her, you'll never want to leave."

"It's not that…" Journey stammered.

Abby looked up from where she was cutting the thick cloth. "At least speak with her. You never know how well things might work out."

Journey searched for an inoffensive excuse. "I don't want to be a bother. If you'll direct me to her house, I'd—"

"It's no bother at all. She lives on a ranch outside of town. Let me get my things and I'll take you there," Abby said, tying a string around the fabric Journey had purchased. "If you like, you can leave your trunks inside until you return."

Fear fluttered like a moth in her throat. "I'm traveling rather light. All I have is my horse tied out front. I'm certain I could find the place on my own."

As Abby patted the package and pulled her coat from a nearby hook, Journey caught her questioning glance but noticed it didn't stop her motion. "It'd be easier to show you. Sam knows I need to get out on days like this, anyway. He can handle the store for a few hours until we get back. I haven't had a chance to visit Miss Rose in a while myself. We'll take some sandwiches and have a nice little picnic. It'll give you a chance to get to know her."

"You can tether your horse around back, if that'll suit," Sam offered. "My wife's a natural guide, born and raised right here in Walten. Montana grows them pretty, that's for sure."

Journey forced her arms and legs to relax. There seemed no way around it, short of racing out the front door and galloping away on Gypsy. "If you're sure."

Sam moved back toward the storage room. "I'll hitch up the team. Oh, and, Miss Smith—"

"Please, call me Journey."

A dimple joined the grin on Sam's face. "Journey, if things don't work out with Miss Rose, come back here. We can't offer much more than a cot, but we might be able to find some work for you."

She nodded once, turning her head in time to catch the knowing smile Abby directed his way. Journey wrinkled her brow, wondering what these people expected from her.

"Thanks. I'll just go and tie my horse around back."

"Wait! Take your cloth—on the house." Abby thrust the neat package her way.

"I don't need charity." Well, that wasn't exactly true.

But she heard the insistence in Abby's voice. "Not charity. I guess Sam owes you for the mess he swept over you. We can't be treating our customers that way or we won't have them long."

She studied Abby. She seemed sincere enough, and she had made a point of not noticing the tattered seams in her dress. "I appreciate your kindness," Journey said, looking away as she slid the wrapped cloth into her satchel.

"I'll meet you around back," Abby said.

Journey nodded. Their kindness overwhelmed her a little. Maybe Hank's training had become more ingrained than she thought. They were just the type of people he had always sought—helpful and unsuspecting. Fortunately for them, she'd rid the world of at least one of his kind.

Journey slid farther into the corner of the narrow wagon seat. Abby had peppered her with a dozen questions before they'd even left sight of town. The sparse grass crackled under the wagon wheel, and she considered her odds of surviving a leap of escape.

"How far to the ranch?"

Abby paused. "Oh, probably three or four miles. Did you live—"

"It's easy to get caught up in the scenery here," Journey said.

"It is beautiful. Some folks complain about it being drab, with all the browns. They don't pay attention to the shades of the mountains in the light, or the pockets of sage tucked in everywhere. I've never wanted to live anywhere else. But listen to me jabber about myself. Where'd you hail from?"

"Back East."

"Yes, of course. I suppose most folks around here do, what with all the families settling in the area. What part?" Abby turned a smile her way.

Most folks took the hint when she answered in such an obviously vague way. "Well, I…I traveled quite a bit before coming here."

"I've never been out of Montana," Abby said. "But my pa's family came once to visit…"

Journey's attention wavered as she tried to ease her pounding heart. She considered making up something but hesitated. Lies had cost her plenty in the past. Weren't lies part of the reason she found herself here now? Hopefully the woman would lose interest.

"I'll bet you have a lot of stories about your trip west," Abby said.

"I suppose I'm one of those who'd rather hear the stories of other folks," Journey countered. She eased her lips into a smile, but it didn't come so easily to her eyes.

"Then Montana's the place for you. Plenty of storytellers around, waiting for a willing ear."

Journey nodded. She'd met grandmothers who adored their grandbabies less than this woman adored her home.

Tension quivered down her limbs. How could she end this line of conversation? "You—y'all do seem real friendly. I do appreciate your kindness."

Abby's thin fingers tapped her knee. "Oh, let me guess—you're from the South, right? Maybe somewhere in Georgia? My aunt Beth lives there. I remember when I was little and she came to visit us. She had the most delightful accent. I just recognized a little of it there in your voice. Am I right?"

"I, ah, I am from the…from the South, but—"

"You'll have to describe it all for me sometime. I always hoped to go back and visit my pa's family, see where he grew up. He and my ma moved back last fall, so to hear about it would make them feel a little closer."

The wagon lurched to the right and climbed steeply, bringing a large two-story ranch house into view. Journey breathed in the dry air, glad for the break in Abby's too-friendly curiosity. She had to stay alert. If something so minute as a tint in her voice could connect her back to Georgia, she wouldn't be safe even through Christmas.

She examined the ranch. A sturdy barn with an empty corral faced the broad porch of the home, with about thirty yards of grass-pocked dust between. The bluff they'd crossed boxed around one edge of the property, but the view beyond scooped across the wide valley. Sage and scrub brush were the only thriving plants she could see across the landscape. The property was secluded from the casual traveler but not closed off.

A pounding hammer echoed and drew her attention to a broad-shouldered figure on the roof.

"That's Zane—Reverend Thompson. He'd said he was going to see about patching some leaks for Miss Rose," Abby said. "The last time Zane visited, it rained, and he said he had to move three times when water started dripping down his back. Each time Miss Rose just pulled out another pot to catch it."

Journey knew what it was like to have to make do with what you had. She watched the man kneeling along the roof, sleeves rolled back over deeply tanned arms, shirt clinging between his shoulder blades despite the cool day. His dark brown hair glistened in the midmorning sun.

"You know him well?" She licked her dry lips.

"Oh, Zane and Sam grew up together. Their families came west together. I knew Zane long before he became our pastor. They say a prophet isn't honored in his hometown, but somehow Zane has made it work. He's a wonderful pastor, a true man of God. And of course those gray eyes of his don't hurt him, either." Abby patted her knee with a light laugh. "You'll get to hear him tomorrow." Journey forced another smile.

Tomorrow? She'd be long gone by then. She didn't need any pastor to make her see her guilt. She knew it well enough already.

"Journey? Is everything all right?"

She nodded, swallowing hard. Everything would be perfect—just as soon as Walten and all of its fine and overly welcoming citizens were miles of trail dust behind her.

Chapter Two

Everything moved so fast—too fast. Abby's chattering wearied her. She couldn't keep up. Journey rubbed her aching temples.

The wagon rolled to a stop beside the porch. "Hello, the house!" Abby called, climbing down over the wheel. Journey did the same and stood close to it.

"Thought I heard a wagon," a deep baritone answered. Reverend Thompson.

She watched Abby dig a sandwich out of the picnic basket and hand it to him as he stepped down the ladder and drank a dipper full of water. "We've come to share a lunch with Miss Rose."

"And this is?"

Journey felt his gaze as he unwrapped his sandwich. With a deep breath to steady her shaking, she tilted her head up to introduce herself. "Journey. Journey Smith."

"Now there's an unusual name. Pleased to meet you, ma'am. I imagine Abby's introduced me already." She stared at the hand he held out for a moment before shaking it. He smiled, crinkling his eyes at the corners and revealing a wide row of straight teeth and a cleft in his cheek. A shock of dark brown hair ruffled off his forehead, and a small thatch tufted at the back, making him look more like an unruly schoolboy than a minister. His square jaw proved more convincing, though his lips curved into a smile that seemed etched onto his face and had a depth she doubted lessened in many circumstances. "I'm Reverend Thompson to most folks, plain Zane to Abby. What brings you all this way?"

"Journey's new to the area, looking to settle in for a while. I thought maybe we could work something out with Miss Rose. She's been talking about hiring some help around here."

"That so?" Zane bit into the sandwich and nodded once slowly as he chewed, as if considering the idea. He swallowed. "Could work fine for you both. Miss Rose is inside. I'm sure she'll be glad to talk with you."

He gazed directly at her, his gray eyes alight in the sun. "So how'd you come by a name like that?"

Breath caught in her throat, choking her. One of the few questions Abby hadn't thought to ask.

"It's a family name."

His eyebrow tilted in a question, one she couldn't read. "Well, that's nice," he said. "I— We'll look forward to having you in our town."

Had they all assumed she'd decided? She wasn't staying here. She couldn't. She scanned the landscape again. Could she?

The young pastor continued. Before she could force a sound from her dry throat, his attention spread to both of them. "I expect we'll see you tomorrow at church. Hope everything works out for you, Miss Smith."

"Reverend Thompson."

"Please, feel free to call me Zane," he said, seeming not to notice her wavering voice. He grinned, glancing up to the roof. Sunshine burnished the planes of his face a deep bronze. "If you'll excuse me, ladies, I have a few more boards to replace. I'll leave you to your visit. Thanks, Abby," he added, waving the sandwich. He snatched another bite as he headed up the ladder.

Journey watched him climb to the roof before following Abby.

An elderly woman with white-gray hair opened the door before they could knock. Her round blue eyes lit with a warm smile for Abby, and with a question for Journey.

"Who do we have here? Come on in, and bring your friend. My, but I haven't seen you in a spell," she said. "What's brought you ladies out today? Come in, come in."

Warm sunlight streamed in two wide windows on either side of the far wall, making the room bright and airy with a view of the distant mountains. A few delicate vases sat on shelves below them. Two daguerreotypes stood on a high shelf, shrouded with a layer of fine dust. Otherwise the room held little adornment beyond the ornate couch and a simple wooden rocker.

The fireplace in the middle of the house glowed with faint embers. On either side, a doorway opened. One led to the kitchen and Journey guessed the other led to Miss Rose's bedroom. Simple in design and decoration, it was so unlike the garish and cluttered rooms she'd lived in up until now. She liked it, quiet and unobtrusive.

They followed the tiny figure into the kitchen. Freshly baked bread steamed through cloths on the sideboard. The scent filled the room to the farthest corners.

"I was about to slice some bread for lunch," the woman said. Journey noted her slow, sure step and the steady voice.

Abby rested the basket she carried on the table. "Then we're just in time, Miss Rose. I've brought some chicken sandwiches for all of us. Zane already took one, and there's plenty more."

Miss Rose sat, then slid out a chair and nodded Journey into it. "I'm assuming your friend has a name you just haven't got around to sharing."

Abby's light laugh held none of the nervousness Journey felt. "This is Miss Smith. She wandered into town this morning, looking for work and a warm roof to sleep under. Journey, this is Mrs. Rose Bishop."

Journey forced her hand forward in greeting. Something about the woman reminded her of the ladies who would pass by the saloon on Sundays, all fine and proper. Except that this woman seemed to possess a kindness, a fairness—confidence born of something more than money and position. She tried to hold her fingers and voice steady. "Pleased to meet you, Mrs. Bishop. Please, call me Journey."

"Only if you'll call me Miss Rose," she said, getting up to set a kettle to heat. "Everybody does. Make yourselves at home, and I'll get the settings."

It seemed Mrs. Bishop—Miss Rose—could well handle the affairs of her own home. It didn't appear as if much needed to be done on the grounds that Miss Rose couldn't find a nearby rancher to lend a hand. She moved slowly but with a fairly steady step. While the house wasn't spotless, it wasn't unlivable, either. What would she want with hired help?

But Journey needed to find a more stationary hideout, and after months on the trail, eyeing every shadow, she was tired. The warmth and comfortable feeling this house offered could seep right in. She'd be inclined to let it.

She couldn't afford to let it.

Abby sat down across from her and placed sandwiches on the three plates Miss Rose brought out. Journey clasped her hands together, squeezing one thumb. Her knee bobbed as her mind raced to come up with a way to bring this meeting to a close before she agreed to something. She wanted to stay. She wanted to think she could belong in such a home. But where had her instincts taken her in the past? She was no longer fit for these fine people.

Miss Rose smiled, skin pulled paper-thin over her round cheeks. She seemed about to say something when Zane's hammer interrupted. Journey caught her motion to take a plate and pass a cloth-wrapped sandwich her way. Then the ladies bowed their heads without a word while she twitched in her seat.

"So you'd be willing to help out an old lady like me?" Miss Rose said when the pounding stopped. "You might find I'm too ornery for your liking."

"I'm not the easiest person to live with, either, ma'am." Hank had shown her that often enough. "I wouldn't want to obligate you."

"Nonsense. I've been looking for someone to move out here and help me some. My old bones can't go like they used to. I've been praying the Lord would send just the right person. To be honest, I'm looking for the company as much as the help."

Journey nodded and drew her eyebrows together. "You really think I could do that?"

From the corner of her eye, she saw Abby's own furrowed brow.

"Now that's hard to tell from this side of it," Miss Rose said. "Can you clean? Wipe windows?"

"Yes."

"Muck out a few stalls?"

"Sure."

"And you're in need of a place to stay?"

"Yes, ma'am."

"Well, then it seems like we're in a position to help each other. I can't believe it's a coincidence that you'd wander into town, into Abby and Sam's store, when here I am looking for someone like you."

"Like me, ma'am?"

Miss Rose looked her over, and Journey sensed the woman knew there was something more than met the eye. "Yes," she said. "Someone just like you."

"What about the preacher? He seems handy enough." Why argue the matter? She couldn't stay. She couldn't.

"Pastor Zane's been helpful to a lot of folks around here. He considers it part of his ministry. But he has plenty ministry beyond playing ranch hand. I found myself expecting it of him, and that's wrong. So I told God He'd have to send someone else along, so I could let Zane focus on more important things."

"You don't even know me." The steadiness of her voice surprised her. "I could only be looking for a handout from you."

A dignified sniff from the woman punctuated the air. "You might find you've gotten the harder end of the bargain. I'm set in my ways and terrible stubborn about some things. My Lord's had many a year to help me improve, and I still struggle with it—" she interrupted with a grin "—so that tells you what I was like at your age. I'll be after you to do some things both here in the house and around the property, but something tells me you're heartier than you look. Pay's not much—maybe a dollar a month, plus room and board, and of course, Sundays off. I'm figuring we could both win on this gamble, if you're willing."

Journey nodded. There was no way this could work. Who was she to involve this woman—this community—in her mess? The pounding on the roof matched the pounding in her head.

"So what do you say?" Abby's voice rose over the din.

Journey's muscles grew stiff. She needed to think. What would it matter if she darted for the door and never looked back? She waited for the hammering to stop.

"I appreciate your kind offer, Miss Rose, but I can't—"

The ring of the hammer interrupted again. It stopped, breaking the rhythm they'd grown accustomed to with a rough scrape. A heavy thud punctuated the instant of silence. For a moment, all three of them sat stock-still. Journey's heart leaped and she grasped the edge of the table, ready to push herself up and away.

"Zane…" Abby voiced Journey's own thought. They jumped from their seats as one.

"Go!" Miss Rose said, her voice calm and firm. "Make sure he's not hurt."

Journey thought that her very tone insisted that he was fine. Somehow that tone was comforting in itself.

But that thought didn't keep her from flying out of the house, close at Abby's heels, wondering why it should matter to her.

Chapter Three

Journey turned the far corner of the house to see Zane struggle to his elbows. His gray eyes searched the skies above, unfocused. She watched as Abby knelt at his side, and followed her glance to the old woman. Miss Rose stood with a white-knuckled grip on the corner porch post, peering over the edge.

"Zane? Zane, are you all right?" Abby grasped his shoulders in both hands, holding him steady.

"What happened?" Journey asked. Zane's head jerked back, focusing his gaze on her. She fumbled for a handkerchief from her pocket and tapped it against Abby's shoulder but couldn't draw her gaze away from his. The woman took it to dab at the wide scrape on his right cheek with the limp cloth.

He blinked several times in his daze, thick lashes fluttering, but a small grin appeared. "Wasn't being careful enough, I suppose. I must have stood too heavy on a loose shingle board."

"If the pupils of his eyes aren't even, he could have hit his head," Journey said. Someone had told her about that once, after a rough bout with Hank.

She looked across the landscape. Even in the months and miles since his death, she couldn't shake the sense that he waited out there. She shivered in the cool mountain air.

A soft groan drew her attention back to the man on the ground as he tucked his feet and stood, taking the handkerchief from Abby. A wince crossed his face when his full weight rested on his ankle. He wobbled a little, but laughed. "Shows how great the wisdom of the Lord is, calling me to preach instead of to become a carpenter."

"Take it easy, there, Zane. Are you sure nothing's broken?" Abby inspected his elbow.

Journey wondered what the congregation might think of their pastor showing up with a nice shiner for Sunday service. He'd no doubt have one.

He pulled the thin cloth from his eye and examined it. "I'm fine, ladies. Really, I rolled right off, nice and gentlelike onto my hammer. Won't look too pretty for a while, but then, I don't reckon any of my parishioners come to see a pretty face."

Journey imagined his handsome face and strong build drew more than his share of coy glances. How could he not know it?

A rattled wheeze sounded behind her. Miss Rose had been forgotten in the excitement. "Well, he's standing and his tongue's working along with his brain same as usual. My goodness, Zane, you might have considered the rest of us. I declare, you took a good six months off my life. Now come inside a bit and rest yourself."

"I'm fine," he insisted, waving the offending hammer toward the roof. "There's only a little more to do before I'm finished. This time I'll pound an extra nail or two in this one." He tapped the fallen shingle with his boot and moved back to the ladder.

"Be careful this time!" Abby smiled at his retreating back.

Journey studied his broad form until he turned, catching her off guard. He shook out the mangled handkerchief to find a clean spot before touching it again to the cut.

"I'll wash this up and return it to you Sunday, ma'am."

"You needn't go to any bother, really."

"I appreciate it all the same, Miss Smith."

She thought to remind him to call her Journey, but then she realized it didn't matter. It would be just as well if he forgot her name altogether. He wouldn't be preaching to her on Sunday. She turned to follow Abby.

"Pardon me, ma'am. You prefer *Journey,* right? A name that pretty, I don't blame you. I'll keep that in mind."

He made her name sound like a complete sentence. But he seemed to look past her, over her. The wind blew his dark hair from his forehead, exposing the length of the hammer's cut.

The faint rustle across the porch drew her attention, reminding her that the others had already returned to the house. She nodded her leave. He smiled again and began pounding.

A job, a place to stay, and nothing more. Lie low for the winter, and be gone with spring thaw. What could be wrong with that? Right now, Walten, Montana, felt a world away from Georgia. Maybe it was.

* * *

"I declare," Miss Rose said, her voice puffing as they stepped into the warmth of the house, "sometimes I think that boy won't be happy till he's knocked his fool head off."

Journey couldn't help but smile at her exasperated tone.

"Anyway, where were we?"

"Maybe Journey would like to see the rest of your place?" Abby suggested.

She flinched, startled at the tug on her sleeve. Before she could protest, Abby drew her across the sitting room to the stairway directly opposite the door. Her brow curled, but thankfully, the woman didn't voice any question. Journey flushed with embarrassment as she followed her up the narrow stairs.

"Well, what do you think?"

Journey peered around. "It's…light," she said. "I've never seen an upstairs so bright."

Instead of being divided into tiny, airless closets, two smaller rooms beckoned with open doors on either side of the hall. Light wooden boards made the rooms appear large and inviting. She walked toward the far end of the hallway, and the space broadened to the width of the house, windows bright with reflected sunlight. The cobwebby corners and dusty floors didn't dim the cheeriness of the room. How could four walls feel so unconfining?

"I haven't been up there in some time." Miss Rose's voice strained to reach them from the bottom step. "You'd be welcome to use the space. We cleared a lot out after my husband passed on."

She felt Abby's hopeful smile on her. "So? What do you say?"

"I think… Well, I just arrived in town, and here I am with a job offer and a roof over my head. It—it's all happened so fast." She glanced around the room and back over her shoulder. "I think I should catch my breath and consider it before I agree to anything. It's all so much kindness."

"It's you who'd be doing the kindness. It's a worry to me, knowing she's alone out here. I know she's lonesome, too. But what with the store and all… Oh, listen to me. You have to do what you feel is best, Journey."

She sounded sincere. Maybe she did want to help them both—Miss Rose and her. But that's not how people worked. A few folks might look out for a dear friend, most would take up a cause for family but no one cared for a stranger. So what did Abby really want? What did any of them want?

"I'll have to take your offer into consideration." She hoped she gave the impression there were other options.

"We've been praying for the right person to come along to help Miss Rose. Then you come along, looking for work." Abby sighed, her hands fluttering. "It's so exciting. Maybe I'll be proven wrong, but the Lord has blessed me with a pretty accurate sense of character. I'd be willing to take the chance. You seem like someone who needs a chance used on you."

Journey stared back, unsure of a response. She forced out a tense breath. "I am obliged for the offer, either way. You've been most kind."

"Will you at least go down and talk with Miss Rose awhile? It can't hurt, right?"

"I suppose not." She hoped not.

Abby stretched her arm toward the stairway. "Let's go, then."

Miss Rose waited in her rocker. Journey noticed she patted her hand over her heart until she saw them.

"Have a seat," she said. "I imagine you have some questions of your own to help you decide whether this would work for you."

Journey sat in the ladder-back chair near the door and tried to keep her breathing even. How could this woman treat her so well? She didn't even know her and yet had offered her so much. What would Miss Rose think if she knew what brought her here?

"It seems you keep the place well enough on your own." She didn't accuse, but she couldn't understand, either.

"I'm not completely feeble yet, but I can't get after this place like I used to. Still, I can't bear to part with what few animals I have left, either."

"You could hire someone from town to clean a few times a week and hire a ranch hand for the animals. Then you wouldn't be bothered with a boarder in your house," Journey said.

Miss Rose's laugh caught her by surprise. "I reckon you're right. It shows you have common sense. But the truth is, I need someone around more than that. It gets too quiet for my liking anymore. But town is too big and busy. I wouldn't be able to hear myself think."

Journey considered that. "I'm not one to chatter much."

Again the laugh. What a shame Mama never laughed like that. "So I've noticed."

Journey found the corners of her mouth curling up

in spite of herself. "Please understand, I can't decide a thing like this before I think it through."

"Take all the time you need, darlin'. It's not like there's a flock of people knocking down my door for the job, Lord knows." Journey felt cool, wrinkled skin pat her hand.

"So when will your nephew be able to visit?" Abby asked. Journey figured the topic must be settled until she decided on her next move.

"Not soon enough for me, but I received a letter from him last week. He's going to try to make it for Thanksgiving, Lord willing."

Journey tightened her grip on the chair. A dollar a month plus board would help her save a little. If she held her purse strings very tightly, she'd be ready to move on by spring with money to get her to Oregon. Or even California. She scanned the warm wooden walls, the solid mantel above the all-but-dead fire. A certainty filled her. Yes. A good, safe home to rest in and regroup. Surely no one would look for her through a Montana winter. She'd be gone with spring thaw. Or, if things worked out well enough, maybe she'd stay on in the spring. Who could find her in a town as small as Walten?

"…some of the cases he works on, I declare. I wish he'd find a safer way to make a living." Miss Rose waved her hand before smacking it down on her knee.

Cases? Her nephew was a lawyer?

"Does he live far from here?" she asked. Her heart skipped a beat.

"Over in Virginia City," Miss Rose said, turning to face her with a smile. "He's a lawman there."

Chapter Four

Zane dismounted without his usual ease. That fall would have him stiff tomorrow but no lasting harm done. With a pat to Malachi's flank, he took off his tack and led him into his stall. After taking care of his mount, he moved to check on the other two horses he kept.

When he had heeded the Lord's call to the ministry, he thought his dreams of owning his own horse ranch were gone. It was a trade he'd been willing to make, but it didn't mean he wouldn't miss it. Sarah had been the one to encourage him to do both.

It hadn't been easy on a pastor's wage to get started, but he and Sarah had both made sacrifices enough to give them a start. He looked around now at the barn with the three horses. Not a grand beginning but room to grow. Without the horses to focus on after the fire and to fill those few hours when he was forced to be alone, he might've lost sight of their dream altogether.

He rubbed his tired eyes, wincing when he nudged the lump on the side of his head. He'd gladly trade it all to be rebuilding his dream with Sarah, rather than continuing it without her.

Zane made his way into the little house he'd built for himself. The Lord had called him to the ministry, and he had believed at one time that Sarah had been the one to be his helpmate in it. But hadn't the Lord shown him otherwise by taking her so soon from him? He'd failed somehow—failed to protect his family when they needed him most.

He rubbed his face and moved his hand back to his neck. He needed to wash up and finalize his sermon notes, then make a visit to the Culpeppers' and see how Agnes was faring with her gout. Then he'd ride upstream a bit and practice his sermon before turning in.

It would be a productive day. It had been a productive week. But it didn't change the fact that he'd come home to an empty house tonight.

Journey gave the ropes a final tug, securing her bedroll to the saddle. The horse sidestepped and pranced. Journey watched the evening sun drip into the horizon behind the peaked hills. She pinched her lips and let go a long breath, then nudged Gypsy toward the west.

Her cheeks ached from holding a tight smile for the better part of the afternoon. It took a firm hold to keep her horse at a walk tonight. They crossed the bridge leading out of town.

"I thanked her for the offer, of course, Gyp." She used low tones to calm the skittish horse. "But there's no way we can stay here. It wouldn't be right to drag her into our mess. Besides, her nephew is the law in Virginia City. We can't risk being caught. I'm not the fool I was when we first left Georgia." Her horse skittered and neighed. "Well, not quite."

Gypsy tossed her black mane and whinnied. "I know. I liked the lady, too. I think we might have gotten a fair shake from her."

She felt guilty taking supper with the Norwoods, but Abby had all but tied her to a chair. Besides, she knew she'd do well to fill up before hitting the trail again. She excused herself before Abby brought out the pie, saying she wanted to explore the town before dark. But the wide, friendly streets and small, boasting businesses didn't attract her as much as the gurgling river and mountain views. They gave her space to breathe. She could appreciate Miss Rose's desire to be away from Walten's streets. There was no way she could stay. But she thought again of Miss Rose's ranch. Was there?

"We'll try the next town," she said. "We can't expect comfortable. Maybe when things have settled down more, we could come back. Everything is too messed up now."

She stroked the horse's brown neck. There was no time to be looking back. She'd had her chance. Stupid, stupid, stupid… Leaving Hank at the start would've been so much smarter. There'd been no reason to stick around after that first slap. There probably hadn't been much of a reason to stick around before it, for that matter.

She shivered, rousing herself back to the moment at hand. With the glow of the sun in the twilight sky being all that remained of the day, the cool of night drew up a breeze. It would be cold sleeping out on the trail tonight. She thought a moment of the airy upper floor of that ranch house. She could picture Miss Rose poking the fire, banking it for the night.

Journey buttoned her coat up to her chin and shifted in the saddle. She'd cut through toward the bluff and camp in the stand of pines there, then keep heading west at first light. Quiet sounds of the night echoed over the bluffs—the hoot of an owl, soft wind from the hills. Her arms and legs lost some of their tenseness. The trail narrowed, but the trees brushing overhead gave the comfort of shelter.

Her eyelids drifted closed until her horse balked, refusing to move on. "A little farther, Gyp, and we'll bed down." She dug her heel into the flank.

But the horse reared back, snapping her fully awake, fingers tensed over the reins. She grabbed the saddle horn before she slid too far. Just as quickly, the forehooves clapped the packed dirt. It jarred the breath from her. The horse raced farther into the trees, heedless of the commands she bellowed. She stretched her arms as far as they'd reach around the horse's neck, muscles pulling as she hung tightly.

She bounced, her vision rattled as she tried to stay mounted and, at the same time, watch the direction the animal was taking.

The horse squealed, then lurched to a stop. Stars, leaves and dirt tangled before her. She felt weightless for an instant, then all of gravity's force came back to her with a crunch. The dimness of sunset faded to dark.

Chapter Five

Zane reined his horse to a stop, breathing hard. "Feels good to stretch the legs, eh, Malachi?" He patted the steamy neck as he dismounted by the stream. Closer to town, the brook broadened and slowed into a river. But here, it still gurgled and bounced over rocks.

He hunched down by the edge and trailed his fingers in the water a moment, then scooped a handful to drink. It ran fresh and cold down his throat, and he smoothed the back of his wet hand over his lips and chin. He'd need to shave before service.

Stretching out on the stubbled grass with his hands clasped behind his head, he stared up at a night sky of the deepest blue, covered with stars high above. Miss Rose would have a piece of his hide if she knew he'd come out without his coat.

For as long as he'd lived here, the beauty of the land had never failed to awe him. "Lord, I thank You for Your hand I see in all creation. It's a comfort to know things are in the order You made them to be." The scent of sage carried on the wind. He traced the swollen lump around his eye with his fingers.

"I pray, Lord, that You'll bless the folks here. Make sure I preach the words You give me to their benefit as well as my own. And thanks for watching out for me today when I fell. It could've been worse, I reckon. Turns out just my pride got hurt. Keep a special eye on Miss Rose, too, Lord. She's a dear old soul who's loved and served You a long while. I'm asking You to send the right person to help her."

Journey seemed an unlikely choice. She reminded him of a colt his father had bought from a rancher known for poor handling of his animals. That colt never lost the suspicious gleam in its eyes. It always flinched when touched, bolted often and busted fences more times than he could count.

"Until You do, Lord, help me look after Miss Rose. And thank You for putting her here to take care of me like she has ever since—"

Since Sarah died. He scratched his chin and sat up, resting his elbows on his knees. A fire blazed in his chest. Sarah. Their baby she carried. The flame that took them burned in him still. Three years without them—where would he be now without Miss Rose's prayer and love and support?

"I still miss them. I know they rest with You, Lord. It makes it easier, but I still ache that they're gone. Help me, Lord."

He stood and brushed himself off, clearing his dry throat. "All these things I lay before You, in the name of Your Son, Jesus Christ. Amen."

He nickered to his horse, who trotted over and nuzzled his shoulder. "C'mon, Malachi. Let's get back. You can listen to my sermon before I turn in."

He'd always been a fair tracker, but when the Lord had called him to preach, he was sure he'd misread the signs. His palms still sweat when he stood before his congregation. Sarah had always listened to the sermon twice—once the evening before so he could practice and again during Sunday service. Her soft laugh would echo through the tiny home he'd been able to provide, and she'd run her fingers through his hair. He could still feel her wide, moist lips on his cheek.

"Preach it with the fire God's given you for His Word, for others, and you'll be fine," she'd say.

Now he had Malachi. Captive audience, little response. He mounted up and spurred the horse to a trot farther along the stream before heading home. It was too nice a night to head back early.

A cry broke through the night. He grabbed the Spencer gun holstered behind his saddle. He hadn't heard any talk of bobcats in the area, but it sure sounded like a woman's scream coming from the stand of trees ahead. He edged Malachi closer, picking his way into the darker night of the woods. What would a woman be doing out at this time of night?

He slid from the saddle and readied the gun in case he'd guessed wrong. A whinny sounded to his right as he drew closer, and it didn't take the brightness of the moon to find the broad, crooked path of broken twigs. Zane followed.

The thrashing horse caught his attention. The mare's eyes rolled back to white in panic as she neighed and struggled to get up from her side. He ground-tied his own mount, then moved toward the frightened animal.

"Easy, easy there, girl." He slid the halter off, stroking her wide brown head. The horse seemed to quiet, kicking only occasionally with her hind hooves.

He patted the heaving side, continuing to comfort the horse in low tones as he slid his other hand along her right foreleg. He grimaced when the bone shifted beneath his touch. Busted.

A soft moan drew his attention to the still, small form lying nearby. Peering through the dimness, he found a floppy brimmed hat lying against a tree trunk. The same one he'd seen on the woman Abby had introduced earlier. Journey? What was she doing all the way out here?

If not for the unnatural angle of her left leg, Zane could've believed she'd fallen asleep. She lay on her side, head cradled on her outstretched arm. A few loosened curls draped over her shoulder. He dropped down beside her and eased her over to her back. A bruise formed near her temple, stark against her pale skin. She moaned again and he leaned back on his haunches, pulling her tattered skirt down from where it bunched at her knees.

"Journey? Miss Smith?" He tapped her cheek. "Journey, wake up."

She tossed her head once to either side as if to refuse him. "Don't touch me. I—I mean it." Her voice slurred.

"Journey? Ma'am, it's me, Zane—Reverend Thompson." Her eyes fluttered. "That's it. Come on now."

He watched her eyes slit open, and she struggled to sit up. He saw her grind her teeth rather than cry out at the pain the movement had to have caused her leg.

"Gypsy?"

He guessed she meant the horse by the way she

searched about with her deep brown eyes. She blinked at him as if he'd just appeared. She moved to touch the lump on her head, but he pulled her icy fingers away and held them in his hand.

"Hold on, there." Zane stayed her with a hand at her arm, not quite touching. "Let's check you out, first. How many fingers am I holding up?"

Squinting, her head wobbled slightly. "Four. How's my horse?"

"Three. And she's not good," Zane said. He slid down and picked up her left foot in both hands. "Neither are you. I need to check your leg."

She didn't protest, only turned her head and squinted in the direction of her whimpering horse. He slid the tattered fabric back to just past the smooth knee. Moving his hands along the leg, he felt the bone move beneath the stockings, much as the horse's had. Fortunately for her, unlike with the horse, it wasn't a fatal injury.

She shivered. Wind blew through the trees. "Journey? Are you with me? Your leg's broken. We need to get you inside."

"My horse..."

Her white skin glistened in the moonlight, like some ghostly beauty from an old story. Her head bobbed with no particular rhythm as she scanned the space around them.

Zane grabbed a blanket from her now-still horse. He balled it up and placed it under her head.

"Ma'am, my house isn't far from here if we cut straight through the field. It seems best if I carry you there, then go for the doc in town."

"I need my horse," she said, as if that should be his only concern.

He moved his head, trying to keep himself in her field of vision. "We'll get you inside, I'll get the doc and then I'll come back and take care of your horse. Ready?"

She stiffened as he moved to lift her. "I'll ride Gypsy." Her voice fairly shook.

He settled back on his heels and slid his hat off to scratch his head. The horse panted behind them, and he knew she hadn't gotten a good look at the damage. But then, she didn't seem to register her own damage.

She scrambled to her feet, slender arms swinging to gain balance. The instant she rested her weight on her broken leg, a low moan ripped through her throat. Zane saw her eyes flutter closed and caught her as she collapsed.

Her breath puffed warm on his neck. He knew he needed to get her indoors but set her back to pull a coil of rope from the horse's halter. He patted the horse's head and she quivered at his touch. "Hold on, gal."

Journey moaned softly. He found a few branches nearby to splint her awkward leg before bending to lift her. "I hope you're as light as you look, ma'am," he said, peering through the pine boughs waving overhead to the starry sky above.

Malachi was a sturdy sort. Not fast, but steady. Zane was thankful now as he lifted Journey to the saddle. He held her head in one hand and pulled himself into the saddle with the other. Her teeth clenched as he reached for the bridle.

"I mean it, Hank. Don't you touch me," she said. He leaned forward, but her eyes never opened.

"Don't worry, lady," he said. He lifted soft curls of

hair to check the cut on her head again. "You'll feel a whole lot better, soon's we get the doc to take a look at you. Giddap, Malachi."

Journey listened, straining to catch the sounds of the room beyond the pounding in her head. Creaking boards told her she wasn't alone.

She opened her eyes a slit, peering through her lashes. She could barely make out a window frame opposite where she lay. The glow at her right side could've been only a lamp, but the warmth made her think of a fireplace. How did she get here? And where was here? She couldn't think with this stampede running through her head.

Gypsy. She remembered the horse stumbling, going down.

A shadow crossed over her. She sat up with a gasp as pain flashed hot like lightning down her leg.

"Take it easy," a voice spoke from the shadow. She jerked her head and opened her eyes wide, but the ache forced her back to the softness of the pillow.

"Abby?" She blinked until her eyes adjusted to the light. "Wh-what happened? Where am I?"

Abby pulled a chair closer to the edge of the bed and smiled down at her. "You're at Zane's. He found you in the woods, thrown by your horse."

"Gypsy? How is she?"

Abby smoothed the blanket over her and leaned back in her seat. "Sam and Zane went to check. Doc Ferris was here. He said your head should feel better in a day or so. It's a good thing Zane was there."

Journey shifted, biting her lip against the pain.

"That leg'll take a while longer. Doc left something to help ease the hurt."

She slid her leg under the quilt, feeling the stiff binding around it. "How much longer?"

Abby's lips quirked to one side. "At least a month, maybe more, Doc said."

She could be snowed in by that time, if the chill in the night air held. Where would she stay? She wouldn't be able to afford a room longer than a week, and that's if she didn't eat. She knew enough to realize Reverend Thompson couldn't extend his hospitality to her that long. And the doctor! How was she to pay him?

She had to leave before that. She'd give herself the day and let Gypsy rest. Then she'd be ready to move on. If she went slowly, they'd make out fine. She could just take it easy, not push the horse too much and keep her leg bound.

"I'll need to settle up with the doctor before I leave."

Abby patted her arm. "Don't you worry. Once you get settled in at Miss Rose's, you can work it out with her. I'm sure she'll help you. You can pay her back when you're on your feet again. Let me get that pain medicine. You're about due."

Abby moved to the table behind her. It seemed this room served as kitchen, sitting room and sleeping area for the pastor. It must be his bed she lay on. Her leg throbbed in time with her head. She had to get out of here.

"Here you go." Abby nudged a spoonful of liquid to her. "This'll help you rest, too. You've had quite a night. I should've told you to stick closer to town."

She swallowed the liquid, but Abby's words burned her with embarrassment. What would she think if she knew there had been no plan to stay? Not that it mattered now. Did it? Was there any way to explain how grateful she was for the kindness they'd shown and make them understand that she couldn't allow it anymore? It didn't seem likely, not without telling too much.

"I'm not one to be hemmed in," she said. She fisted the blankets around her and slid down into the pillow.

"Believe me, I can understand that," Abby said. Her eyebrows lifted, and Journey braced herself for more questions. "I didn't expect you to ride so far out of town. We were looking for you to come back any time when Zane came pounding on the door. He'd found Doc Ferris at the Wilsons' and sent him out here, then came for Sam to help with your horse. I had Sam hook up the wagon and bring me along to see what I could do. I thought you might feel better if you came to with a familiar face around, instead of a complete stranger here."

Journey fought the gathering tears. She nodded and her throat felt tight. "You're right. Thank you." She didn't know this woman well, but it was better than waking up with an unknown doctor prodding around. "Where are they?"

"Doc Ferris figured you'd rest quietly awhile, and he needed to get back to the Wilsons' to check on their new baby before he headed back to town," Abby said. "Zane and Sam should be back any minute now, soon as they get your horse checked over."

Journey felt the bandage over her temple as she brushed a curl from her forehead. She smoothed the blanket at her waist with the other hand even though Abby had already done that. Her leg felt better since taking the medicine, and her head slowed its throbbing. She yawned.

"Did Reverend Thompson—Zane—say how she was?"

"Your horse?"

"Yes." She yawned again. "Gypsy."

Abby turned away, as if she suddenly remembered the spoon and bottle she still held. They clinked together on the table. "Zane didn't say. He was more anxious about Doc Ferris getting out here to see you. He said you were in and out, calling him 'Hank' or something like that."

Journey kept her eyes down, staring at her hands on the quilt. A chill fell over her. She no longer felt drowsy. What else might she have said?

But Abby chattered on, unaware that she'd struck a nerve. "If anyone can patch up your horse, it's Zane. He worked with his father raising horses before Mr. Thompson passed away. What he didn't know about horses wouldn't fill a thimble, and he taught Zane everything."

She slid back down on the bed, pulling the covers all the way over her shoulders, and Abby put another log on the fire. "Keep warm. Doc was worried you'd fall into shock, being out in the cold air like you were. But you look better already than you did when I first arrived. Your color's back."

Boots on the porch boards outside the front door roused her. She and Abby turned as the door swung open, revealing Zane and Sam. Journey caught the shake of Sam's head when he looked at his wife. The sharp whinny of the horse echoed in her memory. How bad could it be?

Zane looked haggard. The bruise around his eye from his fall at Miss Rose's was dark and swollen.

He rubbed a hand over the shadow beard on his chin, and she felt sorry for the trouble she'd caused him. He shrugged her saddlebag from his shoulder and hung it on a peg near the door, then hooked the gun he carried above it. He turned and stared at her.

She grew uneasy, self-conscious, thankful the doctor hadn't needed to disrobe her to splint the leg. She felt bare toes scrape the blanket only on that foot, the other stocking still in place. Why didn't he say something?

He swiped a hand through his hair and cleared his throat, then placed his hand on his hip.

"How bad is she? I have to know."

Zane cleared his throat again and looked over to Sam and Abby. Then his gray eyes turned in her direction and he drew in a deep breath.

"I'm so sorry, ma'am—Journey," he said. "I had to put her down."

The coldness swept through her again, and this time her injuries weren't to blame. She covered her face with her palms.

Slender fingers squeezed her shoulder. Journey looked up to see Abby's teary face. She'd cry herself if she thought it would do any good. She'd come all this way. She couldn't let herself get caught now. But without Gypsy...

"Don't worry about a thing," Abby said. "We'll help you. Miss Rose has plenty of space and a good little riding horse she'll let you use, I know it. We'll work things out with her."

"I have nothing to bargain with. I can't stay here. I'm sorry, I should have said before, but I couldn't possibly—"

"Sure you can," Sam said. "I'm sorry about your

horse. Believe me, I know what it's like to lose a good mount like that. It feels like you lost your best friend. But the Lord works in mysterious ways, right, Zane?"

Zane nodded. "Don't worry about anything, Journey. It'll work out." His voice rasped as he stood in the flickering light.

You don't know! How could you take my horse? She wanted to scream at him. She wanted to shove him out the door and demand he bring Gypsy back.

"I'll stay with you tonight, and we'll let you get some rest," Abby said. "Zane and Sam can stay out in the barn. Then in the morning they can ride over and talk to Miss Rose, let her know what's happened. After church we'll ride you over in our wagon."

"But how can I work for her now?"

"It's the company she needs most," Abby said.

"And we'll be around to give her a hand," Zane added. "I guarantee she'll not consider you a bother."

Her options had been shot out from under her. It was all decided. She'd stay in Walten until her leg healed. Until she could afford another horse. Until she paid all the debts this one night had cost her. She sighed. Or until the law caught up with her.

Chapter Six

Zane dragged his feet across the rug at the door. Journey lay across his bed on top of the quilt Sarah had made. He'd had it in his buckboard the night of the fire, and it was the only tangible thing he had left of her.

"Zane? What's wrong?"

Abby's voice drew him from the memories that never were very far away. "Nothing. I was just…nothing." He nodded toward the patient. "She ready?"

Abby nodded. "She's tuckered out. I helped her wash her hair, so between that and the laudanum Doc Ferris left her, she sleeps hard." She looked from him to the tiny form on the bed. "I get the feeling she hasn't had a good rest for a long time."

Zane remembered her wild-eyed fear the night before when he'd found her in the woods. Something about her tugged at him, and he didn't know himself yet what it was. "Well, maybe that's why the Lord led her here. He definitely wanted her to stick around awhile. What did Doc say?"

"Six weeks. By then the snow will be through the pass and she'll be here until spring."

"Did she say where she was headed yesterday?"

Abby shook her head. "I have a feeling she wasn't planning to be here long, though." Her shoulders rose with a forceful breath. "Does Sam have the wagon ready?"

"He's ready and waiting."

"Good. I'll go out and get the blankets ready, and you can bring her out," Abby said, pulling on her sweater from the back of the chair.

Zane started. He hadn't thought of how they would get Journey to the wagon, but looking at her now, he knew she wouldn't be managing it on her own.

"It'll be good if she stays asleep. I know from experience that leg will pain her these first few days especially." He didn't add the fact that she hadn't been too fond of him the last time he'd tried to help.

Abby grinned and patted his shoulder on the way out. "Don't be nervous, Zane. It's not like she'll bite."

"You didn't see her last night when I brought her in here."

Abby got a strange look in her eyes, the one that told him her thoughts were moving the conversation into a different direction entirely. "Maybe in time both of you will change your perceptions, then. You deserve to give some girl the chance to make you happy again."

He laughed softly as she swept out the door with a wink. Abby, the eternal matchmaker. She'd been the one to introduce him to Sarah.

Striding over to Journey's prone form, he adjusted his hat and bent down to pick her up. Instead of the tense fear that weighed her down last night, she felt no heavier than a new colt. He pulled her head against his shoulder before managing to get a grip under her knees to lift her up.

Her hair followed in a trail that swept past his elbow, a fiery wave of still-damp curls. She smelled of lavender soap, and he knew Abby had been adding any little thing she could to comfort their newest resident.

Standing upright, he felt her shift against him, burrowing her face into his shoulder with a soft murmur. Thick lashes brushed her tanned cheek, which blurred a fine spray of freckles that could be seen only from this close. Her wide mouth parted open slightly, and he felt her soft breath at his neck.

Zane tightened his hold and focused on moving her out the door without jarring her bound leg. But had she been awake and not fighting against him, he knew she would feel his pounding heart in the hand that brushed his chest.

Abby needed to stop putting ideas into a man's head.

The rumble of pans being placed in a cupboard roused Journey. She ran her fingers over the heavy brocade of the couch where she lay. The fire crackled and cast a soft light over the room, which had grown darker since her arrival that afternoon.

Her throbbing head reminded her why she was there. A groan escaped before she could stifle it. She eased into the pillow as Miss Rose came into view, standing in the doorway to the kitchen with a drying towel in her hand.

"Did you sleep well?"

Journey stretched her leg, the one that wasn't broken. "I must've. I forgot where I was for a moment. What time is it?" Her whole body felt stiff.

"Nigh onto seven o'clock."

"I guess I slept the day away."

Miss Rose smiled. "It's the best thing for you. You had enough excitement last night to wear a body out. And I'll bet the ride here this morning didn't help any. Are you hungry?"

Her stomach rumbled before she could deny it. "A little." She mustered a small grin.

"Good. You dropped off before supper and we hated to wake you, so I saved you a plate. Let me warm it a bit and I'll bring it in for you."

Journey pulled herself up further with her arm. "Please, don't trouble yourself. I can come out." She paused as her vision swam.

Miss Rose had already moved back into the kitchen, but her crackling voice carried through. "You'll do no such thing. Doc Ferris said you're to keep that leg up."

"Yes, ma'am."

Doc Ferris's word carried a lot of weight, Journey already knew. Pain medication was given every two hours, no matter how she tried to beg off. No weight on that leg meant being carted to the house by Zane Thompson in his arms, much to her embarrassment. She'd slept through the move from his house, at least. But now here she sat, being waited on by the woman she'd been hired to care for.

The steaming plate placed on her lap aroused her hunger even more. She smiled her thanks and leaned forward as Miss Rose propped more pillows behind her. The chicken leg and green beans smelled delicious, and a thick slice of bread with a generous spread of butter and a drizzle of honey made her mouth water. She calculated the cost of such a meal and made a mental note to keep a ledger. But for now there was nothing to do for it. She'd have to eat if she was going to stay strong and mend quickly. She poked a bean with her fork.

Miss Rose must have been satisfied, because she smiled and said, "I'll leave you to your supper. I figure you'll want some time to ponder your situation." Then she moved back toward the kitchen.

Journey sat back into the cushions, grateful for the solitude. But ponder? There wasn't much she could do. Miss Rose welcomed her with open arms and seemed pleased with the arrangement. Tears fought their way into her eyes as she thought about the kindness these people had shown. How could she tell them why she had run? Didn't they deserve to know? What if they threw her out? What would she do then?

Her options had been cut off. She tried to think what had spooked the horse in the first place, but a fog surrounded all the particulars of the night before. Now here she sat. No horse. No money. No job. Broken leg. She tore a corner from the bread and chewed, trying to slow her jumbled thoughts.

Part of the reason she'd taken up with Hank back then had been because she'd felt she had no choice. But the day she had stood up to Hank was the day she'd realized she was never without options. Even now, looking over her shoulder, waiting to be caught for her crime, she was better off than she'd been with Hank.

Biting into the tender chicken, she thought about her predicament. She couldn't walk around, but there was nothing wrong with her hands. There had to be something. No great loss without some small gain, Mama had always said. Where was the glimmer of hope?

Journey licked the salty crisps from her fingers.

Cooking meant standing. Tending children was out of the question. She drew in a deep breath. Something would come to her. The one thing she did have was time to think—a lot of time to think.

She silently thanked Abby for taking the time to help wash her hair before she had dozed off. She'd need some pins to put it back up. She yawned. Maybe it could wait until tomorrow.

The shuffle of feet from the kitchen drew her attention. "I thought you might want your saddlebag," Miss Rose said, nodding toward the floor by her side. "Zane left it there for you."

She glanced at the buckles. They didn't seem to have been opened since she'd fastened them yesterday. "Thank you, ma'am."

"You might as well get into the practice of calling me Miss Rose," the old woman said.

"I'll work on it." She squirmed under the blanket, trying to shift her aching leg into a more comfortable position. "I appreciate what you're doing, honestly I do. I'd be at a loss without your kindness. I'll make it up to you. I'll pay you back for everything, somehow. I hate to be beholden."

"Nonsense. I'm glad to help. And I don't want you fretting about it. This gives me my chance to play the Good Samaritan." She patted Journey's good leg and took her empty plate. "We'll even it out when you're able, dear."

"You'll find I'm not very 'dear,'" she whispered. "Please, just call me Journey."

"I think there's more 'dear' in you than you give yourself credit for." Miss Rose stroked a hand over

Journey's hair. Like Mama used to do. Warmth for this woman grew no matter how she tried to stop it.

"Zane left this package for you. He brought it in with your saddle." Miss Rose handed her a lump tied in brown paper, then returned to the kitchen.

The fabric she'd bought at the store. She'd have a fine dress, plenty warm for winter. At least she could work on that.

She always could sew a fine seam. Mama had taught her to stitch and to sew in the afternoon hours before she'd go to work. If she could find sewing to do, it might not be much, but at least she could pay something toward her board until she was up and around again. She would ask Abby to post a notice in the store.

She turned her attention to the saddlebag, listening for Miss Rose to return. Looking over her shoulder, she fumbled the buckle open and hefted the bag to her lap to reach the bottom of the deep pocket.

The touch of cool metal brought a sense of relief. They hadn't found it. She pulled the Double Derringer gun from the pack and slid it into her skirt pocket. The smooth nickel barrel and walnut handle felt secure in her fingers.

Yes, there were options. Spring was a long winter away. She had to wait and not tip her hand. Because if they knew she had killed a man, her only options would be prison or a rope.

Chapter Seven

A knock at the door woke Journey. The final glow of sunlight slanted lower through the back window. At least she hadn't slept as long this time. She eased up and swiped the curls clinging against her cheek from her face. Miss Rose stood from the nearby rocker and shuffled to the door.

"Zane! What a nice surprise!"

She slid lower under the covers. Maybe if she closed her eyes…

But Miss Rose's voice called her. "Journey, are you awake? Pastor Thompson is here to see you."

Not Zane this time—Pastor Thompson. This must be a business call. She pushed herself up again but kept the blanket close. The room swam slightly and the pressure in her head felt as if it would push her eyes right out of their sockets. She nodded to Miss Rose, who continued to block the doorway.

"Come on in, Zane," she said as she opened the door wider. "Have a seat and I'll put some coffee on. Journey, I'll get that medicine for you. Your head's probably feeling rocky again by now. I'll be right back."

Miss Rose slid off to the kitchen, leaving Zane to stand in the doorway. He grabbed the Stetson hat from his head and shut the door but seemed to linger longer than necessary before he faced Journey. She watched him rock heel-to-toe once, his eyes scanning the room for a place to lay his hat before sitting in the ladder-back chair at her feet. He finally capped it over his knee and ran his hand over his thick hair.

"Miss Smith," he began, leaning forward. "Journey, I wanted to see you, wanted to tell you how sorry I am about your horse."

She stared at him a moment and he paused. His gray eyes held shadows but didn't flinch. He was looking for something. She rubbed her throbbing head.

"I'm sure you are." She smoothed unseen wrinkles from the quilt.

His broad shoulders sagged a little. "I know horses, been around them all my life. I hate to see that kind of thing happen, but I want to assure you, there was no other option. That foreleg was busted up good."

She bit the inside of her cheek. She would have liked to have made that call herself.

"Believe me, I'd have liked nothing better than for you to have given the order. If you'd been in any shape, I'd have let you. But the horse was suffering. I know you would have done the same."

She nodded. She knew it wasn't his fault, but that didn't change the fact that he'd taken the thing she needed most.

Zane sat up in the chair, crossing a booted foot over his knee. He slid his hat across the bridge of his leg and hung it from the heel. "Could've been worse for you. What were you doing out that far from town anyway?"

"Exploring," she said but refused to meet his gaze.

He tapped the brim of his hat. "If there's anything you need, anything at all, you let me know. Part of my job around here is to help wayfaring strangers…and explorers." He had the audacity to smile.

"I'll work it out." Her voice sounded gritty and harsh to her own ears. The day had been too long. She cleared her throat delicately and tried again. He'd only done what he had to. "It's good you were there to find me."

"Glad I was there. I wish there'd been more I could've done. How are you feeling?"

Miss Rose returned with a tray of steaming mugs. "I expect she has a headache the size of the Beartooths. Here, Journey." She filled the spoon from the tray with laudanum.

Journey swallowed the bitter liquid. "I appreciate you taking me in, but there's no need to fuss over me, too. I'm feeling fine."

But Miss Rose just waved the empty spoon. "Nonsense. You take advantage, missy. Once you're back on your feet, you'll wish it back. Now, what would you like, coffee or tea?"

"Tea, please."

She took the cup and saucer. The pastor was handed a steaming mug of coffee without being given a choice.

"You have to let Miss Rose fuss at you. Otherwise, she's fussing at me." He smiled and took a swallow. "And you do look much better than you did last night. But with the knock you took, I dare say you're not feeling all that fine just yet."

Journey said no more and looked into her cup. It made no sense to argue. Besides, he was right.

"So where were you headed?" Zane asked.

She stared at him over the edge of the mug she held to her lips. She moved it stiffly to her lap, breaking eye contact to glance at the door. "It doesn't matter now, does it?"

He set his cup down on the little table beside him, keeping his fingers wrapped around the handle. She slid back against the armrest but tried to pull herself upright.

His eyebrows shifted and quirked. "I thought if someone was expecting you somewhere, I'd send a telegram for you."

"No!" She jolted forward and pain shot down her leg. Tea sloshed over the blanket that covered her lap. Zane moved to pull it away before the heat could soak through. "I'm so sorry! I'm forever making a mess of things."

"It's all right." He shook out the quilt and brushed at it with his handkerchief. "There," he said, laying it back over her. "Good as new."

"Thank you." He looked down at her, waiting for an explanation. "It's just that, well…there's no one expecting me."

His look told her he was skeptical. "You're sure?"

She looked away from him and Miss Rose. "I'm sure."

Placing his mug on the tray, he stood to go, and for a moment she thought he was angry. But his lips pulled into a smile, though his teeth didn't show.

"If you think of anything—anything at all I can do to lend a hand, you let me know. Like I said, I'm sorry for the way things worked out for you." He squeezed the old woman's thin shoulder. "But you couldn't be in better hands. Miss Rose is a fine woman and very good at taking care of folks."

"I appreciate all your help, Pastor." She shook her head. "Zane. Please don't think I'm ungrateful. It's just…"

"I know," he said, in a tone that told her he somehow did. "Life has a funny way of throwing us once in a while." He turned to Miss Rose. "Thank you for the coffee. Hot and black, just how I like it."

It surprised Journey to see him bow and place a soft kiss on the old woman's cheek. "Let's pray before I go."

Pray? Mama said she had prayed with that skinny little parson at the end of town before she died. It hadn't changed her situation any, and Journey couldn't imagine it would change her own. But apparently the job of pastor required it. If it meant he was leaving, she'd sit through it. He asked questions requiring answers that would only make things more complicated for everyone. It wore her out. The less they knew about her, the better they'd all be. And she never could lie well. No, she'd have to keep her distance from Pastor Zane.

"…Lord, we thank you, too, for our visitor. She's hurting, and we ask that You heal her and help her to find a home here. Be with Miss Rose as she cares for her, and may they find comfort in each other's company. Guide us, Lord, to live lives pleasing to You. In Jesus' name, amen."

Miss Rose startled Journey by echoing his amen. So now he'd leave.

Zane put his hat on and ambled toward the door. The sky was a muted evening gray. He turned as he stepped onto the porch.

"Thank you, ladies, for the visit. And, Journey, I meant what I said. You let me know if you need my help. To tell the truth, I feel responsible for the horse."

Miss Rose nodded to her as if she expected a response.

"It's not your fault. And I'm not your problem," Journey said slowly. "I know it's not something you wanted to do, and I'm glad you were there to do what I couldn't. Gypsy was a good horse and we've seen a lot of trail together. I'll miss her." She paused to steady her voice. "But accidents happen." She tried to spout all the expected responses, hoping she'd get to the proper one quickly so he'd go. The only help he could give would be to provide her a horse.

He tipped his hat. "Glad you see it that way, ma'am. Take care of that leg, and let Miss Rose fuss at you some, like I said. Just so she stays in practice." He grinned and grabbed Rose's hand with a squeeze. "I'll check in on you," he told her.

And then he was gone. But as much as she wished it otherwise, Journey knew it wasn't the last she'd seen of Reverend Zane Thompson.

"Well?"

Zane turned at the bottom step to face Miss Rose, who had followed him out to the porch. "'Well,' what?"

"Is everything set to right between you two?"

He dropped his head to hide his smile. "I don't suppose she's any too fond of me, but she's not liable to shoot me anyway. At least, I don't think so. Why do you ask?"

Miss Rose leaned a shoulder against a post. "She's

a sweet girl. You're a good man. Allow an old woman some hope."

"Now, Miss Rose, don't start. You know I'm not ready to think along those lines with anyone and definitely not with someone I know so little about."

"Caution is good," she agreed with a nod. "I just want to start you thinking along those lines."

They'd had similar conversations before. "Why are you so determined to play matchmaker with me?"

"Because you're too good a man to not allow yourself to make another woman happy. Sarah would not have expected you to live the rest of your life alone."

"I'm not alone. I have my friends, my congregation and this town. That's plenty to keep me busy, and it wouldn't be fair to saddle another woman with that."

"Let a woman make that choice for herself."

He looked to Miss Rose, her eyes lit with the setting sun. She couldn't understand. "It wouldn't be fair. I'm too used to being on my own now. Besides, I'd always be comparing them to her."

"Then I'll be praying in that direction. Remember, you're not replacing Sarah to open your heart to new possibilities." She sighed and stood upright, wrapping her arms around herself in the growing chill of dusk. "Did Journey forgive you for putting down her horse?"

He tipped his hat back and shrugged his shoulders. "She claims she's not upset about it. She knows I wouldn't have put the horse down if I didn't have to, I think. But I'm still the one who did it."

"She'll come around."

"I hope so," he said. The smile on Miss Rose's face hinted at more than his words intended.

"Me, too, young man," she said, turning back toward her door. She stopped before opening the latch. "In more ways than one."

Chapter Eight

Journey's heart throbbed in time with the thud of her foot on the wooden floor as she made her way to the window.

Her request to be awakened before the women left for the church had been denied. The mantel clock chimed ten o'clock, so she guessed they'd return before long. Having been confined to the great room and a cot in the kitchen for the past four days, she was elated when Abby had reminded Miss Rose about the ladies' Bible study or some such midweek church meeting. But Miss Rose wouldn't dawdle in town.

The sunny breeze from the open windows was no replacement for a peek of the horizon. She paused to catch her breath at the door. Sweat broke out across her forehead. Perspiration, Mama would say. Not even pigs sweat.

The day was warm, as summer flaunted itself before giving in to autumn. Journey hobbled out to the porch and sank into the chair beside the door.

She inhaled until her lungs wouldn't stretch any-

more. The scent of sage wafted in the air, and she remembered riding through it with Gypsy. It had filled
the landscape as far as the eye could see, rolling along
with the brown hills, climbing higher and higher. It was
the first time she realized she was alone—no one following behind, no one waiting ahead. It gave her hope
that she'd found her escape. But now...

She listened for approaching wagons and fingered
the pistol in her pocket.

Journey leaned against the chair post, glad for the
chance to rest her leg. Her head barely hurt at all this
morning, and the ache in her leg was tolerable without the pain medication that she'd refused the past two
days. Doc Ferris had been out yesterday to rebind it and
check the lump on her head. He'd proclaimed both on
the mend but recommended keeping the leg raised as
much as possible for another week at least. And Miss
Rose followed his recommendations to the letter.

The stable stood, weathered but sturdy, across the
dusty yard. She remembered Abby mentioning a riding horse and felt a pang of loneliness for her own. She
and Gypsy had traveled the whole way from Georgia
together. The hostler had laughed at her choice, but the
mare was all she could afford, and she took a chance
on the intelligence she thought she saw in the fine dark
eyes. Some of the conversations held with the gentle
brown horse were more enjoyable and wiser than any
of the ones she'd had with Hank. What kind of horses
would Miss Rose keep? It wasn't so awfully far to the
barn.

She stood and lurched to the edge of the porch,
grasping the banister. It took a couple of false starts
before she found a rhythm of dangling the broken leg

before her, leaning toward the banister, then hopping down on her bare foot. She hadn't planned on treading out into the yard, but to go back now would cost precious minutes of fresh air. Her feet would be tough enough to handle the rough ground for the distance.

Hopping several feet at a time before stopping to balance, she made her way to the barn and tugged the door, which caught a bit before sliding open enough to slip through. She leaned against a railing to ease her breathing and let her eyes adjust to the cool dimness inside. A soft whinny to the right drew her attention.

Two horses stood in the stalls, one a broad chestnut with a black mane and tail, the other a smaller paint. She hobbled over and stroked the white blaze across the paint's forehead, holding the harness to steady herself. She blew softly on its nose.

"And what's your name?" she whispered.

"Homer."

She drew the revolver from her pocket, pivoting on her good leg. Reverend Thompson fell back against the open door frame, holding up both hands in defense.

"What do you mean by sneaking up on me?" Her voice came low, ragged. "Moves like that can get you shot."

His Adam's apple bobbed just above his shirt collar, but his voice showed no strain. "I didn't mean to startle you."

"It seems to me you don't mean to do a lot of things you end up doing." She thought her heart would pound out of her throat.

He lowered his hands. "I saw the barn door open and knew Miss Rose had gone with Abby to the Ladies' Mission Society meeting. I thought I ought to check things out. After all, you're to be inside resting, with that leg up."

"Why were you out here?" She didn't know why she continued to question him. Did she really think he'd lie?

He moved farther into the barn with a calm confidence. "I made a call on the Hamlers. Listen, can you put that thing away?"

She looked at the gun palmed in her hand and lowered it into the folds of her skirt, hoping to hide the shake in her hand.

"You—you startled me. And…and, well, I've learned it never hurts to have a little help in backing up your words. I apologize, Reverend Thompson."

"It's still Zane." He shifted and ran a finger along his collar before stepping closer. "You must be feeling a little better if you're making your way outside."

The matter of the gun set aside but not forgotten. "I couldn't resist the sunshine," she said. "I'm afraid we won't have too many more fine days like this one. Then I remembered Miss Rose said she kept horses and I wanted to take a peek at them."

He walked over to the larger of the two horses, and scratched its nose. "This is Zeb, short for Zebulon, and that's Homer."

"Funny names."

"Ah, but fine horses. Homer would make a great mount for you while you're here." He smiled and turned to face her. "That is, once your leg heals. You really should listen to Doc Ferris. It is what we pay him for around here."

She didn't need to be reminded about her debt to the kind, quiet man who had tended to the injury. "I could use a seat," she conceded.

"Can I help you?"

She tensed, wondering if he meant more than the leg. "No. No, I'm fine. I can take care of myself."

She stepped across the dirt, the thin layer of loose hay tickling her feet, then back toward the yard. Journey tensed when Zane reached toward her as she faltered. But he drew back and merely followed close behind.

Beads of sweat dribbled down her cheeks by the time she reached the porch steps. The thought hit her that going up wouldn't be nearly as easy as the trip down. It wouldn't do to have an audience.

She turned toward the preacher, grasping the banister in both hands. "Listen. About the gun... I— You startled me and I reacted too quickly. It won't happen again, I assure you. I'd appreciate it if we could forget about the whole thing."

A shadow crossed his face, as though his mind were a hundred miles from where they stood. As if he could see beyond her secrets.

"Zane? Can't we keep this between us? I'd hate to startle Miss Rose. Or worse yet, have her kick me out."

His attention jerked back as he looked at her, turning his head to either side. "Right. But look, if you're in some kind of trouble, she deserves to know. Let her make up her own mind. Besides, maybe we can help."

"It's no trouble I can't handle, I assure you, Pastor." She leveled her gaze to his.

He rested his hands at his waist and stared at her a moment, then out across the dust-colored bluffs to the east. His jaw twitched. She backed up onto the first step with her good foot.

"Trouble you can handle has a way of turning into trouble you can't," he said, still not looking at her. "If you let us know what's going on, we'll figure a way out."

Her face grew warmer but this time not because of the temperature. "The only thing going on here is I'm trying to figure a way to pay my debts, buy a horse and be on my way. The only thing going on here is a pastor who thinks he can save every soul he meets, fix every problem. Well, there are some problems you can't fix with a sermon." She clamped her lips together as a shiver of fear shot through her. What possessed her to speak to him like that? Hank would have wailed on her before she spoke out. Mama would have been appalled. "We must always be nice to the gentlemen," she would say, in that soft drawl.

Zane bent his head but his stance held no anger. "I'm only trying to help. You may need it more than you think."

His sincerity softened her fear as well as her anger, more than she would have liked. But aggravating him would only increase his suspicions. "I appreciate the offer, but this is my trouble and I'll handle it my way. Getting more folks involved will only make things worse. Believe me, it's not worth it."

He looked at her, his eyebrows quirked. "We'll play this your way for now," he said after a pause. "I won't mention the gun to Miss Rose, but you watch yourself. You have to let us know when you need a hand."

She pulled her shoulders back, determined not to skitter away from him, no matter how her thoughts pleaded with her to. She didn't have to do anything as far as she was concerned. Why wouldn't he just go away?

She gave him a short nod. "I'll tell Miss Rose you stopped by."

He strode to his horse and paused with his foot in the stirrup. "I'd appreciate it," he said, easing his broad frame into the saddle. He grabbed his hat from the saddle horn and clamped it over his dark hair.

She thought he would leave with a tip of his hat, but instead he slid the brown leather brim back from his wide face and looked down at her. "Journey?"

"Yes."

"We have a saying here in the West that you might not have heard. But it's good sound advice."

"What's that?" She crooked her neck to look up at him, squinting an eye to block out the sun, and tightened her grasp on the banister.

"Watch your back."

She stared hard at his retreating form. How little he knew. She was already backed into a corner.

Chapter Nine

"Whoa, Malachi!"

Zane leaned back in the saddle and pushed upright in the stirrups, pulling the reins at the same time.

His thoughts had unraveled from the moment Journey cocked her gun his way in the barn. Lost in a jumble of possibilities, each worse than the one before, he had nudged the horse into a full gallop by the time he'd made it halfway to town. He gave the horse its head until he found himself almost at Norwood's Mercantile. Sliding from Malachi's high back, he landed in front of Mrs. Decker. She stepped back with a gasp, her hand patting her heart.

"Pardon me, ma'am." He swept his hat from his head. "I didn't see you coming."

She tucked her hair back into place with a dainty sniff. "I should think it would be hard to see much of anything coming in that cloud of dust you raised, Reverend."

Zane swiped his face in the crook of his elbow. She would have to be the one to catch him in a moment of recklessness. "Forgive me, Mrs. Decker. I'm afraid my mind was distracted and I allowed the horse too much leeway. I never meant to startle you."

She walked off with a huff, but he heard her mumble. "What that man needs is a good woman to settle him. I should think a minister and widower would maintain greater decorum. Now, my Mary…"

Widower. He hated that word. All the love and joy he and Sarah had shared, all the hopes and dreams and plans, cut down into that one word. He sobered, stroking Malachi's mane a moment before tromping up the steps.

Lost in thought, he plowed into Abby as he stepped through the door, catching her by the elbow. "Whoa! I'm sorry, Abby! You're the second person I've done that to in as many minutes."

She slipped a stray hair behind her ear. "Where's the fire then?"

"I'm in too big a hurry, I reckon. I— Wait, weren't you to take Miss Rose home after the Mission Society meeting?"

"Yes, she needed to pick up some things in town. Did you want to see her? She should be back any minute. I thought I'd straighten up a little while she finished."

"I need to talk to Sam if he's around."

Zane forced his glance to the storeroom, avoiding Abby's level gaze. "He's out back. Is everything all right?"

He smiled at her raised eyebrow. "Nothing you need to pester me about. I just was hoping to catch Sam."

"Fine. But you know he'll tell me anyway."

With a smile and a soft squeeze to her wrist, he cut through the room and around the counter to the back of the store.

He found Sam outside unloading supplies hauled from his weekly trip to Virginia City. "Need a hand?"

"You know I never turn away good cooking or a helping hand." Sam slid a box at him from the rig where he stood.

He hefted the crate and lugged it the few yards into the storage room. After several trips back, the wagon was soon cleared.

"I take it this isn't a social call," Sam said.

Zane watched him hop to the ground, the stubby Irishman who'd been his friend through everything from leaving grammar school to entering seminary and beyond. "What makes you say that?"

"I made you do all the heavy lifting, and you didn't rail at me about it."

Zane laughed. "It's been a long time since I've railed at you. But I did have something on my mind."

Sam folded his arms across his chest and focused on the ground at his feet, a sure sign he was listening intently. "Figured as much. What is it?"

He opened his mouth and then shut it, only to start again. Now that he had Sam's attention, he didn't know for sure what to say. Or leastways how to say it. He scratched the back of his neck. "What do you think of Miss Rose's new boarder?"

The look of surprise on Sam's face was unmistakable when his head cocked up to look him in the eye. "Journey?"

"Yes."

Sam grinned and quirked an eyebrow. "I think she's a pretty lady—seems like a sweet gal that's hit a jagged trail." A sly smile spread beneath his mustache. "Why do you ask?"

Zane shook his head. This wasn't going the way he'd hoped. "Not for the reason you're thinking. I'm asking if you think it's safe to let her stay with Miss Rose."

Sam's mustache twitched. "Since when do we *let* Rose Bishop do anything? What are you getting at?"

He wondered himself. He couldn't exactly cast unfair suspicion. And he had startled her there in the barn. But not just startled her. She'd been downright afraid.

"You don't think she's, well...dangerous?"

Laughter rumbled out of his friend. "Dangerous? The lady's barely five feet tall. She has a busted leg, no horse, no home to call her own. How dangerous could she be?"

"I'm serious, Sam. Don't you think it's a little odd, her coming into town alone? No mention of family. Winds up way out of town on a little evening ride? None of that gives you any cause for concern?"

"It makes me concerned for her. Come on, Zane. I'll admit it's unusual but not enough to put her on trial. This ain't like you. There something you're not telling me?"

He paused. If Sam didn't find any reason for alarm, there was no point in pushing the issue. Sam's sense of character seldom fell short, and if Sam had no qualms about Journey, Zane would try to put his aside as well. "I guess I just wanted your opinion on it."

"You sure that's all that's bothering you?"

"I'm looking out for Miss Rose. I'd hate to see anyone take advantage of her."

"Right."

Sam seemed all too ready to agree. "What is it you're wanting to say?"

"I'm saying she's a lovely young lady in need of help.

I'm saying you're in a place to help her. And I'm saying there's no need for you to feel guilty about that."

"Why would I?"

"You've been dodging every available female around these parts for the past year. It's been three years since Sarah died, Zane. She'd want you to go on." Sam turned to straighten a few boxes.

Zane's chest felt as if it were made of bricks, and he drew in a deep breath to ease the heaviness. "I know."

"You might know it, but you ain't been acting like you believe it. I'm not pushing. I'm just reminding." Sam clamped his shoulder, moving them both toward the rear door and through it into the whitened walls of the storeroom. "But if you're really that concerned, I'll keep an eye out with you."

"Thanks, Sam. I don't want to alarm anyone if there's no need. I just have this funny feeling about her. There's more than she's telling."

"Of course there is. A woman always carries that air of mystery, my friend. Part of the charm. Don't tell me you've forgotten that?"

Zane moved around the counter, but Sam stayed behind it, pounding a soft beat on the weathered wood. The sound of footsteps on the stairway leading to the Norwood home above the store got his attention. Abby smoothed her shawl around her shoulders and adjusted her hat as she stood at Sam's side.

"I'm glad I caught you before you left, Zane," she said. "Miss Rose and I thought it might be nice to have a little 'Welcome to Walten' dinner for Journey. Sunday after church at Miss Rose's."

"I'm not sure—"

"Nonsense. We'll see you there." She moved around

the counter and out to the porch. Zane waved out the door to Miss Rose, who sat waiting in the buggy.

Abby stopped at the bottom step. "Dinner will be served hot and delicious if the minister doesn't get too long-winded." She smiled. "Oh, and, Zane—that blue shirt Miss Rose gave you last Christmas? I'm sure she'd love to see you in it again on Sunday." With a wave and a swirl of her skirt, she climbed into the wagon and headed out of town. Miss Rose winked and waved a hand behind her as they pulled away.

Zane turned in time to see his friend smother a laugh.

"You think Journey can be more dangerous than those two?" Sam said. "Wonder what color they'll have *me* wearing?"

Chapter Ten

The house creaked in the Sunday-morning quiet. Journey hobbled around the couch on the crutches Doc Ferris had dropped off the night after Zane had caught her in the barn. The slender old man with the slight stoop never mentioned the preacher but simply said, "You seem to me to be a woman who's hard to keep down, so I thought we'd better get you onto these. But don't be thinking you can traipse all over creation with them. No farther than the porch for the next couple of weeks, you hear me?"

His fuzzy eyebrows had slouched over his sharp blue eyes. But the crook of a smile added to the stern look made her agree. The fact that Miss Rose stood behind him with her arms folded over herself didn't hurt, either. For reasons Journey could not understand, the woman had made her a personal responsibility and would see to it that she complied.

Hunched over the wooden frames, with dish towels wrapped to cushion the arm supports, she made her way to the cot. Miss Rose had set it in the corner of the kitchen for her, around the doorway from the parlor and near the stove. She sank onto the thick blanket with little grace, wondering if the crutches were intended to make getting around a little more cumbersome to discourage her from moving around so much.

"I should be thankful it wasn't any worse. They could have laid me up the entire six weeks." Doc Ferris assured her it wasn't a bad break, and by keeping the splint and binding tight, she could maneuver around some. Given the rough-and-tumble boys she'd played with as a little girl and her time with Hank, it was more a wonder she hadn't broken something before now.

The injury did excuse her from church, but Journey knew it wouldn't be long, unless Miss Rose thought the verses she read every morning at breakfast from the worn black book were enough. She seemed especially fond of "But as for me and my house, we will serve the Lord." Her soft voice emphasized the *my* as if she couldn't help it. No, part of her job would be to attend services with her employer. But no mention had been made as yet, and Journey didn't bring it up, either. Church was no place for a woman like her.

She stretched a hand under the cot and dragged her saddlebag over, pulling out a tiny mirror. She'd gone the past several days with her hair in no more than a low, loose chignon. The first few days her head had ached to the point where she thought a brush would kill her. But she determined to have it up today by the time Miss Rose, the Norwoods and Reverend Thompson arrived. She moved the mirror around to catch the wild mass from various angles. She should've tried harder before this. Pulling out the brush next, she tugged through the thick tangle of curls.

This whole dinner had her on edge. Why would someone hold a gathering to welcome the new hired hand? Well, not actually working yet, but the sentiment was the same. It didn't make sense. But then a lot of things about these people didn't make sense.

Miss Rose, for all her no-nonsense approach, had something very warm at her core that she couldn't explain. Even her own mama, whom she knew loved her dearly and had never been harsh to her, had been a hard woman. She'd had to be.

Maybe that wasn't entirely true. Those last few days before Mama died, even though she'd been sick, something soft and strong had taken root. Maybe it had something to do with her talk with that parson. Maybe it was just what happened to folks when they knew they were dying. Or maybe the memories had been brightened by her youth.

Journey pulled through the last knot of hair with a jerk when she saw Miss Rose's wagon top the ridge through the front window. Journey swept her hair up with her fingers and tied it in place before adding a few hairpins to hold it in a smooth coil at the back of her head. Then she stowed everything away and pulled up on one crutch so she could bank the fire with another piece of wood.

She heard Miss Rose and Abby being helped from their wagon seats by Zane and Sam and sank down into the overstuffed couch. It seemed rather out of place in this simple wooden house but beautiful nonetheless, with its rose-pink upholstery flecked with tiny blue cornflowers. She eased her broken leg onto the pillow, glad she had already set the table, then blew a wayward curl from her line of vision and rested.

Zane stepped through the threshold first and held the door for Miss Rose. His blue chambray shirt made his eyes look bluer than the stone gray she remembered. She shifted her focus to Miss Rose instead, rather than risk looking him in the eye.

"We're home," Miss Rose said. "How's your leg feeling? I hope you weren't up and around too much while we were gone."

"Not too much," she said. "I'd imagine Doc Ferris will let me out of the house when he stops by later this week."

"We'll see about that," Abby said. She stepped through the door with what looked to be a loaf of bread, wrapped in a cloth. "Let me see that knot on your head. How's that feeling?"

Journey touched the small lump that remained. "Not bad." She forgot about it unless she turned to lie on it in her sleep. The blue swelling had almost faded.

Sam stepped through the door last and wiped his feet on the braided rug, more out of habit than of need, she guessed. "I'd say she looks better than Zane with that hammer mark on his eye," he said, helping Abby with her shawl. "'Course, Journey was further ahead in looks before he had the bruise, too." He laughed as Abby pretended to swat him with her hat.

Journey flushed. She wondered what Zane thought. Miss Rose stood in the kitchen, tying an apron over her Sunday dress. "You gentlemen have a seat while we get dinner on the table. And, Journey, I appreciate your setting the table, but I don't appreciate the fact that you were wandering around on that leg to do it. You have to rest if it's going to heal."

She allowed a small smile to crease her cheek. Somehow that warm spirit of Miss Rose's overtook her words and soothed them down, like taking medicine with honey when she was a girl. "It wasn't much, really. I'm glad to help."

"Well, we'll take it from here," Miss Rose said.

Zane sat on the chair he'd sat to make his apology about her horse. Had it been only a week ago?

Sam remained by the door. "I should have time to unhitch the horses before dinner, right?"

"Here, I'll help," Zane said, moving to stand.

"Nope, I got it." Before the pastor could argue, Sam continued, "Even the Lord Jesus had things that had to be done on the Sabbath. I figure preaching is yours. Besides, no sense in both of us smelling like the barn. It won't take me long. You can give Journey the highlights of your message."

Sam slid out the door with a wink before Zane could protest further. He turned to her and eased back in his seat. She twisted the blanket between her fingers.

"I hope you don't mind, Pastor, if I leave you on your own for a moment. I should help Abby and Miss Rose in the kitchen. There's surely something—"

"Oh, no, you don't." Abby stood at the back of the sofa, tying her own apron. "You've done plenty. Sit there and let that leg mend. We'll holler when we're ready for you all."

"I guess we've been sequestered to the parlor," Zane said.

Journey forced a smile and huffed a breath of air. She watched Abby return to the kitchen, leaving her to face Zane. Now what?

"Listen…"

"I need to…"

Zane gave a full grin, a row of fine white teeth showing. "I beg your pardon, ma'am," he said with teasing propriety. "You first."

She glanced over her shoulder to the kitchen, making sure neither of the women worked near the doorway. The ring of the kettle lid and clink of tin plates confirmed their location near the far window. "I wanted to thank you for not saying anything about the other day. I need this job—well, when I can be up and working—and Miss Rose was very good to take me in like this. She doesn't seem the type to approve of my carrying a gun at all, not to mention pulling it on her pastor."

She licked her dry lips. "Please, believe me, I'm not out to hurt anyone. I'm looking after myself, and I'm counting on your honor as a minister to keep this quiet." She hoped her face carried her sincerity.

"I don't like the fact that you have it, let alone the fact that you feel the need to use it." He leaned forward with a huff. "I know we got off to a bad start when I had to put your horse down. But I have to tell you straight, I don't like the fact that someone with the kind of trouble you obviously have is hiding out here with one of the dearest women God made for this earth."

"There's no trouble here, Zane," she said, hoping she sounded more convincing than she felt. "There's no sense in creating problems where there aren't any."

He seemed to look through her. How much did he see?

"Zane, please—"

He held his hand up to stop her. "I don't like the fact that you won't let me—let any of us— help you." He kept his voice low.

"Most of all, I hate the fact that you're in this trouble, whatever it is. There's not much I can do about any of that, except pray. But let me tell you this," he said, pointing at her with one hand. He leaned even closer to put his other hand on the end of the couch. "I'm keeping my eye on you until I can figure out what kind of trouble you're into. I owe Miss Rose a lot, and I'll not have anyone hurt her in any way if I have it within my power to stop it."

Journey realized she had leaned toward him in an effort to keep their conversation private, but she edged away as he pressed forward. She drew back from the fire in his eyes. Yet his voice held no heat, only concern. What would his sermons be like?

"Answer me this—who will come for you first? The law or someone else?"

"The less you know the better," she said, her voice soft. "You're the one who warned me to watch my back. I can do that fine on my own. All you have to know is that I did what I had to do to survive."

"I'm watching your back, too. I want to know what I'm looking for. I hope you'll come to know there's more folks to rely on here than yourself."

"I won't be here that long, honestly. You've all been so good to me. I'd never want to bring you into my problems."

"You might as well face the fact that you're here until spring. Do you really think your trouble is that far behind?" Zane leaned forward, his voice at a whisper. His gray eyes never wavered.

Blood pounded in her ears and she swallowed hard, drawing back as far as the arm of the couch allowed.

"Suit yourself. You've already answered my question."

Don't cry. Don't let him see you cry. She drew in a deep breath. "I'm warning you to stay as far away from my problems as you can. I can't be looking out for myself and for you as well."

He breathed deeply and the tight lines around his eyes eased.

"Don't you worry about me. I know Someone who can watch out for us both."

Steps on the porch ended any comment she would have made, if any had come to mind. Sam wandered into the room, rubbing his hands together. "It's getting mighty chilly out there. May have our first snow by Sunday next if this keeps up."

Journey shivered in the cold draft. Another reminder that Walten was where she'd be spending the long winter. Zane smiled and somehow she couldn't be angry with him. Wary, yes. Frightened even. But angry proved difficult.

He could ruin everything if he started meddling. And she didn't trust him not to. He was determined to involve himself in her trouble, but how could she stop him? She was thankful when Miss Rose called them to the dinner table, giving her mind a break from her tumbled thoughts.

Chapter Eleven

From Miss Rose's back porch, Zane watched Sam and Abby's wagon disappear over the bluff. He took another bite of apple cobbler and rocked his chair back on two legs. The tangy-sweet flavor on his tongue made him smile. "Sarah loved your baking."

Miss Rose laughed. "I know. She tried many of my recipes, but the poor girl couldn't get the hang of it. You married a good cook, Zane, but she had trouble with the sweets."

He nodded. He couldn't argue with that, though it seemed disloyal to comment. "She was sweet enough herself."

"That she was. But there's no harm in remembering her imperfections. They were part of the woman you loved, too."

True, he thought. But Sarah's imperfections were few and far between, and they lay buried in the ashes. He set his plate on the stand between the two chairs. "Journey still tires easily."

"Some. I have the feeling she uses it as an excuse to

stay away from folks more than being truly worn out. That girl's got a lot on her mind."

Good. At least Miss Rose wasn't totally taken in by her new housemate. "She does seem rather secretive, doesn't she?"

"Oh, there's something bothering her. She's awful quiet most times, keeps glancing around at all the windows like she's waiting for someone to pop through them. I hear her setting the lock every night after I go to bed."

"Maybe it's not such a good idea for her to stay here. I'd hate to see her drag you into whatever problems she has."

"Zane Thompson!" Miss Rose jumped out of her seat and glared down at him, hands flapping. "I'm surprised at you. What would you have me do? Turn that girl out now when she has nothing? She lost her horse. She doesn't have any money. She had me talk to Abby about posting signs hoping to do a little sewing work until her leg mends to help pay for her keep. And you want me to turn her out?"

He held his hands up in a gesture of calm and protest. "Now, Miss Rose, don't get your dander up. I'm just saying maybe it'd be better if she stayed somewhere else, in town maybe. Sam and Abby might—"

"There's not room at Sam and Abby's. Besides, it's not right. They have a business to run, and Journey's under my own hire. She's my responsibility."

She was right. Dear Lord, forgive him, what was he to do? Journey's soft brown eyes and wary glance appeared in his mind's eye. He rubbed his face, hoping to wipe the image away. He had to keep his suspicions in mind. Otherwise it would be too easy to admire her determination.

"I'm sorry, Miss Rose. I know you can't turn her out. I shouldn't have even suggested it. But I worry about you."

Her wrinkled hand rubbed over his and her voice softened. "You can't take care of me any better than the Lord has all these years. You know worry's a sin and can't do you any good anyway. So pray, then stop worrying."

"I will. I have been, but my heart's not been in it. I guess even ministers don't get it right all the time." He smiled at the tiny woman standing over him.

"Being a pastor doesn't mean you're perfect. It means you have a greater responsibility, though. We have to do this for Journey. Whatever her trouble is, God sent her here for us to look after. I don't know what all that means, but we'll need to trust that the Lord knows what He's doing by bringing her to us." He felt the pressure of her thin lips on the top of his head followed by a warm flush over his ears. "But your concern isn't all for me. You care about her, too, Zane. I see it. I know."

He laced his fingers across his stomach and tipped the chair until it leaned against the windowsill. "Comes with the territory."

"I don't know. I've heard a lot of ministers pray with great compassion, but not one looked at me the way you look at her."

He laughed and turned away before she could read something else. "That's how rumors get started, you know."

She did not laugh. Instead, she set her knuckles on her bony hips and gave him a hard look. "That's not my style and you know it. And it's not going to change the subject."

"What subject?"

"The subject of when you're going to move on and give another woman at least half a chance to make you happy."

He rocked forward, both feet hitting the porch floor with a thump. "Hold on, now. I think it's a bit early to be hitching us up. She's not even a believer."

"Maybe not yet. Maybe it's too soon for us to know much of anything about her spiritual life. But it's not like you have to marry her," she said, sitting down in the chair she pulled close to him.

"What?"

"Hear me out before you go jumping to conclusions. I'm saying you're young and handsome. I'm saying there are several young ladies around here who've offered you an invitation to Sunday dinner, and there's no harm in accepting. But Journey's the first lady you've shown that kind of interest in since—"

"Since Sarah died?" He closed his eyes as the remainder of the hammer-bruise on his forehead throbbed a little.

He felt the warmth of her hand on his knee. "Sarah wouldn't want you to be alone for fear you'll not honor her memory. It doesn't give her any honor for you not to go on living."

"All I feel for Journey is a sense of responsibility. It's obvious she needs help, and it's my duty to do that. The Lord has enough for me to do without thinking of courting again."

Miss Rose smiled. "I don't think you believe that any

more than I do. The Lord didn't intend for any man to be alone. You need a helpmate."

"So you're trying to get rid of me?" He glanced her way from the corner of his eye and grinned.

"I love your company, Reverend Thompson," she told him, with a snap of her hand on his leg. "If I was younger, I'd be late for service myself, making that final preen. But I'm not, and it's not right that you should spend so much time with a crumbly old woman."

He leaned forward to kiss her soft cheek. "I'll be fine. Don't worry—it's a sin, remember?"

"I'm not worried. I just wanted to get you thinking. After all—" she lowered her voice as if the sleeping patient could hear "—she is a beautiful and captive audience right now. That should make it easy enough, even for you."

She patted his cheek and wobbled a little until she steadied her feet under her. Zane watched her walk back into the house, catching the wink she sent his way before stepping through the doorway.

He rubbed a hand over his face before resting his forehead on his palm. What had just happened? He had meant to warn Miss Rose somehow. He knew Journey had more trouble than she could handle. As long as she stayed with Miss Rose, they could both be in danger. But Miss Rose had turned his concern into something entirely different.

He cupped his chin and stared out over the bluff as a small smile crept across his face. Leave it to her to suggest courting.

"Christians should find all the clean fun they can, show those unbelievers they don't need all Satan's wiles to have a good time," she often said.

He glanced back toward the door, thinking of auburn curls spilling over the arm of the couch and how she had felt in his arms as he settled her there weeks ago. He stretched to his feet, the smile slipping from his face. He couldn't waste his attention on such things as courting, especially now. There was definitely something more to Journey's story than she was telling. And until he found out what, he'd have no time for anything else.

Chapter Twelve

Journey paused at the top of the mercantile steps to catch her balance as she held her satchel and crutches at the same time.

In another week or so, Doc Ferris said he might allow her to start putting weight on her broken leg. She had taken that as having his permission to finally make a trip into town. Being stuck inside wrangled her nerves, like waiting for a firecracker to explode. So when Miss Rose went to visit Mrs. Hamler, she took advantage of the offer to use the horses.

"What do you think you're doing?" Abby's voice gave her a start and she froze. "I didn't think you were cleared to be walking around yet."

"I thought, with the crutches…"

Abby smiled and Journey relaxed a little. "I see. But I think that's what we call 'following the letter of the law.' Doc Ferris seemed to think it would be at least another week before you'd be able to come into town."

"I had a few shirts finished and wanted to get them to you." That was true enough. She made her way up the remaining steps and hobbled through the door Abby held open.

"I could've picked them up later this week. Sam and Zane are delivering an order, or I'd have brought them today. But since you're here, I've got a few more. Word is getting around about your work. The cowboys heading south through here are glad to find someone to take in their mending. But this'll probably be all from them until spring."

Journey nodded, trying to hide her disappointment as she deposited her satchel onto the store counter, fumbling with the strap. The sewing had held her through the past few weeks at least. Doc Ferris had never mentioned his fee, but she had been anxious to clear the debt. She couldn't let it lie unpaid.

"...post a letter?"

Abby's continued chatter floated back into her consciousness.

"I beg your pardon?"

"I wondered if Miss Rose had given you her letter to post. She usually sends one out the middle of the month to her nephew in Virginia City." As proud as she sounded, Journey would've thought the man was Abby's own kin.

"Uh, no, no letter today. Does she get to see him much?" She focused on the satchel strap, hoping not to sound overly interested. Her leg started to ache.

"Fairly much so, I guess. Of course, can you ever see enough of family? I know she wishes he were closer. He's the son of Rose's only sister, and the last of her family living. She knows he's doing what he's been called to do, so she doesn't complain. But she does spoil him all the more when he gets a chance to visit.

I imagine you'll get to meet him over Thanksgiving." She wrapped the finished shirts in brown paper, fingers flying almost as fast as the words from her mouth.

"That'll be lovely, I'm sure." She'd cross that bridge when she came to it.

"Anything else you need, Journey?" Abby gave her the packet of shirts to be mended.

"No. I'll just take these next orders and head back."

Abby leaned over the wide wooden counter, its honey hues just shades darker than her braided hair sweeping across it. "You didn't tell her you were coming, eh?" she whispered, though they were the only ones in the bright storeroom.

"Not exactly, but—"

The woman waved her hands. "No need to explain to me. I understand as well as anybody how hard it is to be cooped up inside for very long. We're kindred spirits that way. So I won't keep you."

"I appreciate that," Journey said. "I figured it's easier to ask forgiveness than to gain permission."

Abby laughed, light and graceful. "I agree. You really must come for a visit—a good, long one—after you're all mended. Promise you will."

She nodded. "Zane tells me I'll not get beyond the mountains until spring now. I'm sure we'll have plenty of time to get together."

"Good. I'll count on it."

Abby moved to take the parcels out to the wagon. As much as she hated it, Journey had to admit she was grateful for the help. She wanted to be back before Miss Rose returned. It wouldn't be right to worry the woman, and she hadn't left a note.

"Have you made your own dress yet?" Abby asked.

Journey continued to make her way out the door. "I haven't been in any rush, what with working on the other mending and all."

"Well, you'd better get in a rush. You'll want to have it finished for the harvest party, and that's just over a week away. Lots of single, young ranchers from all over the area come into Walten for it." Abby fairly beamed with excitement.

Journey couldn't hide the nervousness in her voice. "Whatever would I do at a harvest party?"

She supposed Abby's excitement could be contagious if she'd let it. The woman smiled at her, hands moving as she described the town gathering. "People bring in some of their crops to share, kind of a way to see who has bragging rights, I guess. Men bring in sheared wool bales, their teams, those kinds of things. Ladies bring baked goods and sewing projects for display. There are games for the children, and the adults, too. Recitations by the schoolchildren, and singing…" Her voice trailed off, apparently lost in memories of previous years. "It's great fun."

Despite herself, Journey found her curiosity growing. What must it have been like to grow up in such a place? Where children were safe and carefree and sent to a real school, where neighbors looked out for one another? The women who'd lived in one-room stalls above the saloon similar to Journey and her mother had formed their own type of neighborliness, she supposed, but it was nothing compared with what she'd experienced in the past few weeks.

While she hadn't missed a word of Abby's description, she must've adopted a rather bewildered expression, because Abby tapped her on the shoulder. "You will come, won't you? I'm sure Miss Rose will want you to bring her, and it'll be a great chance for you to get to meet all the folks around here. You won't get another chance like this until Christmas."

She allowed a tentative grin to pull her lips tight. "It does sound nice." But the last thing she needed was to become acquainted with more people from Walten.

Sometimes the best place to hide is right in plain sight, darlin'. Folks never see what's right under their noses. Hank had told her that. Hank would know. He'd swindled more people in broad daylight than there were stars in the night sky.

She nodded her head once, firmly. "I'll think about it. Thank you for telling me. Maybe I should get started on that dress."

Abby's eyebrows rose as the smile on her face widened. "You let me know if I can do anything to help. Even if you just want to talk, stop in. I love to talk, but I'm not a bad listener, either."

Journey's heart skipped a moment. What had Zane told her? She drew a deep breath. Surely he wouldn't say anything about their meeting in the barn. But she couldn't afford to add to his suspicions.

Thanking Abby, she put her crutches in the wagon bed and hoisted herself into the seat with her arms and her good knee and was soon on her way out of town. She smiled with a small sense of satisfaction and drew her collar up around her as the sharp wind bit at her neck. It felt good to know she had a tight, warm house to go to, especially with autumn nearing an end. The whole town seemed determined to take her in, with or without her permission.

But an icy shiver shook her as she left the town's

borders, one not caused by the winds of coming winter. She glanced over her shoulder. A tall shadow slid behind Norwood's Mercantile. Why it should make her uneasy she didn't know, but she urged the horses to a fast trot just the same.

"So what's put a burr in your saddle?" Zane started, sitting forward on the wagon seat next ~~to Sam.~~ "What do you mean?"

~~we left Walten.~~ "...said more than five words since

"I thought I was here for my strong back, not my conversational skills." Zane grinned at his old friend. "You could've brought Abby along."

Sam gave a wounded look. "I happen to enjoy her chatter. She's lively." He laughed. "Remember that first Sunday drive we took together, you and Sarah, me and Abby?"

Zane nodded. "I wanted her to stop talking in the worst way so Sarah'd be able to get a few words in."

"She was more quiet, like me." Sam gave a sidelong glance as he jostled the reins.

"Sure. And what was it we all called you in school? 'Magpie' comes to mind."

Sam laughed, a deep jolly sound, and Zane joined in. Then he quieted and asked again. "You seem to have something stuck in your craw, is all, and we have a long ride ahead, so you might as well tell me what's going on. Does it have anything to do with the lovely Miss Smith?"

Zane leaned back on the seat. "I suppose so. Something about that lady doesn't sit right with me."

"That's all it is?"

"Of course that's all it is. What are you asking?"

"It's hard not to notice how pretty she is. She's a smart one to have come all that way on her own, determined, kindhearted… No one would think any less of you for being interested in that."

"Don't you start. Miss Rose and Abby have both been hinting. I don't think she's even a believer," Zane argued.

"But if she were?"

Zane rumbled low in his thr̶o̶a̶t̶. ̶.̶ ̶.̶ ̶y̶o̶u̶ ̶k̶n̶o̶w̶ ̶I̶ ̶d̶o̶n̶'̶t̶ condone mission̶a̶r̶y̶ ̶c̶o̶u̶r̶t̶s̶h̶i̶p̶,̶ ̶S̶a̶m̶.̶"̶

His friend slapped the reins lightly, silent for a moment. "After Sarah died, something changed in you—"

"What did you expect—"

"Hear me out, now," Sam said. "You've always been focused on your ministry. I think you had a sense of that even when we were kids. But that focus changed somehow. It's grown so large now I'm afraid it's keeping you from seeing anything beyond it."

"I'm fine, Sam." He leaned forward again, outside of his field of vision. "I'm doing the Lord's work, and that's enough for me."

"So you don't think she's pretty?" Sam asked.

Zane twisted his shoulders so he could look his friend in the eye. "I wouldn't go so far as to say that. But I can't let my judgment be clouded. I can't help but admire her courage, and she's got grit, I'll give you that. But unless she knows the Lord, and until I can figure out the missing pieces to her story, that's all it can be."

Sam nodded. "All the more reason for me to be praying for you."

"And for her, my friend," Zane said.

Chapter Thirteen

Over a week later and Walten's harvest party was in full swing by the time Journey and Miss Rose arrived. Journey carried a pan full of chicken, sizzled in bread crumbs just that morning, into the wagon-filled church-yard. Voices blended with the happy tune of a fiddle somewhere off to the right.

The sky cleared overhead and a strong breeze eased the sun's unexpected heat. The weather might be un-predictable this time of year, but it seemed it would co-operate for the day's festivities.

"Don't be fooled," Miss Rose said, fanning a hand-kerchief over her face. "Tomorrow we could wake to three feet of snow. Winter might tease us for a while, but it's coming. I've lived here long enough to smell it."

"How long have you lived here, Miss Rose?"

She feared she had crossed the line when the pause lengthened. Asking questions too often became a two-way street. Still, in sharing a house with this woman, she'd found her interest welcomed. The woman also was quick to take a hint, never pushing for answers beyond those she offered.

"I guess it's been nigh onto sixty years." Her voice carried a tone of disbelief, and she blinked with a look of amazement. "My Wallace and I were married when I was just sixteen, and we headed west the next day. I'll be seventy-six next spring."

They continued through the maze of booths and tables covered in vegetables and baked goods set in the grassy area behind the church. Children chased one another in the open spaces between. Men grouped near the horses, comparing harnesses. Ladies in bright dresses were busy arranging and rearranging displays.

It felt good to be outside and off the crutches, Journey thought as she placed the pan in a free spot on the table between a plate of crisp potato cakes and a tray of boiled ham. Doc Ferris had cleared her the day before. Even to be out among so many strangers it felt good.

"There you are!" Abby's voice could be heard over the general hubbub as she wound her way through the swarm of people. She took Miss Rose's arm and led them to another table crowded with still more picnic food. "You look lovely, Journey. You chose well for yourself in that color."

She smiled her thanks and fanned her hands over the navy fabric. Fashion was never a great concern, but she had made a point to finish the dress for this occasion. The fitted bodice clasped with simple buttons all the way up to a collar of the same color, but with a scalloped edge. She had been tempted to sew a split skirt for riding but hadn't noticed any other women wearing them in town, and so she resisted. It wouldn't do to stand out.

Besides the work dress she wore for everyday use,

her sparse wardrobe was ragged. She had needed something decent to wear to meet the community. It might reflect poorly on Miss Rose if she came looking unkempt.

"Let me introduce you to our sewing circle," Abby said. Journey found herself pulled into a crowd of women before she could protest. She slipped her fingers along the curls that had already pulled from the low chignon at her neck and tried to tuck them back into the general mass.

"Ladies, I'd like you to meet Miss Journey Smith," Abby said. "She's new to Walten, staying with Miss Rose out at the ranch. Journey, this is Mrs. Phoebe Decker, Miss Sue Anderson and Mrs. Evie Wilson. Journey is quite a seamstress, and now that she's recuperated from a recent accident, I've invited her to join our sewing circle."

Mrs. Wilson shifted her baby from one hip to the other and stretched her right hand in greeting. Journey took it, forcing a smile to her anxious lips. "So nice to finally meet you, since Abby's been telling us about you. I'm sorry to hear you had such a traumatic introduction to our town. We're so glad you're up and about now." Something in Mrs. Wilson's soft grip reminded Journey of her mother.

Sue Anderson's carefully coiffed hair, dimpled face and glittering broach told her story.

The swooping feather of her hat brushed her over-pink cheeks and pointed to an over-wide smile. Her eyes were kind, but Journey had met women like her before. Society. Well-bred. She'd no doubt been born to a life of leisure and had no idea of how hard everyday labors could be. "So nice to meet you, Journey." She held out a gloved hand.

Journey stiffened when Phoebe Decker interrupted with her nasal tone. "After everything we've heard from Rose Bishop, the Norwoods and Reverend Thompson, we've all been anxious to meet you. You've been quite the topic of conversation."

She was not very old, not very pretty and not at all friendly. Journey had a feeling Phoebe was not one to ignore those she could not tolerate.

"I didn't realize I had caused such a stir," Journey said, questioning Abby with a look.

"We're a small community," Abby said. "Anyone new creates a sensation."

"Traveling all that way on your own..." Phoebe clucked her tongue. *Chicken Lady.* The name popped into Journey's mind and she smiled in spite of herself. "I'm certain you'll have stories to share. Surely there are a few worthy of polite company."

Phoebe was not looking for tales of entertainment. This woman had already formulated a few stories of her own about her. But she somehow doubted she had imagination enough to get close to the truth.

Sue stepped closer. "I know I couldn't have done it—traveled alone—without an escort. And then to lose your horse." Sue looked dutifully distressed. "Well, I'm glad to see you're on the mend. We'll see you at sewing circle. Now, if you'll excuse me, I must speak with Mrs. Hamler about the Ladies' Aid Society." With a flounce of her bustle, she moved to the booths, waving a gloved hand.

"I think it'll be wonderful to have a new face in the sewing circle." Evie smiled, and Journey felt her anxiety ease. "We haven't been meeting real regularly through the summer, but now that harvesting is done, we'll start our weekly get-togethers. We talk about as much as we sew, but you'll have to excuse us. We're a bunch of harmless busybodies for the most part, so feel free to tell us to mind our own concerns if we get out of line. Right, Phoebe?"

The woman nodded, drawing a line straight down with the point of her nose. "We have to extend a welcome to you. Especially with all your sewing accomplishments I've heard so much about. You take in mending for the cowboys traveling through town, I hear." She didn't smile. "Please excuse me, Pastor Zane has arrived. He has to have a piece of my Mary's apple pie."

"Never mind her," Evie said, patting Journey's arm as Phoebe hurried off. "She's been after Pastor Thompson for her daughter ever since his wife passed away, and she's jealous of any woman prettier than her Mary."

Journey bit the inside of her lip. "But I don't think—"

"Nonsense. With beauty like yours, who could blame him? Just don't let her get to you and you'll be fine. I'll let you know about our first meeting next week, ladies. I trust we'll see you in services now that your leg has healed, Journey. Well, I had better catch up with my Jimmy. I'm sure he's pestering his father something awful about now. See you on Sunday."

Journey nodded her off, grateful to be away from the inquisition. Her mouth felt dry as she searched the growing crowd, spotting Miss Rose with a group of older ladies sitting near the pie-laden tables, ready to serve.

"Come on," Abby said. "There are plenty more folks to meet."

"I'm feeling easily worn out these first days," Journey said. "I'm not used to so much walking around. Miss Rose has all but tied me down these past few weeks, especially since my trip into town last week. I'll find a shady spot to sit and enjoy the crowd."

Abby did not look convinced. "If you're sure, but everyone's anxious to meet you. We've been praying for you at church, so naturally folks are wondering who you are and how you're doing. I'll find you again later on?"

Journey relented, seeing that Abby wouldn't be content to simply let her be a wallflower. "Maybe this afternoon we can meet more people. I'm not very good with names, so it's easier to go slow."

Her breath left her in a gasp as Abby caught her in a tight squeeze. "That'll be fine. You find a good spot and enjoy the day. I'm so glad you're walking around and that you're here. You'll love Walten. I know it."

Journey watched Abby's tall form slide across the open space, toward Miss Rose. She breathed easier and started off in search of a quiet tree to hide under. There were few to choose from, but anyplace away from the crowd would be welcome. It was going to be a long day.

Chapter Fourteen

Zane arrived to find wagons filling the churchyard. He gazed at the wide expanse of sky, thankful for the clear weather. Snow could be here as early as tomorrow, with the way the wind blew over the mountains, but today the community could enjoy the picnic.

He raised his arms and stepped back, narrowly avoiding some children chasing each other between tables. How Sarah had loved to race with them. "Not dignified," Mrs. Decker had muttered so many times. He and Sarah had talked about having their own children one day. When Sarah had suspected they would soon become a family, Zane had never been a happier man. Sometimes it felt like yesterday. But it was years ago. Three years...

He blinked hard in the sun. Was that Mrs. Decker headed his way? She probably wanted him to have a piece of Mary's apple pie. His mouth puckered at the thought. He hoped Mary wouldn't have to rely on her cooking skills to snare a husband.

Where was Miss Rose? She made a good fence when

it came to keeping Phoebe Decker at bay. He felt sorry for Mary. He doubted her mother gave the shy girl a chance to find her own beau. But he was not sorry enough to eat that pie.

He spied Miss Rose and her friends, sitting in the sunshine. Her silver hair shone, and Zane wondered what she must've looked like when she'd come to Montana as a young bride. He returned her wave when he realized he'd been caught staring, and moved to greet her.

"Hello, ladies," he said. "It looks like the Lord's blessed us with beautiful weather." He relaxed when he noticed Phoebe Decker stop short, then turn to the quilt display. He'd dodged the pie for a moment, anyhow.

Zane squeezed Miss Rose's shoulder as she patted his hand.

"Is Journey here?" he asked.

"Yes." Her smile warned him of where her thoughts were going. "She was with Abby the last I saw her."

"She went to find some shade," Abby said, walking up behind the group. "Meeting Phoebe wore her out, I'm afraid." Her voice lowered, but the gleam in her eye didn't dim.

"Hello. Where's Sam?" Zane asked, searching the crowd.

Abby flicked back her blond hair. "He'll be along. A shipment from Virginia City arrived this morning."

"I'll have to catch him later, then." He craned his neck. "It's good to see so many come out for the day."

"It won't be long until we're all fighting cabin fever," Miss Rose said. "No reason not to get out and enjoy the fellowship when we can."

"I'd better try to find Journey. She doesn't seem one for socializing. With so many people around…"

He shrugged. What did he really think she could do? It's not as if she'd pull her gun in this crowd, would she?

"Right," Abby said. "It'd be a shame to have a pretty thing like her sitting alone with all these gentlemen ranchers and handsome trail hands wandering around."

"Especially in that pretty new dress she sewed for herself," Miss Rose said. He didn't miss the chime in her voice.

He fought with all he had to keep the heat from his ears. The outer ridge grew red enough to give him away every time, no matter how brown his skin turned in the summer sun.

Many of the women in the circle smiled; some even twittered behind gloved hands. Zane swallowed hard. "I'll stroll around a bit, introduce myself to some of the new faces. Ladies, if you'll excuse me."

He ducked his head and cleared his throat as he made his exit from the group. He walked quickly but couldn't miss Abby's voice.

"We really shouldn't tease Pastor Thompson so. He's only doing his duty." Her tone didn't sound very supportive, and several of the ladies laughed outright.

Thank the Lord he'd gotten away when he did. He couldn't decide who tried harder at being a matchmaker, Abby or Miss Rose.

Zane stared at the many unfamiliar faces wandering around the yard. The community had grown over the past year, and the harvest festival gave many new families their first opportunity to relax and meet their neighbors. He remembered how busy his folks had been when they'd moved to Walten.

A few haggard faces testified to a rough start for some. Zane hoped to make his way to all the newcomers and give them an invitation to Sunday services. He also hoped to check in with the cowboys he recognized from those rare Sundays when they could make it to service. Most of them wouldn't be traveling through town again until next fall.

Zane's glance stopped at a shifty-eyed drifter. He looked as if he'd seen more than his share of bad trail and stared through the crowd as if he wanted to find someone in particular.

Zane passed by Evie Wilson, serving up cider.

"How do, Pastor Thompson?" She handed him a battered tin cup. "You look as though you could use some cool refreshment."

He took a sip. "Cold and sweet. That hits the spot, ma'am. Thank you." He set the tin back. "Good to see so many turn out."

"I know. It gives me the chance to see folks there's never time to visit in the busyness of summer."

"Especially with that new little one to watch after," Zane said.

Mrs. Wilson nodded, looking over the crowd.

"Do you recognize that cowhand over there?" she asked, nodding across the dusty clearing at the man who'd caught his attention a moment ago.

"No, ma'am. Why do you ask?"

She shrugged. "He seems lost, looks out of place. You know, I usually recognize the faces around here, even if the names escape me."

Zane squinted against the bright sun. "Probably some cowpoke decided to stop on the way back from Virginia City or somewhere, same as the others. I'll try to catch him sometime today and introduce myself, invite him

to services. Right now I thought I'd check on Journey—
I mean, Miss Smith. Have you seen her?"

Evie shaded her eyes and gestured to the edge of the
yard. "She's under the aspen."

He spotted her, feet drawn beneath her on a quilt. She
wore a navy dress he hadn't seen before, and he found
himself admiring the narrow silhouette she presented.
Her auburn hair shone brightly in the filtered sunlight,
full and rich until tight ringlets fell from her temples to
brush her flushed cheeks. He swallowed hard.

She seemed not to notice the milling crowd as she
looked toward some undetermined spot in the east. Zane
glanced around, trying to decide on what or whom she
was focused. There was nothing but the open range.

"I see her. Thanks." He headed toward Journey.

As he walked, he noticed the drifter's focus on her.
The man's eyes appeared cold and lifeless; the smile
he wore looked as if he'd pasted it on moments ago—a
smile that could be peeled off with his socks that evening. Zane forced himself to look away before he read
too much into the scene. Between Journey's gun, Abby's warning and Miss Rose's insinuations, his mind
had started moving independently from his common
sense. Now his heart seemed to have taken a direction
all its own.

He paused a moment, then moved toward Journey.
Why did he feel compelled to guard her? He laughed
at himself. He continued until he stood within her line
of sight.

"Enjoying yourself?" he asked.

Journey looked up at him slowly, blinking in the
shadow he cast over her face. He waited, wondering if
he'd woken her.

"The picnic is lovely." Her crooked smile shook as her wide brown eyes twitched.

"Mind if I sit down?"

"Suit yourself," she said, sliding over on the blanket.

He sat and rested an elbow on his bent knee. Together they studied the people. The stranger still stood off to the side, away from the other cowboys. Zane watched as Journey's gaze traced a path to the man. Had she noticed the cowboy earlier? She seemed edgier than usual, and he figured that not much made its way past her.

"Nice weather we're having for the picnic," Zane said. "Last year a late storm blew in and chased us all into the church."

Journey nodded, chewing her full lower lip.

"Then we had relay races climbing into the steeple."

"Is that so?"

"Sure is. Miss Rose won and crowed like a chicken from the rafters."

"That sounds nice."

He blew out a breath and chanced a glance at her, then back to the figure that held her attention. He thought about pointing out the man's earlier interest but he didn't have the heart to tease her when she looked ready to bolt as it was.

They sat through the three-legged race in silence. He'd been asked to serve as judge for the pie-baking contest after the noon meal.

He nudged her shoulder with his. "Penny for your thoughts."

She started, eyes flashing with surprise as his arm brushed hers. "I beg your pardon?"

"Are you feeling better, Journey, now that you're up and around?"

"Yes." She turned toward him but glanced over her shoulder. "It feels good to be moving unhampered by those blamed crutches."

Her emphatic response caught him off guard and he laughed. "How are things going with Miss Rose? Is she working you like a mule?"

Journey smiled yet Zane saw her tension grow after a few questions. Was she afraid she'd say too much? "It's more work for her thinking up enough to keep me busy. But she seems happy for the company."

"I know she is." He nodded. "She's not as spry as she once was."

"I couldn't imagine keeping up with her then," Journey said. Her auburn curls caught the sunlight, and he imagined what it would be like to wrap one around his finger.

"It's safer for you to be somewhere warm with winter beating down the door," he said.

She shifted on the quilt. "That's what I hear, but it feels awfully warm to me right now."

"The weather switches as hard as the trails through the mountains. You'll see, we'll have snow soon."

"So I hear." Again, her voice sounded as if her mind was far away. Zane searched her face. For what, he wasn't exactly sure, but hoped he'd know it when he saw it.

She struggled to her feet, and he stood quickly to offer a hand. She pushed curls into place and stood without assistance. "I'd better find Abby."

He stayed her with a hand on her arm. She flinched but didn't pull away. "There are a lot of good people here, Journey," Zane said, staring at her face. How could eyes so wide hide so much? He fought the sudden compulsion to draw her close.

A dimple appeared on her left cheek, one he hadn't noticed before. "I appreciate the company, Pastor. Now, if you'll please excuse me."

"Sure." He watched her limp in Abby's direction, then turn between two tables and around the side of the church building instead. This time, he made no move to seek her out.

Chapter Fifteen

Journey glanced across the circle of people huddled around the bonfire as evening settled on the group of stragglers at the end of the long day. She had hoped to leave hours ago. The strain of seeing so many new faces tired her. But when the fire was lit, and a violin brought out, Miss Rose settled in close, swaying to the music.

She had to admit that the music, combined with the thinned crowd, restored the sense of comfort she'd gotten used to at Miss Rose's house.

A cold breeze picked up when the sun went down. Journey pulled the heavy cape Miss Rose had insisted she bring closer around her. Maybe there would be snow before long. She'd been in the West long enough to know that weather changed quickly. Even though a circle of people blocked some of the fire's heat, the glow kept her nose from numbing.

She scanned the crowd, the faces almost familiar, though she didn't know their names. That thought comforted her, too. Actually, that word could be used to describe the entire town—comforting. She crossed her arms over her knees and stared at her boot tips. Maybe come spring she could afford a new pair before moving on.

Another pair of boots entered her field of vision. She stiffened. Fear shot like ice down her spine.

"Mind if I sit down?" Zane again.

Journey nodded, trying to breathe normally. He said nothing, just stretched his legs out before him and tapped his fingers across his knee in time to the music. Her tension melted as the comfortable silence grew.

The wind switched direction, driving the evening chill a little deeper.

"Bet the cold'll bother you for a while yet." Zane scratched his chin.

"I'm supposing it might." Journey rubbed her leg.

"It might help if you walked around some or sat closer to the fire," Zane said. His eyes were framed with shiny black lashes, and the firelight threw the planes of his cheek and jaw into strong relief.

"Zane, I—"

Loud, coarse laughter interrupted. A wagon drew near the bonfire. Journey recognized some of the men on the wagon from earlier in the day. She stood, smoothing her skirt, and gripped her shaking hands. A sense of dread filled her, but Zane moved and stood behind her, blocking the chill of the wind.

Three men tumbled off before the wagon even stopped. Their singing drowned out the soft violin.

A lanky cowboy with a tan hat strolled her way. His two buddies knocked into each other behind him, with whispers and crude laughter. She edged back, bumping into Zane's solid warmth.

The tall man laughed and only leaned closer. The

smell of alcohol rolling from his mouth made her gag, and Journey pressed the back of her hand to her nose. "Hey, gal, don' be so shy now. I hear you're the right friendly type."

He made a grab for her, but the man tripped and fell as Zane drew her back farther. She stumbled over Zane's feet until his fingers tightened around her arm, as if he knew she would turn and run. Yet there was something in the rumble of his chest that stilled her. "You have no business with her," he said.

The three cowboys howled and slapped their legs, swaying into one another as they helped their friend to his feet. "Business is right, Preacher, from what I hear tell. Ain't that right, missy?"

The crowd grew quiet and the music stopped. Heat rushed to Journey's face, but an icy streak cut the air off at her throat and settled into her stomach. She couldn't breathe. "I'm certain I don't know what you're referring to."

Zane moved from behind to stand between her and the men. "And I'm certain that when you sober up, you'll realize you're mistaken about the woman." His tone left no doubt. "I'll ask you to leave now, before you make bigger fools of yourselves."

The tall one lost his easy smile. He swayed closer and Journey slid back farther, despite the fact that Zane held his place in front of her. "The only fool I see here, Preacher, is you for not knowing when to stand aside."

Cheers from his friends blended to a dull thud in her ears. Zane seemed relaxed, but his feet dug into the dirt. She looked over to the other side of the fire when Abby gasped. She and Miss Rose sat huddled together, hands clasped.

"Zane, don't," Journey whispered, scratching his shoulder with her fingertips barely touching.

"Hold up, fellas." The voice drew her attention to the shadow on the wagon seat. The dark figure didn't step down but let his gruff, sober voice carry his intent. The cowboy who'd been eyeing her all day, the one so familiar and yet…

Sam appeared at Zane's shoulder. "Listen to your friend," he said. "No reason to be stirring up a fuss. Go home, sleep it off. Let these people enjoy their evening."

The lead man half turned, grinning at his friends. "I was hoping to enjoy myself here," he said but turned toward the wagon and the others followed. Journey caught his final glare as he passed through the firelight.

The dark form hovering over the wagon seat tipped his hat in silence. Journey shivered, swallowing back the bitter taste of bile that flooded her mouth. She knew that shadow. Roy.

She shook her imagination back into place before it could run away with her. He was only that cowboy who'd been at the picnic earlier that day, not Roy. She sucked a breath in and heaved it out.

Any other possibility was too frightening to consider.

Zane rocked heel-to-toe on his feet, watching his parishioners return to their homes through the heavy snow that had blanketed the town overnight. Attendance had been down, but he never closed the doors if he could make it, no matter how high or thick the snow.

Conversations had naturally centered around the picnic yesterday, and he had to credit his faithful members for the effort they had put into not adding to the tale of the wild cowboys who'd made an appearance.

But Journey sat through the entire service in misery, expecting someone to.

"Zane?"

Her timid voice caught him by surprise. He thought he'd missed her slipping out ahead of the others. "Glad to see you and Miss Rose could make it out this morning, Journey. I thought maybe you two would be snowed in."

"It was tempting to crawl back under the covers, I have to admit," she said. She gave a short, nervous laugh that made a choking sound. "But I figured I owe you for last night."

She bit her lip, hands fluttering together. Her brown eyes drooped with exhaustion, and he knew she had gotten little sleep after the events of the night before. But her hair gleamed in a wide roll that framed her face, with thick curls trailing from the nape of her neck, some sweeping over her shoulder—the effect disarming. "They passed on through and didn't stay in town last night," he told her.

"You checked?"

"Sam and I took a little ride before turning in. I don't know that they didn't stay close but not in town. Do you have any reason to think they'll be back?"

She shook her head, and he waited for her to say more but she didn't. Frustration built in him, a tight ball in his chest. Then he noticed a thin, wet trail across her cheek. She wiped it away almost before he noticed, and she steadied herself with a deep breath and looked him in the eye.

"Journey, please—"

"I need you to know that I'm not... That is, I never—" She breathed deeply and tried again, her hand shaking now and bunching the fabric of her skirt. "I've done a lot of things I'm not proud of, things that give me no right to be in this church today. But I never did what that cowboy hinted at last night. My mama, she worked as a saloon girl. That and more, you know?"

Her eyes pleaded for understanding, and he nodded without a sound.

"But that wasn't me. I didn't live that way, not exactly…" Her voice faded and her gaze searched the tiny vestibule where they stood. She drew in a breath to continue, but he placed his hand over both of hers, knotted together at her waist.

His other hand brushed the loose curls at her neck of its own volition. "You don't have to explain those men to me," he said. But his mind demanded answers to a thousand other questions.

"I just wanted to thank you, Zane. No one's ever taken up for me before, not like you did. I do owe you for that."

He scanned outside to judge the distance of the others shouting farewells to neighbors in the churchyard. "Then tell me what's going on."

"Oh, Zane," she said, pulling her hands from his grasp and brushing past him. "Not getting you involved is paying you back."

She went down the steps and hopped into the wagon, sitting next to Miss Rose, leaving him with more questions than ever.

Chapter Sixteen

Journey woke at first light and stretched, then curled deeper into the quilts, studying the ceiling. She rubbed the sleep from her face and sighed, stretching the stiffness from her leg.

With the scene in the churchyard one week past, the days had returned to a comfortable routine. She turned to the frosty window, where sunlight peered over the horizon, gleaming from the fresh snow that covered the ground.

The party had broken up soon after the cowboys had wheeled out of town that night. Tiny white flecks, determined dry crystals, had followed the crowd to their homes. Walten awoke to three feet of snow, with fresh coatings each day for the next week.

This morning the skies were clear, calm. Journey felt much that way herself. She hoped the forced seclusion around the community would stop any speculation about her and those men. Her only option was to stay, regardless. She'd never get through that mountain pass on her own now, even if she'd had a horse. But keeping her name out of the local gossip mill wouldn't hurt.

Circumstances held her there. Much to her surprise, she enjoyed the routine that she and Miss Rose established. Clean. Wash. Care for the animals. Cook. Sew. Quiet evenings.

Journey dressed and twisted her hair into some semblance of order. She'd have to do better before going to Evie Wilson's to meet the other ladies in the sewing circle. If only she could get out of it. The weather had been her last hope. But as the sunlight grew warmer and brighter, she knew that was not to be.

She'd been judged before, and likely would be again, but that didn't erase the sting. But by now, nothing they guessed could come close to the reality.

That afternoon Journey realized the forced seclusion had served only to inflame the speculation about her.

"I thought for a moment Pastor Thompson might take a swing at the man himself." Sue Anderson retold the events in grand fashion to the ladies as they sat stitching.

"I don't believe it would have come to that. Reverend Thompson was defending the defenseless, as the Lord would have us do." Phoebe Decker seemed to talk without moving her lips. "It's not like Miss Smith could have known these men would single her out, I'm certain. Don't you agree, Mary?"

Phoebe's tone conveyed anything but certainty, and she flashed a penetrating gaze at her. Journey concentrated on the quilt, bound tight enough in its frame to bounce a thimble on. The only thing sure in this conversation would be Mary Decker's dutiful "Yes, Mother."

She stole a glance at Mary. Her pale skin and black hair created a striking contrast, and had her cheeks been fuller, she would have been a true beauty. Journey felt a stab of sympathy for her. Mary looked a little older than she, and Phoebe's control over her daughter was as strong as Hank's had been over her. Maybe stronger.

With her attention wrapped in the quilt, Journey tried to hide from all the curious stares.

Next time I'll wait for Abby at the store. She pulled another stitch through.

Evie Wilson gave a friendly smile. "I'm sure it's not something we need to review for Journey."

Sue's eyes widened and her hands stopped. "Oh, my, I suppose not. It's just so romantic, I never thought…"

Journey flushed, yet she couldn't hold back her laugh. That laugh never worked right, always slipping out at the strangest times. What could be keeping Abby?

"It didn't seem very romantic at the time," Journey said, glancing around the circle. Blank looks and cool stares outnumbered the smiles that greeted her. She focused again on the quilt. The ladies intended this one as a Christmas present for Zane.

The Wilsons' door opened and Abby breezed through, shaking powdered snow from her bonnet and coat. Journey added her greeting to the others' and shifted her chair, hoping she would accept the invitation. Having Abby act as a buffer between her and Phoebe would make the afternoon much easier.

"I'm sorry I'm late." Abby smoothed her hair and dug a quilting needle and thread from a tiny sewing box as she settled into the space. "We had a late shipment and Sam needed me to watch the store while he unloaded.

I hoped to catch you, Journey, but I'm glad you came along without me."

"Miss Rose cleared the afternoon so I could come." Not that there'd been much to clear. She managed a faint smile. "I thought you'd be here ahead of me." *Hoped.*

"I'm sure you've been entertaining the ladies with tales of your adventures." Abby caught the eye of each woman with her bright expression before turning her attention to the cloth.

Phoebe was the only one to reply. "We haven't gotten beyond Journey's adventures since arriving in Walten. If she brings about this much excitement everywhere, it will take several quilts to hear all the tales."

Most of the women giggled—a high, twittery sound that scraped Journey's ears. Her face grew hot, knowing there was more jibe than jest in the comment.

"If you're so very interested, you'll have to arrange a time to compare stories, I suppose." Evie's voice sounded low and cool. A seamless smile graced her face.

Journey raised an eyebrow to clear a view of Phoebe without staring outright. The flush that came to Phoebe's pinched face helped cool her shame. Several moments of silence passed.

Sue Anderson spoke first. "Please don't think us rude, Journey. We're just interested in all you've seen along your way to Walten." Silence hung for another moment. "At least, I'd like to hear about it."

She searched Sue's face. "Truly, there isn't much to tell. I'd be more interested in learning more about Walten. I haven't had an opportunity to explore."

"So you are staying, then?" Phoebe asked. "I'd heard you were considering it, but I couldn't believe it."

Journey ground her teeth. It wouldn't do to give Phoebe the satisfaction of rattling her. "I have no choice since I have no horse. And with the snow piling and the cold wind blowing, I'm very grateful to have found a job with Miss Rose."

She chanced a look at the group. Abby smiled at her, with a nod so slight that Journey almost missed it. Her face grew warm again, but she turned her attention back to her stitches, a small smile on her own face.

"How is Miss Rose handling this weather?" Evie Wilson rose to her role as hostess, but her eyes never drifted far from her baby, sleeping in a cradle near the fireplace.

Journey thought for a moment. "Miss Rose is a strong woman. I'm sure she'd make out fine without me, but she's very charitable to take me in."

"She needs you more than you realize," Abby said. "There are many in this town who are thankful she has someone living out there with her. Especially to get ready for the holidays."

Sue twittered again and arched her eyebrows in a telling look. "Pastor Zane will definitely be indebted to you. He has a soft spot for the dear woman."

"He always has, and it's the same for her. Even more so since Sarah…" The sentence hung for a moment before Abby continued, this time with a scratch to her voice. "I don't know how he would've made it through without Miss Rose's help."

"He would've found his way," Evie said. "He's always been strong, and his faith even stronger."

Journey's hand slowed. She couldn't help but wonder about the relationship between the pastor and Miss Rose. And who was Sarah?

"That fire burned the heart out of that man. To lose your wife and baby." Abby shook herself, as if realizing she had spoken aloud more than she had intended, and turned to Journey. "Sarah was my best friend."

Journey barely heard her. A lump formed in her throat, but she swallowed it down. Everyone had their stories. This one wasn't her concern. She couldn't let it be.

"I suppose Reverend Thompson will be going to Miss Rose's for Thanksgiving? Is her nephew coming?" Evie asked.

"Zane will be there, and Sam and I are going. Has Miss Rose mentioned if Reed is coming?" Abby tied off a thread and snipped it free.

Journey didn't know. It was news to her that Zane had been invited. And now the nephew—the sheriff from Virginia City—might be coming?

"I— She hasn't said. I suppose I hadn't realized it was getting on that time of year." In truth, she'd never celebrated the holiday before.

"It's only a couple of weeks away. If Reed's coming, he'll ride in the morning before and ride out the day after. Miss Rose never expects him exactly, but she always prepares for him. He always manages to come." Abby clearly looked forward to the holiday.

Most people in Savannah thought it nothing but a Yankee holiday, since Mr. Lincoln proclaimed the first Thanksgiving after Gettysburg. Journey had always figured there was no harm in taking a day to be thankful, but she'd never had cause to before.

She wondered what it would entail. Turkey—she'd have to cook a turkey. Maybe Abby would help. But if Abby were an invited guest and Miss Rose's family would be there, she guessed not. And where would she go? It wasn't as if she could celebrate with other servants. Holidays were for family, and she had none.

Though she tried to squelch it, hope rose in her that she might be asked to stay. Yet how could she sit and share Thanksgiving dinner with a minister and an officer of the law? "I'll talk to Miss Rose when I get back."

The shadows lengthened and the women made their leave. The afternoon had passed with discussions of canning, quilting and raising children, but there were no further comments concerning Journey's past. Mrs. Wilson was a kind and accommodating hostess, but as she stepped from the porch, Journey felt her ease return, one that had been lost when she was among the quilters.

She adjusted the cinches on her saddle, spinning around at a tap on her shoulder. Her hand moved to the pocket of her long coat where the pistol remained. Before she had a chance to pull it, Abby stepped back and smiled.

"I said, can you stay for supper?"

Journey caught her breath and her face grew hot as she glanced around at the other ladies climbing into their wagons. She turned back to Abby. "I beg your pardon. I didn't realize you were speaking to me. Supper?" She searched the sun's position in the sky. "I should be getting back. Miss Rose will be wanting me to get supper ready for her."

Abby sighed. "I told Miss Rose I might try to keep you longer if I could. Won't you come?"

The temptation was strong. If she weren't so different from Abby, they might have been good friends. But she couldn't risk it now. As much as she liked the place she found herself in, it wouldn't do to relax. She couldn't get too comfortable, because it would only be harder in the long run.

"I'm sorry, Abby. I have to go. Maybe another time?" She continued adjusting the reins.

"Can you at least walk back to town with me? I'd enjoy the company." Abby looked hopeful.

Why would Abby want company, having spent the entire afternoon in the midst of half a dozen ladies? Still, she could hardly refuse. Abby had helped her so much. She nodded, adjusted her hat and tugged the halter for the horse to follow.

"The ladies like you."

Journey's step faltered as she considered that. "I suppose someone new passing through is bound to garner some attention. It seems they have some rather exciting notions about me."

Abby laughed. "It's more than that. You have a grace that draws people. Are you really, though, just passing through?"

Melting snow slushed under their feet. "I'll move on come spring."

"We could help you if you want to stay."

Journey froze. "You've all helped me so much already. There's nothing more I need." She attempted to calm her fast breath and pounding heart. "Well, except for a horse and a short winter." She laughed, but it sounded false.

Abby would not be put off. "Are you worried about those cowboys?"

Not all of them, Journey thought. Only the one who should've been a few thousand miles away.

"I'm not worried, because I've never seen them before." She hoped it was nothing more than too much alcohol. Maybe Roy hadn't even recognized her. She'd been the wife of his best friend, if you could consider Hank a friend of anyone. But she never held that much faith in luck or coincidence. She'd never held much faith in anything.

Abby placed a warm hand on her shoulder. "Please, be careful. God sent you to us for a reason. Don't leave before we figure out what that is."

Journey chirped and tugged the horse into motion again. The town came into view as they topped the rise. She fought the urge to nod a promise. "I'll head on from here. I should have that dress for Mrs. Fletcher finished by midweek, and I'll bring it into town. I think Miss Rose wants to pick up some things, too."

"Miss Rose is a hard one to keep down. She manages to finagle a trip to town once a week, no matter what the weather." Abby allowed the subject to be changed. "I'll see you tomorrow morning in church."

Journey guessed she would. She'd avoided it as long as she could, with her broken leg, and last week had been an obligation. She climbed into the saddle and adjusted her skirt around her—a split skirt would have been much easier. She turned to wave goodbye.

Abby waved back. Journey saw her lips move, but the wind had picked up, disguising the sound too much to be sure she'd spoken. But it sounded like "I'm praying for you."

Zane greeted his parishioners from the top of the steps of the church. The sanctuary was already cozy from the tiny woodstove and the heat from the seated worshippers, and it might have made more sense to wait there. But he held at the door, and watched for Miss

Rose's buggy to appear from around the little grove of trees.

He checked his watch and thrust it back into his pocket, then stepped into the sanctuary to nod at Abby, her signal to start playing the battered piano. All the hymns sounded tinny, like music that spilled from a city saloon. If he could sell the yearling colt for a fair price come spring, they could get a new organ. Abby played beautifully, but she couldn't work miracles.

Zane shrugged and smiled at her raised eyebrows. He didn't know where Miss Rose and Journey were. Miss Rose hadn't been late since the time her wagon hitch broke. This delay had to be about Journey. About Journey not wanting to come to church.

She'd been less than thrilled when he made a special point to invite her. Now that she was up and about, without a doubt Miss Rose would have her in church, if at all possible. But if she weren't inclined to come again, he had thought a personal invitation might smooth the way. Something stirred in him at the thought of seeing her face in the pews, and it disconcerted him to know all the reasons for that weren't strictly pastoral.

Zane glanced again at his timepiece. Eight o'clock. He pulled the bell rope, and the deep ring permeated the air. Just as he turned to walk to the pulpit, he spotted them. The wagon fairly slid over the light coat of fresh snow. He gave the bell another tug and made a slow routine of dusting tiny snowflakes from his suit. He'd have time to greet them before he took his place at the pulpit—if they hurried.

The wagon pulled into the yard, and he stepped down to help Miss Rose. Journey hopped to the ground with a flash of navy skirt before he could offer assistance to the elderly woman. She took her responsibility to Miss Rose seriously. If he could fault her on that, he'd have a clear reason to take his concerns to Miss Rose. Not that she'd listen. Striking a balance between concern for Miss Rose and his overwhelming desire to protect Journey hadn't proved easy.

"Good morning! You ladies are right on time." He slid the old woman's arm through his to escort her into the church.

He thought Journey flushed, but perhaps only the chill in the air was to blame. Whatever the cause, he admired the contrast with her navy dress. She limped a little on the healing leg, yet a gracefulness remained.

"These old bones don't move so quick as they used to on mornings like this," Miss Rose told him as they climbed the steps together. "Now, get in there before Sam gets up to take your place."

He squeezed Miss Rose's gloved hand and slipped to the front of the congregation before Abby finished playing. He grasped the front corners of the pulpit his father had built for him when he first took over this church and could feel the smooth edges under his tight grip.

Scanning his congregation, he let his gaze rest for a moment on each member, taking a bit more time at the second pew on the left. He could almost see Sarah as she'd looked that first Sunday after her family moved to Walten. Beautiful, strong, full of life. He'd been only too anxious to make a call on the family that first week.

Her family had filed in beside the woman who still occupied that seat. But today another young woman caught his interest—very different from his wife, but still beautiful, still strong and still full of life. And in the same seat.

Zane snapped his gaze to the Bible resting before him. That wasn't right. His beautiful Sarah; no one could ever compare to her. He hadn't given anyone a chance to, he supposed. So how was it this strange woman managed to seep into his thoughts so often? Journey was pretty enough, with her copper curls and skin pale like china. Eyes of deep brown. But her long, pointed nose gave her a coltish look. And she was far too mysterious, perhaps even dangerous, to be appealing to him.

He smiled at his flock as the hymn ended. "Good morning, and praise God for it. Let's begin with prayer."

He'd have time to figure Journey out later.

Chapter Seventeen

A puff of hot air from the kitchen woodstove hit Journey. The smell of roasting turkey met her as she spooned golden broth over it, humming one of the hymns they'd sung at church on Sunday. She didn't know the words, but the tune was pretty.

She yawned and rubbed her cheeks into the sleeve of her day dress. Awake before dawn, she determined to cook this bird to perfection for Miss Rose and her guests. Then she'd take her leave to the church, certain it would be deserted at that time of day.

"It smells like Thanksgiving already."

She swung around with a gasp as the deep voice startled her. Broth dripped from the spoon and sizzled on the edge of the stove.

"Who are you?" She raised the clutched spoon in her hand and backed away.

"Whoa, there!" The man held his hands up in surrender, stepping back himself. "I'm Reed, Rose's nephew."

Air left her in a rush, and surely he could hear her heart thunder in her chest. She squinted, trying to make out his features in the gray morning light. Nervous laughter bubbled up in the relief of the moment, making it harder to steady her voice. "Then I guess you're safe from my spoon, sir."

His teeth stood out as a smile split his face. "You must be Miss Smith," he said, pulling a chair over for her. "I am so sorry I frightened you. Aunt Rose mentioned you in her last letter. I came into town late last night and figured I'd let myself in to surprise her this morning. Guess I'm the one who got the surprise."

She took the offered chair. "You're not the only one. Miss Rose expected you yesterday."

"I got tied up with some business. I expect my aunt's told you I'm a lawman in Virginia City. There's plenty there to keep a man busy these days." He paused suddenly. "Now, where are my manners? Please, call me Reed."

"And you should call me Journey."

"Right. Journey. How's the turkey coming?"

"I think it will be cooked in time. I'm glad Abby took care of dressing it and all. I've never done anything like that."

Reed turned to watch the rising sun through the windowpane. "From what my aunt Rose tells me, I'm sure you would've managed fine. She and Zane both seem to think you can handle whatever comes your way."

Journey cleared her throat, not knowing what to say to the older man. "They've been very kind." What else might Zane have said about her to this lawman? "Can I get you something for breakfast?"

"No, thanks. I think I'll pass this morning, save room for dinner." He ran a hand over his graying mustache and stubbled chin. "I'm going out to tend to the horses.

It'll keep me from being underfoot. Even an old bachelor like me knows enough to stay out of the kitchen when a woman is cooking."

She smiled, wondering what kind of sheriff this man was. He didn't match the image she'd had of a Montana lawman. He seemed friendly, now that she'd had time to recover from her fright. She watched him put on his hat and head out the front door. Maybe he got more results that way.

The real fright was that she'd not heard him. She hadn't slept so soundly since she was a girl. She thought of the raucous music and giddy laughter of the saloon swelling well into the night and realized maybe not even then. And she'd been caught up in the preparations for the day and missed him coming in behind her. What if he had been Roy? It seemed that the scare of those men at the harvest festival and that feeling of being watched in the weeks following dropped off at the door of this house. She had to stay alert, though. What if Roy really was in town? She hoped not, but she couldn't rely on wishes.

"I thought I heard you up and about." Miss Rose's voice rasped with first morning use and interrupted her thoughts. She'd slept later than usual.

"Good morning. Your nephew has arrived, and I just checked the turkey. It's coming along fine. Would you like a little something for breakfast?" Journey asked.

"I saw Reed on his way out to the barn. I don't believe I'll have anything this morning, thank you. My goodness, as late as I've slept this morning, it'll soon be dinnertime! My Wallace and I never had breakfast on holiday mornings. We'd just have that big dinner meal a little early. It's mighty hard to sleep on a full stomach if we wait until the evening meal. No, no, you go on, do what you need to."

She wondered a moment if she shouldn't fry some eggs anyway, but then decided to take her employer at her word. If she'd learned anything these past two months, she did know Miss Rose wasn't shy about speaking her mind. She started for the stairs.

"Journey?" Miss Rose called after her.

She paused at the bottom step. "Yes?"

Miss Rose stepped closer, patting her hand as it rested on the carved wooden banister. "Why don't you wear your Sunday dress—that deep blue one? It brings out the fire in your hair."

"Ah, yes—yes, ma'am." Her eyebrow tugged upward in confusion. Was she to stay and serve? Miss Rose had never said, but she'd assumed that once the meal was on the table, she'd be expected to take her leave. But if the occasion called for it, she'd wear her navy dress.

She climbed the stairs and washed her face in the tepid water from the basin and changed from her everyday dress. Then she pulled the tiny mirror from her saddlebag and propped it on the stand Abby had loaned her.

Her thoughts turned to the day ahead as she tugged her brush through tangled curls. She and Miss Rose had been planning and baking for a week. "There's always reason to thank the Lord," she'd told Journey. "And it's real nice to think that all across this great land of ours, folks are stopping and bowing their heads in gratefulness to the Almighty."

She had never thought about being thankful, let alone considered God. She'd been happy to find this place for the winter, true enough, though it hadn't been her plan. But she'd run long and hard and made her way.

She didn't blame God, but neither would she give Him any credit.

She stared out the window. The wind blew hard, but the sun felt warmer than the day before. It would be a good day for a ride.

"Journey? Is there anything you need?" Miss Rose's voice carried up to the room and into her thoughts.

"I'm coming," she called, fluttering her fingers up her back once more, double-checking the tiny buttons. It wouldn't do to miss one today especially.

"How can I help?" Journey asked, reaching the bottom of the stairs.

"You've done yourself proud, the way you got everything ready for this day. I wondered if there's anything left that I could help you with before everyone arrives."

She stretched a hand to pat Miss Rose's arm but withdrew it before she made contact. Leave it to Miss Rose to ask if *she* needed anything. "I've got things under control, I think," she said. "I'm going to set the table and lay out the pies. Everything else is ready. You go on and finish your primping. Your guests will be here before too long."

Miss Rose sniffed. "I never primp." But her slow smile took any bite out of her words. She moved toward her own room.

The clock on the mantel soon chimed eleven. From the kitchen window, she could see Zane and the Norwoods follow one another over the hill. Journey brushed her sweeping skirt for any unseen crumbs and patted the moisture from her face. A tangled curl worked its way free again, and she swept it back.

Journey watched as Reed greeted the men with a slap on the shoulder and leaned over to kiss Abby's cheek as they made their way to the house. Frosty breath hung before them.

Cold, fresh air blew in as they clomped wet snow from their feet. "Happy Thanksgiving," Journey said.

Abby swept her into a hug with a quick release. "Happy Thanksgiving! You look lovely, Journey. How did your turkey turn out?"

"I hope it's as big as Abby says," Sam said. His mustache twitched with a smile underneath it. "I believe I could eat the entire bird myself. If it's not burnt, that is."

Journey laughed. "I think your wife and your pastor may challenge you to it. If I didn't burn it, that is."

"I'll eat it, even if it is burned," Reed said.

Miss Rose made her appearance, wearing a deep green wool dress fitted around her narrow figure. Her hair was still mostly dark, with the gray framing her face in a wide roll that circled her head like a halo. Journey wondered about her flushed cheeks and hoped Miss Rose wasn't pushing too hard by hosting such a dinner. Though she'd prepared much of it, the woman had worked along beside her a good bit of the time.

"You look lovely, Miss Rose," Zane said. "Happy Thanksgiving."

Journey excused herself to get the meal set on the table. She smiled and took a deep breath as the steam from the roasting turkey puffed into her face. With Abby's help, she'd learned how to butcher and scald it. It surprised her to have been squeamish about it.

"Can I help?" Abby's voice startled her, and the lid slipped from her hand, clattering to the floor.

"I was about ready to set everything out. You'll want to get a good seat." She wiped her hands on her apron and pulled it over her head.

"That's why I came. We're one place setting short."

Her eyes widened and she mentally checked off the seating arrangement as she pulled plates from the stack. Surely she hadn't forgotten anyone. "I'll get another setting. I'm so sorry."

"I'll arrange it. You've been so busy getting the meal ready that it probably slipped your mind. Everything smells wonderful." Abby lifted the dishes from her hands and sauntered back to the parlor, where the table had been moved to accommodate everyone.

Journey followed with a platter piled high with stuffing.

Placing the steaming plate to one side, she slid the china and silverware to make room for the extra setting. Again she counted—Miss Rose, Abby, Sam, Zane and Reed. She knew she couldn't have miscounted when there were only five to begin with. Miss Rose must've forgotten to mention the other guest. No matter. It looked as if there would be plenty of food for everyone.

"The turkey is ready. Would you like me to bring it out now, or wait until your other guest arrives?"

"Other guest?" Miss Rose asked.

"The one you need the extra plate for?"

Miss Rose looked at each of her guests from where she sat on the edge of her rocker. "We're all here—Reed, Zane, Sam, Abby, you and me."

Journey's lips parted softly.

"Is there something wrong?" Zane asked.

"No, I thought… That is, I didn't expect…"

Miss Rose stood. "What do you mean? You didn't expect to stay?"

"Why, you have to stay!" Abby said. She laid a hand on her arm, as if to hold her there.

Journey smiled. "The hired help doesn't usually eat with the employer. I thought you had me sit with you at supper because you'd rather that than eat alone."

"Nonsense. We're not all that formal here. Not like it is back East. I should've made it plain." Miss Rose moved and motioned the others toward the table. "Besides, you're more than hired help, Journey. Zane, carry in the turkey and let's give thanks."

Journey was scooted into a chair to the left of Miss Rose, at the head of the table. Sam seated Abby across from her. Zane disappeared into the kitchen and returned with the plump turkey, steaming from the platter. He placed it in the center of the table, amid an appreciative dose of sighs. He sat beside her, and Reed took the seat at the end of the table opposite his aunt.

"Zane, will you ask the blessing?" Miss Rose asked. Journey felt her hand clasped in the woman's wrinkled one, and saw Miss Rose stretch her other hand to Abby. Abby placed her right hand in Sam's.

Journey clenched her left hand into a fist. But no one seemed to notice. Zane's outstretched fingers waited.

Her own fingers loosened and trembled. Zane seemed to take that as permission to pull her hand into his. Journey found it warm and rough. He didn't clasp her hand but instead let it rest in his open one. She slipped it back into her lap before he could finish saying "Amen."

Journey reached forward to pass the turkey but stilled as Miss Rose cleared her throat.

"I'd like to take this opportunity to say how happy I am to have you all here," she began. "My nephew, all the way from his big job in Virginia City. Abby and Sam, who bring back so many memories of me and my Wallace. My pastor and friend, Zane, who's done so much for me. And, of course, my new friend and boarder, Journey, who grows dearer to me each day. Yes, the Lord has blessed me with so much more than I deserve. And I'm grateful to all of you for the part you play in that."

Abby squeezed Miss Rose's hand on the table. "I'm glad you invited us. I've been missing my family so much since they moved back East. But since we can't be with them, it's good to be with the next best thing."

"Since we're talking thanks, I have my share, too," Sam said. He rubbed his thick fingers together. "God's been mightily good to me. He's given me a wife prettier than He should have to look at my face, a beautiful country to live in, good friends and a turkey that ain't been burned. Yep, I was doing well before the turkey, but that's an extra blessing."

Laughter rang around the table. Journey looked at each face. Everyone was so kind to her—perhaps the kindest anyone had been since her mother died. With Mama, too, so much of her time had been spent entertaining saloon customers that Journey found herself alone often. And the way decent folk thought of Mama and what she did, they hadn't looked very kindly on her daughter with no papa to lay claim to, either. Her pulse skipped at her temple.

Could she trust them?

She rubbed her hand over Miss Rose's cool, textured skin. "Thank you," she said, her voice straining to reach a whisper. She stiffened, suddenly wanting to say so much more and not knowing where to begin. "Thank you, all, for everything you've done. I'll never be able to make it up to you."

The voices quieted around the table, and her face grew warm under the sudden stares. Miss Rose blinked, emphasizing the wrinkles around her wide eyes. Journey tilted her head to check on her, but Zane drew everyone's attention.

"Making this fine dinner is a start in repayment, so let's not waste it." He stood to carve the large bird.

The meal continued with laughter and stories. Dishes had been cleared in anticipation of the pies that waited in the kitchen. Suddenly a heavy knock at the door drew everyone's attention.

They looked at one another a moment before Zane moved to answer. The light gleamed off the snow through the open doorway.

Something familiar in the voice that returned Zane's greeting froze Journey inside and out. She dug her fingers into the seat of her chair to hold herself still. She'd never forget that voice.

Blood rushed from her face, and her eyes felt too large. The room grew dark as she heard Zane's voice from a muffled distance. "What can we do for you, stranger?"

Stranger... Even in the shadows, she knew him. Recognized the way he ducked into the room. The way the man tugged on his greasy mustache. She jerked to her feet, sending the chair crashing behind her.

"Pardon me." She whirled, bent low, her breath heaving in sharp hitches, and staggered through the kitchen. Tiny black specks darkened her vision. She swayed and banged her hip into the sideboard. Unsteady already, she lost her balance, falling headlong toward the door. But she picked herself up and made her way outside.

She fell down the last step. Her stomach heaved and clenched as she knelt at the bottom of the porch.

Dead...dead...dead.

She'd been so sure. She thrust her hands into the snow that soaked into her dress, but nothing would wash away the blood. Why wasn't he dead? She had swung the iron and left Hank bleeding and still on the bare floor of their room above the saloon. It was her chance to get away from the drunken beatings and conniving schemes.

The law hadn't caught up to her yet and likely wouldn't have, as long as she continued to lie low and mind her own business.

Had Hank risen from the grave?

The landscape around her swirled and darkened. She swayed to her feet but couldn't find her balance. Terror and shock blurred her senses. She fell face-first into cold, wet snow as consciousness faded.

Chapter Eighteen

Zane knelt and rolled Journey to her back. Her skin blended with the snow she lay in. He leaned down and lifted her. Once inside, he'd find out what was wrong. Miss Rose had sent him out to check on her sudden departure.

Journey struggled as he pulled her close, supporting her in his arms. Her eyes fluttered under closed lids, and her breath became swift and harsh again. She lashed out and caught him on the cheek but too weakly to do anything but brush him. "Hank," she murmured. "Hank, you get away from me. You'll never—"

"Journey?" He squeezed her shoulders. "Journey! It's me, Zane."

She shuddered in his arms. "No…no."

He looked into her upturned face, relieved to see a little color returning. Her eyes fluttered open, a solid ring of brown, and her nostrils flared slightly, reminding him again of a wild colt. She gulped air as if she couldn't get enough. A sudden fierceness rose in him to tuck her away and protect her forever.

"Come on, now." He moved slowly, not wanting to startle her. He eased her to her feet, grasping her waist as she swayed. Her hands fluttered over his outstretched arm.

"I'm fine," she insisted. "I—I needed some air, that's all."

Zane challenged her with a look. "There's more to this than feeling penned in. Who is that man?"

"Wh-who?"

He crossed his arms and rocked away on his heels. "Our new visitor. Who is he, Journey? Who's Hank?"

"Don't get involved in my problems," she whispered. "Please."

He drew closer and she ducked, raising her arm as if to ward off a blow. He ran a hand through his hair. "Why can't you let me help you?"

"Where is he?" She shivered as her eyes darted around the horizon.

"He left. He stopped to ask for directions to Virginia City." Zane eased his suit coat off and wrapped it around Journey's shoulders. He let his arm linger at her elbow, nudging her into a walk toward the barn. It might help for her to move around in the cold fresh air before going back indoors.

When she stopped wobbling and he decided she wouldn't bolt, he released her and stepped away before giving in to the desire to gather her close and sweep that one loose curl from her forehead.

"Feeling better?"

She nodded. "You're sure he's gone?"

He stopped and heaved a heavy breath. Instead of the paleness of moments before, Journey now flushed with a bright spot of color on each cheek. She looked embarrassed. No, scared. Vulnerable.

"He said he was headed farther west. I have no reason to doubt him. Should I?"

Journey's breath steamed out in one long puff, clouding her face. "Did he ask about me?"

"I don't know that he even saw you. By the time he'd stepped around the door, you were gone. Why?" He searched her face, hoping for a straightforward answer but not expecting one.

Zane stepped in front of her, forcing her attention toward him. "Who is Hank, Journey? You mentioned him twice now—today and the night you broke your leg."

"Hank's dead."

Why fear a dead man? The more he learned, the more questions he came up with.

"Who was he then?"

"No one who mattered."

Zane coughed, his breath catching in his tight throat. He followed her gaze across the horizon. The sky spread out blue and wide, but deceptive. The wind sliced along the rusty bluffs in the distance. "Let's get you inside. We'll sort it out later. It is Thanksgiving and pie's waiting."

She smiled and nodded, but it didn't ease his suspicions. Instead it only confirmed them, and a desire to help overwhelmed him. Just what that fear had to do with the man who'd wandered by, he didn't know, but he aimed to find out.

Miss Rose and Abby had looked forward to this for too long for this to be hashed out right now. He wouldn't ruin their Thanksgiving plans. Journey's past could wait one more day.

Chapter Nineteen

Journey scratched a hole in the frosted window and stared outside. Wind howled, blowing piles of powder snow into whirling puffs. The storm had hit hard Sunday afternoon and blew strong and steady well into midweek. The bitter cold sliced deeply. She shivered, pulling the shawl Miss Rose had loaned her closer.

Bundling up to face the biting weather as she made her way to the barn each morning and evening made her miss the balmy Georgia winters. Yet she welcomed the coziness of Miss Rose's house and the forced quietness. Journey couldn't hold back a smile. If time to think could solve her problems, she'd have none left to consider.

"No one will be out today." Miss Rose entered the room and interrupted Journey's thoughts. "I think I'll read a bit this morning. Care for me to read aloud?"

"If you like." She sat on the davenport, facing Miss Rose in her rocker. "I think the wind might ease up by afternoon. If so, I might take a ride into town and see how Abby fared during this storm."

The look on the woman's face told her what she thought of the idea.

"You'll freeze solid out on a day like this."

Journey could well imagine what she would think if she knew the entire story.

"I'll bundle up. The fresh air will be wonderful, and you'll be thankful for the break from me." She hoped to make light of her announcement, despite her pounding heart. "I won't be long."

Truth be known, she didn't relish riding out in the strong north winds. The chill settled deep into her bones; shivering was the only motion she could make until the warm fire thawed her. But it was time. Not to see Abby, but to face Hank, if he were to be found. Putting together the sense of being watched during the past weeks with Hank's arrival on Miss Rose's doorstep, she figured he would have sought her out.

The storm had forced her to wait for several days, giving her time to plan. She was thankful, knowing she'd have run if the weather had given her any opportunity.

She realized two things. First, Hank was alive. Hadn't she sensed him the night those cowboys accosted her? She was certain now that Hank's partner Roy had been the cowboy whose gaze she couldn't shake at the church picnic. He'd looked leaner and had shaved his beard, but having Hank turn up on the doorstep confirmed her suspicions. Hank was alive, and he and Roy were up to their old tricks.

Even more dangerous, Hank knew she was in Walten. No coincidence had brought him to the door that day. He knew where she was, and he wanted something from her. It was time to take control because she couldn't run forever. She had to find him first.

Miss Rose read from *Gulliver's Travels* for nearly an hour before her eyes drooped. Journey wasted no time in bundling up and heading into town.

Walten was not large, and Hank was not at all inconspicuous. Tall, with a deep Southern drawl that oozed charm and sophistication, Journey knew the appeal. Knowing how he truly was made her think of the stores she'd seen since coming west. Large and impressive looking from the front but small and plain inside.

Eavesdropping outside the saloon revealed he'd been working at an abandoned mine outside of town. From there Journey had only to ask for directions.

She slid from the horse into snow that buried her ankles and loosened her chinstrap when she spotted the abandoned miner's cabin at the bottom of the slope. It suited Hank, squatting in some tiny hovel so he could afford to maintain his wealthy veneer.

The frigid air stabbed her lungs as a gust of wind kicked and she moved forward. How was Hank handling a Montana winter? She hoped he sat shivering even now. He should've stayed in Georgia. He should've stayed dead.

Suddenly, Journey crashed to the ground, a heavy weight pinning her into a drift. Kicking into the layers of snow, she fought to free herself. She fumbled for the lead rope of the horse, but it slid from her mittens. For a moment she suffocated in the icy wetness. Then with a determined growl, she jolted back, smacking into a firm barrier that echoed her groan. There was a soft thump in the snow beside her as the weight rolled off and she was free.

"I surely do miss that fire!"

Journey whirled to face him, backing onto her feet. "What do you want from me, Hank?" Scared. She could hear it herself.

"Now, darlin', is that any way to greet your dearly departed husband?" He drew to his full height and brushed the snow from his long coat, then smoothed his limp mustache. "I suppose you want to know why I'm here."

"What do you want with me?" She struggled to catch her breath.

"Oh, my dear, don't take things so personally. I didn't know you were here until the night of that quaint little picnic. By the way, your gentlemen friends send their regards," he said. "Roy was quite surprised to see you. Almost as much as you were to see him, I'd gather."

Journey froze as Hank stepped closer. "I won't bore you with details of my premature obituary. But I'll share what plans I have for us here."

"I won't help you, Hank. I didn't then, and I'm not now. There is no *us*." She edged back but not fast enough to escape Hank's grasp. Her arm twinged as he squeezed and jerked her forward.

"You've not willingly helped me, that's true, Maura." His stale breath hung close to her face. "Or should I say, *Journey?*"

"Journey Smith. Maura Baines died the day I thought you did. There's nothing I can do for you, Hank. Ride on and leave me be." She raised her chin, trying to look him in the eye. An icy glare met hers and she flinched. He'd been cruel, but generally his gaze had been dulled with liquor. Not now. His sobriety somehow made him more frightening.

Hank's hollow laugh echoed on the wind. "Oh, I don't think so. You have a delightful setup in this town. You owe me, Maura. You are still my wife, the woman who murdered me."

She jerked her hand from his grasp, stepping out of his reach. "They think you're dead, back in Georgia?"

"Didn't you?" Hank smiled. "Roy convinced the authorities that I'd met my untimely demise at the hands of my beloved. Alas," he said, his face a mask of feigned sorrow, "such a tragic story. It even made the newspaper. But then, you've made some papers of your own."

"I protected myself, Hank. If you were any kind of decent man, none of this would have happened. I never meant to hurt you but was never sorry I had, until now."

Hank shook his head. Waves of hair slid over his shoulders, longer than she remembered. "Such talk... I'm loath to consider what your new minister friend would think to hear you. It'd be a shame to change his perception, when he seems so fond of you."

"He's the preacher here, that's all. He doesn't trust me as it is," she said.

"What about that lawman? I'm thinking he'd be interested to find he had a wanted woman within his very grasp."

"He's the woman's nephew, and he's back in Virginia City. I'm not his concern now."

"Working for his dear aunt makes you his concern. Would Miss Rose enjoy the fact she employs a criminal? Would she keep it quiet?"

"There's nothing tying me here, Hank. I got away from you once, and I can do it again."

He stepped forward, open palm out. She flinched, but his coarse fingers only caressed her cheek, then smacked her lightly. "What a shame if this town lost their pastor and Miss Rose in one fell swoop. And so close to Christmas."

Journey bit her lip against the tension rising in her chest, glad for the cold that numbed her and kept her focused. Hank was out for blood.

"I understand." She inhaled, filling herself with the icy chill. "Tell me what you want me to do. But after this, leave and never come back. I have a chance at something good here, and you won't take that away from me."

Hank threw back his head and laughed. "Little lady, you are in no position to make demands. But we'll try to keep your part in this simple."

"What do I have to do?"

He shrugged, palms open. "You'll introduce me around town to these good people, find me a job to hold me over until things fall into place."

"How will I explain how I know you? They've helped me, Hank, but they don't trust me. Knowing me means nothing to them. You'd be better off on your own. Why do you have to do this here?"

Hank's hand snagged her coat, jerking her forward. "You'll do as I say." His voice thundered and his gaze flared only inches away from hers.

Journey's breath caught. Then his grip relaxed and his expression softened. "Actually, Roy and I were heading toward Virginia City. It's a wild town, darlin'. We could make a fortune before the law even knew what we were up to."

"So go there. Please, Hank."

He grinned. "But *you* are *here*. And a pretty face is always an asset in my line of work."

She couldn't look at him or get her feet to move. "I won't."

A sneer tightened his features. She retreated under Hank's advance, glancing about her.

"Oh, you'll not find a flatiron so handy as you did in Georgia, Maura. Now it's time to pay the piper. The way I see it, you owe me the two hundred dollars in cash you stole from me. Then there's that little matter of the land deal you ruined for me when I became deceased in the eyes of the law."

She fisted her hands in her coat pockets. Why hadn't she brought the gun and ended it here? "Hank, won't you listen—"

His temper flared. She knew it by the widened eyes, the sharp peaks that arched his eyebrows. She ducked on instinct, but no blow followed this time.

"There's nothing to listen to!" He drew in a deep breath and seemed to compose himself. "We'll start simple. You'll do as I say until we seal the new deal. Then I'll be out of your life for good. I only want my two hundred dollars back."

She shivered, silent, hoping it would be enough for him to assume her agreement.

"Good, good." He drew two fingers over his chin, his smile making her flinch. "So, who will I be, Maura? Uncle Hank, Cousin Hank or your dear old brother?"

It didn't matter to her. The only thing Hank could ever be was trouble.

Chapter Twenty

The ride back to the ranch was long and cold. Wind howled, announcing another dose of snow. Journey latched the door behind her as she escaped into the warmth of the house. Within the comfortable walls of Miss Rose's home, she hoped the blizzard would strike quick and hard. With any luck, Hank would be caught off guard and freeze to death in the abandoned shack.

She shook the tiny balls of snow from her coat and hair, hanging the damp coat by the door, and felt a certain sense of relief, knowing she hadn't killed a man. She wished he weren't here now, but she was innocent of his death, at least.

"Goodness, girl! Come by the fire and get warm. You'll catch your death out there," Miss Rose said. The woman came into the main room from the kitchen using her cane. Her hip must have been bothering her again.

Journey curled up on the davenport after removing her damp boots to dry by the fire. "The snow came up so fast."

Miss Rose drew her rocker closer and pushed her

chair into a gentle sway with the tip of her cane. "That's the way winter works out here. Everything can change from sunny and warm to downright blizzardlike within a few hours." Her voice sounded raspy, but she smiled, leaning her head against the high back of the rocker. "It makes me so glad you decided to stay with me this winter."

"When the wind blows like that, I'm glad to be indoors." Journey leaned toward Miss Rose. "Are you feeling all right?"

"It's this winter air getting into my bones. I'll be all right. How about you?"

Journey plucked a strand of thread from her dress. "What do you mean?"

"How well do you know him?"

"Who?" She jerked her head to the door, as if she'd heard something.

"I hoped you would tell me. Maybe I should ask, is he the man you thought he was?"

Journey edged forward. "No," she said. "He's not the man I thought he was. What did Zane tell you?"

"Nothing. He said you'd let us know if there was anything we had to worry about," Miss Rose said. "So you don't know that man?"

She breathed deeply and stared at the woman, who had stopped rocking to fasten her tiny round blue eyes on her. "I didn't say that. I guess no one is really who they seem."

Miss Rose's expression said she didn't agree with that statement. But instead of saying something, she closed her eyes and began to rock, her lips moving slightly. It was strange, not to mention disconcerting, the way the woman would drop suddenly into these silent prayers and pleas.

"I'll work it out. Don't worry about me."

Miss Rose's eyes snapped open and the rocker stopped. She smiled, that sweet smile that hid the strength of character beneath. "I'm not worrying. And neither can you. God's looking out for you, dear, whether you want Him to or not. He sent you to me to help you know that."

"You don't know what a mess I've made of things."

"I don't need to," Miss Rose insisted. "He already does."

By the end of the week, the air had warmed enough to take Miss Rose into town. They rode without talking, soaking in the bright sun overhead, enjoying the chance to be out-of-doors.

She dropped off Miss Rose at Norwood's Mercantile for a visit and supplies. When she helped the woman clear the wagon wheel, Miss Rose gripped her arm. "Go on, Journey. I know you're itching to move about. I'll be a while." Miss Rose patted her arm and moved up the steps.

Journey smiled, eager to slip away and stretch her legs. The open spaces gave her a sense of freedom, but towns provided the reality—she couldn't forget that she wasn't free, not truly. She walked along the boards pounded into the slush, past the handful of businesses along the main street.

The wind blew, sending a shiver up her spine. She pulled the collar of her coat tightly about her neck and quickened her stride.

"I wondered when you'd make it into town."

She stopped at the gruff voice at her ear. "What do you want, Hank?"

"Darlin'," he said, snatching her hand into his own, "I thought I made that clear. This seems like the perfect opportunity for you to introduce me around town. Let's go."

She tugged her fingers free. Doc Ferris caught her eye and nodded a greeting as he walked by. She forced a smile in return and ducked her head. "Not now, Hank. Don't worry, I'll set things up. Give me some time to make the arrangements."

Hank bowed his long frame over her and she shrunk back. "There aren't any arrangements to be made. We'll go back to that quaint little shop, and you can announce your good fortune in meeting your cousin Hank in this speck of a town. What are the odds, really?"

"It would be best if—"

Hank laughed outright. "My dear, we both know you were never the thinker in this relationship. We'll do this my way."

She jerked as he whispered in her ear. "We wouldn't want your friends to suffer because you denied them a chance to cash in on a valuable business venture, right?"

She swung back but couldn't break his hold on her wrist. Grinding her teeth, she struggled, then relaxed before her tears fell. "I'll introduce you, but that's it, Hank. I can't lie to these people."

His heavy hand pushed her ahead. She stumbled but caught herself and tilted her chin as she walked on.

"That's it, Maura," he whispered. "Always the proud one. You just concern yourself with my presentation. We'll discuss how deep your commitment is to this deal as we go along."

He threw an arm around her shoulders, and she stiffened with memories. "It'll be like the old days, Beautiful. Who knows? We were always looking for that one big strike. Maybe this is it. A new beginning for us."

"There is no *us,* Hank. Not now, not ever. The only big strike I looked for was the next one coming from your fist. No, if I do this for you, we're through. For good this time." She strode ahead, wrapping her arms around herself. A few introductions, and she'd be rid of Hank Baines for good.

Zane watched the door. He had felt twitchy ever since Miss Rose walked in without Journey at her side. Ten minutes passed, fifteen—he slid from the counter where he sat and picked up his coat.

He breathed deeply when the door opened and Journey finally poked her head through. The bell jangled in announcement. But the ease lasted only until he saw the dark form saunter in behind her.

Zane caught Journey's glance as her brown eyes flickered around the room, and she started when she saw him. He leaned against the counter, arms crossed.

Miss Rose broke the silence. "You're back sooner than I expected, Journey."

The tall man standing behind her stepped forward. "Excuse her, ma'am. I believe she's in shock. We're just so surprised—"

"Journey?" Zane stepped closer, reaching for her.

She gestured toward Hank. "I—I'd like to, to introduce Hank Baines."

Zane's stomach clenched. "You know him?"

The tall man stepped forward, tucking long black

hair behind his ear and stretching a hand toward Zane. "I'm Miss Smith's—"

"Old family acquaintance," Journey filled in.

Excited questions hummed through the store as Abby and Miss Rose swarmed Journey. Zane straightened his shoulders and took the offered hand. The man's mustache twitched and he glanced around the mercantile with a look that reminded Zane of a rabid wolf he'd tracked years ago. Cunning. Cold.

"Fortunate you should meet Journey here. Are you just passing through?" he asked.

Baines stroked his mustache. Zane wondered if he checked it to be sure it hadn't fallen off. "I'm here on business. It was sheer luck that put Journey in my path this day."

Zane wondered whose luck he meant. "I see. And how are you acquainted?"

Silence echoed as the women quieted. Zane stared at the man but felt similar stares from Abby and Miss Rose aimed in Hank's direction. Journey bowed her head behind Hank, unable to meet his gaze.

"I've known her family for years," he said. "I've been in a position to help Journey on a number of occasions. Why, most folk assumed we'd be married by now." He chuckled. "But I think of her as my younger sister. I hope you'll consider me part of her family." Hank stretched back and grabbed Journey, pulling her to his side. Zane tried to catch her eye, but she stared at the other women and held herself away from his embrace.

"I'm sure Journey will be glad to have a familiar face here. What a shame you missed her when you stopped by the ranch for directions," Zane said.

A dark look crossed Hank's face, gone as fast as it'd come. "Why, to think that we might have been reunited all that much sooner!" Hank squeezed her shoulder, holding her like a possession under his control.

Not if he could help it, Zane thought. "Where will you be staying?"

Miss Rose raised her gloved hand. "You're welcome to bed down in the loft of my barn."

"He'll stay with me," Zane said.

Miss Rose quirked her eyebrow at him, but there was no way he would let Baines stay with them out there alone.

"My," Baines said. "So kind of you all to offer. But, as I am here on business, I'll be staying out at the old Allen homestead."

"That place has been abandoned for years," Abby said. "Deplorable condition."

"True. But I own it now, so it's no longer abandoned, and I'm well-satisfied to stay there." Hank spoke to Abby, but his gaze didn't waver from Zane's.

"That's a large parcel," Zane said. "How'd you come by that?"

Hank smirked, hugging Journey. "An unusually boring chain of events, I assure you."

"Well, tell us all about it when you come for supper Friday night." Miss Rose made the offer before Zane could stop her.

Hank hadn't stepped out of the shadows long enough for Miss Rose to recognize him from Thanksgiving. It was the only reason Zane could think of for her to make such an offer. But couldn't she feel the tension in Journey?

"How kind. I welcome the opportunity," Hank said.

He pressed his lips to Journey's head. "I'll see you Friday, then. Now, if you'll excuse me," he added, bowing to the ladies and nodding to Zane, "I must get back to my property. Journey, my dear, I can't tell you how glad I am to have found you out here after all this time."

Journey didn't acknowledge Hank's departure with anything more than a slight stoop of her frame. Zane slipped closer and laid a hand on her shoulder, softly, fearing she would bolt and run. He stared at her and noticed how her hair kinked tightly on either side of her part, regardless of how tightly she pulled it into the low chignon at her neck.

A strong yearning to lean in and kiss her bent head, as Hank Baines had done moments ago, possessed him. Instead, Zane squared his shoulders and dropped his hand to squeeze her wrist.

Journey peered at him as if she were waking from some strange dream. Her eyebrows curled and tears glazed her eyes, and she blinked hard and turned. "I'll wait for you in the wagon, Miss Rose," she said, walking out the door.

Zane laid a hand on the older woman's shoulder to keep her from giving chase. "I'll go. You finish up here." From the expression on her face, he'd surprised her as much as he had himself.

Did he have any business stepping in? Journey had made it plain she didn't want his help. But that was before Baines made an appearance. Before she was more wary of someone else than she was of him.

Zane stopped short at the door. "Oh, and, Miss Rose—"

"I'll see you Friday evening as well, Zane."

He leaned down to kiss her tiny gray head. "I'll

see you Friday evening, then. I hope you're making chicken. You know it's my favorite."

Journey knew he would follow. Not Miss Rose, not Abby, but Zane. She squeezed the reins and stared ahead, trying to control her breath. The smell of Hank filled her senses, and she rubbed her nose with the back of her palm.

Zane stayed on the sidewalk for a few moments, and Journey wondered if he waited for his sake or hers. She heard him walk toward her, knowing the easy, sure movements of his broad frame. He was nothing like Hank.

She stiffened at the thought. Could that be? She'd been so fooled by Hank in the beginning. His concern had seemed real, but now she knew everything he'd done for her had benefited him in some way.

But Zane had nothing to gain, and his offer of help would only cost him. Yet he wanted to do something. She'd seen it in his eyes in the store. It's the only reason he'd be standing here now. Journey kept her glance strained forward, willing Miss Rose to join her so they could go back to the ranch.

"Journey?" Zane's voice was low, quiet.

She couldn't look at him. "Does Miss Rose need help loading her things?"

"She'll be out in a minute," he said. "Mind if I join you?"

Journey slid away from him on the springboard. She breathed in, trapping the cold air in her lungs and wishing the stale scent of Hank's cigar didn't cling to her clothing.

Zane said nothing for a full minute. She scratched her knuckles. "Is there something you wanted?"

"The Lord works in mysterious ways."

"Pardon?"

The wagon creaked and she turned. Zane leaned a shoulder on the high side of the box, facing forward. "Strong coincidence, running into your old friend in a place like Walten."

"He isn't a friend." She sighed. "I knew him a long time ago."

Zane's gray eyes scanned her face and she turned away. Let him think what he wanted.

"Do you like it here, Journey?"

She hadn't thought about it before, one way or the other. She smoothed the bunched fabric of her coat and loosed her hold on the reins, thankful to see Miss Rose easing her way out the doorway. It would take Zane's attention away from the tears that welled unbidden and clogged her view. She squinted and fumbled in her pockets.

"Journey?"

She gasped and bit her upper lip, searching the horizon. "More than I expected," she whispered. She felt a warm hand on her forearm even through her sleeve and turned to face him. "For all the good it's done me, Zane. More than I expected."

He squeezed her arm with a gentle touch. "We've been known to have that effect." He smiled up at her, winking in the glaring sun moving low in the sky. The light made his eyes reflect blue. "I don't pretend to know where you're coming from, Journey, or what kind of ghosts you've got hounding you. But here's as good a place as any to put them to rest. There's plenty of folks willing to help if you'll let us."

Journey parted her lips, wanting to protest, but he walked away before she could. Who was she fooling? Right now, all she knew is that it certainly wasn't Zane.

Chapter Twenty-One

Journey pulled the collar of her coat around her neck and replaced the pitchfork along the wall. Although the snow held and the sun shone, a bitter wind blew over the mountains from the northwest. The muted land-scape and darkening skies had deceived her eyes, look-ing from the window of the fire-warmed house. Out here, the wind shook the stalls and whistled through the rafters of the barn. But the horses were fed, brushed and blanketed in the cozy darkness for the night. As a child, she would often sneak into the livery to stroke the horses' noses or treat them to a bit of carrot or apple she'd scrounged. She longed now to lie down in the hay with the heavy barn scents that gave some measure of comfort.

Instead, she returned to the house. The fire's calm-ing warmth would die as soon as Hank arrived. Jour-ney was shocked when Miss Rose had insisted he come for supper. Hank, of course, had been thrilled. He no doubt saw the invitation as a prime opportunity to en-dear himself to the woman.

"I've seen how people defer to her aged wisdom," Hank had announced. "And I've inquired about her, discreetly, through the town. She's rich as a troll, I tell you, and she carries a lot of weight around here. We'll seek her out first."

Zane would be coming. Journey held an uneasy hope that his presence would keep Hank from embarrassing himself, and her as well. She climbed the stairs to her room, peeled off her barn dress and washed at the basin. Her navy dress slipped over still-damp skin, and she breathed deeply, one hand at her waist to quell the jittery swirls in her stomach.

A quick knock at the door startled her. "Guests are here, dear," Miss Rose called, interrupting her anxiety.

Journey forced herself down the stairs to answer the door, stepping back as Hank's tall form filled the doorway. Zane stood behind, his broad frame edged out around Hank's. How could he be so at ease? Hank dwarfed him by a good head, yet Zane looked taller somehow.

"You look lovely," the preacher said, nodding Hank through ahead of him.

"I must agree," Hank added quickly. The words slipped over his lips, aided by the heavy oil shining his mustache. "And you, Mrs. Bishop—you're simply ravishing." He swept his hat off with one hand and grasped Miss Rose's fingers in the other, bowing over it. Journey held her breath, but Hank stopped shy of kissing her hand. Hank always knew exactly where the line was and halted short of it when it suited him.

"Your invitation to this wayfaring stranger is beyond all kindness, ma'am," he said. "I surely hope this doesn't inconvenience you."

Could his accent get any thicker?

Miss Rose's blue eyes shone with a peculiar light. "Company is never an inconvenience, Mr. Baines. Come, let's seat ourselves. Journey has everything ready, so I hope you'll forgive the break in Southern etiquette. I've never stood much on formalities."

The scent of venison mingled with smoke from the fireplace, giving the air of an intimate dinner party. If only it felt that way.

"I'm sure I'll find your social graces as refreshing as your boisterous spirit, Mrs. Bishop. Now, if I might escort you?" Hank tucked her hand into the crook of his elbow and turned toward the table.

Miss Rose nodded and allowed herself to be led. Journey watched them a moment before an elbow nudged her side. "Guess that leaves you and me," Zane said, mocking Hank's drawl. A broad smile of even teeth filled his face.

Though her arms felt like wood, Journey forced them to bend around his. Zane patted her hand with his free one and she started. The warmth of his touch gave a comfort she hadn't expected. She looked up, and he went on, his voice soft and deep.

"We'll follow your lead. Let us know what you want. He's your friend—acquaintance. But if you find he's not the man you think he is, we're here. Remember that." His voice lowered, and his gray eyes shone with care.

She looked ahead, forcing her feet to move and fighting to keep her tears at bay. He had summed up the entire problem. Hank was exactly the man she knew he was, and he was about to ruin everything.

* * *

Zane led Journey into the kitchen, which was warm and inviting with wondrous scents filling even the corners. With a sharp pang, he remembered the cozy evening meals Sarah would have waiting for him on cool fall evenings. He knew, somewhere in the far corners of his mind, that most memories of his marriage were colored a little brighter than they might have been had Sarah survived the fire. But it was no exaggeration that they had rarely fought, and it was a fact that her brightness tempered the heaviness and disappointments he faced as a minister. Often now he found himself eating something cooked to less than perfection with his own limited skills from a battered tin plate someone had donated after the fire took everything.

He glanced at Journey, her fine features puckered with tension, face pale as he helped her to her seat. How many home-cooked meals had she shared with anyone before arriving on Miss Rose's doorstep?

Sitting down beside her, he looked at Hank, calm and arrogant and shifty. He hated the feeling in his gut that told him to be wary when it came with no real proof.

Journey held herself stiffly, making herself as small as she could on the chair beside him. While Hank seated Miss Rose at her customary place at the head of the table, Zane touched Journey's elbow, running his fingers along her sleeve to end with a light squeeze to her hand.

She started, fear clouding her gaze for an instant, as if he had woken her from a deep sleep. Her fine eyebrows curled, then smoothed. She relaxed, even if it was forced, and an uncertain smile touched her lips.

He wanted to tell her everything would be fine, that

they'd get through this together with the Lord's help. He wanted to keep his hand over her tiny one until she believed it.

But Miss Rose cleared her throat delicately, breaking the moment, and he felt the weight of Hank's heated glance. He smiled back, then again at Journey, hoping he conveyed the thought anyway.

He squeezed her hand again. "Let's bow our heads in thanks and ask the Lord's blessing."

Journey etched a polite smile on her face, not wanting to give Hank the satisfaction of seeing the fear she felt. She had forgotten how accomplished he was at spinning a tale.

"And so I told her, 'I beg your pardon, but I do believe that's your canary.'"

He could entertain even the dourest of souls with that story. She might have laughed herself had she not heard it so many times or had her stomach not been churning. For now, Hank mastered the conversation. And it wasn't just humor. He could compliment with all the necessary doses of sincerity and affect an attentive ear to the hostess. Yes, he made an excellent dinner guest. Hank knew his game.

"But Journey insisted we offer the poor woman a few morsels before sending her on her way. That's just how she is." Hank patted Journey's arm. "Always thinking of someone else."

She flinched and looked away. That "poor woman" lost everything to one of Hank's hustles. Journey had pleaded for him not to turn her and her young son out in the street. But he'd refused and blackened her eye for the suggestion. That's just the way *he* was.

"That comes as no surprise to us," Miss Rose said, wiping her mouth with a cloth.

Hank certainly endeared himself to her, Journey thought. Maybe she shouldn't hold it against herself for getting mixed up with him in the first place. She'd been so young then, it was no wonder she found him witty, charming and attractive. Even now, he might accomplish it if she didn't know him better.

Zane managed to laugh at all the appropriate places, but Journey sensed his stare throughout the evening. At least he wasn't buying into Hank's facade. Was he?

Miss Rose surprised her. The woman laughed until tears streamed down her wrinkled cheeks. Where had that fiery staunchness gone?

It seemed Hank's scheme would be easy, yet harder than she thought. With Miss Rose charmed by Hank, all Journey would have to do was feed her ideas. Perhaps Miss Rose wouldn't be dissuaded if she tried. From experience Journey knew that once the elderly woman took a shine to a person, she didn't give it up easily. After all, Miss Rose had taken her in without so much as a how-do-you-do and had expected so little in return. No, Hank would have an easy time of it with Miss Rose on his side.

Journey didn't realize she had sighed out loud.

Irritation sparked in Hank's eyes, but he covered it by pulling out his pocket watch. "My, my—the hour is getting late. You really must excuse my lack of manners, Mrs. Bishop. It's been so long since I've enjoyed such fine company, and the venison was cooked to perfection."

Miss Rose nudged her chair back when he stood. "Thank you, Mr. Baines. It's been an entertaining evening for me as well. I'm sorry we've monopolized your time. We left little opportunity for you to get re-acquainted with Journey."

"Not to worry, ma'am. I've taken over quite a lucrative land development opportunity in Walten. I'm sure Journey and I will have plenty of occasions to revisit old times."

"Your business is in brokering land deals?" Zane asked.

"Uh—Hank managed several kinds of business ventures in Savannah," Journey said, hoping she didn't choke. At least she could say that honestly. Although Hank's victims wouldn't have seen his schemes that way.

Zane's eyebrows creased in disbelief. "That seems like a stretch for a little town like ours."

Hank's brown eyes gleamed in the lantern light of the parlor. "Now, that's small thinking, my good man. Think of the proximity to the gold strikes in and around Virginia City."

"You think we're in the same vein?" Zane asked, re-folding his napkin.

"Yes, and I have maps to prove my claim, sir."

"My, that would be something," Miss Rose said.

Journey stared at her crumpled napkin. "Hank has been involved in similar projects in the past. He is experienced." Another truth, but her heart twisted. "*If* there is a strike to be made." Zane nodded, but his gaze never wavered.

"Virginia City's grown too big for its britches," Miss Rose said. "Shooting and stealing are out of control."

Hank extended his arm across the table to Miss Rose, as if to offer comfort. "I agree. That's why the townspeople need to have a say. Everyone buys in, creating one collective claim. The people elect a board to manage the mining process, and everyone takes a share in the profit."

"It sounds like a plan worthy of consideration." Miss Rose smiled as she looked around the table.

Journey glanced at each face, trying to read the thoughts behind each one.

Zane leaned forward. "And that will keep the lawless element away?"

Hank laughed as if a child had shared a joke. "It's not a difficult thing to jump a claim defended by one man. It's quite another to try with a whole town involved." He paused and gazed around the table. Journey knew he read them and was trying to decide whether to forge on or stop while he was ahead.

"Why would you want to do that for this town?" Zane asked, eyebrows furrowed over his gray eyes.

"I'd gain a share, of course, but it gives us all a great opportunity. I trust I can count on your support in this."

Zane choked on the water he'd sipped. "Whoa, hold on there. I'd have more questions I'd want answered before I endorsed this."

"Naturally," Hank said. He didn't bat an eye, but Journey saw the tension mounting in the deepening creases on his forehead. "I can provide all sorts of maps and documents for your perusal."

Zane smiled. "That'd be mighty convenient. But I prefer to check into such matters firsthand. I'm sure a businessman like yourself can appreciate that."

Journey could see Hank's face grow hot even in the waning light of evening. She'd never seen anyone put him in his place so calmly and firmly. She looked at

Zane, his thick hair blocking a full view of his eyes, but she could tell by the set of his jaw and shoulders that the matter was settled.

"You must forgive me." Hank leaned forward in his chair. "I get a bit overzealous when I see such potential. I won't spoil our time with all this talk of business. I'd hate to wear my welcome too thin. After all, it's been such a lovely evening." His words were for Miss Rose, but his fiery gaze bored into Zane.

"Then we must do this again sometime," Miss Rose said. "Maybe when business is not quite so prevalent in your mind."

Journey moved to begin clearing the table. Relief washed through her, allowing a small smile to ease her face. If Hank expected Miss Rose to jump into an investment opportunity right away, maybe he'd lose patience and look for an easier mark.

But Hank was not to be cut off so quickly. "I'd be happy to talk with you about the development at a more opportune time."

"Miss Rose could tell you a few things about this town and the land here, Mr. Baines," Zane said. "She's lived here longer than just about anyone."

"Then I will take that offer, Mrs. Bishop, to enjoy your hospitality again." Journey had underestimated Hank's persistence.

She waited for Miss Rose to extend the invitation to call her "Miss Rose," as most of the community did. But it never came. She continued stacking plates while Miss Rose and Zane led Hank to the door.

"Journey, my dear?" Hank's voice cut through her relief at his departure. "If you'd be so kind as to walk me out?"

Her throat tightened. So this was it: the next step revealed, courtesy of Hank's controlling mind. She turned and nodded, brushing imaginary crumbs from her bodice.

"Hand her my cape, Zane," Miss Rose said. "And don't be out long, dear. I want to speak with you before I retire."

Bless the woman. The departure would be quick now that Miss Rose had given her an excuse.

Zane grabbed the wrap from the peg, and Journey shivered as he settled it over her shoulders, his hands lingering a moment. She turned and saw his eyebrows creased over questioning gray eyes. She shook her head once, cutting off any voice he might put to his concern. He couldn't understand all the stakes. No matter how much she wanted him to. Besides, she was only seeing Hank off. Minutes, that's all. She'd spent years with him—what were a few moments more?

But the closing door thudded with a finality that frightened her, as if she'd just created a barrier she could never cross again.

Chapter Twenty-Two

Journey tugged the heavy wool cape around her neck, burying her hands deep within the thick folds. The wind had died, with only the cold remaining.

Hank stepped off the porch and motioned for her to follow. She avoided the hand he extended to help her down the stairs and walked behind. He didn't force the issue, and she allowed herself a deep breath. She stopped in the yard, halfway between the porch and the post by the barn where he'd tied his horse.

"You might as well get on with it, Hank," she said, mustering any scrap of bravado she could lay claim to. "I can't be out here all night."

He tightened the cinches of his saddle. "Of course not, my dear. We can't have you coming down with something now. We're at a critical juncture."

She flinched. "Which is?"

He didn't bother to face her. "I've laid the groundwork, but Mrs. Bishop is a tougher sell than I'd anticipated. You'll need to convince her to buy into this deal, Maura."

"Journey," she whispered.

Hank turned, loosening the lead and walking toward her. "That's right—Journey. Miss Journey Smith, formerly known as Maura Sojourner Baines, formerly known as *my wife,* currently wanted for murder."

"Please, keep your voice down."

Hank swooped closer. She shivered at the icy fingers of air that pierced her cape.

"Of course, my dear. Keep things nice and quiet. We can't have your new beau finding out he's chasing after a married woman, a murderer and a two-bit—"

"Don't say it, Hank. I never was that and we both know it. And Zane's not my beau, I told you." She glanced back at the house. Warm light glowed from the windows, in stark contrast to the chill outside.

"You may not think so. He may not think so. But he's interested, Journey. A little lost lamb, you are. Pastor Thompson wants to help you find your way. And truly," Hank said, stretching his hand out to spring a curl by her cheek, "you can't blame him, darlin'. My, you are still as beautiful as the first day I saw you in that shop in Savannah."

Every muscle tensed as he touched her. Her face ached from it. She couldn't breathe. Her feet refused the command her mind screamed to run.

Hank backed off. The accent he had worked so hard to cultivate eased, too. "They weren't all bad times, Maura—Journey. Not all of them."

The moment passed, leaving Journey to wonder if she'd heard him at all.

"I'm going out of town for a few days—business, you know," he said, the accent back in place. "I should return by the end of next week, in a few days. You have until then to convince your Miss Rose to buy into this once-in-a-lifetime opportunity. And by all means, let the good reverend know he can get in on this, too. He runs a small horse trade, and there's money in that. More importantly, his congregation has to be convinced to invest as well. After all, who would attempt to dupe a minister?" He laughed and his teeth gleamed, like a wolf's.

"But what if he won't?"

"He has feelings for you. He hasn't sorted it all out yet, but he wants to trust you. Use that."

Journey shook her head. How could she take advantage that way?

Hank's clenched fist drew her attention and she ducked. He chuckled. "I see we still have an understanding."

She glanced back at the house. She'd been out too long already. "Can't you see that this will ruin me? I could have a place here, maybe even a real home. I can't do this. I—I won't."

"I'm sorry, my dear." His voice grew gruff as he swung atop his horse and edged it to stop at her side. He leaned down so close that she could smell the stench of his breath. "I didn't mean to imply you had a choice in this matter."

She pinched her lips together. "I want to be left alone. I'm not helping you anymore, Hank. Hit me if you're so inclined." She drew back. "Turn me in if you want. There's nothing you can say or do this time that will change my mind."

He straightened in the saddle and gathered the reins. "You've been many things, my dear, but never foolish. Don't ruin this."

She glanced away, looking over the snowy waves of bluffs to the west. Would the fear in her eyes give her away?

A jerk on the chin drew her eyes back to Hank's, too close and too cold, like black stones. "And don't even imagine you'll get away again, Maura. Not like the first time. I found you without even trying." He pinched her jaw in his fist. "Believe me. If I have to hunt you down, I will. And the reunion won't be nearly so joyous the next time."

She tore herself from his grip with a shake. "You do what you have to. But you'll do it without me."

"How noble you've become! Perhaps I can't force you to cooperate." He pulled his coat tighter and stared at the skyline with a faint smile. "But I can make you wish you had. Such a fine young minister. Such a shame for him to be out on his own so much, checking on his congregation, shepherding the fine people of this community." Hank clucked his tongue and his shadowed form shook in the darkness.

"Whatever would they do without him?" He paused. "Remember, I gave you a chance to protect your new friends."

He galloped off, dark coat, hair and horse blending in with the black horizon. She blinked back tears. Minutes passed before her frozen mind compelled her into the warmth of the house. Once Hank had his way, only coldness would remain.

Zane raked his fingers through his hair, peering out the window into the darkness, and chuffed out a breath.

"She's only on the other side of the door, Zane. What could happen?"

He turned to see Miss Rose hobble into the great room, having stacked the supper dishes for Journey in the kitchen. "Hard to tell. Everything's been flying like robins caught in an early snowstorm ever since she rode into town."

"You have been spending a fair amount of time keeping your eye on her. There's no one who could fault your ministerial concern for her, but you've done what you could. You have no further obligation toward her." Miss Rose settled onto the couch. "Some folks are determined to cause themselves trouble."

"You're the last person I would've thought would ask me to forget about her problems." He sat in the rocker and pulled it closer to her side.

Miss Rose rested her head against the tall cushion, her gray hair pressed wide around it. "I'm not telling you to forget, Zane. Not about Sarah, not about Journey's problems. I just want you to see that your concern is beyond what your job as our minister requires. Journey certainly doesn't expect it. What's more, she doesn't want it."

"She's alone and needs someone to help," he insisted.

"See, even as a boy, if anyone needed someone to come to their defense, you were there. Your mother told me once you gave a boy a black eye for throwing stones at that old stray dog." She smiled. "But now that Hank is here, I would think you'd be happy to pass along the responsibility." Miss Rose closed her eyes.

"What if this is only the start of her problems? That man leaves a bitter taste in my mouth. What if I let her face this trouble alone and it turns out to be more than she can handle? What if the very thing she's running from has found her here?" He leaned forward, tugging his hair and resting his elbows on his knees. "How can I let her stand against him by herself?"

"I'm glad to hear you say that. I wouldn't expect anything less." Miss Rose smiled without opening her eyes.

"You don't trust him either?" He raised his head in surprise.

"Not further than I can throw him."

"But—"

"He's entertaining, I'll give him that." She wiggled down into the cushion. "There was nothing false in enjoying his tales. But it doesn't mean I think we should sell the ranch and give him the proceeds. The whole deal smells too sweet—like fruit when it's starting to rot."

Zane rocked back in the chair and boosted himself up, resting his hands at his waist. "I agree. I'm taking a trip to Virginia City the first of next week to see what I can dig up."

Miss Rose opened her eyes and leaned forward, tapping her cane on the floor. "What if you get snowed in? Can't this whole business wait until spring? Mr. Baines won't be pushing anything before Christmas, surely."

"That's the trouble. We need to know what we're dealing with so we can protect Jour—protect the town, before he starts pushing." He stood and walked to the window.

"There's no shame in wanting to protect her," Miss Rose said.

"It's not only her. There's a whole town to consider. What if we're wrong and this is a legitimate offer? Folks around here—"

He turned at the feel of a warm hand on his shoulder. Soft blue eyes met his. "You've been thinking about me, about Sarah, about everybody else but yourself for too long, Zane."

He grasped Miss Rose's hand. "I couldn't help Sarah the night she died. She cried for me, Miss Rose. She cried for me to get out of that house without her, and I did…and she died."

Miss Rose stretched a bony arm around him. "We've gone over this before. You were hurt, too. We could've lost you both. The Lord had other plans."

His breath caught on the hard knot in his chest. "I know that. It's taken a lot of time and a lot of prayers. I still don't understand it, but I know it. But maybe this is my chance. Maybe the Lord needed me here to help Journey, to keep whatever mess Baines is set on bringing to Walten from happening."

Miss Rose gasped, a soft puff of indrawn air. "You think the Lord took Sarah so you'd be more focused on Him, don't you? I wondered why all those young gals at church never caught your eye before now."

"I'm willing to live life as a bachelor if that's what the Lord requires," he said, his voice straining. Surely Miss Rose understood that. But the ache he never had been able to dismiss entirely burned around his heart. "If I had only known before we married, I would've spared her." His breath caught on the ache in his chest, and he rubbed his hand over his face.

"Oh, honey," Miss Rose said, draping a warm arm around him. "I didn't realize. You have to know that God planned that man and woman would help each other to get through this old world together. If ever a woman was created for a man, it was Sarah for you.

"Now, I'm not saying Journey can't fill that job. She's not a suitable choice at the moment, but I don't know what the Lord has in store for the two of you ahead. All I'm saying is you need to let your heart open to the possibilities, not close yourself off because you're afraid."

He faced the window. The two shadowed forms outside drew closer, then suddenly apart. He wondered about their conversation. "All I know is that I have to follow this trail until it forks or flat out stops. I'm not being stubborn. I've prayed and I believe I'm where God would have me."

"In that case, my boy," Miss Rose said, pushing herself away with a firm grip on his forearm, "let me pack some biscuits for you to take along. I'll send a wire to Reed so he knows to expect you. Whatever storm's brewing, I'll feel better knowing both of my boys are working it out together. And I'll be praying for you both."

He focused on the window, watching Journey's shadow pull away from the other. Fear seemed very real any time she was near Hank. Zane knew she needed help.

But the question never stopped nagging at the back of his mind: what if she was fooling them all?

Chapter Twenty-Three

Zane nudged his horse closer to the wooden boards along the wide street. Buildings rose up and pressed in on him, blocking his view of the mountains surrounding Virginia City.

A stiff wind blew through him, but the sun shone overhead, trying its best to offer a little heat. He pulled his sheepskin coat closer around his neck and drew a slow breath. After two frigid nights on the trail, he wanted nothing more than to stretch out in a soft bed and sleep until the light of day woke him.

Virginia City had grown more civilized in the years since the gold strike in 1862. The town had sprung up overnight, but there had been over a hundred murders in the first two years. Now, Wallace Street's main thoroughfare boasted three churches, a fine courthouse and several good hotels. The town had tamed considerably.

Two cowboys slammed out from a saloon, trading blows and rolling from the sidewalk. Zane sidestepped the men and crossed to the other side of the road. *Well, maybe it's not totally tamed yet.*

First things first, he thought. Let Reed know he'd arrived, then stable his horse.

Moving along the mile-long street toward the courthouse, he stopped at the sturdy building of stone that sat next to it. Reed met him outside, the word SHERIFF inscribed in block letters above the door where he stood.

"Well, what brings you out this way, Pastor?" Reed slid his hat back with one hand. The other held a rolled wad of handbills. "Or should I say, 'horse trader'? I'm guessing it's only one or the other that would bring you to town in this weather."

Zane joined the older man on the open porch. "Guess you could say neither this time. Or maybe a little of both."

"Come on in and set yourself by the stove a bit, then."

Zane tramped into the warm office, guided by Reed's handshake and a welcoming clasp on the shoulder. "I trust Aunt Rose is well."

"Fit as a fiddle. She'll outlive us all."

"If spunk will do it, then I'm sure she will. Have a seat," he offered.

Zane pulled his hat down and drew his fingers through his matted hair. "I need to find somewhere to stay, get settled in. But I figured I'd talk to you first, let you know I was in town."

"Aunt Rose sent a telegram." He reached into the narrow front drawer of his desk and pulled out a pale yellow paper. "Zane arrives Wednesday STOP Watch for him STOP Love Aunt Rose STOP."

Zane laughed and tugged his gloves from his frozen hands. "That's like her." His fingers soaked up the heat, making them tingle.

"I figure this must be pretty significant if you're

coming here this time of year." Reed handed him a steaming mug of coffee from the stove. The scent roused Zane from the drowsiness that'd crept up after the long, cold ride. The sheriff pulled up a chair and propped his boots on the low stool at his feet, tipping back and clasping his hands behind his head. "How long are you planning to stay?"

"I head back tomorrow if I'm to make it for Sunday service." Zane gulped the rich coffee, melting his insides. He hunched over the steaming mug, digging his toes into his boots as they began to thaw and burn.

"So this must be some kind of important," Reed said again. He tilted back a little farther and scratched his jaw. "What's on your mind?"

"What have you heard about more gold strikes along Alder Gulch?"

"The stories turn out better than the strikes, for the most part. But I suppose the luck is still fair. More folks are arriving down along the way. Especially since we've settled down a mite. But I'm guessing you're looking for something more specific."

"Have you heard about the likelihood of a strike near Walten?"

Reed laughed, a deep, rich sound. "Wouldn't that be something? So many folks moved out to get away from all the trouble gold's caused here. I guess stranger things have happened, but I'd be surprised if the line played out that far. Why do you ask? You figuring on going into prospecting?"

Zane shook his head. "Not hardly. We had a visitor come to town who claims he has maps that prove there's gold right near Walten. He's talking of selling shares to the people to set up a gold-mining company of sorts. Everyone pays in, everyone shares in the profits." He followed Reed's gaze to the fire, watching him consider the information.

"Do the people seem inclined to buy in?"

"It hasn't been set out before everyone yet. I know he wants to get a few of us on board first. Me, your aunt, people who have been around long enough to have some say."

Reed straightened in his seat. "He picked the wrong crowd then. Gold nuggets have never been what you've searched for."

"But what if it's there? Word's bound to get out. The man says if the town sets up as one big claim, it'll keep lawlessness from taking over our town." Zane rubbed his tired eyes with the heel of his hand. "You remember what this place was like a few years ago, Reed. I'd hate to see that come to Walten."

The sheriff stared at the fire. "Not much better now," he murmured. "No, I'd hate to see that, too. But do you think his plan would stop it?"

"Let's just say, I don't think the man would have a problem with a criminal element coming into the town. In fact, I get the feeling he would be the forerunner."

A pause lengthened before Reed spoke. "Are you going to give me a name?"

He stretched, feeling each ripple of his spine, and cracked his knuckles, absentmindedly thumbing an old rope burn.

Reed cleared his throat and his boots pounded the floor as he stood. "Does this have something to do with Journey?"

Zane jerked his head up. "What makes you say that?"

"Never mind. You just answered my question. Aunt

Rose has been concerned," Reed said, walking over to fill his mug from the coffeepot on the stove. Zane waved off the offer of a refill.

The sheriff sank to his seat and curled his lips over the bitter drink. "It doesn't surprise me that she'd make a difference. Listen, Zane, I can't help you if you don't tell me what you know. Especially if Journey's involved."

"I don't know that she is."

"But you suspect—"

"I suspect she could be in danger if she is. She's been acting peculiar lately. Ever since this Baines fellow found her."

"Found her?" Reed asked.

"Remember the stranger from Thanksgiving? Turns out Journey knows him. I knew she was running from something. Turns out it's a someone. They claim he's an old family friend. Well, he claims that and she doesn't correct him. She isn't very excited about him being there. I've had colts that had been whipped before I got them that didn't act as skittish as she does." He bent low in his chair, rubbing his temple.

"So she's asking for your help?"

He scratched his eyebrow and grinned. "Not exactly. She'd be happier if I signed up for foreign missions."

Reed laughed and stood to stoke the fire. "I was there, Zane. I saw her, and I don't think you could be further from the truth." He took another gulp of coffee. "What can I do to help?"

"I thought we could look through some old posters."

"You came all this way to look through posters? Why not send a wire?"

"I've seen this guy. I thought it might move things

along a bit, in case he hasn't always gone with the same name."

Reed eased back into his seat, rubbing his thick fingers along his lip. "This isn't like you to be so suspicious."

"I know. That makes me even more sure that something's up. I've prayed about this. I believe the Lord sent me here."

"I've never known you to miss on something like this, Zane. But you look done in. Why don't you settle in over at the hotel? Get some hot food in you and come back over after supper to look through the posters."

Zane stretched and stood, swirling the last of the coffee in his cup before draining it down. "You won't get an argument from me. If you could point me in the direction of the livery, I'll untack my horse and get him settled in."

"You'll find it down a piece from the hotel. Tell Beans I sent you."

Zane pulled his heavy coat back on, now toasty from its placement near the roaring fire. His fingers felt stiff as he tugged on his still-damp gloves. Supper sounded good. Sleep sounded better. But too many questions still rumbled in his head, and he'd come for answers. A pale, freckled face framed by tight rings of ruby-brown hair came to mind. Yes, the sooner he figured out her story, the sooner he could put Journey out of his mind.

The wind grew stronger as the sun set. Clouds billowed in overhead, promising more snow. As he walked toward the courthouse, Zane was thankful for the muffler Miss Rose had forced on him before he'd left. The sidewalk changed its width and rise seemingly at will but was easier to walk on than the snowy street.

Passing up the nap for a bath had been a good choice, he decided. The hot water had eased aches he'd gotten from sleeping on the ground that the lumpy bed would not have. *I'm getting soft,* he thought.

The streetlamps had not been lit yet, but inside the jailhouse Reed had lanterns burning brightly. They'd need the light if they were going to search through the stack of wanted posters Reed had pulled—an entire year's worth.

His friend turned as he walked in, a pile of papers in one hand, a cup of coffee in the other. "Have a seat, Zane. I figure we might as well start with the most recent posters and work our way back."

Zane took the offered seat with a nod and tipped it back, pulling the first poster closer to the light to study the face drawn on it.

"It might be helpful if I knew what we were looking for," Reed said. "Does this guy have any distinguishing marks?"

"He has really dark hair. Wears it longish, with a mustache to match. He's tall. I suppose some ladies might consider him handsome." Zane flipped to the next poster.

"I'll warn you, the likenesses usually aren't as helpful as the written description, and even then you probably know ten other folks who'd match it."

"I see that," Zane muttered. "But I still think we need to try. It could prove important to a lot of people. My parishioners could lose everything."

Reed slid into the chair across the narrow table. Zane

looked up when he cleared his throat. "Your only concern is your congregation?"

"Walten is a good town. I want what's best for it and the people who live there."

"And that's all there is to this?"

"You're fishing."

Reed harrumphed. "A devout bachelor like myself?"

Zane settled back and flipped to another yellowed leaflet.

"But no one would blame you if you happened to notice how pretty she is."

He shook his head, never lifting his attention from the papers in his hand. "Journey needs me to get her away from this guy."

"Are you so sure she wants to get away from him? And what makes you think I'm talking about her?" Reed slid closer to the heat of the stove.

He snapped his glance to his friend. "Because no one likes to live in fear." He grinned. "And because I know you."

Reed nodded, his expression sober. "I reckon you're right, Zane. Reckon you're right. Can you use some more coffee?"

He nodded and turned his full concentration back to the papers on the table.

A few hours later, night had taken a firm hold over the city, and Reed turned up the lanterns. Zane rubbed his eyes.

Reed's voice broke the silence. "You want to finish up tomorrow?"

He tilted his head, holding out his mug for a refill. "Are you kicking me out?"

"No," he said. "Just checking."

"So make yourself useful." He laid the last of his posters on the pile at the table while the sheriff disappeared down a narrow hall.

"You want to go back another six months?" Reed called from the back room of the office.

"We might as well." He stretched his legs, pacing around the dusky outer room.

Reed returned with a smaller stack. They settled in to search the ink pictures. Zane feared they were all melting together in his mind. One big criminal. He wondered how Reed dealt with it all.

"Zane? Look at this."

He stood and looked over Reed's shoulder at the poster he held, pulling it from the sheriff's hand to ease it under the light. The hair was drawn loose, but the curls were unmistakable. The lines were harsh but the composite utterly recognizable.

And under that familiar face, he read the words: "WANTED: Maura Sojourner Baines."

Chapter Twenty-Four

"Name's different, Zane. It could be someone else. What do you make of it?"

"It's her." He barely recognized his own voice. *What kind of trouble are you in, Journey?*

Reed smacked his shoulder. "We don't know the whole story. What else does it say?"

"Wanted for murder, arson and theft. In the state of Georgia," Zane read. "There has to be some mistake. She wouldn't do those things."

"It's hard to say what some folks will do under the right circumstances. You have to admit it yourself, Zane, she's awfully skittish for someone with nothing to hide."

"But murder? Tell me you think she's capable of killing someone. Even physically—she's so small." He laid the poster on the table but couldn't tear his attention from it. He didn't want to remember the gun she'd drawn on him in the barn.

Reed peered out the window, shaking his head. "No. No, I don't think she's capable of it. But that's not the point. She's a suspect at the very least, and I think it's best if we bring her in and get this settled."

"You can't arrest her. She's finally starting to trust us."

Reed read the poster again. "Maybe we have reason to not trust *her*."

Zane locked a fist in his hair and blew out a heavy breath. "Does it have to be right away? If she were going to run, she would've done it before now. She's stuck in Walten until spring breaks. That gives us time to find out what happened. Besides, it'll soon be Christmas. I get the feeling she hasn't had many nice ones."

The sheriff scratched his mustache. "If she's convicted of murder, she won't have any more Christmases, nice or otherwise. But it isn't her name. And it would explain the connection between her and this Baines fellow. They must be related somehow. Maybe a brother or something. I agree it's not likely she'll run for a few months yet."

"Thanks, Reed. You don't know what this means to me." Zane rubbed a hand over his face.

"I expect you don't know what it means to yourself."

Zanc thought he would elaborate, but Reed turned back to the fire and sat in the closest chair.

Zane stood to go, pulling his muffler around his neck. "I appreciate your help with this. I'll stop by in the morning on my way out of town."

Reed looked up, coffee cup midway to his mouth. "You're leaving now?"

"I already found out more than I wanted to know. I need to turn in early so I can start fresh tomorrow. I have a congregation to get home to."

"What about Baines? You want me to keep hunting

for more on him? It would help to know Journey's connection to him. Until we know more, we can't count her out."

Zane pushed his hair back under his hat. "I'd appreciate it. You'll wire me if you learn more?"

"Sure enough. But remember, this could have nothing to do with the gold maps," Reed said.

"I think we're both too skeptical now for that." Zane grinned and pulled on his gloves. "But I'll keep my eyes and ears open, and I'll be in touch. Pray about it, won't you? I don't want to force Baines's hand, I don't want my judgment clouded about Journey's involvement and I don't want to put the town at risk by holding on to what I know for too long." What if they were working together?

He pulled on his warm coat. "But, if this man's claims are true, many people could benefit from the money a mine could generate, even if there's a fraction of the gold in Walten that's been found here. It's going to take more discernment than I have."

"Deciding when to come in out of the cold takes more discernment than you have," Reed joked, then sobered. "I'm always praying for you and Walten. I grew up there, you know."

Zane nodded and moved to the window. "Looks like the wind has picked up."

"You'll have a hard ride ahead if you want to miss the next snowfall."

Zane moved to the door. "Should I head out tonight?"

"I think if you don't get some sleep you'll fall off your horse before you hit the trail." Reed leaned back in his chair. "You'll make it. It won't do to take the scenic route, is all."

"Thanks, Reed. For everything."

"You stop by in the morning. I'll have a letter for Aunt Rose."

"Will do. See you bright and early." He stepped out into the night. The wind pierced through his heavy coat. Its howl silenced all other sounds around him.

Street fires burned low and at wide intervals, providing little light and even less heat. Zane expected they would soon be smoldered to prevent the risk of spreading to nearby buildings as the night winds picked up.

A noisy shuffle came from the left as he passed a narrow alley. He felt the crack of a heavy board across his back before he could turn. Surprise forced the air from his lungs. He twisted, trying to get away, but only felt himself dragged farther and farther from the dim fires.

A flash of pain at the back of his head, and his feet became useless. Blackness threatened to blow in with the storm, but stones cut into his cheek, rousing him again.

An arm pinned him to the wall. He sensed that his attacker was at least a head taller. The voice that rumbled down to him confirmed it. "If you were as smart a man as you think you are, Pastor, you wouldn't have been digging around where you have no business."

He tried to pull his scattered thoughts together, to make sense of it all.

"Come, come, now—has the cat got your tongue?" Another jolt knocked his head into the wall. Something solid pressed against his throat, making it hard to breathe. "I'll make it real simple, real simple. Let this alone, and stay away from Maura."

He heard a mumbled response, then realized it was his own.

"All you need to know is your precious Journey isn't so innocent. Or do you know that already? Stay away from her. Mind your own business, and you stay alive. I'm sure we understand one another," the voice said. Zane tried again to identify the tone, but the echo resounded in his head, tinny and far away as he spun around into the harsh wall again.

Zane swung out, determined to get away. Reed… Reed could help. One fist found only air, but the other clipped a shoulder—at least, he thought it was a shoulder. The way the light and darkness danced around in his head, he couldn't tell for sure.

A fist in his gut doubled him over, leaving him unable to recover before a slash of pain cut across his head once more. This time, he fell down through the darkness, into something cold and wet.

Lord, he prayed. But his thoughts went no further and the darkness consumed him.

Chapter Twenty-Five

Journey stared out the window above the kitchen sink and scrubbed furiously at a pot. A cold sliver of ice sank to the pit of her stomach, despite the dishwater that steamed around her. The snow blew white on the horizon, blending with the sheeted clouds in the sky.

Where was Zane? Tucked in somewhere warm, she hoped. She'd been surprised at his sudden decision to make a trip to Virginia City. Even more worrisome was the fact that Hank had left on his business trip the day before him.

She couldn't bring herself to ask questions. Not knowing for sure was easier. If Hank tried to work another angle, she'd have to tell others of her involvement with him, especially Zane. Could he help? What would Hank do? Best not to think about it.

Miss Rose had insisted on a rare Monday-afternoon trip into town. She seemed her spunky self but a mite quieter than usual. Something had her worried, too. Journey wiped the last plate and stacked it, then grabbed the dishpan to throw out the lukewarm water.

"Oh!"

Miss Rose stood behind her. The mucky water sloshed over the kitchen floor.

"I didn't mean to scare you. I was just going to get another log for the fire. That wind is blowing right through the cracks."

"I'll get it. You should stay bundled up and close to the heat. It's drafty out here."

Miss Rose smiled. "I'll tell Zane you were dutiful in hovering over me in his absence."

Journey swallowed and bobbed her head, setting the pan of water back into the sink. "It's the least I can do. Will he be back for Sunday's service?"

"Oh, yes. He expects to be back Friday evening, late."

She walked behind Miss Rose, carrying a few extra logs into the sitting room. "I'm sure you'll be relieved to see him."

The woman paused, adjusting her shawl over her shoulders.

"Oh, I miss him, but I'm not worried about him. The Lord will watch out for him, and He can do the job much better than I could. I notice your friend Mr. Baines hasn't been around, either. I hope there's nothing wrong."

Journey concentrated on stoking the fire, wanting to protest the use of the word *friend.* But better not to draw more attention to it. "He's out of town this week."

Miss Rose settled back in her rocker, adjusting a pillow under her head. "It is a funny coincidence, you meeting up with him again all the way out here."

Journey swallowed hard and brushed her hands on her apron. "I suppose so."

"Don't worry. They'll both be back before you know it, itching to be around underfoot." Miss Rose closed her eyes for a nap.

Journey slipped into the kitchen. She didn't know which bothered her more, the fact that Miss Rose was probably right or the fact that deep down she didn't believe it could be that simple.

A blinding white…

Cold. Darkness. Each registered in his mind as separate ideas, but he thought no further than that.

Someone rolled him over. Light stabbed his eyes and he tried to raise both hands to block it but only one responded. Someone lifted him by his coat lapels, and he swung at his attacker. But his feet slipped, unable to support him.

"Zane! What happened?" He knew the voice that echoed in his head. "It's me, Reed."

Zane swung his head up and leaned forward, determined to balance himself. The bleary form of Reed Knox swam before him, and he wondered what he was doing.

"Cold out here." His words slurred together, like his tongue had grown too large for his mouth.

"I know, buddy. Come on, let's—"

He dropped again into the cold darkness.

He waved to Sarah, sitting by the fireplace. She smiled at him but didn't say a thing.

Suddenly, fire slithered along the floorboards, creeping up the rockers of her chair, and he darted forward. But as he fought the burning heat, a scream rang out.

He looked through the flames to see Journey falling into their grasp.

"Whoa! Whoa, there."

Zane felt a weight at his shoulder, pinning him down. He gasped when he tried to throw off the heaviness, and pain ripped through his head and side. He opened his eyes and found Reed staring, his eyebrows curled together and mustache scrunched tight. He looked to be in need of a shave, too.

"Do you really look that bad, or is my vision that blurry?" It sounded like someone else's voice saying his thoughts.

"What kind of fool question is that? I've been up all night with you carrying on. Do you remember what happened?"

Zane glanced around the room, having learned not to make any sudden moves. He was in the sheriff's office; they were looking for something here last night. Wasn't it last night?

"How long have I been out?"

Reed pulled up a chair and sat. "You kind of roused when I dragged you in here, I think. I found you half-way down the street, half covered in snow in the alley by the bank. If it weren't that I keep an eye out for Old Petey, I might've missed you."

"Old Petey?"

"Let's say he's a regular. He's sleeping off a drunk in the back right now. He walked in on his own not long after I dragged you in here. How do you feel?" Reed gave him a scrutinizing look.

"Like I ran into a wall."

"From the looks of it, you did—a couple times. What happened?"

"What time is it?"

"It must be getting close to noon. Why?"

Zane shifted up on the bed, not easy with one arm in a sling. "Last thing I remember, we were looking at wanted posters. Then I woke all trussed up like a turkey." He managed a smile. "So what'd you do to me?"

"You go around smiling like that in the shape you're in, folks will think you've lost every plum in your pie."

Zane swung his feet out to the floor and cradled his head in his hand. "Honestly, Reed, I don't remember. You didn't hear anything?"

"Lie back down. You wouldn't be going anywhere now even if you were right as rain. The snowstorm's raging out there," Reed said, nodding toward the front windows.

"I guess that's a no, then?"

Reed shook his head. "I'm just glad I found you when I did. It's a wonder you didn't freeze to death."

Zane eased to his feet, swinging his good arm out as his view got shaky.

"Sit down!"

He shook his head. "I'll be fine. I need to move around some."

"I knew I should've had the doctor take your pants. That'd keep you in place."

"You'll know better next time," Zane said with a grin. He shuffled to the window, ignoring the stitch in his side. "How long do you reckon this storm will last?"

"Not long. It's moving fast. But then I don't imagine you'll feel much like sitting on a horse for a couple of days, anyway."

Reed stepped over and set a chair by the window.

Zane sank into it, lips curled together. "I'll have to wire Miss Rose."

"I figured I'd wait until you roused before I sent word."

"Good. Don't tell her anything that will worry her. It's probably just a thief looking for money."

Reed laid a heavy hand on Zane's shoulder. "I'll tell her you'll be home sometime next week, and not to worry. She'll figure the storm delayed you. But we both know this isn't about robbing a preacher."

Zane turned back to stare at the driving snow through the windowpane. "Reckon you're right. Maybe I did get hit harder than I thought, because I'm thinking someone didn't want me to make it home too fast."

"Who knew you were coming?"

"Miss Rose, Sam and Abby, Journey…"

Reed looked at him.

Zane leaned back in the chair, trying to ease the ache in his ribs. "It wasn't Journey."

"So tell me how you know this."

"Because," he said, rubbing his temple with his thumb. "Because it was a deep voice."

"You remember now?" Reed slid forward on his seat, waiting.

"Not much. Just that the voice was deep and came from above me."

"Like the voice of God?"

Zane grinned. "Real funny when you're not the one wearing the sling."

"Sorry. But we know it was a man taller than you with a deep voice. Strong, too, I'd say, by the looks of you."

"I wasn't exactly expecting a fight. Besides, we don't know what *he* looks like this morning," Zane said.

"True, but we do know he walked away." Reed walked over to his desk in the corner of the dim room and opened a drawer. "Anyway, I think I'll search back a little further in the posters. Where's Hank from?"

"Georgia. Abby said Journey had lived there, too."

Reed scratched his mustache with his thumb. "I'll send a wire and see if anyone's heard of Baines. It's worth a try."

Zane nodded and smothered a yawn. It stretched his ribs too much. "Think it's time for a nap."

"Terrible to get old," Reed said, giving him a hand up.

He stood without help, caught his balance and wavered back to the bed. "I reckon you're the one who'd know."

Chapter Twenty-Six

Journey peered through the frosted glass at the swirling snow from the rocking chair where she sat.

"I don't know that he'll get back today," Miss Rose said.

"Who?" She let the curtain slide from her hand.

"Zane. It could be more like late Saturday night, I'd expect, what with the storm and all."

"I wasn't—I mean, I didn't... He never said when he'd be back or even that he'd be going. You don't suppose he's caught out in this?" She focused on the tiny stitches of the suit she was sewing.

Miss Rose rocked, head back, the rest of her buried in quilts. "No, he'd miss it, or at least the worst of it, if he left when he planned. But it could slow him down some."

Journey watched Miss Rose close her eyes. Another nap. She had been so tired lately that Journey thought Doc Ferris should stop in and check on her.

The creak of the rocker stopped, leaving only the tick of the mantel clock and the crackle of the fire inside the snug house. Journey looked up from her work to see Miss Rose sleeping and eased off her own chair, walking to the window to draw the curtain aside.

The sun rested behind the saddle of mountains in the west. The cold, flat disk radiated light from the fresh snow through the day but provided little warmth. Something moved and caught her eye.

"Rider coming," she whispered, glancing at Miss Rose, who hadn't stirred.

Pulling her cloak from the hook, Journey slipped outside. The wind had calmed through the day but seemed to be picking up with the setting sun.

She peered into the dimness. The rider blended in with the shadowed mountains, almost invisible. But still, she watched. It could be Zane. She shivered, trying to shake the uneasiness.

The figure rode close to the window, and she drew back as horse and rider emerged into the faint light. "Hank."

He swept his hat off. The balance of light from the house and the remaining rays of the sun mixed to give him an eerie glow. His eyes glittered black and tiny. *Snake.*

"Hello, my dear. I wanted to drop by and let you know I've returned. Please forgive the lateness of the hour." His accent lacked smoothness, as if he were very tired.

"Where were you?" she whispered, her heart pounding.

Hank shook his head. "Oh, but, Maura, you're my wife even yet. It's good to hear your concern."

"It's Journey. And please answer the question."

He chuckled but it ended in a cough. "My, my, I

admire this new spunk you've acquired here in Montana, *Journey.* I've been looking after our interests in Virginia City."

"*We* have no interests there." *Keep your voice steady,* she thought. "*We* have no interests anywhere."

"Oh, but we do. Roy has come to help us with all the details of the little investment we're going to make available to the fine people of Walten," he said.

Any fight she'd gathered evaporated from her.

Hank didn't seem to notice, but surely he felt it. "Roy found me lying on the floor after you'd belted me with that flatiron the night you left. He'd come to warn me our fine sheriff was about to appear at our door with a warrant for my arrest."

She hoped Hank could not make out her expressions in the darkness. She knew he'd been up to no good when she was with him in Georgia.

"The sheriff would have caught me good," he continued. "Then Roy concocted the plan to get out and set fire to the place. He testified as witness to your part in my murder and in the blaze that harmed all those dear neighbors." He paused to clear his throat.

"You should have stuck around for the trial. The community was quite irate. Quite ironic, isn't it? If you hadn't tried to kill me, you would have been rid of me anyway. Rather amusing, don't you agree?"

Could it be that she had found her way out when true escape had lain so close at hand? Stupid, stupid woman! But then, she'd had little choice at the time. Kill or be killed. If she'd been better at it, she wouldn't be in this predicament now.

Hank paused. He'd always been a master at effect.

She waited, drawing her arms around herself under the cape.

"Roy and I were able to make our way out before the whole place burned to the ground. Pity about the place. We had some good times there, Maura."

"If you consider beating me a good time," she said, her voice quiet and blending with the night.

"Can't you just once remember something good?" His voice flared. "I loved you, Maura. I still do, you know. I miss your fire. It's only that you made me so—"

"As I recall, it was the whiskey that made you so…"

He smiled, faint light glistening from his teeth. "Either way, the fact is now we're together for as long as I say. Turn me in, and you'll be tried for attempted murder, at the very least. There's the little matter of the arson, too. Not to mention the fact that a good sum of money went missing. You'll be sent back to Georgia, where we'll still be married."

"Turn me in. I don't care anymore. I'm tired of living in your grasp."

"Perhaps I will." He swiped a hand over his mustache. "Perhaps you'll have no reason to stay regardless. I think you'll find your new beau not quite so attentive as before."

The coldness around her was nothing compared with the chill that shot through her. She cleared her tight throat. "What have you done?"

"Don't count on the help of your young Pastor Thompson any time in the near future."

Her heart dropped.

"Hank, if you—"

He cut her off with a laugh. "I don't think you're in any position to finish that thought. I'll be in touch."

Journey called to him as he turned to go. "Hank, you didn't..." She couldn't say it, but she knew he'd done as much before.

"Let's not raise a fuss, Maura. It would be a shame to disturb the delightful Miss Rose." He turned, an envelope offered by his shadowed hand. "I almost forgot. Telegram from Virginia City, dear. Addressed to Mrs. Rose Bishop. From her darling nephew, I'd suppose. I picked it up in town." He clucked his tongue. "I do hope it's nothing serious."

Her eyes felt wet and frozen, like her breath. She clasped the envelope to her. By the time she drew her gaze from it, Hank was gone.

Chapter Twenty-Seven

Journey swept through the warm room. Miss Rose slept, her face turned toward the fire's heat. Journey moved up the stairway, straining over the creaking fourth step.

A sliver of moon shone through her bedroom window. She grabbed her satchel and tugged the latches open, coins jangling inside the pockets. Precious few. Still not enough for a horse of any kind, and how far could she get on foot?

She threw in her navy dress and jerked the straps tight. Miss Rose's horses would get her anywhere she needed to go. The thought ripped through her head before she could quell it. She padded back down the stairway, her mind racing. Take the horses, ride off and never look back. And the money Miss Rose kept in her rosewood box on the mantel would go a long way in helping her get lost once again. She could…

The sight of Miss Rose asleep on the rocker stopped her. Miss Rose would want to help, would understand. And once she settled again, she'd pay everything back.

Walking over to the fireplace, she pulled the money from the box. She couldn't stop to count it but knew from the thickness it would take her far.

Stuffing the wad of bills into her coat pocket, she passed Miss Rose's chair and out the door, easing it closed behind her. The bitter wind kicked in her face and made it hard to breathe as she ran across the yard to the barn.

Puffs of air clouded her view. Hank would never let her go if she didn't do it this way. He'd already hurt Zane; he—

Zane. How far had Hank gone to get what he wanted? He had never displayed too many limitations before. Gambling, stealing, pursuing the magnificent plan— whatever struck him at any given time as the best way to make the most money in the least time with the least amount of effort. And yet, how many months behind on the rent had they been when she left Georgia?

Zane had to be fine. Surely Hank had only meant to frighten her. She patted the money in her pocket. Maybe she could give Hank the money he craved, and he would leave everyone alone. Could it be so simple?

"What will she do when she finds out Zane's hurt and I'm to blame?" she muttered. Her fingers froze, her harsh breath echoing in the quiet of the barn.

She grasped Homer's dark mane, pulled her fingers into it and rested her forehead against his neck. "What will we do if he's worse than hurt?"

The image of Zane lying cold and in pain somewhere along the empty trail crushed her heart. She'd look for him and find Reed. Reed could help. But would he help a woman who had tricked his aunt, taken advantage of her hospitality and fallen in love with his friend only to endanger his life?

Wait. She didn't love Zane. She didn't. He invaded places in her life he had no business being. She told him to stay out of her way and stay out of her life. He hadn't listened to her. And now he paid the price.

"Journey?"

The sound drifted through the thick barn walls. Miss Rose must be awake, and calling her. Would the darkness hide her if she sneaked out the side door? What if Miss Rose tried to find her?

She wiped a tear with the back of her hand and walked outside. She'd stay, just a little longer, until they had word from Zane. It would give her time to think things through, to lay tracks that Hank couldn't follow.

Nothing mattered beyond that. No one would care what happened to her once they knew about her past. A past that Hank knew all about: being raised in a cat-house with no father to speak of. Selling herself into Hank's service at fifteen. Had it really been worth the trade to avoid the life her mother had led up until the week before she died? When she turned seventeen and Hank married her, she thought her chance at a respectable future had finally arrived. But that was all lost now.

"Journey? Are you out there?" Miss Rose called again, her voice wavering in the wind. Her shadowed form stood in the open doorway of the house.

"Yes, Miss Rose. I'm coming."

Journey drew the bills from her pocket and, with a glance back at the house, slid them into the edge of the carrot bin inside the barn door.

She walked across the yard. The wind whispered through the porch eaves as she stamped snow from her boots and shook it from her skirt hem. She hung her coat on a peg, her gaze catching the box on the mantel. The heat of shame burned her face.

Miss Rose sank into her rocker, wiggling closer to the fire. "Whatever were you doing out there, Journey? You'll catch your death of cold out on a night like this."

She swiped a stray curl from her forehead and tucked it behind her ear. "A messenger delivered a telegram for you, Miss Rose." Her voice felt trapped in her throat.

The woman coughed and leaned back in her chair, sending it to motion as she closed her eyes. "Read it to me."

Her voice sounded calm, but the blue-veined fingers tightened over the arms of the chair. Journey's hand trembled as she opened the seal and scanned the brief message.

"Zane delayed STOP Be home early next week STOP Don't worry STOP Delay gold mine STOP Reed," she read. "Oh, Miss Rose!"

"Don't fret now, child."

How could she be so calm? Journey blinked a hot tear away. "But if Zane were truly fine, he'd send his own telegram. What if—"

"The only thing we can do now is to pray. Will you do that with me?" Miss Rose stared at her, no longer rocking.

Journey sank into the closest chair and forced the thin paper into the envelope with shaking hands. "But God won't listen to me. He's never listened to me. He'll answer your prayers. You do it."

"Zane needs us both. Please." Her voice was gentle but raspy, and a soft smile graced her face. "What can it hurt to try? God never stops listening. Never."

She nodded. If it made Miss Rose feel better, she'd try it. She felt her hands engulfed in the too-warm grasp of the other woman and watched as she bowed her head. The smile never broke as Miss Rose talked to the Lord as if He was sitting next to her.

Journey bowed her head and remembered to close her eyes. Her thoughts didn't form a prayer, exactly, but she wished with all her heart that God would listen to Miss Rose's prayers, given on behalf of a man who certainly deserved His mercy.

Chapter Twenty-Eight

Zane held his arm stiffly at his side. He didn't need the doctor from Virginia City to tell him how fortunate he'd been. A broken arm. Ribs bruised, wrapped tight but not busted. His headache had hung on through the better part of Sunday, but he'd been kicked by horses and hurt worse. He smiled, knowing Doc Ferris would not favor his decision to head back to Walten. Or Miss Rose, he supposed. But it felt as if he'd been away for a month, instead of a week.

Had Journey missed him? He thought of the poster and the telegram from Georgia folded carefully in his pocket. Everything came down to questions only she could answer.The modest steeple of the church rose over the final ridge and above the other buildings that made up the little town of Walten. His town, his church. He longed to be there but had other stops to make first.

Pulling up to the post in front of Sam and Abby's store, he slid from the horse and dusted snow from his coat with one hand.

"Zane!" Abby flew from the porch, grabbing his

good arm in both hands. "Are you just getting back? We've been wondering about you. When Reed sent the telegram, we thought… Well, he didn't tell much. What happened to your arm? To your face?"

He lifted a hand to the bruise at his eye. He thought it looked remarkably better when he'd shaved the morning before leaving Virginia City. "Never mind that now. You'd better get in from the cold. Is Sam around?"

"Around back. Go on, and I'll make coffee."

Moving around to the storage shed, he found Sam stacking crates of supplies. "Hello!" he said, not wanting to startle his friend.

Sam didn't turn. "Grab a crate and join the party."

"Not today, I'm afraid." He smiled and lifted his broken arm a little when Sam faced him.

"What happened?"

"Have you heard anything about investing in a gold claim in Walten? From that Baines fellow Journey knows?"

Sam sat on a crate, pushing his hat back and slipping his gloves off. He kicked another crate over and motioned for Zane to sit.

"Some. Most folks around here don't have the money for that kind of thing, though. There's talk Mr. Baines will take land as collateral if people are willing to sign over, but I haven't heard of anyone who's taken him up on that offer. I'd imagine some will."

Sam sighed and scratched his jaw. "He seems awful sure there's enough gold to make us all rich as trolls. Some folks are worried about what could happen to the town if word gets out before we have a plan in place. Baines has everyone shook up with tales of 'crime and avarice' to follow."

"A lot of these people lived through those early days in Virginia City. They know he's right on that count." Zane passed on the seat, not willing to subject his stiff side to getting up from it later.

"How busted up are you?" Sam asked.

"Bruised ribs, broken arm. Had a little run-in with a wall or two one night. Baines wanted my stamp of approval on this deal. I told him I'd want to check things out for myself first." He leaned against the doorway of the shanty. "I'm thinking he took exception to my doubts. And he wants me to stay away from Journey."

"He's been out of town himself."

"How long?"

Sam rubbed his neck. "He left same day as you, maybe the day before. I guess he was back in town sometime Saturday. He ended up delivering Reed's telegram. I heard he headed back to Virginia City, though. I'm surprised you didn't see him on the trail."

"He and I wouldn't ride the same path."

"What do you mean?"

"I mean, if he left right away, he'd have made it back in time to—"

"You think he's the one who beat you?"

"I found out enough to know that if we were sitting on a gold mine, Hank wouldn't be looking to cut the town in for the profits."

"So how can I help?" Sam asked.

"Right now I have pieces, but nothing fits together yet. Keep your ears open, see what folks are saying and tell them to hold off until we can get a town meeting together. I'll let you know when I find out anything for certain."

Zane cocked his head toward the main building. "Abby promised coffee, and I could sure use some."

"Right. But the minute you need me, I'm there."

"Thanks, Sam." He shifted, then winced as the pain grabbed his side. "Could have used your help in that alleyway," he said with a grin.

An hour later, warmed inside out by the coffee, Zane rode out to Miss Rose's. Abby's fresh bread with preserves hadn't hurt his outlook, either.

He slowed his pace as he drew near the ranch. As much as he wanted Journey to answer his questions, he didn't relish the confrontation.

"Dear Lord, show me how to talk to her. She's scared, and I reckon she has every reason to be. Show her, Jesus, that she has no reason to fear me. She hasn't exactly been happy with my help to this point. But, Father, I have the town to think of, too. I think— God, I'm asking you to work this out because I know You can and I know I can't. You've said that when we seek Your will, we'll find it. Help us all. In Jesus' name I ask. Amen."

He scanned the rolling mounds of snow, knowing the whiff of smoke rising from over the next hill belonged to Miss Rose's chimney. He nudged his horse onward.

It's good she has Journey this winter, especially since she's been down with that cold, he thought. How would she feel when she discovered her boarder was mixed up with Baines?

Zane made his way into the frozen yard. The wind had swept a path between the house and the barn. The sky, wide and gray, promised another dose of snow. Maybe they'd have a fresh coat for Christmas, if this weather held. He went into the barn and tied Malachi to a post.

"Here, boy," he said, reaching into the carrot bin. His fingers swept over soft paper, and he pulled it out. Instead of the knobby carrot, he held a stack of bills.

Hundreds of possibilities swarmed, but only one lodged in his mind. He tucked the bills into his sling and stroked the horse's face. "We could get kicked out mighty quick, if Journey has anything to say about it. But she has a lot of explaining to do herself."

The door slid open, and he turned to see her slip through it. "Journey," he said, hoping not to startle her.

"Zane." He couldn't decipher the tone in her voice. She sounded almost relieved, but maybe the surprise of finding him in the barn brought the lilt to her voice.

She stood still for a moment. Then, drawing a deep breath, she said, "Oh, Zane, I'm so glad you're here."

He stepped forward, grasping her arm with his good hand. "What is it?"

"Miss Rose—she's sick, been sick, but today, I have to get Doc Ferris." She pulled herself away, stumbling toward the stalls.

The importance of any questions he had paled. "I'll go. You go back to Miss Rose, make her comfortable. I'll fetch him."

She sagged with relief and drew closer as he slid his hand up to caress her cheek. It felt damp and soft.

He almost lost his balance as she leaned toward him, resting her cheek against his chest. He brought his free arm around her and patted her shoulder, almost out of instinct. He soaked in her warmth, rubbing his fingers in small circles at her shoulder. A dam inside him cracked, and a wave of protectiveness surged through.

She shuddered in his arms, as if trying to compose herself. "I'm sorry. I didn't know what to do. I've made such a mess of things. I never meant to—"

"We'll talk about that later. I'll go for Doc." He felt her draw away. He pulled himself into the saddle with one arm.

She opened the door for him to ride out. Light filtered down, casting a glow over her face. She looked younger with her freckles more pronounced against her pale skin. Her brown eyes were wide, frightened.

"It's only to town and back. I'll be here with Doc before you know it. Then we can talk, all right?"

She nodded, looking up at him with wet trails marring her cheeks. "She's so hot. I'm afraid for her."

"It'll be all right." He hoped his words assured her. With a squeeze of his legs and a duck of his head, the horse took off across the cold terrain.

Zane prayed.

Chapter Twenty-Nine

Miss Rose rested under a mound of quilts, her breath so shallow they didn't stir. Journey threw another log onto the fire, where it crackled and popped. The sound of a fast-moving buggy drew her to the sitting room. How long had Zane been gone?

The men brushed snow from their pant legs and dusted it from their hats as they stepped through the door.

"Where is she?" Doc Ferris asked.

She led him to Miss Rose's room, off the sitting room in the front part of the house. "I'm sorry to call you out so late, Doc. I didn't know what else to do."

"You did right, sending for me. I'll take a check on her. Wait here with Zane."

"Can't I help?"

He patted her arm and smiled. "Could I bother you for some coffee? I surely could use a cup."

She nodded but didn't move until he went in to Miss Rose's room and slid the door partially closed. She put the kettle of coffee on in the kitchen and then returned to pace the floor in front of the couch. Zane sat, almost swallowed in the cushions, eyes partially closed.

"Sit down, Journey," he said. "You must be exhausted. I had no idea she was so ill."

"What took you so long?" She stopped in the middle of the braided rug, hugging her waist.

"Doc was out at the Andersons'. I told him about Miss Rose and he came right away. Said it sounds like the same thing Mr. Anderson has, and Mrs. Hamler, and the Wilsons' son, Jimmy. Influenza."

She sank to the end of the couch, opposite Zane, and rocked forward, unable to hold back any more tears. She was too tired to try.

He shifted and she heard his muffled gasp. "Zane?"

She wiped her face, noticing his. "What happened to you?" she asked, thumbing the bruise near his eye. How had she missed it when she'd first seen him standing in the barn?

"We have to talk."

She drew her hand back. His gray eyes held her focus. He knew. She slid from the cushion and backed away. "Please, don't—"

"I have to, Journey. I have questions and there's too much at stake. It's not just about you or me." Slowly he stood, his bound arm pressed tightly against his side. He drew a page from his coat pocket with his free hand, unfolded it and held it out to her. Waiting.

She peered at the wrinkled paper, afraid to touch it. Hank's sketchy face stared back. The likeness was rather good, though he wore his hair much longer now. She choked. "The law did know about him in Savannah. If I had only realized."

Doc Ferris stepped out from the bedroom, cutting off

all but thoughts of Miss Rose. Journey pulled the poster from Zane's fingers and slid it behind her. "How is she?"

Doc shrugged into his coat before answering. "It looks like influenza. Tricky thing. I'm thinking of pulling everyone who's come down with it into one place, so I can treat them all at the same time. It's too hard to keep up with everyone spread out as they are."

"How many are there?" she asked, her voice shaky.

"Maybe ten. Mostly children and older folks, but it'll spread. We'll need someone to take word out to some of the outlying farms, tell them what to look for, and what to do if they come down with it. We'll need blankets and buckets, food and water, cots and mats." He adjusted his glasses.

"I'll talk to Abby. Where should we tell folks to go?" she asked.

"How about the church?" Zane offered.

The doctor gripped his chin in his hand and nodded. "It *is* the largest place. We'll need wood for a fire out back and someone to tend it. We'll need hot water."

"I'll ride out and check on the families farther out, then Sam and I can get a fire going," Zane said. "I don't know medicine, Doc, but I'll help any way I can."

"I'd be obliged," Doc Ferris said. "I'll go back to town, start getting supplies together. Let Miss Rose rest a few hours, then bundle her up and bring her to town at dawn. Rest as much as you can until then, and I'll send some telegrams, see where we can find more quinine should we need it. It's going to be a long few weeks before this runs its course, I'm afraid. We'll need all the help the Almighty can give us."

He clamped his hat tighter and tapped the brim toward her. "It was good you sent for me, miss. You both take care, now. And, Zane, take it easy on those ribs. Once people start coming into town, we'll need all the able hands we can find."

Journey closed the door behind him. Thick flakes of snow fell, the lazy kind of shower that signaled a break in the storm.

Zane grabbed her shoulder as she passed him, moving toward Miss Rose's room. She ducked with a gasp, her heart pounding.

He released her as if she'd burned him. She focused on the fire glowing in the hearth, embarrassed by her snap reaction.

"I'd never hurt you. Never." He stepped back. "But we need to sort this all out before we get to town. How do you know Baines? And why is he here?"

She whipped her coat from the peg, punching her arms through the sleeves and tugging her hair out from the collar. She grabbed her saddle pack, which was leaning against the wall near the door.

"Where are you going?"

"I'm leaving before I cause more trouble. I should've gone a long time ago," she said, clamping her hat down on her head.

He stepped in front of her before she could reach the door latch. "Don't you think you owe us an explanation?" A handful of bills waved before her eyes, swirling in time with her thoughts. "You're going to leave now, like this, after all Miss Rose has done for you?"

She looked away and swiped back her tears. "I would have paid it back. I swear it. I've brought nothing but problems for this town, and I need to get away before things get worse. Look at you. You never answered my question. What happened to you in Virginia City? How do you explain that welt by your eye? The sore ribs?"

Zane stood back, his lips drawn into a tight line.

"Never mind. I already know. Hank came by. You're lucky you got off so easily. He could have killed you. I thought…"

"Thought what?"

"I thought he had." She palmed the rough warmth of the fireplace stones behind her. "I thought he killed you and left you lying out on the trail." Each word squeezed from her throat. "But you're safe. We prayed—that is, Miss Rose prayed—and here you are. I can't take a chance of you getting hurt again."

"How will your leaving make everything right?" He made no move toward her, but she moved another pace away from him.

"Hank won't have any hold over me if he doesn't know where I am."

"What hold does he have on you, Journey?" His voice softened and he stepped toward her. She felt his hand on her shoulder, drawing her to him. She felt safe in his arms, holding her strong and warm.

"Tell me about that poster." His jaw rubbed her head as he spoke.

She looked up at him. This would be easier if he were angry. Hank had trained her to face that. Instead, his gaze held, firm but compassionate. His eyes crinkled at the edges, eyebrows furrowed.

She looked away and pulled from his hold. "I can't."

He moved away a moment, and she fumbled with the lashings on her pack. She looked at him again when he blocked the light from the lantern in the window.

"Then maybe you can explain this one."

Her own likeness greeted her. Not a very flattering one, but hers nonetheless, staring from the wrinkled parchment.

She closed her eyes and fought to draw a breath. "It's not how it looks. Please, let me leave."

"So it is you," he said. "I figured, but I've been wrong before. Hoped this was one of those times."

She opened her eyes to see his outstretched arm. Glancing toward the door, she allowed him to guide her to a chair by the fireplace. She knew she owed him an explanation.

He wasn't demanding that she leave. He hadn't hauled the law in to come and take her away. Was he really giving her the benefit of the doubt?

She sat down, picking at the brim of her hat. "How much do you want to know?"

"Everything."

Tell him, a silent voice pleaded. *Tell him why you have to run.*

"Hank's my husband."

Zane would think everything had been arranged from the start, that she had tricked them all, but it was better that way. It would be easier to go if he hated her.

Zane sat in the chair beside her and smoothed out another paper. He stared at it a moment. "If Hank Baines is your husband, that makes you a widow according to this."

He laid the page on her lap as he stood. She read without touching it. "You don't know how I wish that were true."

"So tell me what is true. Let me help you sort this out."

"Does Reed know?"

"Where do you think I got the posters?"

"Are you taking me to the sheriff?" Her breath came fast and short. A year of looking over her shoulder—ended. The thought almost brought relief.

"Not unless I have to." She cried in earnest when he fingered the curls draped down her back. "I convinced Reed you deserved a chance to explain your side of things. Won't you tell me, Journey? If you leave now, there's no way I can keep you safe."

She folded over in the seat, burying her face in her skirt. "I can't be safe. Not here. Not anywhere Hank is."

"What are you saying?"

She lifted her head enough so her words weren't muffled. "I'm saying that you should call Reed and have him lock me up. Maybe jail is the only place where Hank won't be able to hurt me anymore."

"I don't think it's that simple. Is it true, what the poster says? Did you kill a man by burning down a hotel? Are you Maura Baines?"

"I am Maura Baines, but I never burned a building. And I never killed a man, but it doesn't mean I never tried. That's enough for God to punish me, I suppose."

"Tell me how you got here, Journey—Maura—whoever you are." He sounded as confused as she felt. "At least let me try to help." Zane's tone didn't plead. It sounded firm and comforting, like his arms had been moments before.

"My mother's maiden name was Sojourner. I borrowed from that when I needed to get away. And Smith could be anyone. Miss Smith would never attract attention. Being away from Hank was all that mattered."

"You didn't know they declared him dead?"

She stood and walked away, arms crossed. "I knew

because I was the one who'd killed him, or at least tried to kill him."

She whirled on Zane, trying to judge his thoughts. What did it matter now? He'd have to notify the law. Bars that kept Hank away would be better than living like this, always waiting for the day he'd find her. It was too hard, and she was too tired to fight anymore.

"You must've had a reason. The judge could take that into account. Besides, if he's not really dead—"

"He's not, but apparently someone died that night. Do you think a judge will care what happened? 'Certainly, Your Honor, I'm innocent. I never intended to kill the man who died. I believed I had killed someone else.' Not only thought it, was glad of it."

She moved to the window, staring out into the blackness. Miss Rose hadn't stirred. Thank goodness she wasn't awake enough to hear this.

Zane stood beside her, looking straight ahead through the window and she tensed. "How'd it happen?"

He didn't deny her involvement, she noted. But he still tried to wrap his mind around it, still tried to understand. She touched his shoulder, ashamed that he should care.

"It's not your fault," she said. "I made bad choices after my mama died. She was a…a saloon girl. I was fifteen when she died." It seemed so long ago.

"Fifteen?"

"I was scared and Hank offered me more than the life my mother had. At least it was only him." She didn't go into details.

She remembered her mama's smile. "She seemed different, those last days. She made me promise not to go the way she did. I don't think I could've anyway, but then, look at where I am now." Her laugh sounded hollow, even to her.

She turned to Zane, sensing his gaze. The compassion she saw was more than she could bear. Her resolve faded.

"I met Hank when I was so young," she continued with a heavy breath. "But he wasn't always mean like he is now. He always had that drive for more, the fierceness to make things happen. He treated me as well as Hank knows how. I don't expect he grew up much better than me, but he never spoke of it. Then plan after plan to make things good fell through, and he started drinking more. He grew angrier at life. I was in the way, I suppose. The fierceness I thought would protect me turned against me."

"He hit you." Zane didn't ask, he knew.

She nodded. "Quite often. I stood it for three years, waiting for him to turn into the man I wanted him to be. But it only got worse. I thought he was going to kill me many times those last few months. Maybe it would've been better that way. Easier for him."

"No."

She pulled back at the anger in his voice. His hand fisted against the windowpane.

"No one deserves that."

"Most women live with being hit. My mama lived through worse and for longer than me. She was stronger."

"You're strong, too. No one deserves a life like that."

She dismissed him, moving back to the seat by the fire. "I started saving what money I could, so I could buy a ticket to someplace far away. I figured Hank would be happy to see me walk out. But he came home one night, full of plans and hope and liquor. He found my satchel with the money I'd hidden. He was furious. He would've killed me that night, but he was drunk and he tripped. When he did, I grabbed the flatiron and I—I hit him." Over and over.

She pictured the dingy room above the saloon even now, wrinkled her nose at the coppery scent of blood that flooded her memory. She would've sworn Hank was dead when she left. He certainly wasn't moving. But then, her only thought at the time had been to get away. She shivered against the chill of the memory.

She forced her mind back to the present, to the warmth that surrounded her in this room. She cleared her throat and twisted her head to look at Zane, surprised to find him sitting close.

"I've made so many mistakes in my life, never a good or right decision. But my biggest regret is that I didn't make sure Hank was dead before I left. It's haunted me ever since. I didn't want him to die, not really. But I wasn't sorry, either."

Her breath shook. How could she explain? "Things would be so much easier now if he had."

"We'll work this out, you'll see," Zane said. "But I can't help if you leave. I can't protect you out there."

"You can't protect me anywhere, Zane. That's the whole point."

"Let me try. Don't give up now."

She sank into the cushions and shook her head. Didn't he realize it was pointless? "They'd lock you in the cell beside me."

"It'd be worth it if it helped you."

A tear dripped on her hand. "I'm not worth it. And Miss Rose needs you. Just let me leave."

Zane slid to the floor before her. "You know I can't do that. Reed already knows about the posters. Do you really want to live like this, always running, always waiting to be found out?"

Wasn't he listening? Of course, she didn't want to live that way. But what else could she do? If she could just get away and rest....

"I'm tired, Zane."

"I know you are. All the more reason to stay." His gray eyes caught her attention.

"Will you give me a few days? I can help the doctor. I need to be sure Miss Rose is well." She looked at the dying fire. "Then you can wire Reed."

She strained for any sounds of discomfort coming from Miss Rose's room. But it was silent except for the whispers of wheezy breathing, the ticking clock above the mantel and the fire as it crackled.

He weighed the decision in his mind, she could sense.

"All right. Miss Rose will need you. The whole town will." His voice was low but determined. "Then we'll contact Reed. He can help us sort this out. He could talk to Hank. Maybe he'd help to clear you—"

"No." She shook. "Hank won't help me. Not without a higher price than prison. Jail would be better."

Zane opened his eyes, as if he had been praying. Then he pushed her hair back, searching her face. What did he expect to see? She relaxed into the warmth of his touch in spite of herself.

"We'll do it your way." He took the satchel from her grasp. She had forgotten she still held it. "We'll pray. God can work this out in ways we can't even imagine.

You have to believe that. I'm praying that you will. In the meantime, you'll promise you'll not run?"

She nodded her head in agreement. What was one more broken promise?

Chapter Thirty

Journey leaned back on her knees and swiped a hand across her forehead. She hardly recognized the church sanctuary. Instead of pews facing the pulpit in neat rows, they lined the edges of the room, some with patients resting precariously on them, a few holding tired caregivers. Other patients slept or tossed on cots and piles of blankets scattered about the room.

The heat Doc Ferris ordered to keep the sick comfortable made the room oppressive for those trying to keep up with the continual washing, cooking and treating of those in need. The odors of sickness and the smell of turpentine the doctor had used as an antiseptic mingled in the air.

She heard the outer door open and turned toward the entryway. Where could they fit another person or find the energy to care for another patient?

Zane tapped snow from his hat with his free hand as he entered. She stretched to her feet, grateful to see he came alone. A three-day growth of beard darkened his face, and she could see the sag of his eyes from across the room. With a weary smile, he wound his way through those lying on the floor.

"How are you holding up?" he asked. He clasped her warm hand in his cool one.

"I could ask you the same. Have you rested at all?"

He grinned. "Guess that's a 'no' for us both."

"I slept after you left this morning. We've been taking turns between us."

"But there're fewer workers than we started with." He glanced around the room. "You have to take care of yourself, too." He squeezed her arm lightly and heaved a deep sigh. "How's Miss Rose?"

She looked over to the cot in front of the pulpit. Under the high pile of covers, Miss Rose's pale form lay. "She's been awful quiet. Too quiet, but Doc says she's no worse."

"Let's go outside and see how Sam's coming with the bonfire. You could use the fresh air," Zane said.

She hesitated. The patients seemed to be settled for a moment, or at the very least were being cared for by another attendant. But Miss Rose, what if...?

"C'mon." He squeezed her arm. "We'll be right outside. Doc will call us if there's any change." His voice grew louder as he looked toward the doctor, stooped over a patient in the back corner.

"Sue Anderson isn't doing well," she whispered.

Journey thought of the day they'd quilted together. She couldn't help but think that Sue's notions of romance might thrill at the idea of having her fevered brow mopped by some handsome benefactor. Instead, she had a kindly old doctor who likely was as poor as a church mouse for her attendant. The influenza hadn't taken note of her privileged status nor held any illusions of romance.

"Go on," Doc Ferris said. "Rose'll rest easy for a while. Bring in more hot water when you return." He nodded them out the back door.

The cold air felt clean and fresh after the heat of the church. She slipped into the coat Zane handed her. Sam poked at the fire blazing under a large kettle, boiling bed linens and cleaning cloths. Both the chill of the air and the warmth of the fire reddened his face.

"How you holding up?" Zane asked him.

Sam greeted them with a nod. "Tending fire's the easy part. Journey's the one that's got to tend the folks inside."

"How's Abby? I haven't seen her lately," she asked.

He wiped the sweat from his brow and replaced his hat. "She's tired this morning—been busy keeping the store open, making sure folks can get what they need. And she's been cooking and baking up a storm in that kitchen. But she misses you and wishes she could help here. I let her sleep this morning."

"She deserves it," Journey said.

"We're all in this together." Sam rubbed his hand over his face. "If you can take over the fire, Zane, I'm heading out for Virginia City. Doc needs more quinine."

"You want some company? That's a lot of snow to get through on your own."

"It'll be faster sending one man, I think. Besides, you shouldn't be out gallivanting around the country with that arm busted and all. I'm packed for the trail already. Just wanted to give Doc a hand before I left."

Zane took his fire prod and nudged his friend's shoulder with his own. "Then by all means, get going. We'll take it from here. You take it easy out on that trail."

"Will do," Sam said, clamping his hat down. He walked to the tree where he'd tied his horse and mounted. "I'm riding straight through, so I aim to be back late Thursday night, no later than Friday morning."

"We'll be expecting you." The men shook hands and Sam headed out.

Journey watched him nudge his horse into a trot back through town and off to the north and west. "How long have you known him?"

"Sam?" Zane stopped poking logs to toss another one onto the fire. He took his time brushing his glove off on his denim pants, as if his mind couldn't remember that far back. "We've been friends a long time. Our families came west together during the gold rush in California and then moved to Montana when that played out and things got crowded. He's like my own family. He even introduced me to Sarah. She and Abby were best friends."

For a moment, all was silent save the water bubbling in the large basin perched over the fire. His eyes took on a faraway look, and a smile appeared on his face—Journey found herself wondering about his wife.

Everyone had loved her. Just hearing them say her name made that plain. She imagined what Sarah must have looked like, pretty and tall, with sleek brown waves falling around a porcelain face. Miss Rose and Abby had mentioned Sarah's beauty both of face and spirit many times.

Journey poked a loose hairpin into place. When had she brushed her hair last? She must look a sight. And likely smelled worse. She wiped the smoke and grime from her face.

"You have a smudge," he said, pulling her from her reverie. The pad of his thumb brushed against her cheek, and something in his gaze changed. He leaned forward, his hand cupping her cheek.

Then he blinked and his lips parted in a gasp. He turned back to the fire, clearing his throat.

"What about you?"

Her heart jumped. "What about me?"

"Do you have any family?" He concentrated on the glowing blaze, but she sensed her answer mattered.

"No, not really. There was a woman who…worked with my mother. She helped me to leave that place. I always thought she must be what an aunt was like. I don't know much about Mama's family." She hugged her arms around herself. "After she died, Hank became the closest I had, until—"

Until Walten? When had she started thinking of them all as family?

She turned back to the church. "I need to tend Miss Rose, make sure she's warm enough."

Zane turned also. "Didn't we just come out to cool off from that heat?"

"To see that she's not too heated, then—"

"Why not stop over and see if Abby can use a hand? Let her know how Miss Rose is doing?" Zane tipped his head to look under the brim of her hat, with a hand on her shoulder to still her. He leaned the tree limb he used to stir the fire against his bound arm. "I'm sure she'd like the company."

She glanced across the snow to the mercantile, squinting against the sun's reflection. Abby had done so much over the past few days to make sure food and supplies were on hand. "I could run over for just a few minutes."

She headed off without a backward glance. The packed snow under her feet marked the path worn by many trips between the two buildings. Her feet felt like lead as she pulled herself up the few back steps to the mercantile.

"Abby?" she called out, easing her way through the door. Hearing no response, she moved into the tiny kitchen in back of the store, which connected the business to Sam and Abby's home. A small pile of wood lay scattered near the low flames. Rags littered every flat surface. Abby certainly had been busy to let this mess happen. She couldn't remember a time when Abby's home wasn't meticulously clean. She walked into the shop, coming in behind the counter.

"Abby!"

Her long form lay on the floor, stretched on her side in an odd slump. Journey knelt down and shook her shoulder.

"Abby, can you hear me?" Her skin felt hot, even through her woolen dress.

She grabbed a heavy blanket from the shelf and spread it over her. "I'll be right back." She ran her hand over Abby's clammy face. "I'm going for help." Abby sighed but Journey sensed she didn't realize anyone was there.

"Zane! Zane, where's Doc?" Journey called, running from the store to the church.

She found him pushing a wad of sheets into a steaming pot.

"Zane, it's Abby! She's sick."

He abandoned the boiling pot and met her halfway up the path.

Together they moved back to the shop. Abby hadn't shifted. Zane bent down on one knee, grasping the blanket to pull under her as he scooped Abby up from the floor.

"Get another blanket to throw over her, Journey. We'll get her to the church."

"You can't, Zane. You're hurt."

His head snapped back. "I can if you help me. Lean her up."

Journey pulled Abby's arms carefully, holding her head as it lolled to the right. Zane braced in behind her and clutched Abby around the waist with one arm so that her upper body balanced against his broad chest.

"Grab her legs."

She obeyed, biting the inside of her cheek as she struggled to balance under Abby's long form.

Lurching and stumbling, they made their way down the steps and across the yard to the church's back door. She heaved a sigh of relief when Doc Ferris appeared at the corner and took a firmer grip on Abby.

She raced ahead of them into the church, tripping up the steps into the sanctuary that seemed to shrink with every new patient.

Doc and Zane followed close behind. Zane's labored breathing echoed above the pounding in her ears.

The doctor's chin jutted toward the pulpit. "Set up a cot over near Miss Rose. It'll save you from running between them."

She swallowed over the tight knot in her throat. Her eyes washed with tears, and she couldn't tear her attention away from Miss Rose's tiny, hidden form. The doctor's hand grasped her shoulder.

"Come on, now," he said gently. "We need to stay focused. They need us."

She nodded yet couldn't seem to make her feet move, until Zane sank onto the floor by the door, Abby limp in his arm. She scrambled to the pile of blankets the women of the community had brought in and traipsed back through the patients to set up the last available bed. Unfolding one blanket only partially made for a thick pad to soften the rough fabric of the cot. She helped Zane and Doc slide Abby onto it.

"I found her lying on the floor," Journey said, her voice low. "She's so hot, Doc. Burning up."

She nudged Zane aside to lay a heavy quilt over Abby, then stood back, wiping sweat from her forehead.

Restless movements from around the corner of the pulpit drew her to Miss Rose's side. The woman shivered; her eyes opened a slit but remained unfocused. Journey grabbed a cup half full of tepid water and held it to her lips, supporting her head with her other hand. Only a few dribbles made their way down Miss Rose's throat before leaking from her lips over her cheeks.

Tucking the blanket closer to Miss Rose's chin, she moved back to help with Abby. She seemed paler, if that were possible, except for bright spots of color on each cheek.

Doc Ferris handed her a bottle of white powder. "Mix one spoonful of this into a tin of water for her."

"I'll do it, Doc," Zane said, pushing up from Abby's side with one arm.

Doc looked at her, then back to Zane. "No, right now

I need you to rest a minute so you can go for Sam. He can't have gotten far."

Zane moved to get his coat, before realizing he still had it on. "I'll be back quick as I can," he said, pausing at the door.

Journey stepped over to him. She sensed his urgency. The thought that his best friend could lose his wife, as he had, brought a flicker of something to his soft gray eyes. Was it fear? She put her hand on the arm of his coat to stall him.

"You'll pray, won't you?" She pulled back and wrapped her arms around herself. Why did he look at her like that? Like she'd lost her mind? He prayed all the time, didn't he?

"I mean," she stammered, "when you were gone and then Hank said... Well, Miss Rose prayed for you and you came back. A little worse for wear, maybe, but all right." Still, he stared. "Zane?"

"Right," he said. His voice sounded dry, far away. "You're right. I will be praying. I have been. And when I get back, maybe we can pray together."

She looked around the shadowed room filled with fevered bodies and weary workers. Could her prayers help at all? God never stops listening, Miss Rose had said. "Go on," she said, turning him around and all but shoving him from the room. "Catch Sam. Abby needs to know he's here. Besides, we need you here. Go on, now. Hurry."

She shut the door behind him. If her prayers worked, he'd find Sam before he got out of town.

Chapter Thirty-One

Zane picked his way along the path, surrounded by ghostly figures of snow-covered rock as he moved into the mountains. When Sam said he'd be moving quickly, he wasn't kidding. He'd covered a lot of ground in an hour, but Zane expected to reach him soon, if the tracks gave any indication. Though he'd only been a fair tracker, his friend had left an easy trail to follow.

Despite the drive to push on and get back, the beauty of the land never failed to calm him. The land rose up to the west, the valley rolled out toward the east. The skies, clearing from the heavy snow clouds of the past few days, were brushed blue and white, sweeping along with the wind that blew, a little warmer than it had been. But the snow would keep the ground white for months to come. It promised to be a beautiful Christmas, though little thought had been given to it over the past few days.

C'mon, Sam. Where are you?

A thud and a groan answered him from ahead. Sliding from his horse with one hand, he headed into the scrub pines up the knoll on foot.

One shot rang out. Zane ducked and heard the bullet whistle through the tree behind him.

"I believe you've come far enough, sir." Hank's voice wheezed from behind snow-covered shrubs.

He slipped back and raised his arm slowly.

"I'm not carrying a gun, Baines, and I have no intent to hurt you. I'm looking for Sam. He's on his way to Virginia City, but his wife took sick and needs him. Has he passed through?"

Hank shook his head, his face glistening in the streams of light. "I haven't seen him. An' I'm tired of seeing you, Preacher. I should have finished you off when I had the chance."

Zane watched Hank stumble into the shrubs, gasping for air, and moved forward to catch him.

"Don't you come any closer, I say." Hank's revolver bobbed a little before his grip steadied. "I got plans for you, Preacher. Plans for you, for Maura, for this whole little town of yours. As soon as Roy gets here, you'll see."

He forced his muscles to relax, easing away. Hank didn't appear too focused, yet he held the gun.

"Let me help you, Hank. You're sick."

"Ah, you'd like that, wouldn't you?" He laughed. "I wouldn't imagine that act of kindness would endear you to our darlin' Journey, now, would it?"

A glimpse of deep blue fabric caught Zane's attention. Sam was out there. Baines made no sign that he'd noticed. *Keep him talking.*

"You know it was Roy that found her in the first place? He tried taking up honest work, riding herd up here when he spied her. I understand there was a little trouble that night. Roy didn't take so kindly to the good parson cozying up to his buddy's wife."

Hank's mustache drooped and his eyes glazed over. He slumped toward a tree to support himself, but the revolver barrel seemed plenty steady.

Zane caught Sam's attention as he appeared through the trees. He lifted his chin a little, signaling Sam to move in.

"You know that's not how it is, Hank. Besides, it seems to me she wants to be left alone—"

Hank's head snapped up. "She told you that?" He took several slow steps forward.

Zane held his ground. "I can see for myself she's afraid of you."

"That was before. We were in a bind—things were tight. It'll all be different this time." Hank's voice grew louder, more insistent.

He ducked his head and shuffled his feet, hoping to distract Hank as Sam edged closer. "I don't reckon she'll be going anywhere with you."

The storm that smoldered in Hank's eyes washed over his pale face. "I daresay she will. She'll recall how good things were, soon as we are away from here. Away from you!"

Hank lunged forward on unsteady feet, finger tightening on the trigger. From the corner of his eye, Zane watched Sam's dash, and he tucked his arm in close to dive at Hank's feet.

Strange how the quietness of the snow magnified the echo of the gunshot. It was Zane's last thought as he fell into the unmarked snow.

Chapter Thirty-Two

Journey jolted, startled from her sleep by unfocused dreams. She glanced around, finding herself at the church, and eased back against the pew.

So many were sick. Evie Wilson, looking pale, spooned water into her son, Jimmy. The first day they brought people into the church to set up the makeshift hospital, the boy had thrown up until she wondered what could be left. Now she found his stillness unsettling. She would try to get Evie to rest a little—as soon as she could force her own limbs to move.

Abby's quivering form caused Journey to cast aside all weariness. She got up and brushed her palm against her friend's face and found it scorching. Grabbing the cloth from a fresh bucket of snow, she laid it over Abby's forehead. Pale green eyes, fever-bright, blinked open.

"Sam?" Her voice cracked and she struggled to sit up. "Sam!"

Journey pulled the covers higher and tried to settle her. "It's me, Journey. Sam's on his way, Abby. Zane went after him, and they'll be back soon. You need to rest."

Abby didn't seem to hear but fell back with a sigh. Journey hadn't thought to get her to drink some water. Doc Ferris said that was important.

"Journey? Journey, are you there, dear?"

She grabbed the corner of the heavy wooden pulpit to drag herself around to Miss Rose's side. The woman's blue eyes opened only a slit but appeared clear. "Let me get Doc," she said.

Miss Rose grasped her arm with bony fingers. "In a minute. Where's Zane?"

"Sam went for more quinine, but when we found Abby collapsed in the store, Zane set out to fetch him. They should be back any time."

She could almost feel Miss Rose's exhaustion as she rubbed the woman's head. *Any time now, Zane. Please, please get back here. Miss Rose needs you.*

She almost missed the weak voice. "Miss Rose?"

A cough with a tight, dry rattle answered. "Tell Zane I said to take care of you."

Journey shook her head. "You concentrate on getting yourself well. I'm not telling him anything."

The warm hand stroked her sleeve. "Don't be stubborn. He'll be stubborn enough for both of you. He cares for you, Journey. Let him."

Forcing a smile on her face, she rose with a squeeze on her arm. Miss Rose couldn't know all that had happened since Zane's trip to Virginia City. "I'll get some tea for you. We'll see how it sits."

"Fine, dear. I'll be here a while yet." Her eyes closed and a smile eased the lines on her face. At least she seemed peaceful.

Lengthening rays from a cold disk of sun cast an eerie light through the window. She went for her coat and headed outside for some hot water to make the tea. The weight in her pocket reminded her of the pistol she'd started keeping there since Hank's last visit.

She searched the path Zane would have taken and then looked toward town. The whole community seemed to hold its breath, waiting in the quiet to see how the epidemic played out. Looking west, the jagged spines of the hills lay under a blanket of white, rising to blue-toned mountains farther back. It struck her as odd that she hadn't thought of the land that lay beyond them in quite some time. The urgent plan to get as far west as solid land allowed no longer drove her.

The calmness of Walten had crept in on her, and she found herself wishing that she could belong there.

She shook her head. Where were Zane and Sam? Shouldn't they have returned by now?

God... she began. She concentrated on the fire. What could she say? That she wanted to stay? It seemed too big a miracle to ask. For Hank to leave her alone? That was more than she deserved. She had brought this mess on herself, after all.

God, please be with Zane and get him back here soon. I wouldn't ask it for myself. But Miss Rose needs him around, and Abby needs Sam. She paused, wondering how to end her prayer. *And if I could stay until I know they'll be all right, I'd consider it a real gift. I appreciate it, God.* The name sounded strange coming from her lips. Who was she to call on God?

Journey threw another log onto the bonfire. The need for hot water for cleaning the sick, boiling cloths and making tea never ended.

Dipping into the kettle of water warming over the fire, she poured it over the willow bark powder at the bottom of the mug and set it on the pile of wood to steep. She leaned back and rubbed the tired muscles in her lower back. She'd gotten more sleep those cold nights on the ground coming west than she did on the hard pews these past few nights.

Motion caught her eye, and she turned to find three riders trotting into the far end of town. She ran around to the front of the church for a better view. The figures looked tiny, framed by the buildings on either side of the street, the sky wide and blue-gray overhead. Two men rode upright, the third lay over the back of his horse. Her throat tightened. Then her feet pounded forward, until she met the riders in the middle of the road.

She looked up at Sam, who didn't seem to notice her as he traveled on to the church. His mustache twitched, and his eyes blinked in rapid succession.

Zane, on the other hand, stared down at her, looking like he had in his cabin the night Gypsy had gone wild, crashing through the trees, leaving both her and the horse with broken legs. The night he'd had to shoot Gypsy. His jaw worked in and out with tension under the shadows of his hat brim.

"What's happened?" She craned her head, trying to see around him and his horse. Who else had fallen sick?

Zane slid from the saddle and stood in front of her. Only then did she see the fresh bruise forming over his eye. She reached up to brush his thick brown hair away. "Zane?"

"It's nothing. I fell, is all." He cocked his head in the direction of the other horse that trailed beside and slightly behind, out of her view. "Journey, it's Hank."

She narrowed her eyes and stepped away, arms stiff at her sides. He reached out to grasp her, but she jerked back, freeing herself. Could he hear her heart pounding?

"How could you? How could you bring him here, Zane? After I told you—"

"Listen to me. He's sick. I couldn't leave him out there in the hills to die."

"I trusted you. And now you've brought the fox to the henhouse!"

"We'll keep a close watch on him. He won't be able to hurt you or anyone else anymore, I promise. But he's burning up with influenza, like the others. He needs a doctor."

"If this God you're always telling me about is truly just, he'd have died out there."

"We're better off with him here, where we can keep an eye on him. He won't be turning you in to the law anytime soon, and he won't be trying to sell shares in some nonexistent mine."

"No!" She tried to catch her breath. Miss Rose had said he would take care of her. Thankfully, she knew better than to rely on him. It seemed only right that his concern lie with the town. She understood that.

She couldn't blame him for not trusting her, but at the same time something heavy settled over her. The fear that slipped away when Zane held her close and safe that night in the barn returned with a vengeance.

She shook until she thought she'd rattle apart. Hank couldn't win. She fumbled in her coat pocket and touched cold, sharp metal. She lunged forward, holding the revolver steady in her hands.

* * *

Zane watched Journey's expression change in an instant. Fear aged her more than mere years would show.

A flash of metal appeared as she darted forward, hands withdrawn. Her fingers shook from the weight of the pistol in her tiny hands.

He stepped close, thankful that the deserted street kept them from prying eyes. Hank's eyes blinked open, looking like muddy puddles. They focused on the barrel pointed high at his chest.

Zane's heart hammered. He laid a hand on Journey's arm, grateful when she didn't flinch at his touch.

"Leave me be," she said, her voice deep and tight. She never looked away from Hank, whose mustache trembled and throat convulsed.

"You know it can't end this way." He kept his voice low, stretching his other arm around her.

"It can end any way I want. You're the one who reminded me to watch my back. That's exactly what I'm doing."

"Not this way."

"Once Hank's gone, I'll never have to worry about him again. You'll never have to be bothered with *me* again. I'm already wanted for his murder. For once in my life the stories about me will be true."

Zane shifted his weight and nodded Sam off when he turned back toward them. "If you do this, you'll never be free of him. He's here, Journey, but he can't hurt you. Look at him. He isn't going anywhere. We'll contact Reed—get him to come and tell us how to handle this. We'll get a lawyer from Virginia City to come if you need one. We'll—"

"No!" She thrust the barrel closer to Hank's heart.

Hank wheezed. "Listen to him, Maura—Journey. I promise you, I won't stay around to bother you anymore."

"You lie!"

Zane stretched an arm forward, pushing the barrel tip toward the sky. The jolt knocked the gun from her hand, and it fell to the ground, slowed by the thick folds of her skirt.

She turned on Zane. Her fists pounded against his chest, and he crushed her to him. This only served to free her feet, which she dug sharply into his shins. An elbow poked his tender side, and he released her, sucking in a breath.

"Journey?" Zane edged closer. "C'mon, sweetheart, come inside. We can work this all out."

Hank silenced her response with a moan. His eyes darted like a cornered cat, and he sucked in a great breath of air and held it, bowing low over the saddle. Only the slightest movement told Zane he hadn't stopped breathing.

Zane watched Journey, her bottom lip quivering as great tears gathered in her deep brown eyes. He leaned forward, hoping to offer comfort. But she staggered back, then turned and ran before her tears made good on their threat to fall.

Chapter Thirty-Three

Zane moved to follow her, until he heard Hank tumbling from his horse. Zane went to his side but kept an eye out for Sam, who'd already made his way up the front steps of the church.

"C'mon, Baines," Zane said, nudging him with his boot. Hank didn't move.

It took several failed attempts before he managed to pull Hank to his feet. Together they wobbled to the church. The main street of Walten had never seemed so long. Finally they were met by a puff of warm air and Doc's helping hands.

Zane stomped snow from his boots before stepping into the welcoming heat of the sanctuary. His shoulder throbbed, and the ache in his ribs made it hard to breathe. Even more painful was the feeling he'd abandoned Journey. Would she ever trust him again? But how could he have done anything but bring Hank to town?

After Hank's warning shot had ricocheted off a tree to skim Zane's forehead, Hank had collapsed under the fever and ache of the grippe. Leaving him would have meant certain death out there in the snow. Journey wanted him dead, but he had brought Baines to town for help. Had he destroyed any trust Journey might have had for him? Had he taken mercy too far?

Sam knelt at Abby's side, brushing her long hair back from her damp face. Doc Ferris held Miss Rose's head up, coaxing something steamy into her cracked lips. *Jesus, be with all these things going round in my head. Help us, each one, to focus on the task at hand, and give us wisdom to know just what that should be at any given time.*

"Sit down, Zane," Doc called over to him. "You look like you've been ridden hard and put away wet yourself. I'll check your arm and that wrap on your ribs in a minute."

He obeyed, finding a spot in the corner and struggling with the buttons on his coat.

The room was an odd balance of quiet and chaos. The heavy steps of tired workers echoed across the floors. An underlying drone of raspy breathing filled the room. Strange how a church that seemed plenty large every Sunday morning when he stood before all those peering eyes could shrink so much. He closed his eyes and leaned his head back.

Doc Ferris roused him. He darted up, cradling his side when he felt a stitch.

"Hold on there," Doc said. "You slipped off a bit. You're entitled." He frowned, looking at the welt Zane felt above his eye. "Trouble on the trail?"

"You might say that."

"I might say this looks like a bullet nicked you."

Doc's eyes concentrated on the slice on his forehead, but the rest of his expression demanded an explanation.

"I ran into Baines in the little piney. He fired off a shot and I took heed, but he wasn't himself. I could see he was feverish, not thinking real clear. But then, I'm not exactly his favorite person these days, as it is. Sam came up from behind to get the pistol away, but Hank shot again. I ducked and slipped on a patch of snow, but the bullet ricocheted off a branch and creased me."

"Did you lose consciousness?"

"No. Things got a little blurry there for a minute, but I didn't pass out."

Doc stood and turned back to a pile of bandages behind him. "You're fortunate. It'll be sore, but no stitches. Take off that shirt and I'll check those ribs. They'll need to be rebound after that fall, I'd expect."

Zane looked at all the ladies shuffling to feed broth to the patients who were awake. "Here?"

"I doubt you'll garner much notice." Zane could hear the tired smile in his voice. "Come on, now. I haven't got all day."

Zane eased his shirt off, and the undershirt beneath that, as his ears grew warm. In no time, Doc had the binding loosened off. He winced as the doctor prodded his tender side but convinced him it felt much better than it had a week and a half ago.

"I'm going to wrap you again, just the same," Doc said. "There's no sense in being hasty."

"Where's Hank?"

Doc nodded to a cot on the far side where Hank lay with his head toward the front door. "He's been quiet ever since you brought him in."

"Good. Has Journey come back?"

"Zane?" A low voice from the back of the room interrupted them.

"Miss Rose?" He stood, pulling his flannel shirt around his shoulders, and moved over to her bed. Sam sat on the floor nearby, his head leaning on Abby's shoulder, their hands entwined. Both slept.

"Zane? Are you there?" Miss Rose looked as though she were trying to sit up on the cot and failing.

"I'm right here. Settle back and tell me what you need, and I'll get it. You rest."

"Journey? Where's Journey?" she asked, lying back.

He glanced at Doc, who shook his head and continued gathering his supplies. Zane pulled the blanket up under Miss Rose's chin.

"She stepped out for a while to clear her head some. Sam and I, we brought Hank in. He's sick, too."

"And Journey?"

"I haven't seen her since," he said. "She wasn't happy to see Hank and not pleased with me for bringing him here. She said I should have let him die out there."

"And maybe you should have, Lord forgive me," Miss Rose said, her voice sounding much like his grandmother's had, but she had smoked cigars. Zane tilted her head to give her some water.

"I know," she said, rolling her eyes a little at him.

He leaned back. "I didn't say anything."

She coughed and her face scrunched up, making her wrinkles even more pronounced than usual. "You've been my pastor…long enough. I know what you'd say."

He grinned as she closed her eyes again. For a moment he thought she'd fallen asleep. But she slid her hand over his and squirmed under her blankets.

"Go after her, Zane. Look out for her. She needs you."

"What about you?" He brushed wiry gray wisps from her face.

"I need to know you're both fine and looking out for each other. The Lord has something in store for you both, Zane. Don't be afraid of it. I don't know when she'll be ready for you. But let yourself be ready for her if the Lord allows it."

He stood, finding her blue eyes focused on him. "I'll find her. We'll help her through this, whatever happens. Don't worry. Just rest." He moved to get his coat and hat.

Her fragile voice followed him over the growing din of the room. The light through the windows slanted, casting a reddish tone over the golden wood of the sanctuary walls. It lit Miss Rose's face.

"Go on," she said. "Like I told Journey, I'll be here a while yet."

He pulled his shirt closed and fumbled through the buttons, managing to slide most of them through by the second try, even with his fingers moving stiffly from their sling. He grabbed his coat.

"Preacher?" A quiet drawl caught his attention, and he turned to see Hank's foggy eyes focused on him.

Anger flared within him, to his surprise, but he went to the man's side. *Lord,* he thought, *give me the right words to say—and keep me from thrashing him myself.*

He pulled a chair up to the low cot. Hank's breath came in shallow gasps that didn't rustle the blanket over him.

Where was Journey? He shifted in his seat. The sun

would soon set. His knee bounced and he looked toward the door. But he sensed the Spirit wanted him here.

A low voice called his attention back to the bed.

"I would suppose," Hank said, "that you're happy to see me here. Rather fitting, right?" His eyes remained closed, as if he hadn't the energy to open them.

"Fitting, no. Believe me, Baines, I take no pleasure in you being here." He rocked in his seat. *Where was Journey?*

"You don't find the least satisfaction in my illness?" Shallow breaths interrupted his speech. "After I lied, tried to cheat your town, and am married to the woman you're in love with?"

"Don't forget our little meeting in Virginia City, Hank. And I care for her, but I'm not *in love with* Journey."

"So you say. And I'm to believe you forgive me for all that? No one has that capacity to forgive."

The flames that took Sarah came to mind. The rescue he should have been able to make. "I've had to forgive things a lot worse than anything you've done. But what I do isn't what matters here." *Maybe Journey had only gone back to Miss Rose's to think things through.*

Hank licked his lips. "I didn't intend for things to turn out this way. My ma took me to church when I was a boy. I know about God."

Zane glanced at his pocket watch and leaned close to Hank's pasty face. He sure looked worse than the other patients. Where was Doc? "But do you know His Son?"

The dark eyes widened. "It's too late to feed me that line, Preacher. I always meant to get my life together, to make things right. It never seemed the proper time, though."

Doc Ferris came over and placed his hand on Hank's head. Then he dug Hank's hand from under the covers and checked his wrist against his pocket watch.

"Anything I can get you?" he asked. Hank shook his head.

Zane cleared his throat and looked at the doctor.

Doc nodded him over to the dim corner before answering. "He's not going to make it, Zane. He's too hot and drying out. His pulse is weak and out of beat, and there's nothing more I can do. If we had more quinine, maybe. But I think he was too far gone when you found him. Sounds like pneumonia has settled in his lungs."

Rubbing a hand over his face, Zane looked back over at the patient. "Hard to figure how a man gets to the place where he is."

He let his gaze wander around the sanctuary. "I was heading out to Miss Rose's, figured Journey might have gone that way. But if you think he hasn't got long, maybe I'll sit with him a bit, try to talk to him again."

Doc nodded. "I know you'd rather be with her. But you won't have another chance at Hank, unless I miss my guess. I'll say a prayer for him."

"Throw one in for me, too, Doc," he said. "I'm afraid my compassion's about to run out."

He patted the doctor's stooped shoulder and moved back to the seat by the bed where Hank lay.

Chapter Thirty-Four

Journey slipped into the church entry without a sound, pausing at the door to the sanctuary. Her breath clouded before her, but she felt warmed by the shame that burned her face. Why did she always make everything worse by her actions?

She rested her forehead on the rough door frame, then pushed the door open. Lanterns had been lit but not enough of them to conquer the growing darkness. Most patients seemed to be resting, with workers waiting to attend any need that might arise. The room was quiet, and only Doc Ferris seemed to notice her. Still, she couldn't force herself through the door.

She spotted Zane's broad back, sitting next to a cot by the wall. He blocked the view of the patient, but she could tell from the size of the feet hanging off the edge that it was a man. And she could well guess which man, even before she heard him.

"You still here, Preacher?"

"Thought maybe you'd like to talk some more." She heard Zane's low reply.

"There's nothing more to say. You think I don't know how this is going to end? You expect me to come blithering to the Lord's feet, begging Him to take me now, when I know I can't do a thing to earn my keep?"

"It's not about 'earning' anything, Hank," Zane said.

Did he really think he was dying? Or was this some unexpected trouble that he planned to turn to his advantage?

"That sounds very well, but that's not the way life works," Hank said.

"No, but that's how God works. There's still time for a change, if you want it."

Could he change? Journey wondered. Could God forgive someone like Hank? Would He?

"The only thing I want, Preacher, is to be left to myself."

She caught a glimpse of Hank's face, which held a grayish cast in the waning light, as Zane shifted and lowered his head.

"Let me sit awhile and pray for you. I won't say a word. But just in case you change your mind—"

"Suit yourself, Preacher. I expect you have a job to do." He chuckled, but it came out in a gasp. "At times like this, I'd imagine you'd rather have found another line of work."

She watched Zane raise his head and detected a grin from the dimple on his cheek. The thought must have crossed his mind. He stood and walked over behind the pulpit, pulling out a worn Bible and returning to his seat. He opened the book over his knee with one hand. She watched his lips move silently in profile.

Hank shifted, turning to draw in more air. He seemed

to have trouble with that. Would the same happen to Miss Rose and Abby as the illness lingered?

"One thing, Preacher."

"Yes?" Zane held the Bible closed with his finger marking the place.

"Tell Journey…" She leaned forward to catch every raspy word. "Tell Journey I'm sorry. She's a wonderful woman, kind and full of life. At least, she was before I changed that in her. She deserved someone good." Hank's dry cough interrupted him.

She slipped a step back with surprise. Her mother had been a prostitute. She'd grown up in a saloon and taken up with Hank before she'd married him at seventeen. Even now, with the mess she'd made of her life, she'd never thought it wasn't all she deserved.

"It's not about deserving. God forgives us in spite of what we deserve. That's what I'm trying to tell you," Zane said.

"Too late for me. I won't come groveling to the Lord this way. But Maura…maybe Maura. Journey deserves someone like you, Preacher."

Zane slid his chair forward, but Hank waved him off with a finger that barely moved. "I believe I'll sleep for a while now. You'll be sure and tell her what I said?"

She didn't stay long enough to hear Zane's response. She couldn't face him, not now.

Shutting the door without a sound, she left the church. The cold fresh air would clear her head. The last thin rays of sunset clung to the snow-sculpted hills and peaks.

Did Zane truly believe Hank could be forgiven? She wanted to scream her denial of the thought. But what if there was hope for someone like Hank? For someone like her?

She stepped down to the ground and headed for the shed, where she'd left the horse. She needed to feel the cold on her face, needed to breathe in the open air, away from town. She needed to think. She needed—

But all thoughts flew from her mind as hands clamped around her waist and over her mouth, stifling her scream. Then light burst behind her eyes, and darkness fell.

Chapter Thirty-Five

Icy cold seeped in, drawing Journey awake. Shivering overtook her and her teeth chattered. She blinked her eyes open but only darkness greeted her. Rough wood bit into her cheek as she shifted on a lumpy pillow. She couldn't feel her hands, couldn't tell if they were in front of or behind her.

She struggled to keep her breathing slow and even, but her gasps echoed around her, unnaturally loud in the hollow air. Where was she?

Hearing no sounds that would indicate another's presence, she shifted to her side until her back met with solid wall, and muffled a groan as sensation returned to her hands with jagged tingles. Only then did she realize they were bound, along with her feet. It took several tries before she managed to rock herself upright.

Not even the barest flicker of light could be seen. Maybe it was night outside. How long had she been unconscious? Would whoever brought her come back for her?

It couldn't be Hank. He was too sick, wasn't he?

Roy! All control left her at the thought, and she blinked, trying to dispel the darkness. The air wafting by smelled dank and seeped through cracks around her. The walls around were close, leaving her boxed in where she felt suffocated by the darkness. She drew her legs up, trying to conserve any heat her shaking could muster. What did Roy want with her?

Hank's kindnesses had been few and far between, but at least they had existed before he'd met Roy. Hank became cruel, but Roy truly frightened her. Hank's temper ruled him, especially once he began drinking more. Roy never lost control; every cruel act sprung fully planned from his mind to be carried out. And that made him terrifying.

Tears spilled down her face in icy trails. She hugged her knees to her chest, rocking to and fro in the narrow space. *Think!* She commanded her pounding head. What would Miss Rose do?

Pray? Come sniveling to the Lord when she found herself between a wall and, well, the blinding blackness that lay beyond?

"You expect me to come blithering to the Lord's feet, begging Him to take me now, when I know I can't do a thing to earn my keep?" Hank's words echoed in her mind.

Zane said it wasn't about earning anything, that God would forgive, that it wasn't too late for change.

She thought back to the week before her mama died. The owner of the tavern where her mother worked had been furious when Mama refused to take any more gentlemen callers. Not gentlemen, she corrected herself. Not men like Zane and Sam. Those men had been like Hank and Roy, taking only for themselves.

Mama had been sick, but she'd never have returned to that business. She had tried to explain why, but somehow those lessons had been lost in Journey's efforts to get away after Mama died. Within that week, when she was hungry and cold and tired of living in the streets, Hank had befriended her and taken her to live with him. Could God forgive all that she'd done since that time? So many deceptions.

There's always a chance, she reminded herself. She pushed into the wall at her back as the darkness crushed in tighter.

She buried her head in her bound hands. "Oh, Lord," she whispered, her voice unnaturally loud as it cut through the overwhelming silence. "I've made such a sorry mess of my life. Then I tried to hide it, and that's only made it worse."

Rocking harder in the enclosed space, she paused to catch her breath. "Jesus, I don't know You, not really. I only know I've made so many wrong choices that I can't make any right ones anymore if You don't help me."

She stopped, listening, arms trembling around her knees. Her breath caught. Was that a creak she heard? But if there'd been anything unusual, it made no other sound.

"I know You can forgive me, Jesus, if You only would. And whether I make it out of here or not—" she gulped, hoping the latter would not be the case "—but even if not, Lord, I want to be Yours, and to know Your forgiveness. Uh, thank You, and…amen."

She lifted her face. The throbbing in her head moved from the back where she'd been struck to a point behind her eyes. Sniffling, she managed to fish a handkerchief from her pocket with her hands tied.

Cold air still wafted around her. No light threaded its way into the blackness in which she was submerged. A rescue didn't appear any closer at hand than it had a few moments before. But the cold knot of fear and confusion and sorrow that had gripped her heart began to loosen…and soften…and grow warm. Peace filled her as the happy tears fell.

Chapter Thirty-Six

Z ane jerked his head up at the sound of feet stomping in the door. How long had he dozed? He needed to find Journey.

"Reed?" Zane watched him make a beeline from the entry to his aunt's side and followed. The sheriff sat at Miss Rose's side and held her hand, his gaze resting on her tiny form. He swallowed hard and blinked several times.

"How's she doing?"

"She's resting. How'd you hear?" He adjusted the sling around his arm.

"I met a man on the trail who said there's been sickness and that you had everyone holed up at the church. When I didn't find anyone at Aunt Rose's, I thought—"

"I'm sorry. I should have wired before."

But Reed waved him off. "No matter now. I'm glad you were with her." Zane caught his glance. "Besides, I'm here on business. I had a visitor. A man came in by the name of Roy Clemson. He claimed to be a lawman from Georgia investigating the case of Maura Baines, otherwise known as Journey Smith."

"He came all that way to find her?"

Reed shook his head. "Something didn't sit right with me, either, so I did some checking of my own. He's no lawman and I have a poster on him."

"He's looking for Journey?"

"She ever mention him? Do you recognize the name?"

"No, but Hank may. He's sick and Doc says he doesn't have long, but we could ask." Something clicked in his mind. "You said no one was at Miss Rose's place? You checked the barn?"

"I looked around a bit, hoping. But I didn't see anyone. Why?"

Zane shook his head and scratched his eyebrow. "Journey was none too happy with me for bringing Baines here. She ran off, and I thought she'd go there."

"Preacher?"

He glanced over his shoulder at Hank and stood, looking at Reed.

"I'm sure she'll turn up, soon as she's had a chance to think things through," Reed said.

Zane watched him pull his seat closer to Miss Rose's side. Sam knelt near Abby. Both women were still and asleep, but Abby's color had already improved since they'd found her. He wished the same for Miss Rose.

"Preacher? Are you there?"

He shuffled to his chair beside Hank. A lantern flickered its light over his gray face. "I'm here, Baines. What can I do for you?"

"Maura," he gasped. "Where is she? I have to talk to her." Hank kicked his blankets off.

"She's not here. You have to settle down." He held the man with a hand at his shoulder. "Doc?"

The man appeared at his side, with Reed right behind. Doc grabbed Hank's wrist with one hand and pulled out his pocket watch with the other. "You can't carry on like this, Mr. Baines. What can I get you?"

"Maura. I have to tell her—Roy's coming. He said he—could persuade her—to help us."

"Help you how?" Zane's voice sounded unnaturally loud to his own ears in the quiet room.

"Mining deal. We had maps, drawn up special." Hank puffed. "Never had a chance to use them."

He leaned forward, clenching his hand in the blankets covering Baines. "What will he do?"

Doc Ferris nodded him off with a furrowed brow. "Take it easy, son. She was here earlier."

"When?"

"You were talking with Hank. She didn't stay long."

His fingers tightened into a fist. "Where would he be, Baines? What will he do if he finds her?"

"Don't know." Hank coughed hard and fell back, his breath shallow. "But he'll find her, unless you do… first." Air gurgled in the back of his throat and his face grew dark as he tried to inflate his lungs. "Tell her I—tried." He choked and his lips went white. He brought a trembling hand to his chest and his eyes rolled back. He struggled again with the blankets. "Too hot…"

Zane tried to pull the man upright, awkward with one arm in a sling, but lost his leverage as Hank grew heavier and slumped to the bed, eyes closed. He looked to Reed and then Doc, who shook his head and replaced Hank's hand at his side. "He's gone, Zane."

He wanted to kick the cot and make Hank tell him

more. He blew out a frustrated breath. His muscles tensed, and he felt Reed's hand on his shoulder.

"You might as well rest yourself. There's no way we could pick up any trail tonight," Reed said, stretching to his feet. "You know that."

He fell into a chair by the window, cradling his ribs. "All I know is that she's out there. What if this Clemson guy has found her? We have to do something."

"And she could be tucked in at Aunt Rose's place by now for all we know."

He gave a ragged sigh. "I know. I should've gone out to check myself. Maybe she—"

"Look at yourself. When's the last you slept?" Reed asked. "Your ribs must be killing you."

"Not so bad that I can't ride."

"Ride where? Unless you know right where she'd be, we could mark up any tracks we might find if we wait until daylight." Reed eased into the seat by his side in the corner.

Zane remembered Journey's fury as she had stormed off, thought about Hank's warning about Roy Clemson. Somehow he didn't hold out hope that she could be sleeping, safe and sound. Wind rattled the window.

"I know," he whispered. "But something's not right. I feel it. Tell me you believe she's fine."

Reed cast his gaze toward his aunt, shielding his eyes in the shadows of the room. He kept his voice low. "I believe we can only trust the Lord to take care of her until He guides us to find her. But we can't head out until daybreak. You get some sleep, and we'll leave at first light."

Miss Rose's voice barely crossed the room. "Zane? Zane, are you there?"

He moved to her side and knelt. "Right here, Miss Rose. What can I do for you?"

"You can settle yourself. You're no good to Journey or anyone else if you go off half-cocked." Her weak voice was painful to Zane's ears.

"I have to find her. I hate to think she's out there and I can't—" His chest burned and he swallowed over the knot in his throat.

Miss Rose slipped her hand over his. "She's not Sarah."

He focused his gaze on the lantern on the far windowsill. "I know that. I don't want her to be."

"You think if she's not Sarah, you can't love her," she said. "But that's the one thing they have in common."

He looked down at her pale face, blending in with the pillow slip. "I only want to help her. She needs me."

Miss Rose managed a dry laugh. "You need her. She's the only woman to get any of your attention since Sarah died." She shifted under the covers. "Besides me, that is."

He leaned down and smiled. "No one deserves the attention more than you."

"I won't always be here to look out for you. You need someone, Zane. Journey loves you, you know."

"She'll be gone the minute the snow melts."

Her blue eyes blazed with fever and irritation. "Only if you don't give her a reason not to. You love her. Or you're starting to. Don't let Sarah's memory blind you to a future she'd want you to have. Go after Journey."

"She's not even a believer. I can't just— She's not—"

"Trust God. He's working on her. Trust Him and go after her."

"I will," he said. He looked at her pasty skin and

heard her shallow breathing. He leaned down to kiss her cheek. "I will."

Morning couldn't come soon enough.

Chapter Thirty-Seven

"Journey!"

Sunlight had only begun to kiss the horizon when Zane and Reed were saddled and ready to head out. The night air still hung cold and frosty, and he wondered, not for the first time, if Journey was somewhere warm. They pushed the horses hard on the ride out to Miss Rose's place, but the careful search of the ground for even the barest of tracks garnered no leads.

"Journey! Can you hear me?"

Reed reined in beside him. "She's not here."

"Jour—"

"Zane!" He felt Reed grab his coat sleeve and pull him around, carefully because of his ribs. "We're wasting time. We need to backtrack this Clemson guy and see who's talked to him, where he'd go if he did have her, where he'd be now if he doesn't. Maybe if we talk to him, we could at least take out some possibilities. We can't go out searching all over creation and hope to find her," Reed said. "It'd be like looking for a needle in a haystack."

"Your way could take days." He kept his voice low and tight. "That's time Journey might not have."

"Do you have a better idea?"

He swiped a knuckle over his forehead. *Dear Lord, where is she? Guide us, please, Father. Why, if she were mine, I'd—*

Mine.

"Zane? You feeling all right?" Reed shook him out of his daze.

"I will be when we find her," he said with a nod. "And I think I know where we can look. Listen, you go ahead into town, ask around and see what you can learn about Clemson. Baines has been stirring up interest in the old mine. He's been staying out there. Maybe Clemson is, too, and if so, maybe he's taken Journey there."

Reed shifted in his saddle. "I don't know, you with that arm? What if you meet up with Clemson without me?"

"I'm not looking for trouble. I only want to find Journey, make sure she's not hurt. I'll be careful."

His friend still looked doubtful. "You're sure? Aunt Rose'll kill me if anything happens to you."

"I'm sure. I'll see you back at the church."

Journey shivered and felt her stomach flop, shaking to stay alert. She blinked and tried to stretch before remembering her bound hands. The darkness prevented her from seeing anything more than shapes, but the impenetrable black lightened with streaks of sunlight winding through the loose boards in the walls. It must be morning.

What was that noise?

The wind moaned, piercing the cracks at her back,

but she could have sworn there was something else. *Lord, am I losing my mind?* Day and night all tumbled together. She slid until she felt the press of boards at her shoulder.

Again she heard it. A voice. Maybe voices.

Would someone be looking for her? Would they even notice she was missing after the way she'd run off? What if Roy came back for her? What if—

Wait a minute, she told herself. What about faith? Wasn't part of believing in God remembering that He had control over everything?

Her hands no longer had any sensation, but she clenched them to bring the feeling of pins and needles back at least. If someone came, she'd need to attract attention. If Roy returned, he already knew where she was, and calling out would do no harm, she reasoned.

"I'm here!" Her voice filled the space around her, sounding raspy and weak to her own ears. She coughed as the chill air suffocated her. "I'm in here!" she called again, louder.

She strained to hear over the odd moans and creaks of the closet. Weren't the voices getting closer?

Rocking back and forth, she tried to stop the trembling that chased down her spine. "Zane!" She couldn't stop the tears that rolled down her face. "Please, Jesus! Let it be Zane!"

Zane pulled his horse back into the stand of trees near the old mine. He squinted across the clearing to the mine shack standing in all its dilapidated glory near the mine entrance. *Please, Lord, let Journey be there.*

* * *

Steps sounded closer, and Journey held her breath. "Zane?"

The closet door creaked open and a match flared. She screamed.

"'Fraid not, Maura," Roy said, his face eerie in the soft glow. "By the time your preacher man figures out where to look for you, we'll be long gone."

Cold dread formed a lump that sank to her stomach when he drew closer, settling back onto his haunches and blocking the doorway. The glimpse she had of the room that lay beyond told her little.

He grinned without a single tooth showing. "Your prince won't be arriving anytime soon."

"What do you want?" She struggled to catch a deep breath.

"You. You're going to straighten out this whole mess." He leaned closer until she could smell a strong lack of soap on him.

"There wasn't a problem until you told Hank where I was."

"No problem at all," Roy said. "You flitting about with your new beau under your husband's nose. And Hank was still going to cut you in on the deal."

"It wasn't like that. I didn't want to be a part of any deal. And Zane—"

"That's not the point, is it?" He struck another match and watched it add its glow to the first as it burned out, then used it to light a cheroot held between his teeth. "The money you took from Hank that night you left belonged to me. So I figure it's me you owe, after all."

"I don't owe you anything," she insisted.

A third match lit the lantern that rested at his feet,

still necessary in the morning grayness. He drew a long puff and let the smoke swirl slowly from his lips and nose.

He continued talking then, as if he'd never heard her. "You'll come with me. I'm sure we can find something for you to do until you pay your debt." She felt his gaze on her, moving from her boots to her face, lingering longer than it should. "I'm sure we can come to some kind of agreement." His tone showed he didn't care about being agreeable.

"I'm not going with you, Roy. We'll settle this here."

"Hmm...that might have worked if you had helped Hank like he said you would. As it stands, maybe it'd be best for you and me to move on, head to California. Some towns are starting to get right civilized—makes the folks more willing to be fooled. With looks like yours, they'll fall in well enough." He stretched a stubby finger and stuck it into one curl. "Yes, Hank certainly knew what he was doing when he took up with you."

She stiffened, her heart pounding in her throat in the pattern of her uneven breaths.

"Yep, you're a fine-looking woman, Maura." He drew forward, eyelids heavy.

He caught her bound wrists and pulled her up close. The scent of tobacco gagged her.

He leaned closer. She squirmed, moving her arms between them, and pushed him away, scrambling to her feet in the tiny closet. She slipped down on her tingling feet. Roy moved closer and yanked her back up. She staggered as he shoved her away, managing to right herself against the wooden doorjamb before she toppled over completely.

"You could do worse than taking up with me." His lips brushed her ear as he spoke. Bile rose to her throat.

Sparks of panic flew behind her eyelids, which were squeezed shut as his hand slid around her waist and up her back. The other hand trailed through her loose hair brushing either side of her face. She panted and thrashed, striking out with her bound hands.

Roy grabbed her waist again and thrust her away. Sharp pain gouged her back and forced air from her. She cringed when he stepped forward, beefy fist raised.

She ducked and rolled against the wallboards to the floor. He grabbed the hem of her dress and yanked her back over the uneven floor, pulling her upright against him despite her kicks. *Lord...*

"Let her go, Roy."

A voice boomed against the unnatural light as she struggled free. Zane! His shadowed form blocked most of the morning light as he stood in the outside doorway.

Journey squirmed and thrashed until Roy's grasp loosened and she felt him pull away. She dropped to the cold dirt floor of the cabin and rolled to her knees, squeezing into the corner.

Roy spun free of Zane's grasp on his collar and whirled, shoving him against a rickety table. He gasped as his bound arm twisted.

Then Roy stepped in, wielding a board at his head. She squealed and Zane managed to avoid the swing. The sickening crunch of wood against wood muffled his groan as his tender ribs battered the rough edge of the stand.

Roy swung again, this time catching the side of the preacher's head. "Zane!" Journey yelled as he slumped to the floor.

But he kicked out, knocking Roy's legs from under him. The man fell to the floor and scrambled to some dark corner.

Zane pulled toward her, and she reached out to help him lean against the wall beside her.

"Did he hurt you?" he asked, panting and trying to stand.

She helped him up, holding her bound hands over his side to check for further damage. He worked to catch his breath, swaying slightly. "No, he— I'm fine. Zane!"

Roy swung the wooden club again. This time it connected with the end of Zane's chin, forcing his head back and into the rough wall. He dropped to the floor, unmoving.

Journey wobbled to his side on her knees. She ran her fingers over his face, hoping to rouse him. "Zane?"

But a cold, hard grasp jerked her to her feet. Roy pinched her jaw in his grimy hand, bringing tears to her eyes.

"Don't bother. You'll be a lovely memory for him, if he has a memory after that hit. Now, you're coming with me."

"No!" She pulled away, moving to Zane's side. "Please! Please, you have to let me help him. I'm no good to you, I'd only slow you down."

"I said—"

"They'll follow if I'm with you, Roy. They came this far. If you go now, you'll be in the clear. They'll never catch you, they'll—"

Roy slapped her and she sank to the floor. "Fine. You make a good point. But if you say a word about me to a soul, I'll be back and I'll kill you and your darling pastor—and anyone else who means anything to you. And you know I can."

She shook, unable to speak.

"I see we have an understanding." Roy grabbed the lantern and moved to the edge of the waning shadows. "Be sure it stays that way."

He left her in gray silence.

Chapter Thirty-Eight

Zane roused as pain seared through his head. He opened his eyes, his vision murky at best. Gentle hands smoothed his face.

He sat up carefully, leaning against the rough board behind him. Where were they again? He moved his good arm around to push himself up and away from the wall.

"Journey? You there?"

The soft sound of crying echoed between the walls of the almost empty cabin. He brushed her shoulder and pulled her into the crook of his arm. She curled against him without any argument. He leaned his head back with a deep sigh.

He breathed deeply, choking with the staleness of the air in the shack.

"Journey?" He nudged her. "Journey, where'd Roy go?"

She continued crying and he shook her. "Journey! Where is he?"

"He said if I sent the law after him he'd come back

and kill us. Then he took the lantern and left. How badly are you hurt?"

"Never mind me. We have to go now if we want a chance to catch up to Roy. Come on!"

He pulled himself upright, using the sturdy beam at his back for leverage, and dragged Journey up behind. "Let's get out of here."

Her head nodded against his chest, and he wrapped an arm around her shoulders. She followed a few paces, then stopped short. Her wide eyes gleamed in sudden panic.

"What if we don't find him?"

He ran his fingers down her arm to clasp her hand. "We will. We have to, or you'll be looking over your shoulder for him every day for the rest of your life." He tried to calm her with slow, even tones. "We have to move now. Maybe he headed back to town for Hank, or maybe he's camping somewhere close, but we can't know until we get out, all right?"

"What about Hank?"

Her warm arms trembled and tightened around his waist. She didn't falter, but he sensed she wanted the truth.

"One thing at a time, right? Let's get out of here and get help. Reed's in town. Then we'll talk. There are a lot of things I need to tell you." He felt strength grow in her and wondered at it.

"Oh, Zane. You haven't any idea."

Journey felt Zane's arm wrap around her shoulders and relaxed into his embrace. His muscles tensed under his coat sleeve, but she couldn't tell if this was from pain or something else.

She watched Zane carefully, saw his struggle to stand upright and not crash to the floor. She tried to support him, but a night of sleeping bound in the cold had caught up with her. Her legs cramped fiercely.

"Zane—"

She cringed, rubbing her legs with frustration. He tugged her onward and she skidded to her knees, gasping as tears streamed down her cheeks.

"Journey! We have to—"

"I'm trying. Give me…a moment."

They wouldn't get anywhere at this rate. He'd move faster alone. "Go," she said, exhaustion sweeping over her. "Go on without me."

He drew closer and she heard his voice in her ear, soft yet firm, as he stooped on one knee, wavering at her side. "No! We have to stay together."

He helped her to her feet and again they stumbled on. The distance seemed to grow as he staggered and turned without pattern. Only his determination kept him upright as he tugged her along.

Zane pulled Journey closer as they stepped onto the porch, where the roof lowered above them, sunken near the entrance. He motioned for her to follow behind, and she nodded her understanding, unable to read his eyes anymore. They appeared as two black caverns in his face.

Two turns around the corners and the glow from a lantern shone in the still-darkened woods ahead. Roy must be waiting for them.

"Zane?" Where would they go now?

He muffled a cough and clutched his side. How much farther could he manage? "This way!" he whispered.

She followed. Where was he going? The path narrowed and she glanced back. In the early morning mist she could make out the outline of the cabin where Hank had been staying. Roy, too, most likely.

A crack sounded up ahead. Gunshot? She started, feeling Zane drag her behind a tree.

Then another crack, this one a sound breaking in her ears from much closer. Zane's arms shook around her and loosened as he slipped to the ground.

Zane whipped around at the sound, dropping to the ground. "Journey!" He grabbed her hand and dragged her down beside him.

He heard her scream, a shrill echo in his pounding head, and swayed to his knees behind the tree. Holding her down with a hand at her head, he peered into the dim array of trees, searching for Roy's location. The growing light sliced through his head. He turned back, a finger to his lips to tell Journey to be quiet.

"I know you're out there, and I know you're listening." His mouth dried up, making it hard to swallow. "This has to end here, Roy. Hank's dead." The roaring in his head distorted all other sounds. "Turn yourself in and help Journey clear her name. Hank would've wanted that, and things'll go easier with you if you talk to the judge."

Journey struggled to her knees in spite of his warnings. He managed to grasp her waist and hold her tightly, edging around the tree that hid them. He squeezed Journey closer, black dots swarming his vision between them. She squirmed from his grasp, and the sound seemed to explode around them.

He peered out again, hoping for a glimpse of the man, but instead the sound of a gun being cocked met his ears. He froze, keeping his arms up and away from his sides as he turned to face the end of Roy's gun.

Close. They were so close. But Roy drew back, smashing the pistol at his head again, and Zane's vision grew black, the sparse light slowly overtaken by gray dots that obliterated all else.

I'm so sorry, Journey, he thought. *I couldn't save you, either.*

Chapter Thirty-Nine

Several moments passed before it registered in Journey's brain that Zane hadn't followed her. The sun had replaced the blackness overhead, but no movement of shadow behind her could be seen. She dropped back to her knees, scanning the trees for any sign of motion.

Zane. She spotted him now, lying at the tree where she had left him, unmoving. His wide eyes stayed closed, their long, dark lashes brushing his dirt-streaked face. His shirt and free hand showed torn patches, and a scrape along his chin bled readily. She worked her way back to him, darting tree to tree until she collapsed at his side. Another gash caught her attention on the other side of his head, one she hadn't noticed before.

Exhaustion weighed on her and her eyelids drooped. They needed help. Once she rested, maybe she could—

Her eyelids snapped open. She had to stay alert. *Oh, Zane. Wake up!* She wanted to scream at him, wanted to see those gray eyes. Instead, she rubbed a smudge from his cheek and tried to jostle him awake.

If Zane had come looking for her, maybe he wasn't

alone. He wouldn't come himself in his condition, would he?

"Help." The word came out soft and weak and raspy from her dry throat. She drew in fresh air for long moments and tried again. "Help!"

Trees rustled and footsteps rushed from the surrounding brush. She twisted around to find the source of the noise as it drew closer.

One last scrape of limbs and she shrieked as Roy stepped out into the flat where she and Zane lay sprawled.

Her heart pounded in her ears as he stopped short. His lips drew into a sneer. "I knew you wouldn't let well enough alone. Stirring things up in this charming little town, too, eh, Maura?"

"Stop it, Roy. You know I haven't done anything. You know I didn't kill anyone. It wasn't me that set that fire. Please, we need to get him help."

He stepped closer and she trembled. If only Zane would wake up. His chest lifted and breath puffed shallowly, but his face remained lax. She tried shifting her legs to rouse him. *Please, Zane.*

Roy stood over her. His hand ripped through her ragged hair and jerked her head, tilting her face to his. He pulled his stump of cheroot from yellow teeth and breathed more smoke into her face. "I know you didn't set any fire. That's part of the fun for me, you see. You didn't kill Hank, but he's dead now. You didn't start that fire, but a man was burned to death in it. You'll never be able to prove—"

"Clemson! Put your hands up and step away."

Reed? Reed! *Thank You, Lord!*

Roy's hand gripped her even tighter and yanked her

up, which sent Zane rolling to the ground with a muffled moan.

Reed stepped into the path. A gun flashed in his hands. She struggled, feeling Roy's grip loosen with surprise.

He shoved her and she sprawled against Zane. Landing on her side, she saw Roy's own pistol draw upward in his hand, cocked and ready. She heard the thundering echo at her ear as she tried to reach him in time to thrust him away, saw the puff of smoke drift from the end.

"No!"

Roy smiled and lowered his gun to her face and she felt an instant cold streak settle in her stomach. No time to pray, no words to fill the instant of time that seemed to hang frozen. Roy's hand continued to drop and he slipped a step, falling over a tree root to land on his back. His eyes closed, but that evil smile held for a moment before easing away with the slump of death that took him. Only then did Journey notice the dark stain of blood growing in the center of his chest.

And then Reed was there, squeezing heat into her arms and lifting her to her feet once again. She hovered as he knelt by Zane, who still hadn't opened his eyes, and watched him lay an ear to his chest. Her breath caught, unable to draw in or release. Zane had to be all right. Dear Lord, nothing else mattered, so long as Zane lived.

Warmth. A cool hand. Each sensation made itself known slowly in his foggy head.

Sarah waved to him from where she sat by the fireplace. Zane waved back and she smiled. She stood then and drew her rocker closer to the flame, pulling another chair beside her own. She pulled a tiny pistol from Journey's saddle pack and threw it into the fire. Then she lifted the pack to the chair.

Journey appeared and sat with her. He moved forward to join them....

"Doc, he's awake."

A cool hand held him down as he struggled to turn.

"Let him up. He's likely queasy after that knock to the head." Doc Ferris's voice punched through the throbbing walls of his head.

He lost the contents of his stomach and felt the hands guiding him back into bed. His eyelids felt like wagon wheels as he shifted them open.

Journey's smile greeted him. He thought he managed a smile back and patted the hand that rested over his chest. "We're all right," he said.

She must not have understood, because she leaned closer and said, "You rest. We can talk about this all later, when you're feeling better. You're going to be fine, Zane. We're both going to be just fine."

When Zane roused again, his stomach still felt wobbly, but he did open his eyes without getting sick. Journey sat in a chair at the foot of his bed, asleep with her head tilted against the wall, one arm resting over his foot. She looked like he felt.

"You awake, Zane?" Reed stepped into his line of sight.

He managed a small nod. "Reckon I am." He paused to think, which seemed a lot more difficult than usual. "'Cause surely something prettier than you will be there to meet me at Heaven's gates."

Reed managed a chuckle and sat down. "What do you remember?"

He searched his foggy memory. "We were looking for Journey this morning." He stopped to draw in a slow, shaky breath. "So what'd you do to me this time?"

"You do an awful lot of talking for a man in your condition," Reed said. "Do you remember the mine?"

He closed his eyes and tried to think. "You mean Hank's mine? Wait, he's dead, isn't he?" He pushed his brain to recall more. "Roy! Roy Clemson—"

"He's dead, too. There was nothing I could do."

Zane nodded his understanding.

"The pieces will fill in later, Doc says. You'll feel fine in a week or so, be up and around before that."

"What about Journey?"

She had slipped around to sit next to Reed before he realized she was awake. "It's all going to work out. I have a lot of things to tell you once you're feeling up to it." Her voice was quiet but her smile spoke loudly.

"Reed?" he asked, not taking his gaze away from her almond-brown eyes.

"She's a free woman. Both her accusers are dead, and I heard enough from Clemson and Hank to clear her name. I expect the fact that she ran will be forgiven by the courts, under the circumstances."

Zane smiled, his eyelids feeling heavier by the moment until he could no longer keep them pried open. "How are the others?"

"Abby's feeling better. Doc says she had a mild case, but it was good you brought her in when you did. Sam's with her now. Jimmy Wilson still has a long row to hoe, but Doc thinks he'll pull through. We haven't had a new case in over a day, since you found Abby. Doc thinks we may be through the worst of it." Journey's quiet voice soothed his aching head.

"And Miss Rose?"

Silence. He opened his eyes to catch the tail end of a look Journey and Reed exchanged. He struggled to his elbows. "How is she?"

"Not good." Reed didn't mince words. "She's developed pneumonia. She's weak. Doc Ferris says it's out of his hands. She's been asking to see you. She said she wants to talk to you and Journey both."

"She awake?"

Reed glanced to his aunt's cot and nodded.

Zane struggled to sit, in spite of Journey's and Reed's hands trying to hold him back. "No, let me see her, let her know I'm well."

He thought he held steady but must have wavered, because Journey's strong arms drew around to support him. Together with Reed, they helped him move to a chair beside Miss Rose's cot. He managed the short distance and sat with a heavy thud.

"'Bout time...you got here," Miss Rose whispered. Her skin tinged with blue and her blankets barely moved as she panted. "You had us scared silly."

"Sounds like you've been doing the same," he said. Journey settled on one side of him, and Reed on the other, sitting on the end of Miss Rose's cot.

"Nothing to be afraid of, Zane. You know that better than anybody, I suppose." She puffed several times before she could speak again and her legs shifted restlessly. "Journey knows that now, too."

He stared in confusion a moment before understanding flooded him along with surprise. He turned to Journey. "You believe?"

"I heard you with Hank, saying there's nothing God can't forgive, even with all he had done."

"But Hank didn't believe, Journey. He hardened his heart and wouldn't accept God's forgiveness." Zane ran a thumb over her hand.

Journey placed her other hand over his with a light squeeze. "Reed told me. I'm glad you tried, though. I guessed if Jesus' death could cover Hank's sins, that maybe there was a chance for me, too. I prayed, in that mine shaft when I woke up. I prayed, Zane," she said, her eyes growing damp as the deep joy he'd just now noticed shone from them. "I prayed and God forgave me. I know what you were talking about now. And, oh, I have so much more to learn."

Miss Rose gasped, her face scrunching with pain as she turned to Zane. "And you'll be around to teach her. I believed the Lord had something special in mind when He brought you here, Journey. This one's about as special as they come. You've both been given an early Christmas gift."

She grew paler and her eyes closed. Zane wondered if she'd fallen asleep, but she forced them open again. "I won't be around…to see how…things progress. But… you can be sure…I'll be keeping an eye…on you all. So long as the Lord…allows it."

He leaned forward and stroked her cheek, ready to deny that this was her time. He glanced at the tears pouring down Journey's face with disbelief, then watched Reed take his aunt's hand in his own.

"I've had a life far better…than I deserved," she continued. "But I'm ready to see my Lord…in person. And see my Wallace again, my family."

Her eyes drifted closed and Zane leaned forward

even farther, cupping her cheek in his hand. "No, Miss Rose—"

"Yes. You've been...like a son to me, Zane," she said. "But don't you...ruin this. It's a time...to have joy."

She shifted enough to peer up at Reed. "And you... have been...a wonderful...nephew...so strong and bright...true to God's calling...brave." She paused again, her eyes drooping. "I love you—both my boys."

Journey lost control then, weeping openly and loud in the tiny sanctuary that seemed hollow in its emptiness. He gripped Miss Rose's knotted hands in his own, stroking the fingers.

"And you...missy. Only just met you...but you're to me...all I fancied...a daughter of...my own...would be..."

Journey choked out a "Thank you" on broken sobs.

"Don't go...thanking me. You want to say...thanks, you take...care of my boy." Miss Rose pushed her head back into her pillow, arching slightly as she tried to draw in enough air. "You all...take care of...each other..."

A sudden slump and an easy smile across her face announced her passing. Reed drew his aunt into a final embrace as Journey sobbed, rocking in her seat.

Zane drew Journey close and shed a few tears of his own.

Chapter Forty

December 1870, Montana

Journey stepped from the lukewarm water and toweled herself dry. She donned her dressing gown and brushed her damp hair back to dry in the heat of the fireplace. Tomorrow would be Christmas Eve, and the last of the patients had been sent home a couple of days ago. The epidemic had hit the town hard, but Doc Ferris thought it might have been worse. Another note of praise in the joyous season.

Curling onto the rocking chair—Miss Rose's rocking chair—she thumbed her Bible open to read. She'd been working through the Gospel of John on Zane's suggestion.

There was so much to learn, so much she didn't understand. But each week she'd take her questions to Zane. And each week he'd shed more light.

She read for an hour, maybe more judging from the way the fire's flames had subsided. She stood and stretched, then pulled on her long coat and twisted her hair under her shapeless hat. The bathwater would be cool enough by now to dump.

Dragging the metal tub through the back door, she tilted it into the snow. Her gaze scanned along the moonlit ridge as a shadowed form of horse and rider appeared on the rise above the kitchen. Zane.

She returned the tub to the pantry and buttoned her coat over her robe, then moved to meet him at the front door.

He pulled up short next to the porch, and she saw another horse tethered behind Malachi when Zane dismounted. He nudged his Stetson from his head just enough to peer up at her. "Evening, Journey," he said.

"What brings you out this time of night?"

"I apologize for the hour. I meant to get by earlier but got called over to the Hamlers' to help shore up the barn roof. Can we talk?"

"Do you want to come in?"

His eyes caught the light and a grin tugged on his lips. "'Avoid every appearance of evil,' Journey. I can't. You come here."

Her cheeks grew warm as she moved down the steps. She fished a crumbling lump of sugar from her pocket and offered it to Malachi, scratching his nose as he ate it. "I'm sorry I don't have any for your friend," she told the horse. "What's her name?"

"Actually, she hasn't been named yet," Zane said, speaking of the mare. "That's up to you."

She turned to face him, almost knocking into his broad chest. She stepped back to a more comfortable distance. "What do you mean?"

"Merry Christmas, Journey. The mare is yours, if you want her."

She looked at the sturdy little horse with surprise. "For me?"

He nodded. "I didn't have anything ready at the time, but I do feel kind of responsible for your horse. I mean, there's not a thing I could've done different to save it, but I felt bad that it had to be done, just the same."

"I was angry at you for a long time because of that, you know." She smiled, moving toward the tethered horse. Her honey-gold coat shone, brushed carefully over sleek muscles.

"Even yet?"

"No. There have been a lot of changes in me since September. But you didn't have to do this. Homer's mine now, I guess." She shook her head, blowing softly on the mare's nose. "I still can't believe Miss Rose left this whole place to me. She was a good woman."

Zane looked toward the barn and nodded in agreement. "That she was." A moment passed. "I wanted to talk with you, Journey, about your plans."

"Plans?"

"You know, now that you've been cleared of charges. Now that you're free to come and go as you please without watching over your shoulder." He shrugged. "I know you've been waiting for spring so you could move on. I guess it's…well, is that still the case?"

She stroked the horse's tawny hide. "I hadn't really considered it much. I've been sorting through things, trying to move on without Miss Rose here. Learning more about God and what He wants from me. I've spent most of my life running from something or other, Zane. I guess I'm trying to learn how to sit still."

"So you're staying?"

She concentrated on the horse's dark mane. "How important is it to you?"

His hand on her shoulder turned her to face him. He stared hard a moment, his gray eyes looking almost black in the darkness, then drew her close. Sweeping the hat from his head allowed the moon to create a halo of light on his brown hair. He ducked, tilting her chin so he could slip under the wide brim of her hat.

She closed her eyes as the warmth of his lips melted hers. Their pressure brushed along her cheek to her ear, into her hair as her hat slipped back, letting several heavy curls escape. He smelled of leather and wintergreen, filling her senses. Her body relaxed and she leaned toward him only an instant before he pulled away.

"I'm sorry," he whispered, but somehow he didn't sound completely sincere. "This isn't the order I meant to take."

She squeezed his arms, pulling him in to kiss his cheek. "What are you saying?"

He smiled and placed his hat back on his head, adjusting hers as well. "I learned a lot since September, too. I learned that I love you more than I wanted to admit. I learned that I can do that without forgetting Sarah. I want—that is, what I'm trying to say is—"

"I love you, too." She smiled, happy tears blurring her vision.

Zane laughed, a deep, rolling sound. "So now, for my Christmas present—will you marry me?"

Joy filled her. But... "What about my past? There'll be those who aren't so willing to forgive as you. What will Mrs. Decker say? She's had you picked for her son-in-law for a long time."

"It doesn't matter. I'll preach a series of sermons on gossip and forgiveness, and we'll work through it. Just say you'll have me and that you won't leave." He gathered her in his arms and held her close. She heard his heart pounding at her ear, strong and true.

It felt like home.

"Yes," she said. "Yes, I'll marry you."

His arms drew her tighter, his chin caressing her head. Would she ever begin to comprehend God's goodness?

She stood with him in the moonlight, happy in the love she felt. Never had Christmas meant more, knowing Christ's heart, and that of this wonderful man. A sudden thought brought her back to peer into his eyes, teasing. "Why bring the horse? Is it a bribe?"

"Not exactly." He sighed. "I didn't want your not having transportation away from Walten to be an excuse for marrying me."

She giggled. "You're saying taking this horse and heading west might be a smarter option?"

"That could well be." He laughed. "But she won't love you like I do."

His arms slid from her and she shivered in the sudden chill. His hand gripped hers. "So have you come up with a name for your mare?"

She hugged his arm, leaning against him as they looked the horse over together, standing under the light of the Christmas moon shining down over the crests of snow on the ridges around the ranch.

"I think I'll call her Dweller, Zane. Because we're both here to stay."

* * * * *

Linda Ford lives on a ranch in Alberta, Canada, near enough to the Rocky Mountains that she can enjoy them on a daily basis. She and her husband raised fourteen children—four homemade, ten adopted. She currently shares her home and life with her husband, a grown son, a live-in paraplegic client and a continual (and welcome) stream of kids, kids-in-law, grandkids and assorted friends and relatives.

Books by Linda Ford

Love Inspired Historical

Big Sky Country

Montana Cowboy Daddy
Montana Cowboy Family
Montana Cowboy's Baby
Montana Bride by Christmas
Montana Groom of Convenience
Montana Lawman Rescuer

Montana Cowboys

The Cowboy's Ready-Made Family
The Cowboy's Baby Bond
The Cowboy's City Girl

Christmas in Eden Valley

A Daddy for Christmas
A Baby for Christmas
A Home for Christmas

Visit the Author Profile page
at Harlequin.com for more titles.

THE PATH TO HER HEART

Linda Ford

Jesus Christ the same yesterday,
and to day, and for ever.
—*Hebrews* 13:8

To my friend Alma, who has always been such a faithful encourager in my faith walk.

Chapter One

Favor, South Dakota 1934

They represented all she wanted.

They were everything she could never have.

The pair caught twenty-four-year-old Emma Spencer's attention as she made her way home. The way the tall man bent to the sweet little boy at his side, the tenderness in his gesture as he adjusted the child's hat and straightened his tweed coat brought a sting of unexpected tears to her eyes.

The child said something, and the man squatted to eye level, took the boy's chin between long fingers and smiled as he answered. Even from where she stood, Emma could see strong and assuring depths in his dark eyes. Then he straightened, his expression determined, and stared across the street.

Emma ducked, afraid he'd notice her interest and think her unduly curious. But she couldn't resist a guarded look at the pair.

The boy took the man's hand. The man picked up a battered suitcase and they continued on.

Emma's throat closed so tightly that she struggled to breathe. An ache as wide as the Dakota prairies sucked at her thoughts. Just a few steps away, across the wind-swept, dusty street, stood the embodiment of all she longed for—a strong, caring man and a dear little child. She mentally shook herself. Although it was not to be, she had no reason to begrudge the fact. She loved being a nurse. She loved helping people. Most of all, she had a responsibility to her parents and brother, struggling to survive the drought and Depression on the farm back home. They depended on the money she sent from her wages each month. She thought of her brother, Sid, and drew in a steadying breath to stop a shiver of guilt. She waited for her lungs to ease and let her usually buried dreams subside into wispy clouds she knew would drift across her thoughts from time to time, like the straw-colored autumn leaves skittering past her feet.

The pair turned in at Ada Adams's boardinghouse and stopped at the front door, side-by-side, tall and straight as two soldiers. She smiled at the way the boy glanced at the man to see if he imitated the stance correctly.

The door opened. Gray-haired Ada reached out and hugged them each in turn, then drew them inside.

Emma gasped and halted her journey toward the boardinghouse. This must be the nephew—a widower— Ada expected. Somehow Emma anticipated an older man with a much older son. Truthfully, Emma had paid little attention when Ada made the announcement of their impending arrival. She'd simply been relieved Ada finally decided to get help running the house. The work was far too much for the older woman, suffering from arthritis. Now Emma wished she'd thought to have asked some questions. How old was the man? How old his son? How long was he staying? What had Ada said happened to his wife? Ada might have answered all her questions but Emma had been dashing out the door and hadn't stopped to listen to the whole story.

Emma hesitated, calming her too eager desire to follow this pair. She glanced at her sturdy white shoes. Her white uniform revealed the evidence of a hard day at the hospital. The weather had been cool when she left before dawn and she'd worn her woolen cape, but now the sun shone warmly and she carried her cape over her arm.

She needed a few minutes to collect her thoughts and seek a solution to this sudden yearning. Rather than cross to the boardinghouse, she continued along the sidewalk with no destination in mind, simply the need to think in solitude.

She passed yards enclosed by picket fences. Mr. Blake fussed about his flower beds, preparing them to survive a bitter South Dakota winter. She called a greeting and he waved.

Praying silently, she circled the block. *Lord, God, You know the road before me. You know I don't resent my responsibility. In fact, I am grateful as can be for this job and the chance to help my parents. It's only occasionally I wish for things that might have been. This is one of those times. I thought I had dealt with my disappointment and buried my dreams, but it seems they don't have the decency to stay dead and buried. Yet I will not fret about it. I know You will give me the strength to do what I must. In Thee do I rejoice. Blessed be Your name.*

A smile curved her lips as peace flooded her heart.

She knew what she had to do, how she had to face the future, and she would gladly do it.

Her resolve restored, she walked back to the boardinghouse. Only for a second did her feet falter as she remembered Ada's nephew's dark eyes and the way he smiled at his small son. A tiny sound of disgust escaped her lips. She wasn't one to let fanciful notions fill her head. No. She was the kind to do what had to be done. No one and nothing would divert her from her responsibilities. She tipped her thoughts back to her prayer. God would help her. Yet, it might prove prudent to avoid as much contact with the nephew as possible. Certainly they would sit around the same table for meals but apart from that...

She suddenly chuckled. The man might be unbearably rude or snobbish, even if in those few moments as he encouraged his son, he'd touched her heart.

Her smile flattened. Rogue or otherwise, she needn't worry. He'd probably not even notice her. She was no china doll. Her eyes should have been blue to go with her blond hair. Instead she had dark brown eyes, equally dark lashes and brows. Too often people gave her a strange look as if startled by the contrast. She'd been told many times it gave her a look of determination— a woman more suited for work than romance. Yet...

She pushed away useless dreams, straightened her shoulders and stepped into the warm house.

She thought of slipping up the stairs to change, but she would only be avoiding the inevitable. Sooner or later she'd have to meet the man. Besides, despite the rumpled state of her uniform, wearing it made her feel strong and competent. A glance in the hall mirror, a tuck of some loose strands of hair into her thick bun and she headed into the kitchen.

He stood with his back to her. He'd shed his coat. He was thin as were many people after years of drought and Depression prices. His shoulders were wide and square, and he was even taller than she'd thought—six foot or better, if she didn't miss her guess. His hair was brown as a warm mink coat.

She blamed the hot cookstove for the way her cheeks stung with heat.

Ada leaned to the right so she could see past her nephew. "Emma, I told you my nephew, Boothe, was coming."

The man faced her. His eyes weren't dark as she first thought; they only appeared so because they were deep-set and gray as a winter sky, filling her heart with a raging storm to rival any blizzard she'd ever experienced.

"Boothe Wallace." Ada's voice came like a faint call on a breeze as Emma's emotions ran the gamut of longing, loneliness and finally into self-disgust that she couldn't better control her thoughts.

"Boothe, this is one of my guests, Emma Spencer."

Emma, her feelings firmly under control, stepped forward but halted as his expression grew forbidding.

His gaze raced over her uniform, pausing at the blotch where she'd tried to erase evidence of a young patient's vomit.

She wished she'd taken the time to change. "I'm sorry," she murmured, forcing the words past the blockage in her throat. "I just got off work."

"A nurse." Boothe's words carried a condemning tone, though Emma could think of no reason for it.

She'd given him no cause to object to anything she'd done or not done.

"She works at the hospital," Ada explained. "And this little fellow is Boothe's son, Jessie."

Boothe showed no sign of moving over to allow Emma to meet the boy, so she stepped sideways. Jessie perched on the table. He gave her a shy, glancing smile, allowing her a glimpse of startlingly blue eyes. She wanted to sweep the adorable child into her arms. She wisely restrained herself. She loved working with children best. Her superiors praised her rapport with them.

The boy wore an almost new shirt of fine cotton and knickers of good quality wool. Compared to his father's well-worn clothes, Jessie was dressed like a prince.

"I'm happy to meet you, Jessie," she said in the soft tone she reserved for children and frightened patients. "How old are you?"

He darted another glance at her and smiled so wide she ached to ruffle his sandy-colored hair. "Six." His voice had a gritty sound as if he wanted everyone to forget he was a little boy and think he was a man.

That's when she saw the deep slash on his arm and the blood-soaked rag that had recently been removed. "You've been hurt. What happened?" Instinctively, she stepped forward, intent on examining the wound.

"Ran into a sticking out nail. Daddy got really mad at the man pushing the cart." He gave the cut a look, shuddered and turned away, but not before she got a glimpse of his tears. The wound had to hurt like fury. It was deep and gaping, but a few stitches would fix it up and he'd heal neatly as long as he didn't get an infection—and unless it was properly cleaned, he stood a good chance of just that. Dirt blackened the edges of the cut. "I'll clean it for you, and then your father can take you to the doctor."

But before she reached Jessie's side, Boothe stepped in front of her.

"No doctor. No nurse." His harsh tone sent a shudder along Emma's spine. "I'll take care of him myself." His stubborn stance was a marked contrast to the tenderness he'd exhibited a short time ago on the street.

She thought she must have misunderstood him. "It needs cleaning and stitching. I can do the former but a good doctor should do the latter." Again she moved to take over the chore.

Again he blocked her. "I'll be the one taking care of my son."

The challenge in his eyes felt like a spear to her heart, but she wouldn't let it deter her. "Your son needs medical attention."

"I don't need the bungling interference of either a doctor or a nurse." He'd lowered his voice so only Emma heard him.

She recoiled from the venomous accusation. "I do *not* bungle."

He held his hand toward her, palm forward, effectively forbidding her to go any farther.

She clasped her hands at her waist, squeezed her fingers hard enough to hurt and clamped her mouth shut to stop the angry protest. How dare this man judge her incompetent! But even more, how could he ignorantly, stubbornly, put his son at risk? Too many times she'd seen the sorry result of home remedies. She'd seen children suffer needlessly because their parents refused to take them to the doctor until their injuries or illnesses

pushed them to the verge of death. She shuddered, recalling some who came too late.

He turned back to his aunt. "Would you have a
basin?"

Ada's eyes were wary as if wondering if she should
intervene then she gave a barely perceptible shrug,
pulled one from the cupboard and handed it to him.

Boothe's demanding gaze forbade Emma to interfere. When he seemed confident she'd stand back, he
turned to his son. "Jessie, I'm going to clean this and
then I'll bandage it."

Boothe filled a basin as Emma helplessly looked on.
It took a great deal of self-discipline to stand by when
little Jessie sent her a frightened look as if begging her
to promise everything would be okay. Unfortunately,
she couldn't give such assurance. The wound continued
to bleed. One good thing about the flow of blood—it
served to cleanse the deeper tissues.

Boothe dipped a clean cloth in the water. Jessie
whimpered. "Now, son. I won't hurt you any more than
I need to. You know that?"

Jessie nodded and blinked back tears.

"You be a brave man and this will be done sooner
than you know."

Jessie pressed his lips together and nodded again.

Emma admired the little boy's bravery. She watched
with hawk-like concentration as Boothe cleaned the
edges of the wound. He did a reasonably good job but
it didn't satisfy Emma. She itched to pour on a good
dose of disinfectant. Iodine was her first choice. She'd
never seen a wound infect if it'd been properly doused
with the potent stuff. She opened her mouth to make a
suggestion but Boothe's warning glance made her swal-

low back the words. The boy would have a terrible scar without stitches, and the wound would keep bleeding for an unnecessarily long time.

"Aunt Ada, do you have a clean rag?" Boothe asked. Ada handed him an old sheet.

No, Emma mentally screamed. *At least use something sterile.* "I could get dressings from the hospital," she offered, ignoring his frown.

"This will do just fine." He tore the fabric into strips.

Anger, like hot coals to her heart, surged through her. How could this man be so stubborn? Why did he resist medical help with such blindness?

Ignoring her, though he couldn't help but be aware of her scowling concern, he pressed the edges of the wound together and wrapped it securely with the cloth, fixing the end in place with the pin Ada handed him then stepped back, pleased with his work.

Emma watched the bandage, knowing it would soon pinken with blood. By the time Boothe had washed and cleaned up, the telltale pink was the size of a quarter. She could be silent no longer. "Without stitches it will continue to bleed. You need to take him to the doctor."

Boothe, drying his hands on a kitchen towel, shot her a look fit to sear her skin. "We do not need or want to see a doctor. They do more harm than good."

Emma shifted her gaze to Jessie, saw his eyes wide with what she could only assume was fear. Her insides settled into hardness. "May I speak with you privately?" She addressed Boothe, well aware of Ada's tight smile and Jessie's stark stare.

"I don't think that's necessary."

"I do." She moved to the doorway and waited for him to join her in the hall. She wondered if he would simply ignore her, but with a resigned sigh, he strode across the room, his movements and expression saying he hoped it wouldn't take long, because he was only doing his best to avoid a scene.

She went to the front door so their conversation wouldn't be overheard in the kitchen. "I am deeply concerned about your attitude toward the medical profession. Not only does it prevent you from taking your son to the doctor for needed care but it is instilling in him an unnecessary and potentially dangerous fear of doctors. There could come a time when it is a matter of life or death that he seek medical attention." She couldn't shake her initial response to the man, couldn't stop herself from being attracted to his looks, his demeanor and his gentleness toward his son. Yet he was ignorant and stubborn about medical things—the sort of man who normally filled her with undiluted anger.

"Do you realize this is none of your business?"

She didn't answer. A person didn't interfere with how a man raised his children—one of the unwritten laws of their society. But she could not, *would* not, stand by silently while someone was needlessly put at risk. *Never again.*

He suddenly leaned closer, his gray eyes as cold as a prairie winter storm. "I've seen firsthand the damage medical people inflict. I will not subject my son to that."

She drew back, startled by his vehemence. "Our goal is to help and heal, not damage."

His nostrils flared, his eyes narrowed. He sucked in air like someone punched him. "My wife is dead because of medical 'help.'"

His words filtered through her senses as shock, surprise, sympathy and sorrow mixed together. "I'm—"

"Don't bother trying to defend them."

She had been about to express her sympathy not defend a situation she knew nothing about, but he didn't seem to care to hear anything from her and rushed on.

"They poisoned her. Pure and simple. Overdosed her with quinine. The judge ruled it accidental. He reprimanded them for carelessness, but they got away with murder. So you see—" he took a deep breath and settled back on his heels "—I have good reason to avoid the medical profession and good reason to teach my son to do so as w ell."

Emma wondered why quinine had been prescribed. It was often used to treat fevers or irregular heartbeats. Adverse reactions were common but reversible. Although she'd never seen toxicity, she knew it involved heart problems as well as seizures and coma. How dreadful to see it happen to a loved one. And so needless. An attentive nurse should have picked up the symptoms immediately.

Determined not to let her tears surface, Emma widened her eyes. "I'm sorry. It should have never happened. But it's not fair to think all of us are careless."

"Do you think I'm going to take a chance?"

They faced each other. His eyes looked as brittle as hers felt. He was wrong in thinking he couldn't trust another doctor or nurse. It put both himself and Jessie at risk. But she didn't have to read minds to know he wasn't about to be convinced otherwise. Her shoulders sagged as she gave up the idea of trying. "I'm sorry about your loss, but aren't you spreading blame a little too thick and wide? Allowing it to cloud your judgment?"

He snorted. "I realize we are destined to live in the

same house and I intend to be civil. But I warn you not to interfere with how I raise my son."

Emma scooped her cape off the banister and headed up the stairs, her emotions fluctuating between anger and pity. But she had to say something. Her conscience would not allow her to ignore the situation. She turned. "Sometimes, Mr. Wallace, a person has to learn to trust or he puts himself and others at risk."

Boothe made an explosive sound. His expression grew thunderous.

Emma met his look without flinching. There was no reason she should want to reach out and smooth away the harsh lines in his face. Except, she reluctantly admitted, her silly reaction to a little scene on the sidewalk.

"Trust." He snorted. "From here on out, I trust no one." He pursed his lips. "No one."

He'd been badly hurt. But he verged on becoming bitter. Silently, she prayed for wisdom to say the right thing. "Not even God?" She spoke softly.

He stood rigid as a fence post for a moment then his shoulders sank. "I'm trying to trust Him." His head down, he headed back to the kitchen.

"I will pray for you, Boothe Wallace."

Chapter Two

Boothe stayed out of sight of the kitchen door to compose himself. Jessie had enough fears to deal with without seeing his father upset. He hoped seeing Emma in her nurse's uniform wouldn't remind Jessie of that awful time two years ago when Alyse had been murdered by a negligent doctor. Aided and abetted by a belligerent nurse. The doctor said it would stop her fluttering heartbeat that left her weak. Instead, it had succeeded in stopping her heart completely. The judge might have ruled the incident accidental, but Boothe considered it murder. There was no other word for giving a killing dose of medicine. Alyse hadn't stood a chance. He shuddered back the memory of her violent seizures.

And for Emma to suggest he should trust! She didn't know the half of it. He'd trusted too easily. It cost him his wife. No. He would not trust again. Ever.

Not even God? Her words rang through his head. Even trusting God had grown difficult. One thing forced him to make the choice to do so—Jessie. He feared for his son's safety if God didn't protect him.

Hopefully, his trust would not be misplaced. *Trust in the Lord with all thine heart; and lean not unto thine own understanding. In all thy ways acknowledge Him, and He shall direct thy paths.* He knew the words well. However, reciting verses was far easier than having the assurance the words promised.

He drew in a deep breath. Why hadn't Aunt Ada warned him one of her guests was a nurse? But then what difference would it have made? Leaving Lincoln, Nebraska, and moving to South Dakota had been the only way to escape the threat he faced back in the city of losing Jessie. Besides, there was no work back there and he'd been evicted from his shabby apartment. Here Jessie was safe with him. He could put up with an interfering nurse for Jessie's sake. He would forget about Emma and the way her brown eyes melted with gentleness one moment and burned with fury the next. He smiled knowing he'd annoyed her as much as she annoyed him. Why that should amuse him, he couldn't say. But it did.

He paused outside the kitchen.

"Where did my daddy go?" His son's voice had a brittle edge signaling his distress. Poor Jessie had dealt with far too much in the past two years, but these past two weeks had been especially upsetting with losing their home and then being snatched away from his Aunt Vera and Uncle Luke. Jessie did not understand the reasons behind this sudden move. But it had been unavoidable. Trusting his sister-in-law had almost proven a disaster. Boothe only hoped Favor would be far enough from Lincoln.

Aunt Ada, bless her heart, answered Jessie soothingly. "He's just in the other room. He'll be back shortly."

"Is my daddy mad?"

Aunt Ada chuckled. "I can't say for sure, but I don't think it's anything we need to worry about."

"Is my arm going to fall off?"

Boothe stepped into the room intent on reassuring his son. The bandage already needed changing. "Your arm is going to be all right." He kept all traces of anger from his voice even though he silently blamed Emma for frightening Jessie.

"But that lady—"

"Emma?" Aunt Ada prompted.

"Yes, Emma—"

"*Miss* Emma to you," Boothe said.

"Miss Emma. She's a nurse. She said—"

"I'll wrap your arm better. It will be just fine." *Thank you, Miss Emma, for alarming an innocent child.* He gently took off the soiled dressing, tore up more strips and created a pad. "Aunt Ada, do you have adhesive tape?"

"In the left-hand drawer." She pointed toward the cupboard. He found the tape and cut several pieces, using them to close the edges of the cut before he applied the pad. He wrapped it with fresh lengths of the old sheet and pinned the end. "There. You'll soon be good as new."

Jessie nodded, his blue gaze bright. "I don't need a doctor, do I?"

Boothe kept his voice steady despite the anger twitching at his insides. "Jessie, my boy, a man does not run to the doctor every time he gets a cut. Okay?"

"Okay." He slid his gaze to Aunt Ada. "Miss Emma lives here?"

"Yes. Did you like her?"

"She has a nice smile."

Boothe shot Aunt Ada a warning glance. "Where do you want us to put our stuff?"

Aunt Ada winked at Boothe. "She's a nice woman. Knows her own mind. I admire that in a person."

Jessie nodded vigorously. "Me, too."

Boothe grabbed the suitcase, wanting nothing more than to end this conversation. He did not want Jessie getting interested in Emma.

"I've made space for you in the back of the store-room. Sorry I can't offer you a bedroom but the upstairs ones are all rented, for which I thank God. And I don't intend to give up mine."

"I'm sure we'll be more than comfortable." Boothe fell in beside Aunt Ada as she limped toward the back of the kitchen. Jessie followed on his heels.

The room was large, full of cupboards stacked with canned goods, bottles of home preserves, tins and sacks of everything from oats to bay leaves. Spicy, homey smells filled the air. He tightened his jaw, remembering when such aromas, such sights, meant home. With forced determination he finished his visual inspection of the room. Two narrow side-by-side cots and a tall dresser fit neatly along the far wall. A window with a green shade rolled almost to the top gave natural light. "This is more than adequate. Thank you."

"Is this our place?" Jessie asked.

"For as long as you want," Aunt Ada said.

A load of weight slid from Boothe's shoulders. They would be safe here. And maybe one day in the unforeseeable future, they might even be happy again. "I can't thank you enough."

Jessie kicked off his boots, plopped down on one bed, his bony knees crooked toward the ceiling. "I had a room of my own at Auntie Vera's."

Boothe had been forced to leave Jessie with Vera on school days and often on weekends as he tried to find enough work to make ends meet. He hadn't liked it, though he appreciated that Jessie had a safe place to stay.

He hadn't expected it to be a complete mistake.

"No thanks needed." Ada grinned at him. "You'll be earning your keep sure enough. Things have been neglected of late. I can't get around like I used to."

"I'm here to help. Tell me what you need done."

"I'd appreciate if you look after the furnace first. Emma's been kind enough to do it but she's a paying guest."

"I'll tend to it. Jessie, your books and toys are in the suitcase. I'll be back in a few minutes."

Jessie bolted to his feet and scrambled into his boots, ignoring the dragging laces as he scurried after Boothe.

Boothe should have known the boy wouldn't let him out of his sight. He squatted down to face Jessie. "I don't want you to come downstairs with me." He had no idea what condition the cellar was in. It might not be safe for a six-year-old. "You go with Aunt Ada and wait for me. I'll be back as soon as I can."

Jessie's eyes flooded with fear.

Boothe squeezed his son's shoulder. He hated leaving him but Jessie was safe. Sooner or later he'd have to get used to the fact his father had to leave him at times. But he'd learn that Boothe would always return.

Aunt Ada took Jessie's hand. "I have a picture book you might like to see."

Boothe nodded his thanks as his aunt led Jessie back to the kitchen table. Only then did he venture down the worn wooden steps. He found the furnace and fed it, dragged the ashes into the ash pail then looked around the cavernous cellar. Bins built along one side contained potatoes and a variety of root vegetables. He hadn't been to Aunt Ada's in years but as a kid had spent several summers visiting her. He remembered her huge garden in the adjoining lot. But she had been quick and light on her feet back then. Now she moved as if every joint hurt. Did she still grow everything the household consumed?

Boxes were stacked on wide shelves. He opened one and saw a collection of magazines. The next held rags. Another seemed to be full of men's clothes. He couldn't imagine whose they were, seeing as Aunt Ada had never married. Perhaps a guest had left them behind. He pulled out a pair of trousers and held them to his waist. He found a heavy coat, a pair of sagging boots and a variety of shirts. He'd ask Aunt Ada about the things. They were better than anything he owned. Despite his disappointment at Vera's treachery, he allowed himself a moment of gratitude for the fine clothes she bought Jesse.

He carried the pail of ashes upstairs and paused, breathing in the aroma of pork roast and applesauce. The furnace hummed and the warmth of coal heat spread about him. This was a good place to be. Safe and solid. He tilted his head toward the kitchen as he heard Jessie.

"When will my daddy come back?" His voice crackled with tension.

Boothe hurried to the back door to get rid of the ash bucket.

Emma's gentle voice answered Jessie. "Your daddy is taking care of the furnace so you'll stay warm. What did he say when he went to the cellar?"

"He said he'd be back as soon as he could."

"There you go. Even when you can't see him, you can remember what he said."

Boothe stood stock-still as Emma reassured Jessie. A blizzard of emotions raced through him—gratitude that she dealt with Jessie so calmly, soothingly. Anger and frustration that Jessie had to confront the fear of loss. Children his age should be secure in the love of a mother and father. Most of all, emptiness sucked at his gut making him feel as naked, exposed and helpless as a tree torn from the ground by a tornado, roots and all. The future stretched out as barren as the drought-stricken prairies. This was not how he'd envisioned his life. Nope, in his not-so-long-ago plans there'd been a woman who shared his home and made it a welcoming place.

He clenched his jaw so hard his teeth ached. He'd come here to find peace and safety. In the space of half an hour, Emma had robbed him of that, not once, but twice. Thankfully he wouldn't have to see her more than a few minutes each day—only long enough to share a meal with all the boarders.

He deposited the bucket on the flagstone sidewalk where it would be unable to start a fire. The wind made the ashes glow red. Dust sifted across the backyard. Late October often meant snow, which would settle the dust. But this year the snow had not come. Only the endless wind. He lifted his face to the sky. *God, when will this end?* He couldn't say exactly what he meant. The drought? The nationwide Depression? His loneliness? Jessie's fears? He supposed he meant all of them.

Not that he expected divine intervention. Seems a man just did what he could and hoped for the best. He hadn't received what he considered best, or even good, in a long time. He tried to find anything good in his life. Right now, about all he could give that label to was Jessie. He paused…and this house. He headed to the kitchen.

Jessie sat at the table, a coloring book and crayons before him, but he paid more attention to Emma than his coloring. Emma stood at the stove stirring something while Aunt Ada carved the pork roast. Emma had changed into a black skirt and pale blue sweater. She glanced up as he stepped into the room and her gaze collided with his. Her dark eyes were a surprising contrast to her golden hair. If he didn't know she was a nurse, he might think her an attractive woman.

He hurried to her side and reached for the spoon. "I've come to help Aunt Ada. Now that I'm here, there's no reason for one of the boarders to work." His voice was harsher than he intended and caused the two women to stare at him.

Jessie stiffened. His eyes grew wide and wary.

"What I meant is you're a paying guest. You shouldn't have to help." He forced a smile to his lips and tried to put a smile in his voice. He knew he failed miserably.

He felt Emma, inches away at his elbow, studying him, but refused to meet her gaze until she laughed and he jerked around in surprise. Her eyes glistened with amusement, and her smile seemed to go on forever. He couldn't breathe as it brushed his heart. He shook his head, angry at himself and his silly imaginations.

"Here you go." She handed him the spoon and a jar full of white liquid. "You do know how to make gravy?" Her words were round with barely restrained laughter.

He looked at the pot of bubbling liquid on the stove and the jar. He had no idea what he was expected to do.

Emma laughed low and sweet, tickling his insides. He fought his reaction. He could not allow a feeling at such odds with how he felt when he saw her in a nurse's uniform.

She laughed again. "A simple yes or no would suffice."

Behind him Aunt Ada chuckled.

"Daddy, you can make gravy?" Jessie's surprised awe brought more low laughter from Emma.

"I'm sure I could if someone would tell me how."

"Very well," Emma said. "Stir the juice and slowly pour the flour and water mixture in. The trick is to keep it from going lumpy."

Boothe followed the instructions as Emma hovered at his elbow watching him like a hungry eagle waiting for some helpless prey. A reluctant grin tugged at the corners of his mouth. His experience taught him nurses didn't care for anyone showing they might know a thing or two. He'd do this right if only to prove he was as capable as she.

The gravy thickened. "Smells good. How am I doing?"

She stepped back and considered him. "Are you sure you haven't done this before?"

He grinned, glad to have succeeded in the face of her doubt. "Cross my heart."

Aunt Ada laughed. "Maybe you could teach him to mash potatoes, too."

Emma didn't seem the least bit annoyed at his success. In fact, if her flashing smile meant anything, she seemed rather pleased about it.

He couldn't tear his gaze away from hers as something inside him, both exciting and alarming, demanded consideration. His stomach growled and he freed himself from her dark eyes. He was only hungry. Nothing more. "I'm sure I can learn to mash potatoes with the best of them."

Emma handed him a masher and pointed him toward the big pot. Not only was there pork roast, gravy and potatoes but there was a pot of turnips and a bowl of canned tomatoes. His mouth watered at the prospect of so much to eat. For months he'd been forced to ration every scrap of food he scrounged, glad Jessie was being well fed with Vera and Luke. All this abundance was unbelievable. God's blessing? A flash of hope and belief crossed his mind before he focused his attention on Emma's instructions.

"I think everything is ready," Aunt Ada said a few minutes later. "Jessie, do you want to help me ring the bell for supper?"

Jessie bounced off his chair and followed Ada into the hall. At the bottom of the stairs, she handed him a little brass bell and instructed him to shake it. He laughed at the racket it made. From upstairs came the sound of doors opening.

Emma scooped the potatoes into a bowl and poured the gravy into a large pitcher. "Help me carry in the food." She nodded toward Boothe.

He grabbed the platter of meat in one hand and the

gravy jug in the other and followed her into the dining room where the table was already set. He counted nine chairs. That made six paying guests. Quite a load for Aunt Ada. He intended to ease her load and find a job as well. He'd heard there was always work in the town of Favor, on the edge of the irrigation area.

Aunt Ada took her place at one end of the table and indicated Boothe should sit at the other end, Jessie at his right. "As soon as we're all here, I'll make the introductions."

People filed in, taking what seemed to be appointed places. As soon as each chair had a body behind it, Aunt Ada spoke. "I told you all that my nephew, Boothe, agreed to come and help me run the boardinghouse. The young man beside him is his son, Jessie."

Jessie pulled himself to rigid attention at being called a man.

Boothe grinned. His heart filled with pride.

One by one, Aunt Ada introduced the others starting on her right. "Loretta, one of my oldest and dearest friends."

The older, thin woman smiled at Aunt Ada before she turned to Boothe. "I'm glad you've come."

Beside her stood a woman, probably in her forties, Sarah, who had a dress shop downtown. Next, Betty, a chambermaid at the new hotel, a girl fresh off the farm if Boothe didn't miss his guess. He turned to those on the other side of the table. Beside Jessie stood Don, a man in his late twenties or early thirties, and next to him, Ed, an eager-faced young man who could barely tear his gaze away from Betty long enough to greet Boothe. Both men worked at the brick factory.

And then Emma. She grinned at him. "Boothe made

the gravy, so if you have any complaints, direct them to him, not me."

Don chuckled. "Emma's teasing you already. Best be careful. She can have you running in circles."

Boothe kept his expression bland. "I don't run in circles." Maybe not literally but she'd already proved her ability to send his thoughts down useless rabbit trails.

Aunt Ada cleared her throat. "Shall we pray?"

They all bowed as she offered up thanks for the food and for Boothe and Jessie's arrival. Her gratitude soothed away Boothe's tension.

Only then did they sit down.

The meal proved excellent, the conversation interesting. Ed and Don told him of the work in the factory.

"You could probably get a job there," Don said.

"I'll look into it." Boothe planned to check out a few other prospects first.

He expected the boarders would disperse as soon as they finished. Instead, everyone grabbed a handful of things and headed for the kitchen. The women began to wash and dry dishes while Ed and Don shook the tablecloth and arranged the chairs. Boothe tried to keep up but it seemed each knew what he or she was expected to do.

"Aunt Ada certainly has you organized."

"Not Ada," Don said. "She was reluctant to accept help. But when Emma saw how much pain she had, she got us all doing our share."

Emma. Boothe tried to think if it surprised him. She seemed the sort who liked to organize things. Or—his jaw tightened—did she like to be in control? Was it an innate part of being a nurse? Always in control. Always right.

As soon as the dishes were done, the guests moved into the front room. Emma carried in a large tray with a teapot under a knit cozy and cups for everyone. Aunt Ada brought in a plate of cookies. Again, everyone seemed to know what to do. They prepared tea to their liking, served themselves cookies and settled into one of the many chairs. Aunt Ada and Loretta sank into the burgundy couch.

"Do you mind if I give Jessie tea?" Emma asked. She held a cup almost full of milk.

"Can I, Daddy? Please."

Boothe nodded. He sat on one of the upright wooden chairs and edged another close for Jessie.

Emma sat beside the table and pulled a book to her lap. "We've been reading the biography of a missionary to China. You're welcome to join us."

"It will soon be Jessie's bedtime."

"We'll stop when it's time for him to get ready for bed."

Boothe didn't know if he liked the gentle way Emma smiled at his son. He wasn't about to trust another woman getting close to Jessie. He'd learned his lesson, but Jessie's eager expression convinced Boothe to agree to let him stay for the reading.

Loretta and Aunt Ada knitted as Emma read. Sarah sewed lace to a dress. Betty sat, her reddened hands idle, her expression rapt as she followed each word. Both Ed and Don leaned back, simply glad to relax. Emma read well, giving the story lots of drama, and Boothe was drawn into the tale.

Soon Emma closed the book. "End of chapter. I'm going to stop there so Jessie can go to bed."

Boothe jumped up, guilt flooding his thoughts. What

kind of father was he to forget his son's bedtime? "Come along, Jessie."

Jessie took his hand but stopped before Emma. "Thank you, Miss Emma. It's a good story. Is it really true?"

"It is. It's exciting to see how God did such wonderful things for them. Doesn't it make you feel safe and loved to know God does the same kinds of things for us?"

Jessie nodded vigorously.

A few minutes later, Boothe tucked him into bed.

"How long do we have to stay here?"

Boothe smoothed the covers over the small body. "I already told you. We're going to live here."

Jessie's eyes were dull with sleep yet he had enough energy to flash his angry displeasure. "Auntie Vera said we could live with her." His words quivered. "I want to live with her and Uncle Luke. I want to go home."

"This is home now. Besides, if we leave, you won't be able to hear the rest of Miss Emma's story." Boothe couldn't believe he'd used Emma as a reason to stay. *Only for Jessie's sake.*

Jessie rubbed his arm and gave Boothe a watery, defiant look. "My arm hurts. I want Auntie Vera."

Alarm snaked up Boothe's spine. Were Jessie's cheeks flushed? Was he fevered? He pressed his palm to his son's forehead. Did he seem warm? Boothe didn't know.

He pulled the covers down and looked at the dressing. A spot of pink stained it. He touched the skin on either side of the white cloth. Did it seem hot? Or was it simply warm from Jessie having his arm under the covers?

Boothe eased the blanket back to Jessie's chin. He had Emma to thank for stirring up unnecessary fears. The wound would heal just fine. Jessie was safer without the interference of any nurse or doctor.

He'd seen Emma eye Jessie's arm several times throughout the meal and afterward. She would do well to respect his wishes for his son. He would not allow an interfering woman—no matter how kind she seemed—to put his child at risk. Nor let his heart wish things could be different.

Chapter Three

Her bedroom lay in late fall darkness. Emma rolled over, turned on her bedside lamp, pulled her Bible to her chest and read a few verses. She prayed for her parents and her brother. *Lord, make sure they're warm and have enough to eat.* Last winter they'd run low on coal and used it so sparingly that the house was always cold. While she was grateful for a warm, safe place to live, she felt guilty knowing Sid and her parents did not enjoy the same luxuries.

As soon as she finished her prayers, she'd run down to the basement and stir up the furnace. She paused. Was the house already warm? Had Boothe already stoked up the fire? How pleasant to waken to a warm room. She returned to her prayers, bringing her patients before God. A couple had been in the hospital for several weeks, fighting dust pneumonia. *Lord, a good snowfall would put an end to the dust. But You know that. Just as You know everything we need.* She prayed for friends and neighbors. Finally, when she couldn't put it off any longer, she prayed for Boothe. There was something about him that upset her equilibrium. She didn't like it. *Lord, help him learn to trust again. And heal Jessie's wound.* She'd heard Jessie crying in the night. It was all she could do not to run down and check on him. That wound was nasty and no doubt painful. But Boothe had forbidden her to do anything for his son.

She took time to thank God for all the good things in her life. Unable to avoid the truth, she thanked her Lord for Boothe. *He's an answer to prayer for Ada, even though he is certainly not the man I would have sent to help. But again, You know best. Perhaps he needs something he will find here.*

She jumped from bed, dashed across the hall to the washroom and splashed water over her face. Back in her room she pulled on white stockings, slipped into her uniform and pinned a clean apron on top. She toed into her white shoes, tied them neatly then headed downstairs to help Ada with breakfast.

At the kitchen door, she halted.

Boothe presided over the stove, frying bacon. Ada tended to the toast. A pot of coffee bubbled. Emma turned to the dining room, intent on setting the table. She stopped at the doorway. "The table's set."

"Boothe did it," Ada said. "He's catching on quickly."

"I noticed the house is already warm. That's nice." Emma glanced at Boothe. He looked smug as if expecting he'd surprised her.

She shifted her gaze away. She wasn't sure what to do with herself nor where to look, and headed for the window. The square of light revealed the yellowed grass scattered with dried leaves. Emma shivered then turned to catch Boothe watching her.

"It's going to be cold today." He offered her a cup of coffee.

She took it and cradled her hands around its warmth. "I heard Jessie in the night. Is he okay?"

"He's sleeping. I'll leave him until he needs to get ready for school."

"Was his cut hurting him?"

Boothe glowered at her. "He had a nightmare. It will take him a few days to feel secure here."

"It's got to be hard for him." Losing his mother and moving to a strange place. "But please keep an eye on that wound. Infection can be deadly."

"I know enough to take care of my son without your help, if you don't mind." His expression grew darker but she refused to be intimidated. As a nurse, she faced disagreeable patients and families and dealt with them kindly, realizing their anger wasn't directed at her personally. Only with Boothe, it felt personal. She smiled as much to calm herself as to convey kindness to Boothe. She would act professionally even with a man who despised her profession.

The boarders trickled in for breakfast. Loretta never joined them. She had no reason to be up so early. The others gathered round the table, for the most part eating without speaking.

"No snow. That's good," Betty said. "Do you know how much mess snow makes on the floors?" She seemed to be the only one who woke up bright and cheerful.

"Snow would settle the dust and perhaps end the drought."

Emma jerked her head up at Boothe's soft voice, surprised by the emotion hidden in his words. His eyes darkened as he looked deep into her soul. She felt a connection, a shared sorrow at the sad state of the economy, an acknowledgment that life was difficult. Then he shuttered his feelings and his brow furrowed as if she'd overstepped some boundary.

She turned back to her breakfast. He didn't need to fear she'd be intruding into his life. She had more important things to attend to. Besides, she did not want to feel a connection to this man. He was dismissive almost to the point of rudeness and refused medical attention for his son. He'd branded her and the whole medical society because of a terrible accident. Tears stung her eyes at the stupidity that caused the death of his wife. She blinked them away and forced her thoughts to other things—like her responsibilities. She would do all she could to make life more tolerable for Sid and their parents.

Don spoke, thankfully pulling her from her troubled thoughts. "Boothe, did you want me to ask about a job at the factory?"

"Not yet but thanks for offering. I'm hoping to find a job that allows me to be home until Jessie leaves for school. I don't expect I'll be able to be home right after, but I'm grateful Aunt Ada will be here."

The smile he sent his aunt filled Emma with alarming confusion. A man of such contrasts, full of tenderness to his son, warmth to his aunt, cold disapproval to Emma.

Betty jumped up and gathered her dishes. "Gotta run."

Ed followed hard on her heels. Emma grinned after the pair. Ed moved in a couple months ago, fresh off a dried out farm, and had fallen instantly in love with Betty. Betty, although kind to the boy, did not encourage him. She vowed she'd spent enough years on a farm and stuck in a small town. As soon as she saved enough money, she was off to the city.

Boothe asked Don about other job possibilities. He spoke in an easy, relaxed manner, his tone warm, his expression interested.

Emma's errant thoughts repeated her initial reaction at her first glimpse of him approaching the boarding-house. *A strong, caring man.* She slammed a mental door. She had her duties. They excluded useless dreams, especially ones that included a man. Emma sobered. She would not let herself be another Ed, longing for something that was impossible.

"Don't worry about the dishes," Ada said as Emma hesitated at the sink. "Boothe will help me."

"Do you want me to bring up a basin of potatoes?" She normally brought whatever vegetables Ada needed to prepare during the day.

"Boothe will do it. I expect to make him work for his keep." Ada's voice held a teasing note.

Emma realized how good this arrangement would be for Ada.

"I'll see you later, then." She wrapped her cape about her and headed out into the cold darkness. The sun breathed pink air over the horizon as she entered the hospital.

At the end of her shift, Emma hurried back to the boardinghouse, shivering in the cold wind and cough-ing in protest of the dust particles in the air. The end-less dust grew tiresome. It would be worse for Mom and Dad and Sid on the farm. Relentless. *God, please send snow. Please end the drought.*

She was getting home later than she should have been thanks to the demands of her job. And she was exhausted—more so in mind than body. It had been one of those days that made her wish she could change people's thoughts.

Two elderly patients died—their deaths not entirely unexpected, but the woman might have survived if she hadn't refused to see a doctor until she was too weak to protest when her daughter insisted she must.

And then a woman came in to have her baby. She'd been in labor seventy-two hours before she finally decided she needed medical intervention. The baby had been delivered and both were alive, but Emma wondered about the long-term effects on the baby. The infant girl had been slow to start breathing and seemed sluggish in her responses.

Emma wished she could erase the mental images of the worst scene of all—a young man who had been ill for some time but only when he could no longer respond did his parents decide to seek help. By then the skin on the young man hung like a sheet draped over a wooden rack. His eyes were sunken. She couldn't help thinking of Sid, remembering how vigorous he'd been at that age. She smiled past tears. Sid had been so eager for life and adventure—with an attitude that led him to take reckless chances just for a thrill. She stilled a shudder. The consequences of taking such risks had gone beyond harmless adventure.

She'd worked feverishly over the young man in her care, determined she would not let his life slip away. He showed little improvement, even with all her efforts.

Later, in private, Dr. Phelps shook his head. "He's so dehydrated I wonder if his kidneys are even functional."

"I don't understand why people wait so long to get help." Emma's voice was sharp with frustration. "So much of this suffering is unnecessary."

Dr. Phelps sighed. "The greatest disease of all is ignorance."

The young man had still been alive, struggling for each breath, when she'd finally left the hospital, chased away by the matron who insisted Emma was of no value to them if she wore herself out.

Emma paused before the front door of the boarding-house. She would not drag her frustration and sorrow into the house. *Lord, take my concerns and replace them with Your peace.* She waited until she had a sense of God's comforting arms about her then stepped inside.

From the kitchen came the sound of Jessie's crackling voice, high with some protest and Boothe's lower, calmer response.

As Emma headed for the stairs, she could hear the conversation more clearly.

"Daddy, I want to go home." The irritable note in Jessie's voice alerted Emma's instincts.

"This is home now." Boothe explained in gentle tones with just an edge of impatience.

Emma smiled, guessing this conversation had gone on for some time and Boothe had about reached the end of his rope.

"I don't like it here." No mistaking Jessie's stubbornness. "I don't like the school. I don't like anything." She heard a small thump, as if Jessie kicked something.

Emma hesitated part way up the stairs, curious to know how Boothe would handle this.

"You'll learn to like it. You'll learn to be happy."

"No. I won't."

Emma tilted her head toward the kitchen. Obviously, Jessie was finding the transition difficult, but it sounded like more than that. He sounded like a child who wasn't feeling well.

She wanted to check on him, but Boothe had made it doubly clear he would tolerate no interference with his son, yet she could simply not ignore the needs of a sick child. Remembering the young man at the hospital, remembering an earlier time when she'd failed to intervene, she spared a moment to pray for wisdom then headed back down the stairs and into the kitchen, not giving herself a chance to change her mind.

Boothe peeled potatoes. He gave her a brief glance, his mouth set in a tight line. "Aunt Ada's resting."

Jessie sat at the other end of the table, a book before him.

Emma took a few more steps into the room so she could see Jessie better. He glanced at her, his mouth pulled back in an angry frown, his hair mussed as if he'd been pushing it back in frustration. There was no mistaking the glassy look in his eyes.

"Hello," he murmured, his voice croaky as if it took effort to get the word out.

Emma itched to press her palm to his forehead, but she didn't need to touch him to know he ran a fever. She turned to Boothe, undaunted by his glower. "Your son is sick. You need to look after him."

Jessie jumped from his chair. "I want to go home," he wailed and raced for the storeroom where they slept.

Boothe's mouth pulled down into a fierce scowl. "I warned you to stay out of my affairs."

"Strictly speaking, you said not to interfere with your son, but I can't stand by and see him needing medical attention and not getting it. I've seen enough needless suffering for one day." She stopped short of providing any details from the hospital. "Your son has a fever. You should attend to him. I'll finish the potatoes as soon as I've changed."

His eyes darkened with anger, but she met his gaze boldly, unflinchingly. They looked at each other a long time. She felt as if they dueled with unseen weapons. She would not let him win this silent war. This was not about him proving he didn't need the help of a nurse. This was about a sick little boy needing care. She would not back down and let Jessie or anyone suffer needlessly.

Muttering under his breath about interfering women and controlling nurses, he tossed the paring knife on the table and strode after Jessie.

She called after him. "You might want to sponge him with cool water to lower the fever. And check his cut. If it looks infected, try an old-fashioned remedy like a bread poultice."

She waited to hear Boothe murmur to Jessie. The shrill whine of Jessie's answer sent skitters of alarm up her spine. She hoped home remedies would be enough.

Guessing Boothe might not want to return to the kitchen until she left, and knowing he needed to get water to sponge Jessie and probably prepare a poultice, she headed to her room to change into a warm sweater and skirt.

A wave of discouragement swept over her and she fell to her knees. *God, I can't stand to see so much suffering because of ignorance or stupidity. And it's difficult for me to stand by when I see Jessie needing attention. He's such a sweet boy and is dealing with so much. Heal his cut. Heal their inner hurts.* She didn't question that she meant both Jessie and his father in her last request.

Chapter Four

Boothe fumed at Emma's insinuation that he didn't know how to care for his son. He might not be as quick to figure out medical needs as she was, but even before her comment, he realized Jessie wasn't just whining because of the move and a new school, though Boothe figured it was more than enough reason to cause the boy to fuss.

He paused outside the storeroom, pulling his angry thoughts into submission before he faced his son.

Jessie lay face down on his bed, sobbing.

Boothe shifted Jessie and perched on the edge of the cot beside him. He rubbed Jessie's back. "I'm sorry things are so hard right now, but I promise they'll get better."

Jessie scrunched away making it plain he cared little for Boothe's promise.

Boothe swept his hand over Jessie's forehead. It did seem warmer than normal. He checked under Jessie's shirt. Again, the boy seemed a bit too warm. "Jessie, I need to check your arm."

Jessie wailed and drew into a ball, pressing a hand to his shoulder as if to prevent Boothe from touching him.

"I have to look at it."

"Leave me alone." Jessie turned his tear-streaked face to Boothe. "I don't want you. I want Auntie Vera."

Boothe's heart stalled as the words pierced his soul. He pulled his hand back and ground his fist into his thigh as if he could force his mind to shift to the pain in his leg. Jessie had no idea how his words hurt, how losing his son's love to Vera and Luke seemed like the final injustice in a list of unexpected, undeserved tragedies.

Ignoring his son's resistance, he turned him to his back. "Do you want to take off your shirt or do you want me to?"

"No."

"I won't hurt you." He unbuttoned the shirt.

"Owwwww."

Boothe ignored the pathetic pleas and sat Jessie up to remove the shirt and lower the top half of the long underwear. He gently touched the arm on either side of the dressing, but he couldn't tell if it seemed unduly warm.

"I have to take off the bandage."

Jessie batted at Boothe's hands. "Don't touch it."

"I have to." He began to unwrap the cloth.

When Jessie realized his protests wouldn't stop Boothe, he settled back and glowered. "You don't care if it hurts."

"Son, I don't want to hurt you. You know that. But if your cut is infected, it has to be treated."

"You don't care."

Boothe's eyes narrowed as he pulled off the pad of cloth and saw the reddened edges of the wound. "I'll have to put a poultice on this." He didn't need Emma to tell him what to do. He knew about poultices because Alyse had put one on his leg when he tore it on barbwire. She'd ignored his protest that it would heal just fine left alone. Silently he thanked her for insisting; otherwise he would not know how to treat their son now.

He tilted his head toward the kitchen and when he determined it was quiet, hurried in and put a small pot of milk on the stove. He had no desire to see Emma or listen to her unwanted advice. Knowing she was a nurse who played with people's lives made his tongue curl with a bitter taste.

As he waited for the milk to heat, he prepared a thick slice of bread and gathered up clean rags.

He heard Emma's steps on the stairs as he carried his supplies back to the storeroom. The skin on the back of his neck prickled with tension, and he picked up his pace even though he doubted she'd follow him. He put the milk-soaked bread on the wound and wrapped it in place with a length of sheet. According to what he remembered Alyse saying, it had to be left until morning and by then would have drawn out the infection. If not, he would do it again. He would fight for the well-being of his young son. And he would not let someone interfere because they had an education that they thought gave them the right.

Jessie continued to glower at him. "You should have taken me to the doctor like Miss Emma said."

Boothe finished pinning the cloth in place, giving himself time to calm his thoughts. He gently took Jessie's shoulders and squeezed. "Jessie, don't ever think you can turn yourself over to the care of a doctor or nurse and you'll be safe. You must promise me to use your head and do what you need to look after yourself and those you care about."

He waited for Jessie to agree but the boy only whimpered. Boothe didn't like to press him when he was feeling poorly but this was too important to let go. "Jessie, you have to take care of yourself or let someone who loves you take care of you. Don't trust strangers. You must promise me."

"Okay, I promise."

Boothe wondered if the boy understood, but he would be sure to repeat the warning time and again until Jessie had it firmly in his mind. He did not want to lose his son to a careless nurse or doctor concerned more with their medicines and diagnoses than with the patient. Alyse was not simply a patient. She had been his wife and Jessie's mother.

He sponged Jessie until he seemed less restless. He would have done it without Emma's instructions. He focused on Emma's interference, hoping to keep his fear at bay. It was only a cut. Nothing out of the ordinary for a small boy. He himself had many scars to prove children endured cuts that healed sometimes without so much as being cleaned.

Yet Boothe had overreacted when Jessie ran into the nail on the side of the baggage cart. When he saw the deep tear in Jessie's flesh, he'd roared at the innocent baggage handler. It had taken a long while for his inner turmoil to settle down, for his fears to subside.

Jessie was all he had left. He intended to protect him from danger and interference.

But now he had an infection and Boothe was powerless to fix it.

He felt inadequate trying to be both father and

mother. He didn't feel adequate as one parent, let alone trying to be both. But one thing he knew without a flicker of doubt—his son would not ever be subjected to the careless ministrations of a nurse or a doctor.

He let his anger, fear and frustration narrow down to Emma. Just because she was a nurse gave her no right to interfere in his life. Or Jessie's. He'd warn her again to mind her own business. Surely there were enough people at the hospital wanting her help without her having to play nurse at home. Apart from having to sit at the same table for breakfast and supper, he could see no reason for the two of them to spend time together or even speak for that matter.

He sat at the bed until Jessie drifted off to sleep.

When Aunt Ada had admitted she hadn't slept well because of her arthritis, he'd sent her to bed promising to make supper. He returned to the kitchen to fulfill his duty.

Emma stood at the table cleaning up the last of the potato peelings. She glanced up as he entered the room. "How is he?"

"Fine."

"You might want to—"

"Stop. If I want your advice, I'll ask. I want to make myself very clear here." He stood at the doorway, his fists on his hips, and gave her his hardest look. "I don't want your help looking after my child. *I* will see to his needs. Do you hear me?"

She quirked one disbelieving eyebrow. "Of course I hear you. But—"

He shook his head. "No buts. Stay away from Jessie and me. Find someone else to fix if you have such a need."

Her eyes darkened like the approach of night. Her nostrils flared.

He waited, expecting an outburst, or perhaps a hot defense of her abilities.

But she swallowed hard and then blinked twice in rapid succession. "I am not trying to fix anyone, though I wish I had the ability. Believe me, many times a day, I wish I could."

"So long as we understand each other."

"Oh, I think we do, and I don't think keeping out of your way is going to prove too difficult for me."

Her gaze slid past him. He understood she thought of Jessie.

"Leave Jessie alone."

Before Emma answered, before he could guess what the sudden flash in her eyes meant, Aunt Ada entered the room.

"It's almost time to make supper." She patted a yawn. "I can't believe I slept so long."

"The potatoes are ready to cook." Emma headed for the door, obviously ready and anxious to get away from Boothe. "I'm going to run over to the Douglases."

She left and Boothe turned his attention to supper preparations, slicing pork for frying, pouring applesauce from a jar into a bowl and generally, in his inept way, doing his best to help Aunt Ada.

The meal was almost ready when he heard Emma return. A tightness across his shoulders relaxed. For the past twenty minutes, he wondered if he'd offended her so badly she decided not to come back. Perhaps she would find somewhere else to live. It would prove a relief for him if she did but he knew Aunt Ada needed her boarders, and despite his personal dislike of Emma, she was, no doubt, the sort of boarder Aunt Ada preferred.

Emma slipped into her place at the far end of the table.

He glanced her way as he placed a bowl mounded with creamy mashed potatoes in the center of the table. He'd done a good job with them, if he did say so himself, though it had taken some direction from Aunt Ada.

He'd expected Emma to be subdued, even a bit sullen after the way he'd spoken to her, and the look of eager anticipation and excitement on her face made him narrow his eyes. Had she found somewhere else to live? Somewhere more welcoming? For Aunt Ada's sake, he hoped not.

"Where's Jessie?" Betty asked.

"He's not feeling well. I've had to sponge him a couple of times to get his fever down." He kept his voice firm to convince one and all he was competent to care for his son without medical interference.

Emma studied him soberly but offered no more advice.

The others murmured sympathy for the little boy.

Loretta, the old dear, offered her own solution. "The boy needs a good dose of salts. That will fix him up in a snap."

Boothe almost laughed at the shock in Emma's face. "I'll keep that in mind." Though he had no intention of doing such a thing.

Emma's eyes flashed. She opened her mouth, but before she could speak, he shook his head ever so slightly, silently reminding her of his warning. She shut her mouth and fixed him with a deadly look.

He ducked to hide a smile. He almost enjoyed seeing her bristle.

Amidst the general discussion as people dug into the food, complimenting both he and Aunt Ada, Boothe stole several glances at Emma. Her anger at him had disappeared as quickly as it came, replaced with the same eagerness she'd had when she returned. He wondered what sparked the flashing light in her eyes and again hoped she wouldn't decide to move out.

The food disappeared quickly. He helped Aunt Ada serve the butterscotch pudding she'd made earlier in the day. As everyone enjoyed the dessert, Emma leaned forward.

"Listen everyone," she began.

Boothe waited for the announcement.

"I went to visit Pastor and Mrs. Douglas this afternoon. You all know how difficult things have been for them this year with Pastor Douglas recovering from a stroke."

Boothe listened to the murmurs of acknowledgment. Was she going to move in with them?

"They always make gifts for each child at the Christmas concert." Emma edged forward and glanced around the table, her expression eager as she looked at each one until her gaze settled on Boothe. Then her eyes grew wary.

Then she skipped past him and continued. "With all they've had to deal with, they haven't got the gifts made. Mrs. Douglas was fretting about how to get thirty or forty gifts done in time. I thought we could do something to help. What do you think?"

There was silence for a moment while everyone digested her request. For his part, Boothe had to work hard to keep from exhaling his relief over her announcement. Her excitement was only about taking over a project and getting them all involved.

Betty spoke first. "Forty gifts? How on earth did they ever do it themselves?"

Emma nodded. "I know. I wondered the same."

"What sort of things do they normally make?" Sarah asked.

"Generally, wooden toys for the boys, dolls for the girls. and Mrs. Douglas said they also like to make sure every child gets a pair of mittens."

"Goodness," Ed said. "Forty gifts."

"I thought if we worked in the evenings, making it a group project instead of reading our book… Just until this is done," Emma added as the others protested. "Pastor Douglas sent the pattern for trucks and trains. He said if anyone can carve, you could make airplanes with little propellers that turn. Wait, I'll show you." She hurried out to the hall and returned with a large wooden box that she put on the floor by her chair. She pulled out pieces of wood. "He even got a few cut before his stroke. They only need to be sanded and painted." She finally sat back, quiet, waiting for the others to respond.

"Forty toys," Ed said again.

Loretta clapped her hands. "Well, of course the children must have their gifts. I can certainly knit mittens."

"I'll knit some, too," Aunt Ada said.

"I can sew things," Sarah added.

"Thank you." Emma turned to Ed and Don. "Can you help with the wooden toys?"

"Forty gifts?" Ed said.

Betty snapped her fingers in his face. "Ed, get over it. Say you'll help. I'm going to."

Everyone laughed at how quickly Ed agreed. Don added his promise to help.

Emma slid her glance over Boothe. "Good." She rubbed her hands together. "As soon as the kitchen is cleaned, let's get started. We have a lot to do."

Boothe stared at her. Was he invisible? Wasn't he allowed to be part of this? His eyes narrowed. Did she think he'd refuse simply because it was her idea? Or because she'd be there? Admittedly, a part of him rebelled at the idea of working with her. But what was he supposed to do? Sit by idly while everyone else made gifts for the children? And he was the only one with a child of his own. It simply wasn't right. "I'll help, too."

Emma gazed in his direction. "That's very generous of you." Her words sounded like she'd dragged them from the icebox.

"You're welcome. I'm proud to do my part." Not giving her a chance to respond, he grabbed a handful of plates and strode to the kitchen.

As he washed dishes, having appointed himself chief cook and bottle washer, his thoughts mocked him. *Avoid her. You only have to see her at supper and breakfast. Stay away from her and her interfering ways. And the first time something comes up where you don't have to be in the same room, jump right in and volunteer.* Oh yes. He certainly made a wise move there.

The evening barely got underway before he knew he'd made a mistake. Emma took control of the proceedings in such a high-handed way that he bit his tongue to keep from protesting. Only Aunt Ada and Loretta escaped her control as they retired to the front room, sorted through yarn and started on the mittens.

Emma put out fabric on the table, some already cut

into rag doll shapes, and gave Betty and Sarah each a job. She ordered Ed and Don to the corner of the room. "We don't want to mess up Ada's kitchen any more than necessary." Ed and Don obeyed like young boys and immediately began sanding pieces. She looked at Boothe, shrugged and left him to decide what he wanted to do.

He didn't want to be ordered about, but he also didn't want to be ignored as if she didn't care to acknowledge his presence—maybe even his existence. "I'm going to try my hand at carving a propeller." He grabbed a chair and joined Ed and Don in the corner.

As they worked, they talked. And Boothe listened.

"Any news from Kody and Charlotte?" asked Betty.

Boothe learned that Kody was the Douglas's son and he and his wife owned a ranch in the hills.

"I haven't seen them in a while," Emma said. "I might have to go out there on my day off."

At the lonesome tone in her voice, Boothe glanced her way. Did nurses feel the same emotions as others? Somehow he expected they functioned like machines— bossy machines—with no concern about how people felt. That she'd reveal ordinary emotions surprised him.

Two hours later, she stood. "That's enough for tonight." She looked at the doll Sarah was working on. "This is sweet." Boothe glanced over. Sarah had embroidered a lifelike face.

Betty threw down the doll she worked on. "Mine looks stupid. It has button eyes."

Emma retrieved it. "This is fine. And your sewing is so strong. It will stand up to a lot of loving. Why don't you, Sarah, do the faces and you, Betty, stitch them together? That way you both get to do what you do best."

Betty puckered her mouth. "You aren't just trying to butter me up?"

Emma laughed. "I'm being practical."

Ed chuckled. "Betty, you know Emma doesn't say things she doesn't mean. Hey, look at my truck. Vroom, vroom."

Everyone laughed as he played with the wooden automobile he'd sanded to satin smoothness.

Don exhibited his project—train wheels. "Now show us what you did," he said to Boothe.

Reluctantly, Boothe held out the propeller he worked on. "When I'm done, it should spin freely."

"We accomplished a lot." Emma gathered together the sewing. Don put the wooden pieces into the box Pastor Douglas sent.

Boothe assessed the toys. He tallied the items already cut out and did a quick estimate. Once the shapes were cut out, the work went quickly and could be done in the evenings. However, there needed to be a lot more pieces cut.

Emma wiped the table. Boothe grabbed the broom as she reached for it and swept the floor.

She paused at the box of wood and looked thoughtful. "We need to find someone to cut out more shapes for us."

The others had left the room so Boothe felt compelled to answer. "I'm sure you'll think of something."

"You sound disapproving. Why?"

He concentrated on sweeping up the wood dust. He hadn't meant to sound like a man with a mouthful of vinegar.

"Do you think you can protect yourself by pushing everyone away? Aren't you afraid you'll get lonely?"

Her words slammed against his heart. Boothe stopped sweeping. He closed his eyes and squeezed the broom handle so hard that he felt a sliver stab his palm. No, he wasn't lonely.

Jessie cried out. Boothe dropped the broom and headed for their room. He'd checked Jessie several times throughout the evening and figured the temperature remained down. He resisted the temptation to take the poultice off and look underneath. Only Alyse's words stopped him. She'd laughed at him when he tried to pull the poultice off his leg. "Stop trying to rush things. Let it do its work."

As he soothed Jessie from his nightmare, relieved his son seemed only normally warm from sleep, Boothe felt a great tear in his heart. He would endure loneliness to protect Jessie. He heard Emma still tidying. For a moment, he considered returning to the kitchen and her company. Instead, he stared out the window in to the dark, feeling the gloom settle into his soul.

Chapter Five

Emma hurried into the kitchen and laid out the yard goods she'd purchased at the store. If she cut out several dolls, the work would go faster. As Ed said, forty gifts was a lot. As she pinned the pattern pieces, Jessie bounced into the room singing a tuneless song. Boothe had assured everyone over breakfast that his son had slept well, but he'd let him stay home from school.

Emma smiled at Jessie. His eyes were bright and clear, his color good and he seemed about to erupt with pent-up energy. His eager smile made her want to hug him. "You must be feeling better."

Jessie stopped jumping about and pulled his face into a dark frown. "My arm sure hurts a lot. I don't think I'll be able to go to school. Won't be able to write, you know."

Emma laughed at his sudden change in demeanor. Jessie's recovery appeared to depend on being able to stay home. To test her theory, she said, "No more school today."

Immediately Jessie went from a lifeless wooden puppet to an animated little boy. "What did you do today?"

What a fun child. She loved children who showed a little spark. "I went to work." She paused, wondering how much of Boothe's anger toward medicine Jessie absorbed. "At the hospital, remember?"

"My daddy says I must never go to a hospital."

"Sometimes it's the best place to be."

Jessie squinted at her. "My daddy says you have to take care of yourself or let someone who loves you do it."

Emma fought hard to mind her own business. She'd promised herself to do her best to get along with Boothe. Teaching his child the benefits of modern medicine would not accomplish that goal. She wouldn't go so far as to directly go against his wishes but perhaps she could plant a little seed of reason. "Sometimes only a doctor can help you." She decided to change the subject before it went any further. "Where's your daddy?"

"He's downstairs making something. I'm not 'lowed to go down there." Jessie sighed long, communicating how sad it made him to have to obey his father's orders.

"And Aunt Ada?" Emma continued to cut out the fabric.

"She went upstairs to check on Miss Loretta. Whatcha doing?"

Emma paused. Jessie would be one of the children receiving a gift. Should he see them before it was time? She glanced at the box holding the wooden cars and trains. Someone had covered it with a blanket. "We're making rag dolls." She guessed he wouldn't care about the girls' gifts.

"Dolls? Ech!"

Emma laughed. "Do you want one?"

Jessie scooted backward. "I'm no girl."

Emma pretended to give him lots of study. Again, she noticed his fine clothes. From what Aunt Ada said, she gathered Boothe struggled to care for his son. "No work and trying to be both mother and father. It's been rough," she'd said. And yet the sweater and trousers looked expensive. Jessie regarded her with a wide-eyed expression. Something about this child appealed to her at a deep level.

She recognized her denied maternal instinct. She'd love a child of her own with the same spunk, the same golden glow, the same—

God, I again give You my desires. I want only to do what is right. I know You have set before me a responsibility, and I will not shirk it or regret it.

She waited a moment for peace and contentment to return.

"I ain't no girl," Jessie repeated.

"I'm *not* a girl," she corrected. "And I can plainly see you're a big strong boy."

He pushed his chest out and lifted his chin.

Behind him the basement door clicked and he spun around. "Daddy, are you done now?"

Boothe stepped into the room, carrying a box. "For now." He saw Emma at the table and his eyes narrowed. "What are you doing, Jessie?"

"Me and Miss Emma were talking."

Emma's cheeks burned with guilt. She kept her head down, afraid to meet Boothe's gaze as she waited for Jessie to tell his father about their discussion over hospitals.

"She said I could have a doll." Jessie's comment dripped with disgust.

Boothe chuckled, pulling Emma's gaze from her work. His eyes seemed softer, like the first gentle light of morning. He held her gaze for a heartbeat and then another. Her heart felt as if it stopped beating as something passed between them, something fragile, tenuous, unfamiliar and slightly frightening.

"I told her I'm not a girl." Jessie's voice sliced through the moment.

Boothe grinned at his son.

Emma's blood rushed to her limbs with a jolt. She grabbed the edge of the table as her legs shook. How could she explain what had just happened? For one brief moment, it seemed as if they'd both forgotten their differences and—

What? She grabbed the scissors and resumed cutting.

They only acknowledged shared amusement over Jessie's disgust. Nothing more.

"Jessie, would you go to the bedroom and find my knife? I think I dropped it on the floor this morning."

As soon as Jessie ran from the room, Boothe crossed the floor. Emma told herself she wasn't any more aware of him then she'd been this morning, or last night. He was a rude, backward man who relegated her profession to something akin to a snake oil salesman. She couldn't believe she gave him more than a passing glance the first time she saw him.

But as he passed, her cheeks burned and she shifted sideways to avoid looking at him.

"Lift the blanket off this box for me, would you?"

She jumped as if he'd snuck up on her and shouted *boo!* The scissors clattered across the table. She spun around. He stood beside the box of wood and waited, his expression watchful. She took a deep breath and prayed he hadn't noticed her foolish reaction.

"The blanket?" He nodded toward the box.

She snatched it off and clutched it to her chest.

He dumped the contents of the box into the larger one on the floor.

Emma gaped. "You've cut out more trucks and trains."

"I had nothing else to do. I haven't found a job yet. And Aunt Ada doesn't need help for more than a few hours a day."

She stared at him. "Boothe Wallace, you surprise me."

"How so?"

"I—" It didn't sound very nice to say she expected him to criticize her project. "You—" Saying he didn't seem the kind to help didn't sound any better. "You just do."

He considered her long enough to make her squirm, then reached for the blanket. As his fingers brushed the back of her hand, she jerked back a step.

"I'm assuming Jessie will be one of the children receiving a gift. The least I can do is help." He rubbed his hands together as Jessie returned waving the knife.

"Found it under the bed."

"Good job. Now let's get your things ready for school tomorrow."

The two of them left the room, Jessie protesting loudly. "My arm hurts. My stomach aches."

"You'll be fine."

"No, I won't."

Emma grabbed the scissors and returned to cutting

out rag dolls, pushing her thoughts firmly back in place. Boothe made it clear as glass what he thought of her being a nurse. She might as well expect the moon to land at her feet as to think he might show a speck of interest in her.

Emma stood before the front door and took a deep breath. Thankfully she'd been too busy all day to dwell on how silly she'd acted yesterday. For the most part, she'd been able to pretend her heart hadn't given a quick little kick against her ribs every time she glanced at Boothe. But standing on the step, her cheeks burned to think how she'd reacted to his soft smile. She feared her eyes revealed a glimpse of her dreams for love and family.

Lord, help me be sensible. Give me Your peace. She waited a moment then stepped inside.

She heard Jessie and Boothe talking in the kitchen. She hurried up the stairs to change, ignoring the way her heart clamored for a glimpse of the pair. She took her time pulling off her uniform and selecting the outfit she wanted. Then she brushed back the strands of hair that had fallen from her bun.

She was a nurse. He hated nurses. It was as simple as that.

Yes, an inner voice argued, apart from that, he's a good man, he loves his son and—

Enough of that. You're a practical person, Emma Spencer. There is no room in your life for such things, even if Boothe liked you, which he most certainly does not.

Her responsibilities could not be changed. And she got a great deal of joy out of nursing. She'd had the satisfaction of seeing that very sick young man improve before she left the hospital. He stood a fair chance of a complete recovery. Tucking her practical acceptance about her, she headed down the stairs.

Boothe bent over Jessie, who was seated at the table, running his finger along a page. "What's this word?"

Emma sucked in a deep breath at the sight of the pair.

"Daddy, I can't read." Jessie sounded ready to cry.

"No one can at first. But you already know this word."

"I forget." Jessie practically choked on a sob.

Boothe's lips grew tight. Emma feared the man would be angry, disappointed with his son, but when he looked up, she saw he wasn't angry but hurting for his son's frustration. "It's okay, Jessie," he said. "I'll help you." He squeezed his son's shoulders and kissed the top of his head.

Swallowing hard at the sudden emotion clogging her throat, Emma glanced away. All her life she'd had a dream—two actually. She'd dreamed of being a nurse and helping others get better. She had always planned to do that for a time before she pursued her second dream—a man who loved her and showed her tender feelings. She knew her father loved her, but he didn't show it in touches or words. He only showed it in acknowledging her successes and commenting on her accomplishments. Secretly, she longed for more.

She would get even less if he knew—

She stopped herself from following that trail.

With a gentle touch, a kiss, Boothe assured Jessie of his love even when he couldn't do a task. Had he shown the same love to his wife?

She forced her thoughts in a safer direction. She

would never be able to experience her second dream. Speaking cheerfully, she said, "Hello, everyone," and went to Ada's side where she stirred a simmering pot of soup. "Anything I can do to help?"

She would not allow herself to look at Boothe.

Jessie scrambled from the chair and rushed to her side. "Daddy made me go to school today."

"Yes, I heard." She bent to his level. "How did it go?"

He shrugged. "I've had better days."

She hid a smile and glanced at Boothe. A grin tugged at his mouth, making it impossible for Emma to pretend indifference. Tearing her gaze away, she turned back to Jessie. "I'm sure it will get better."

He looked unconvinced.

"What was the best thing about your day?"

He thought for a moment then brightened. "At recess we practiced throwing sticks and I threw mine the farthest. Even farther than some of the big boys." His chest expanded. "They said I could play ball with them." His shoulders caved in. "But we had to go inside and we didn't play ball at all."

Emma ruffled his hair, liking its fine texture. "I'm sure you'll get a chance. They aren't likely to forget you were the best thrower, now are they?"

He grinned. "Uncle Luke taught me how to throw good."

Emma glanced toward Boothe again, wanting to share her pleasure in Jessie's pride, but instead of smiling, he scowled, his expression dark, almost angry. When he saw she watched him, he turned his back. Why should he get upset at the mention of an uncle?

Jessie tugged at her hand. "I've forgotten how to

read." He pulled her toward the table and showed her his reader. "I could before we moved."

She stood beside him, aching to pull him close and assure him things would get better. "I wouldn't worry too much. I remember one summer I forgot some real easy words like 'the' and 'how.' And I was in fourth grade. It soon came back." She also remembered how afraid she'd been her father would find out and be unhappy with her.

"I guess so."

"I heard your daddy say he'd help you."

Jessie turned the book round and round studying it from each direction. Suddenly he sat up. "Maybe you can help me, too."

Emma couldn't answer. Her chest felt tight. A rush of longing flooded over her as she acknowledged her impossible dreams—a man to love her and show that love in concrete ways, a man like Boothe, a child to pour her love over, and a child like Jessie. She forced herself to take a deep breath, chasing away her foolish thoughts. "I'd like to, if your father doesn't mind." She finally dared raise her gaze to Boothe, uncertain what to expect. Would he resent her interference or welcome her help? He'd made it clear he didn't want her medical advice. Would this be any different?

He stared at his son, a bleak look on his face.

Emma lowered her gaze back to Jessie's reader, unable to bear the pain she saw in Boothe's eyes, wishing she could ease it.

Mumbling something about needing to check the furnace, Boothe strode from the room.

Jessie watched every step that took his father out of sight. He gave a shaky sigh. "Where is Daddy going?"

"To the basement," Emma said. "He'll be back in a minute."

"He's been up and down at least a dozen times," Ada added. "Found a box of clothes I said he could have. I can't even remember who left them. He's fixed a leaky pipe and stopped a hole where the mice were getting in." She chuckled. "I'm liking the idea of him living here more and more."

"I don't want to live here," Jessie whispered. "I want to go home."

Ada limped over and sat across from him. She took his hands between her own. "Jessie, we're family. My house is your house."

"But I want my Auntie Vera."

Ada opened her arms and Jessie scrambled from the chair. Sobbing, he threw himself into her embrace. "I miss my auntie. Why did we have to go away?"

"There, there, child." Ada's eyes filled with tears. "You'll be safe here."

Safe from what? Emma wondered at Ada's choice of words.

Boothe rattled up the stairs. Jessie flew into his arms. "I don't want to stay here. I want to go home. Why can't I?"

Boothe hugged the boy tight.

Emma's eyes burned with tears she would not allow to fall. Everything in her called to hold Jessie, rock him and soothe away his fears. But to him, she was only a stranger in an unfamiliar house.

She spun around and headed for the closet under the stairs where Ada stored books and games. She found the one she noticed weeks ago. A story of Joseph written for children. She plucked it from the shelf and returned to the kitchen.

Boothe stood over the stove. She sensed tension in his stiff posture. Again she wished she could do something to ease his pain. Medicine relieved physical pain, but time seemed the only cure for emotional pain.

She turned to Jessie. "I have a story here about a boy whose mother died and he had to leave home even though he didn't want to."

Jessie's eyes grew round. "What did he do?"

"Do you want me to read it?"

He nodded eagerly.

Emma glanced at Boothe, silently seeking his permission.

His eyes dark, his expression bleak, he nodded.

She pulled a chair to Jessie's side, put the book on the table in front of him and read how Joseph was sold to slave traders and taken far away from his father and home.

Jessie put his hand on the book before she turned the page. "That was really mean, wasn't it?"

Emma agreed. "But that wasn't the end of the story because, you see, God had a plan for Joseph."

She turned the page and read, "'But the Lord was with Joseph.' You see, no matter what people did to Joseph, they couldn't stop God's plan." She read the quick summary that took Joseph from Potiphar to prison to the Pharaoh's throne. And then the final scene with his brothers. "Listen to what Joseph says, 'You thought to do me evil but God meant it for good to save His people.'"

Jessie looked thoughtful. "What does that mean?"

"It means God uses everything for our good and the good of others."

Jessie looked surprised and then pleased. He bounced off the chair and raced to Boothe's side. "Did you hear that, Daddy? God will make everything turn out good."

"I guess that's right." He lifted his gaze to Emma, his eyes full of dark mystery she couldn't interpret. She turned away first, uncomfortable with his intense look.

Thankfully, Ada spoke and broke the tension. "Emma, how thoughtful of you."

Boothe cleared his throat. "Yes, thank you."

Just then, the other boarders trooped in. A short time later, supper was served. Afterward, as Boothe supervised the cleanup, Jessie edged close to Emma, his reader clutched to his chest.

"'Member you said you'd help me?"

Emma bent over to look directly into Jessie's blue eyes. "Did you ask your daddy if it's okay?"

He turned toward Boothe. "Daddy?"

Boothe, his hands submerged in water as he washed the dishes, glanced over his shoulder. "If Miss Emma doesn't mind."

Emma didn't mind a bit and followed Jessie to the table. He placed the reader between them and smoothed the pages open. "It isn't as good as the story you read me." His voice crackled as he bent over the page.

Emma sensed he was tense because he couldn't remember how to read, so she talked about the pictures in the book, laughing at the expression on Dick's face.

"That's Dick's name." Jessie said, his voice round with excitement. "I remember that." He bent over the page, struggled to form the words in his mind. *"See Dick. See Dick run."*

Emma clapped. "I knew you'd remember."

Jessie grinned so widely that his eyes squeezed shut.

Boothe paused at the table. "That was great, son. You did well. Thank Miss Emma for helping you." Boothe's gray eyes warmed with what she took for approval.

"Thank you, Miss Emma," Jessie said.

Emma forced her gaze to Jessie. "You're most welcome." She couldn't bring herself to look at Boothe again, afraid her face would reveal how much she reveled in his appreciation.

Life settled into a routine. After supper, when Jessie had gone to bed, the boarders worked on the Christmas toys. Every day Sarah brought home a little dress she'd made for the dolls and fancy material to make others. Boothe carved half a dozen propellers and affixed them to wooden airplanes. Daily, the pile of toys grew larger.

Emma smiled as she entered the house. They all seemed to enjoy themselves as they worked together. As Boothe relaxed around them, she discovered he was an amusing storyteller.

Recalling his story last night, she laughed softly.

"I found work helping haul logs out of the woods. The man I worked for had this knothead of a horse. It seemed to me the horse went out of his way to complicate matters so he could rest while we tried to fix things." He chuckled.

Emma noticed his expression grew gentle, making him look younger. He had a strong chin and a wide smile when he forgot his troubles. She'd wrenched her thoughts back to the rag doll she stitched together.

Boothe continued his story. "Old Barney had a knack for getting stuck on a stump. Then he couldn't seem to remember how to back up or turn around. I tell you, I've never seen a horse act so stupid when he was just plain smarter than either of us wanted to admit." He laughed, his voice deep with amusement. "One time he got himself all tangled up in the traces. Mr. MacLeod told Old Barney the only reason he was still standing was because he hadn't brought a gun. MacLeod sweated and grumbled and Old Barney played dumb. We finally got him straightened round and MacLeod was so angry that he shook his fist in Barney's face and threatened to knock him cold. Wouldn't you know it? Old Barney pretended MacLeod frightened him and took off like a shot, knocking MacLeod off his feet. The horse stopped a few yards away and put on a great show of being scared half to death. I laughed so hard I had to lean against a tree. MacLeod picked himself up, grabbed a hunk of tree and brandished it. I wasn't sure who he wanted to hit most—me or Old Barney."

Emma's smile deepened. Boothe seemed the kind of man who had been able to find humor in most situations. She wondered if he still had the ability.

It was a good thing she had to go to work each day. Too much time spent in his company might make it hard for her to remember her responsibilities. Once Emma was inside, she went for the mail Ada always left on the tiny table in the hall. Emma shuffled through the letters and found one from home. She opened it and skimmed the two tightly written pages. Mom wrote almost every week—always including a detailed weather report. "Wind on Monday. More wind on Tuesday and falling temperatures. It was so cold we couldn't get more than two feet from the stove. Even staying close, we baked on one side and froze on the other. Wednesday, it snowed a little. Not really snow though. Just hard little pellets." Emma skipped the rest of the weather news, looking for Sid's name. She found it near the bottom of the second page. "Sid misses you. Says to tell you to come home soon."

Emma read the rest of the letter, then returned it to the envelope. She missed her brother. She'd make plans to visit in the near future.

But would she ever see Sid without experiencing as much pain and regret as she did pleasure?

Chapter Six

Boothe hurried toward the boardinghouse. He'd planned to be home by the time Jessie got back from school but Mr. White at the garage had been interested in Boothe's ability to tinker with engines. He'd taken Boothe into the shop and asked him to look at a 1928 Dodge. Boothe had breathed deeply, contentedly, of the smell of grease and oil, then bent over and poked around the engine. He made a few adjustments then cranked over the motor. He listened, adjusted the choke and nodded. "Sounds good."

Mr. White handed Boothe a rag to wipe his hands on. "Does indeed. You say you're looking for a job?"

"Could use some work all right."

"Then show up here tomorrow morning around eight."

Boothe hesitated.

"There a problem?"

"Got me a boy with no mother. I'd like to see him to school before I come in." Jessie whined and fussed if Boothe wasn't close by. Boothe couldn't be there every waking moment but neither could he expect Aunt Ada to get the resisting child off to school.

"It's gotta be tough for you both." Mr. White shoved out a meaty, grease-stained hand. "Nine will be fine. Nothing that can't wait until then."

Boothe paused on the step of Aunt Ada's house. He wasn't looking forward to Jessie's complaining about Boothe's absence. He didn't know how he'd deal with it day after day now that he had a job. But having a steady income was essential in order to keep Jessie.

He stepped inside and stood still. He'd expected whining but heard Jessie laughing. Emma's voice joined. Surprised and curious, he dropped his cap on a hook and edged toward the kitchen door.

The pair sat on the floor facing each other, their attention on something between them. He strained forward trying to glimpse what it was without alerting them to his presence. Seeing Jessie playing happily, laughing and relaxed even though Boothe was absent, gave him a queer twist of pleasure and relief. He'd almost forgotten what it was like to come home to such a scene.

"My turn," Emma said, leaning forward to scoop something toward her—dominoes. She lined them up like soldiers in a long squiggly row. "Now."

Jessie tipped the first one and laughed as the row fell in a chain reaction. He reached out to pull them close. "My turn." He saw Boothe and jumped to his feet. "We're playing knock 'em down dominoes. It's fun." He grabbed Boothe's hand. "Come and play with us."

Emma pulled her feet beneath her and began to stand. Jessie caught her shoulder. "You have to play, too."

Boothe sensed her reluctance and wondered if she

objected to being in his presence. He'd given her plenty of reason. He'd warned her repeatedly to stay away from him and his son. Nevertheless, he was glad she hadn't taken him literally. She'd soothed Jessie's fears by sharing the Joseph story. Jessie had repeated it many times to him, finding comfort in the words, "God will make everything turn out for good."

"What are the rules?" he asked.

"See who can make the longest chain fall down," Jessie said.

Emma settled back to the floor. "See how much fun we can have," she murmured.

Fun. When was the last time he'd done something just for fun? It seems he'd forgotten how.

"You go first," Jessie said, pushing the dominoes toward Boothe.

"Put your foot out and hold still. I'm going to build a fence around it." He set up the dominoes, gauging how far apart to place them in order for them to still tip each other. Jessie giggled as Boothe placed one close to his ankle.

"There." Boothe sat back and pulled his knees up to lean on. "Don't move."

Jessie looked surprised at his order. And then he realized Boothe teased him and chuckling, touched the first domino in the line. He broke into peals of laughter and fell sideways to the floor as the chain snaked around his foot.

Joy, uncommon and unfamiliar, unfolded at Jessie's pure enjoyment of the moment and somewhere, deep inside Boothe's heart, a crack mended. Boothe grinned wide enough to stretch his cheeks. And then he chortled. He chuckled. He laughed until his sides hurt.

Emma's eyes widened with what he could only assume was surprise. Was it that strange for him to enjoy himself? Her surprise faded, replaced with a warm glow, and she chuckled softly.

His laughter abated, though he couldn't stop smiling, and he studied her. He'd never noticed how thick her hair was, the color of ripe straw. Strands hung loose from her bun, trailing down her back almost to her waist.

She blinked and jumped up.

He sobered. He'd been staring rudely. He jerked to his feet. "Pick up the dominoes, Jessie, and put them away." He tried to sort his scrambled thoughts. "Emma—" He didn't want to say he was sorry. He wouldn't take back one fraction of the last couple minutes—laughing with Jessie, sharing the moment with Emma, enjoying a short time in which he forgot his troubles. "I've never thanked you properly for reading Jessie the story of Joseph. He got a great deal of comfort from it."

She nodded and smiled, her eyes following Jessie as he put the game away in the cupboard under the stairs. "I'm glad." She shifted her gaze to Boothe and he felt her growing intensity. "It's a good reminder for us all."

His heart beat hard in his chest. He wanted to believe as he used to—simple, unquestioning, untried belief in God's goodness, in His promise to turn everything into something good. "How does the murder of one's wife turn out for good?"

She reached out, her expression filled with pain.

Shrugging away from her hand, he walked out of the room. He didn't want to hear empty platitudes. What did she know about dealing with such useless, painful loss?

* * *

"I don't want to go to school," Jessie said, as he and Boothe walked in that direction. Every day it was the same but his protests grew less demanding; now mere words he repeated out of habit.

"Looks like it might snow today."

Jessie looked into the sky with sudden interest. "Do I have to go to school if it snows?"

"Unless we have a storm, yes."

"I hope it storms."

"Storms can be nasty, you know."

"I could stay home and play games with you and Emma."

"You'd like that, would you?" He and Emma had played games several times with Jessie. Old Maid, Snap and Go Fish. But Jessie's favorite remained dominoes. Boothe also held a special regard for the game. It had signaled a change in his relationship with Jessie.

Jessie let out a long-suffering sigh. "I wish you got home earlier so we could play more games."

"Me, too." By the time he returned from his job, he felt duty bound to help Aunt Ada with supper, though often Emma had done much of it. "How about after supper tonight we play whatever game you want?"

"Goodie." Once they reached the schoolyard, Jessie allowed Boothe to hug him, then ran to join the other children.

Later, his day at the garage finished, Boothe hurried home. He looked forward to spending some time with his son. He hoped Emma would join them. He slowed. What did it matter if she did or not? She was, he reminded himself, a nurse. He had no use for anyone involved in the medical profession. But his silent protests got all tangled up with mental pictures of her playing with Jessie, sharing a laugh with him over his son's enthusiasm.

He shook his head, trying to clear his thoughts but succeeded only in giving himself a headache.

He rushed into the house with unusual haste, tossed his cap to the hook and shed his coat so fast the arms turned inside out. A murmur came from the kitchen and he hurried in that direction.

Jessie sat at the table making a puzzle Aunt Ada had given him. His aunt sat before a basin of carrots, peeling them and slicing them into a pot. He glanced around. There was no one else in the room.

"Hello," he said, a little louder than necessary. In the back of his mind, where he didn't have to admit it to himself, he hoped to alert anyone who might be elsewhere in the house.

Jessie bounced from the chair and rushed to Boothe's side. "Miss Emma can't come home." He tugged Boothe's hand.

"Oh?" Curiosity mingled with disappointment. He turned to Aunt Ada, silently seeking an explanation.

"Didn't you hear about the accident?" she asked.

Accident? Alarm roared through his veins. Emma? And she was at the hospital? His first thought was to rush out the door and snatch her from that place. Away from doctors and nurses who cared only about their medicines. He shook his head. "I've had my head buried under the hood of a truck all day."

"Surprising," his aunt said. "I thought everyone in town knew."

"I heard at school," Jessie said. "Even though the

teacher warned the big kids they shouldn't talk about it in front of the little ones." He puffed out his cheeks. "I'm not a little kid."

"What happened?" Boothe barely managed to squeeze out the words.

"A car was hit by the train south of here. A whole family in the car was injured. I heard there were three children besides the parents." Aunt Ada tsked. "It's a miracle they—" She glanced at Jessie and paused. "That they survived."

"Miss Emma has to help," Jessie said.

"Someone brought us a message," Aunt Ada explained. "I don't know when she'll be home."

Relief warred with anger. Emma wasn't at the mercy of someone who considered themself a miracle healer. No. She was one of *those* people. A bitter taste burned the back of his throat. How could he have almost ignored the fact she was a nurse just because she made him laugh? Made Jessie laugh. Gave him looks that turned all his firm determinations into warm butter. How could he have encouraged her friendship with Jessie?

"Daddy?" Jessie jerked Boothe's hand. "Are you sad?"

"I need coffee," Boothe mumbled, pulling away from his son to pour a cupful from the pot on the back of the stove. The brew tasted like the dregs from breakfast, but he forced himself to swallow one mouthful after another.

Jessie watched, his eyes round.

Boothe turned and met Aunt Ada's curious look. No doubt they found his sudden need of old coffee as strange as his reaction. "It's been a long day." He pulled out a chair and sat down.

"She promised to play dominoes with me." Jessie sounded like he'd lost his best friend.

"I'll play with you."

"You aren't as much fun."

Boothe swallowed another mouthful of coffee as bitter memories assaulted him. Alyse was gone because of a nurse and doctor who insisted they knew more than Boothe. He'd never be able to completely shut from his mind the horrible pictures of her last hours.

He'd almost lost Jessie because he'd blindly trusted someone. And yet he'd been lulled into letting Jessie grow fond of Emma. "We'll play something else then."

"Okay."

Boothe ignored the heaviness in his chest rendering his lungs inadequate and forced a smile to his mouth. He turned to his aunt. "What can I do to help?"

Aunt Ada listed some chores.

Boothe dove into them hoping work would banish thoughts of Emma from his head. But when they sat down to eat, Emma's empty spot at the table mocked his efforts at dismissing her. He forced his attention to his anger at the medical profession. He focused on remembering Emma in her uniform. He filled his memory with bitter thoughts of Alyse's death.

The conversation centered on the accident.

"I wonder how they're doing," Betty said. "I heard the little girl was hurt the worst."

Aunt Ada put down her fork. "Let's pray for them and for Emma. We all know how broken she'll be if they don't pull through."

Boothe bowed his head last. He wanted to believe

their prayers held some value, but God certainly hadn't listened to Boothe's desperate pleas for Alyse. But perhaps He listened to the prayers of others. Aunt Ada prayed aloud. The others murmured, "Amen." For himself, he felt only doubt and disbelief, silently drowning the things he'd once believed with such blind faith.

He washed dishes, tended the furnace and played a short-lived game of Old Maid with Jessie, who said he preferred to do his puzzle. Later, he tucked his son into bed, listened to his prayers and helped work on the Christmas toys, silently listening to the others talk about the accident. All the time he seemed to be waiting, listening for something.

The others finished their work and wandered off to bed. The house creaked as it settled into the cold night.

Boothe sat at the table. He couldn't even say what it was he waited for. He only knew something kept his mind on edge. The night ticked away. He drummed his fingers on the table.

Hinges squeaked and he leaped to his feet so fast the chair tipped. He righted it then strode to the hall.

Emma leaned against the front door, her eyes closed.

"You look tired."

She didn't bother to open her eyes. "I am."

"Do you want tea or something to eat?"

She sighed and pushed herself upright. "Tea might be good." She shrugged out of her cape and draped it over the banister. There were blood spatters on her apron.

Boothe tried not to think what it represented—injury, pain, death. He hurried to the stove and pulled the kettle to a hot spot.

Emma sank wearily to a chair, propped her elbows

on the table and leaned heavily into her palms. "It's been a long day."

Boothe poured boiling water over the tea leaves without answering.

"Thank God they are all going to be all right, though it was touch and go for the youngest girl."

Boothe put two teacups on the table, set out cream and sugar and added a plate of Aunt Ada's raisin cookies. So they all pulled through. Because of prayer? If so, why did God grant *this* prayer and deny another? Didn't Boothe need a wife and Jessie a mother as much as this family needed each other?

"Thank you." Emma gave him a weak smile. He sensed it took almost more energy than she had left.

"Have some cookies." He shoved the plate toward her.

At first she looked at them with little interest, then took one as if it required too much effort to refuse.

Boothe watched her swallow tea and nibble at the cookie. And waited for what he still didn't know.

"It was a miracle any of them survived," Emma said. "As we worked over them, I prayed harder than I've ever prayed before."

"Maybe it was plain good luck or—" He wanted to think God had no hand in it, but if he took God out of the picture, he didn't know what or who else to give credit to.

"You don't really believe that, do you?"

He turned his teacup round and round. "Makes as much sense as believing prayer makes a difference."

"Doesn't make any sense at all."

He shoved the teacup away and stared at her. Despite her weariness, fire flashed through her eyes. She believed wholeheartedly. He wished he could. "What use are prayers if some are answered and others are ignored or denied?"

Her expression softened. "You're talking about yourself, aren't you? About losing your wife?" She didn't give him a chance to deny it. "Was she a Christian?"

He nodded.

"Then she's gone to heaven. Perhaps she's escaped something in the future that would be horrible."

He snorted. "So if someone dies, it's for their good? That doesn't make any sense. How is Alyse's death good for Jessie?"

She sighed wearily. "Boothe, I honestly don't know the answer to why some people die early, others suffer a long painful death or why any sort of tragedy occurs. I only know I have to trust that God's ways are higher than my ways, that He plans good and not evil for my life." She yawned. "Sorry."

"You'd better get to bed. Do you have to work tomorrow morning?" He glanced at the clock. She would only get a few hours sleep if she had to be up for the morning shift.

She nodded. "I'm off to bed. Thanks for waiting up for me."

He blinked. Had he waited up for her? He only wanted to make sure she got home safely…

It didn't make any sense. But he couldn't deny the truth of it.

He turned out the lights, checked the door and strode into his room. Jessie slept peacefully, his arm now completely healed. Without any help from a nurse or doctor. Sure, Boothe was happy that medical people had helped save that injured family. And if Emma played a part in it, well, he was sure it made her feel good.

If only he could believe in God's goodness and help as plainly as she. But he couldn't. God didn't take care of everyone. And everything did not work out for good. Which left a man no choice but to handle things on his own.

Despite the late hour, it took him a long time to fall asleep. He woke with a start thinking it was the middle of the night, but a glance at the clock revealed morning had arrived.

He hurried into his clothes and dashed downstairs to stoke up the fire. In the kitchen he put on the coffee, pulled a frying pan from the cupboard and sliced strips of bacon.

"Morning."

At Emma's cheerful voice, he jerked around. Half-moon shadows darkened the skin under her eyes, but she grinned and seemed full of energy.

"Shouldn't you be tired?" He'd had to force himself from his own warm bed.

She stretched her arms over her head. "Nothing like a good night's sleep to refresh. Coffee ready yet? Maybe you should have some."

He filled her cup and poured himself some of the brew. Emma's eyes fairly burst with teasing as she watched him over the brim of her cup.

One sip and he began to feel better. At least he preferred to think it was the coffee and not her smile. Deciding it was too early for deciphering his feelings, he hummed as he turned back to the bacon.

Sunday dawned cold and crisp. A light dusting of snow teased of a break in the drought. Boothe prepared for church. He wanted Jessie to know about God. He wanted God to protect Jessie. And so he went to the service even though he no longer believed as easily and unquestioningly as he once had.

Pastor Douglas's speech was halting. He sometimes fumbled for words, and Boothe remembered Emma said the man had a stroke. It hadn't taken Boothe long to discover the man had a favorite theme—God's faithfulness—and Boothe learned early to take his thoughts elsewhere during the sermon.

This Sunday was no different.

"My text," Pastor Douglas began, "is from Philippians chapter four verse four. 'Rejoice in the Lord always: and again I say, Rejoice.' How many of us have asked 'how'? How, Lord, are we to rejoice when things are going terribly wrong?"

Boothe shifted his mind to other things in order to block out the words. Yet the one word, *how?*, kept calling to him. He didn't, he tried to convince himself, need an answer. He had his own. *It wasn't possible.*

The pastor paused for prayer. "Let us lay our concerns before the Lord so He can speak to us in our need." Among the things he laid before the Lord was the family hurt in the accident. It seemed many of the congregation knew them and a couple of sobs rent the quietness as Pastor Douglas prayed. For a moment after his "amen," the man didn't speak.

"How can we rejoice when a senseless accident leaves a family struggling to survive, when children lay injured and hurting? For each of us, the answer might come in different ways at different times."

Boothe strained forward in his seat, barely breathing as he waited for Pastor Douglas to provide an answer—one enabling Boothe to recapture the assurance of faith he'd once known.

"It's possible only if we forget the past and look ahead to the right things."

Boothe closed his mind. Forget Alyse, forget the pain she suffered? He couldn't even if he wanted to. And he didn't. He didn't ever want to forget what happened when a man turned over the care of his loved ones to someone else.

Boothe shifted so his gaze wasn't drawn to the front of the church. Emma sat ahead of him, across the aisle, and he studied her. She stared straight ahead, nodding slightly at something the pastor said. For a change, she'd pinned her thick hair around her head. Her brown hat sat in the middle of the bouffant roll, a fuzzy feather of some sort waving as she moved her head.

He'd seen little of her the past few days. She'd worked late four days in a row. Last night she came home early, but when she sat down to help with the gifts, Boothe excused himself and went to the basement to cut out some toys. The day of the accident, or more correctly, the morning after, he'd realized how far he'd allowed his thoughts to wander. Emma was a nurse, which was reason enough to avoid feeling anything for her, but she was controlling as well. She organized the residents at the house as completely as she organized the toy-making project. He knew he wasn't being entirely fair in his judgment. It seemed they gladly let her organize them. But being annoyed about it proved the only way to keep himself from admitting the thoughts buried deep under his resentment and anger. The truth was he craved her company. And admitting it caused his stomach to clench.

* * *

Emma paused inside the door to the boardinghouse and listened—something she never used to do. And totally unnecessary. Boothe wouldn't be home from work for an hour or more. But there she stood, even forgetting to close the door, which she did now with a quiet click. It was silly, she scolded herself, to be prepared to slip up to her room if she heard his voice. She paid to live here. She could come and go in any of the public rooms as she wished.

But she didn't want to encounter Boothe. For days he'd been terse around her to the point her skin prickled if they were in the same room. For the life of her, she couldn't explain why he had gone from laughing and waiting up for her to treating her like she had the plague.

Her memories dipped back to that night. That special night when he'd waited up for her. At least it had felt special to her. And they'd talked about what they each believed. She'd allowed herself to think something had changed between them. Despite her weariness, her heart had reacted in a foolish, eager way when he poured her tea and made sure she had something to eat.

The next day he seemed glad to see her. Their eyes connected for a beat longer than usual.

But now this…this cold distance. She couldn't find a reason for it. Except he'd reverted to his earlier opinion and what he thought of her being a nurse. Though she thought saving all those involved in the accident should cause him to change his mind about the medical community. The father and two older children had gone home. The mother remained with her younger daughter.

Emma wondered why Boothe didn't acknowledge the benefit of medical help in this case. The whole family might have perished or if a couple of them had survived, it would have been with major handicaps. Dr. Phelps had done an excellent job, and the nursing skills of herself and others on staff played a huge role. But she might as well save her breath as say all this to Boothe. He wanted to believe what he wanted to believe. Perhaps it was easier than dealing with reality. She'd faced that choice, too, but accepting the facts of life, adjusting to them, doing what one could to deal with them made a lot more sense in her mind then clinging to futile denial and unfair blame.

And that's what she needed to do now—accept the reality of the situation and be practical about it.

She heard Ada and Jessie's voices in the kitchen. None other. So she stepped into the room.

"Hi, Jessie." She ruffled his hair. Thankfully the boy didn't share his father's opinion of her. They had become good friends. "Ada, how arc you? Can I help with anything?"

"No, my dear. Sit down and relax. I just made tea."

Emma poured a cupful, then at Jessie's begging, prepared him one of mostly milk. "How was school today?"

He shrugged.

Emma chuckled. She guessed Jessie would never admit to liking school. "Did you do anything fun?"

"We're building a snow fort."

The needed snow had finally come, reluctantly, miserly, but the wind created drifts the children enjoyed.

"Do you know your part for the Christmas concert?"

"I'm a star that burns warm," he repeated in a sing-songy voice. "Ruthie gets to say she's a star that shines bright." Jessie crossed his arms over his chest and glowered. "I don't want to burn. I want to shine."

Emma blinked and shot a surprised glance at Ada, who sputtered her tea. Laughing, Emma pulled Jessie into her arms and hugged him. "Oh, honey, burning is good. Think of how nice the flames are in a fire. Warm and dancing." She grinned at Ada, her eyes burning with delight at Jessie's reasoning. Or—her grin widened as she thought of Jessie's Christmas recitation—were her eyes shining? "You're so sweet," she murmured against the boy's hair.

He leaned into her shoulder. His arms stole around her neck.

She closed her eyes and breathed in his little boy scent of wool, milk and the soul-deep need for hugging. Boothe hugged him lots but Jessie missed his mother's hugs or maybe his aunt's. She'd never heard him ask for his mother but often for Auntie Vera.

Suddenly aware of how she clung to the child, she drew a shaky breath and eased out of his clasp.

"Will you read to me?" he asked, his eyes large with earnestness.

How could she refuse either of them the pleasure? "Did you have a book in mind?"

He nodded and hurried to the cupboard. He brought back the Joseph storybook and laid it on her lap, leaning heavily against her shoulder as she read.

Soon she finished and closed the book. Glancing at the clock she realized Boothe would soon be home. She handed Jessie the book. "Put it away when you're done."

"I will." He turned pages, studying the pictures.

"I have to change." She hurried to her room where she remained long after she'd removed her uniform and put on a sweater and warm skirt, struggling with her emotions. She fluctuated between disappointment at the way Boothe had pulled back, reverting to his cold demeanor, and anger at herself for caring. Like a sprinkling of snow over it all lay her deep-seated longing to love Jessie. But she couldn't let herself. Not like she wanted. *Lord, I want to be obedient to You. I want to accept my responsibilities wholeheartedly, with nothing causing me to wish for anything else. But Jessie is such a sweet boy.*

The feel of his arms about her neck, the way his hair tickled her cheek—

She allowed one fleeting, honest emotion to surface. She wanted to be more to Jessie than a fellow boarder.

More to Boothe than—

She gasped.

Oh, God. Forgive me for wanting things I can't have. In You I trust. I know somehow You will take the mess of my life and turn it for good. Be with Mom and Dad and Sid. Keep them safe.

The outer door clicked. A few minutes later, it clicked again. She heard the murmur of voices, footsteps going up and down the stairs, hall doors opening and closing. Four times the outer door clicked. Everyone must be home now. Certain she heard Boothe's voice, she stayed in her room, her Bible open, her finger at a verse. *No man having put his hand to the plow, and looking back, is fit for the kingdom of God.*

She hadn't asked for things to be the way they were. If she could undo one hour—

But she couldn't. She'd accepted her responsibility in what happened, had put her hand to the plow and would not turn back. But there came times like now when regrets assaulted her.

Only one thing gave her the strength to put aside her regrets—she believed God had His plans for good even in the midst of trials.

Thank You, Father. In You I trust.

Someone rang the little bell signaling supper. Smiling, her heart calmed with God's peace, she closed her Bible and went downstairs.

Jessie rushed to her side. "Where you been?"

"Upstairs."

"I want you to look at my elbow. It hurts." He pulled up his sleeve and crooked his arm toward her.

She saw no sign of injury and leaned over to run her fingers along the bone. "Where does it hurt?"

"There."

She moved her fingers to a different spot. "How about here?"

"Yes."

Wherever she pressed his arm, he said it hurt. "I think I know exactly what it needs." She touched her lips to his elbow and made a loud kissing noise. "Best medicine in the world. Is it better now?"

Jessie nodded. "I think so." He rolled down his sleeve and faced her. "Thank you for fixing it."

Boothe stepped into the hall. His eyes narrowed. "Jessie, are you bothering Miss Emma?" From the thunderous look on Boothe's face, she wondered if he'd heard the word *medicine*.

She glanced at Jessie's crestfallen face and wanted to hug him. "He wasn't bothering me. Not at all." She wanted to grab Boothe and shake him hard. She had no intention of interfering with the medical care of his son.

The kind of medicine she'd just dispensed didn't require any training, only a little sympathy and understanding. "Didn't I hear the supper bell?" She swept past Boothe without giving him another look. Let him think what he wanted. Unless he forbid it, she would continue to give out free hugs and kisses to Jessie.

Jessie needed her as much as she needed him.

She tried not to feel the strain of Boothe's silent disapproval over supper and refused to blame herself. She didn't need his dark, glowering looks to warn her she flirted with impossibilities when she thought of him as more than Ada's nephew and helper.

Jessie hopped around from foot to foot as the boarders cleaned the kitchen. "I can help."

"You sure can," Betty said. "You can put this pot in the cupboard for me."

Jessie rushed to do it. "What else?"

Emma wondered why this sudden urgency. She glanced at Boothe to see if he understood, but he met her gaze and gave a tiny shrug.

"Are you all done?" Jessie demanded a few minutes later as Boothe wiped the counter and Emma hung the tea towels on a line behind the stove.

"I think we are." Boothe said. "What's your hurry? Do you have homework?"

But Jessie rushed from the room before Boothe finished.

"He has something up his sleeve." Emma laughed nervously hoping her words wouldn't remind Boothe of the little scene in the hall. She wasn't sure how much he'd seen or heard.

Before Boothe could respond, a beaming Jessie returned bearing the box of dominoes. "Let's play."

Emma smiled at the eager boy. "You and your daddy have lots of fun."

Before she could slip out of the room, Jessie grabbed her hand. "I want all of us to play—you and me and Daddy."

At the pleading in his eyes, the quiver of his mouth, she stopped and faced Boothe, silently seeking his decision.

He studied his son then slowly brought his gaze to her, uncertain, as if he wanted to refuse but couldn't bear to disappoint Jessie—the same confusion she struggled with. She wanted to spend time with Jessie but Boothe had not shown any desire for her company in a long time. She couldn't quite pinpoint when it had happened or why. She wished she knew the why. But whether she did or not, she wouldn't refuse Jessie unless Boothe made it clear he didn't want her there.

Finally, Boothe's eyes softened and he smiled. "I could use some fun. How about you?"

She grinned, fearing her sudden rush of joy would make her glow. Why did she feel as if her heart had suddenly been freed from a short tether? "I think I could stand some fun, too."

They played a game of matching like-ends on the tiles then Jessie insisted on a game of "knock 'em down." He laughed so hard each time the row of tiles fell that Emma laughed, too. Her enjoyment doubled when Boothe's laughter joined in. Suddenly she couldn't look at Boothe without her eyes feeling hot.

Later, as Boothe tucked Jessie into bed, she put out

brown wrapping paper. The gifts were finished. They only had to be wrapped for the upcoming party.

Betty poked her head in the room. "Is Jessie gone?"

"He's off to bed."

Betty ducked back to the front room. "Come on, people. We have work to do."

The others came in.

"Let's set up a system," Emma said. "We can work around the table in teams. One wrap, the other mark the gift for a boy or girl." She laid out scissors and string. Ed made sure he paired up with Betty. Don and Sarah went to the other side of the table. Loretta and Ada carried in the forty pairs of mittens.

"These are lovely," Emma said. The others added comments of praise.

"We'll just be in the way," Ada said. "Come on, Loretta."

"How can I help?"

She jumped at Boothe's question. She didn't expect him to join them. Lately, he'd found reasons to avoid the gathering, though he continued to make toys on his own. "You could —— " She glanced around the table.

"He'll have to be your partner," Sarah said, barely taking her attention from the doll she wrapped.

Emma's heart turned into a heavy lump. She didn't want to work with him. She'd been far too aware of him as they played with Jessie. She'd hoped for a respite from her stubborn longings. Having put her hand to the plow, she would not look back. Nor wish for things not available to her. Not that Boothe represented those things. Her mouth grew dry as she tried to speak.

Thankfully, Betty rescued her. "You can work at the end of the table."

"Sure." She grabbed a roll of brown paper and a ball of string. "Do you want to wrap or write on the parcel?" She avoided looking at him as she edged closer, realizing with a burst of alarm how narrow the end of the table was they'd have to share.

"I'll let you wrap." He stood beside her, so close she smelled coal dust from his last trip down to the basement. He must have put an awful lot of coal on the fire because her skin felt overly warm.

"Fine." She grabbed a pair of mittens and struggled to fold the paper around them neatly.

Betty noticed and laughed. "Sure hope you're better at bandaging then you are at wrapping."

Emma laughed, too, her voice high and nervous. She made herself stop, sucked in air and held it, trying to calm her jittery heartbeat.

"I got started wrong." She smoothed the paper and started over. She grabbed a length of string to tie the bundle shut. The string knotted. She struggled to undo the tangle.

"Let me help." Boothe's low voice seemed full of amusement, which only increased her discomfort. Their fingers brushed as he pulled the string from her and sorted it out. A flame of embarrassment shot straight up her arm and burned into her heart like a raging fire. Why was she letting his nearness, his touch make her act so foolishly?

Because, she admitted, she had opened the door to her dreams and desires the first time she saw him on the street and noted his tenderness with Jessie. It reminded her of everything she wanted and couldn't have.

She accepted that some things could never be hers. Her commitment would be required the rest of her life.

She wrenched shut a mental door, grabbed the scissors and cut the thread as Boothe successfully tied the parcel.

If he wondered why her hands jerked as she worked, he gave no indication. In fact, he seemed perfectly at ease as if he felt none of the chafing tension between them. Yet he could hardly miss it. Sparks fairly danced in the air at the end of the table they shared.

She sighed in relief when all the gifts were wrapped and stacked in boxes ready to be delivered to the church. "Thank you, everyone."

Sarah, in her soft gentle way, spoke. "It's as much our responsibility as yours or the Douglases to see the children of the community get gifts at Christmas."

"That's a fact," Boothe said.

Emma shot him a look. Darted it away so fast her head spun but not before she saw a gleam in his eyes she couldn't interpret.

Ed, Don and Boothe stored the boxes in the hall closet, out of sight until they could be delivered.

Emma clasped her hands together. The job had united them each evening. Now she felt at loose ends. She should be glad. Boothe would no longer feel he had to spend his time with her—them, she corrected herself.

She would no longer have any reason to expect to see him for more than mealtime.

But she wasn't a bit glad. Something good and precious had ended. And she didn't want it to. "What about tea and cookies?"

"Good idea," Ed said as he withdrew from the depths of the closet. His gaze lingered on Betty, and Emma felt a burst of sympathy for the man. It hurt to care about someone when it was futile or foolish.

Emma tightened her jaw. She had no room for foolishness. Time to get on with the realities of her life. With determined steps, she filled the kettle and put it to boil.

Chapter Seven

Boothe hummed as he headed back to the boarding-house. He pulled his collar up and closed the neck of his coat more tightly against the nasty bite of the cold. He wouldn't mind the bitter temperature so much if it brought more snow.

Life had settled into a familiar routine of work, time spent with Jessie and helping Aunt Ada care for the house. Since the gifts were completed, the boarders returned to sitting in the front room as Emma read aloud. He hated to admit it, but he enjoyed the evenings. Emma had a good reading voice. The story she read held compelling qualities even if the simplistic, un-flinching faith of the characters bothered him. If only life could be as uncomplicated as it had been when he kissed Alyse goodbye in the morning, went to work, kissed her again upon his return and tossed Jessie in the air until he squealed. Do the same thing six days a week and go to church on Sunday with a wife at his side, a son in his arms and his faith intact.

After a period of whining about school and complaining about missing Aunt Vera, Jessie now seemed happy enough. His change was due, in part, to Emma's influence. Boothe had mixed feelings about her involvement with his son, but he didn't want to spoil the gentle contentment of today by analyzing the situation.

He stepped inside the boardinghouse and shrugged out of his winter coat. A few letters lay on the small hall table, and he rifled through them to see if any were for him. His name stood out, stark and black, on a long linen-weave envelope. The return address gave the name of a legal firm back in Lincoln. The skin across the back of his neck tingled as he pulled his pocketknife out, slit open the envelope and drew out the single sheet of heavy paper.

He read the contents twice. Skipping all the fancy words, it plain and simply said Vera and Luke had filed for custody of Jessie.

His arms grew numb. The inside of his head felt scraped hollow. His heart pressed against the soles of his shoes. They wanted to adopt Jessie. He jammed the letter back into the envelope, not caring that he crumpled them both in the process, and stared at the closed door. He thought this was over. He thought he'd put an end to it by moving to Favor.

But he was wrong.

"Daddy, you're home." Jessie raced to him, pulling on his arm and demanding attention.

Boothe shook free. "I have to go out again. See if you can help Aunt Ada." He grabbed his coat and hat and stepped into the cold. He strode to the street before he realized he carried his coat and jerked it on. He jammed the hat to his head and half ran, half staggered toward the center of town.

He reached the office he subconsciously sought just as a man pulled the door shut and turned the key in the lock.

Boothe rushed to his side. "Are you the lawyer?"

"I am." The man looked wary, and Boothe guessed the man must think him mad.

"I have to talk to you immediately."

"My office hours are over. Come back tomorrow." The man started to walk away.

"Wait, mister. This is too important. They want to take my son."

The lawyer paused, and Boothe dug the tattered letter from his pocket. "Here, read it. Tell me what to do."

The lawyer hesitated then nodded. "Come inside."

Boothe jerked off his hat and twisted it. "Thank you." He practically trod on the man's heels as he followed him into the small office.

"Sit." The lawyer slipped out of his topcoat and waved toward a straight-backed chair. He went around the desk and sat in a creaky, wooden armed chair. "Let's start with the basics. I'm lawyer Ashby Milton and you are…?"

"Boothe Wallace. It's about my son."

"Pleased to make your acquaintance." Ashby held out a hand.

Boothe shoved the letter into it, then realized the man meant to shake hands. "Sorry." He stuck out his hand and they shook.

Ashby settled back, pulled a leather eyeglass case from his inside pocket, adjusted his lapels, hooked the spectacles over one ear and then the other, sliding them up and down his nose until he seemed happy with the position. Only then did he carefully pull the letter from the envelope and unfold it.

Boothe barely contained his impatience at the needless delay. "They can't do it, can they?" Afraid they could, he added. "How can I stop them?"

Ashby harrumphed and smoothed the letter to the top of his desk. "They allege they have a good home, are well off and able to provide extras for the child whereas you—" He checked the letter. "Have no home, no job and no wife. Is that correct?"

"It was, but I work at White's garage now and we live with my aunt. She owns Ada's Boardinghouse."

"Fine woman." He harrumphed again. "No wife?"

"I'm a widower."

"So who cares for the child when you're at work?"

"Jessie. His name is Jessie. I take him to school, and Aunt Ada is there when he gets home."

"Isn't your aunt rather, well, old?"

Boothe sat forward. This conversation was not going how he wanted. "She's not too old to run a busy boardinghouse. I guess she's not too old to watch a six-year-old child for an hour or two. Besides, Emma Spencer is often around to spend time with him." He never thought he'd be grateful for her interference.

"Mr. Wallace, let me be quite honest with you. Judges favor a two-parent family, especially if they have a permanent home and are well off. It seems in the best interest of the child, wouldn't you agree?"

Boothe jerked forward and planted his fists on the desktop, not caring that he almost tipped over a fine gold-encased clock. The lawyer reached out and straightened it. "No, I don't agree. He's *my* son. He belongs with me."

"I understand your emotions but let's be practical. Your job could be gone tomorrow. Your aunt Ada isn't a young woman. You see how the judge will view this?"

Boothe sank back. Desperation sucked life from his heart. "So what do you suggest I do?"

"It depends on what you're willing to do to keep your son."

"I'm willing to do anything."

"Then I suggest you find a wife. A judge wouldn't be likely to take your son if you were married."

"A wife? I don't know anyone I want to marry." But his mind flooded with pictures of a practical nurse with heavy blond hair in a thick bun and brown eyes that shifted through a range of emotions. Emma? She practically bolted from a room when he entered.

"It's my best advice. I'd give it serious consideration if you want to keep your son." Ashby removed his spectacles and slid them into the leather case. He again pulled the lapels of his suit into precise alignment then stood. "I can do no more. It's up to you to help yourself."

Knowing he'd been dismissed, Boothe lurched to his feet. "A wife?" An absurd idea.

He realized Ashby waited at the door. He thanked the lawyer, planted his hat on his head and stepped into the cold. Slowly his thoughts cleared.

He'd do whatever he must to keep Jessie. Even marry. He considered the idea, turning it over and over, pushing it into various shapes to see how it felt. A marriage of convenience held certain appeal. A home again. A family again. All without emotional pain. But who would agree to such a thing? He ignored the face laughing at him in his thoughts. Emma would be his last choice.

There was Betty, of course, but she was young and

full of dreams of travel and adventure. Sarah, she was older—perhaps too old—and so quiet she scared him. Whenever he talked to her, he got the feeling she'd burst into tears if he raised his voice a fraction. She wasn't what he needed. He needed someone—

Practical.

The word slapped against his brain. Emma and practical were synonymous.

His steps lagged as he let himself explore that direction. Emma would see the advantages of a marriage of convenience. Although she didn't seem to hold Boothe in high regard—more like an unwelcome infection—she showed genuine affection for Jessie.

The wind caught at his collar and shivered down his neck. He picked up his pace. He'd ask her. For Jessie's sake. She would see the practicality of such an arrangement.

Now to plan a time to broach the subject. But when he reached the boardinghouse, he had come up with not one good idea of how to approach her. Not even a half good one. For that matter, he hadn't dredged up even a bad idea. It had been far too long since he'd courted a woman. And with Alyse it hadn't been so much courting on his part as hanging about with her brother, Luke.

Luke was his friend, or so he'd thought. That Luke supported Vera in trying to claim his son seemed the final insult. He'd trusted them to help care for Jessie—not steal him away.

He crunched his teeth together. He would find a way to get Emma alone and propose to her, though he supposed propose was hardly the right word. More like offer a practical proposition.

Emma stood over the stove as he stepped into the

house, Jessie hovering at her side. He turned at Boothe's entrance. "Miss Emma's making me hot chocolate."

Boothe assessed Emma as if he'd never seen her before. Her features were dainty, her eyes framed by dark lashes that gave warmth to her face like fur lining in a pair of mittens. The smiles she reserved for Jessie seemed to come from a golden light within. She'd make a good mother for his son.

He almost blurted out his plan right there in the kitchen until he realized Emma had asked him something. "Sorry?"

"I asked if you wanted some hot chocolate, too?"

"Oh, yes. Sounds good." He was as awkward and confused as he'd been at nineteen.

She filled three mugs and set them on the table. She and Jessie grabbed chairs and sat down. He fumbled with the chair closest to him and managed to get himself seated.

"How was your day?"

Jessie answered. "Only two more days until the school concert. Then I don't have to go for two whole weeks." He sighed expansively.

Boothe shifted his gaze to Emma. He'd really meant the question for her.

Her eyes narrowed before she lowered her gaze.

"And you?" he prodded.

She shot him a look ripe with disbelief. "It was fine."

He understood her hesitation. He'd been pretty forceful about his dislike of the medical profession as a whole. But he was prepared to overlook it in Emma's case. "That's good." He felt her uneasy stillness. No doubt she found his behavior as strange as he found it embarrassing.

He gulped his hot chocolate, gasped as it burned his mouth.

"You have to blow on it. Like this—" Jessie illustrated "—before you drink it."

"*Now* you tell me." Boothe waved his hand at his open mouth to cool his tongue.

Jessie and Emma glanced at each other and attempted to hide their giggles.

Boothe stopped trying to cool his mouth and grasped the hot cup between his palms. Now. Now, he told himself. Do it. He looked squarely at Emma. "What are your plans for the evening?"

She turned from grinning at Jessie. "I told the Douglases I'd decorate the church. Why do you ask?"

He shrugged. "No reason." Did he expect she would be available because he suddenly had a burning need to talk to her? "Could you use some help?"

Her mouth dropped open. She shut it with an audible click. She mouthed words silently and finally got them out. "Are you offering?"

"I might be of some use."

"It would go faster with help."

Jessie bounced forward. "Can I help, too?"

"It's a school night, son." He hated to disappoint Jessie but this was all about what was best for him. He returned his gaze to Emma. "Can we go after he goes to bed?"

"Certainly." She lifted one hand, and shook her head as if confused.

The church was warm. A naked pine tree stood in one corner. Someone had put boxes on the front pew. Emma hurried to them and started to pull out tinsel, red bells and fragile balls. She lifted a golden garland over her head and laughed. "I love this job."

Boothe hung back. He'd been nervous and jumpy all evening and hoped no one noticed. Even as he tucked Jessie into bed, he'd been trying to think how to ask Emma the question. He could hardly wait to be alone with her. But now he couldn't think why he'd been so anxious for the moment to arrive or how he'd spring the question.

"Here." Emma handed him a box of bells. "Hang those on the tree while I put up the balls."

He knew from doing this with Alyse that he had to balance the placement and, anxious to please Emma, studied the tree before he placed the first bell then he stepped back for more study before he put up the second.

Emma laughed. "Do you want a yardstick to measure it?"

He grimaced. "I'm just trying to do a good job."

"Let's be practical here. We have to get the job done tonight, not next year."

Practical. What he intended to propose was simply that. He tried to hang the bells faster while keeping them balanced. Emma scurried around dotting balls in between the bells all the time talking about how happy the children would be with their presents, how this was her first year celebrating Christmas in Favor. She paused and stared into space. "I hope I can make it home for Christmas Day."

He realized he knew nothing about the woman he planned to ask to marry him. "Do you have a large family?"

"No, only my parents and my brother, Sid."

"They must miss you."

She returned to her task. "No more than I miss them, but I can help them more by working."

"Where do they live?"

"On a farm in North Dakota."

"They've been affected by the drought?"

"It's been awful for them. They haven't grown enough for seed the last three years. They wouldn't have enough money for food and coal without my help." She drew in a long breath. "What about you? Where is your family?"

"My parents are both dead now. My father died when I was nineteen, my mother five years later. No brothers or sisters."

"That must be lonely. No family."

"Alyse—that was my wife's name—had family. Her parents and a brother and sister-in-law live in Lincoln. That's why we were living there."

She straightened from tucking a bell to a lower branch. "Why did you leave?"

"No job. Lost my apartment. Aunt Ada said she could use some help and give us a roof over our head." It seemed like a perfect opening to pop the question. Instead, he said, "And things weren't going good."

"Here, help me wind these garlands around the tree." She held the end of one toward him.

He took it and let her wrap the lower branches while he wrapped the taller ones.

"Now the angel for the top."

He looked at the tree. "Do we have a ladder?"

"I don't know. Would a chair work?" She hurried to the back room and returned with one.

He pulled it as close as possible to the tree and

stepped up. She handed him the white robed angel. He could barely reach the top. He stretched an inch more and dropped the angel into place just as the chair scooted away. He leaped aside to keep from falling into the tree and crashed into Emma.

She staggered back, grunting under his assault.

He grasped her shoulders to steady both of them as they struggled to regain their balance. He held her arms and looked into her wide, startled eyes. She really was quite beautiful. She'd make a fine wife. "Will you marry me?"

Chapter Eight

Emma broke from his grasp and stepped backward until a pew blocked her retreat. "Are you crazy?"

Boothe scrubbed his hand over his chin, the rasping of his whiskers scratching along her nerves. He'd been acting strangely all evening. But this was the crowning act.

She laughed nervously. "I know you don't mean it, but it's not funny to pretend."

"No, I mean it. I just didn't mean for it to come out like that."

"We don't even like each other. Why would you want to marry me?" At the untruthfulness of her words, heat raced up her veins leaving a hot spot on her cheeks. She'd tried to tell herself otherwise, but she liked him. Might even admit she'd grown slightly fond of him. Okay. Truth time. She might even be a little attracted to him. Had been since her first glimpse, even though she knew it to be foolish.

He took a step closer and stopped, correctly reading the alarm in her eyes. "I like you just fine."

"I'm a nurse. Have you forgotten?"

He hesitated. "Well, as nurses go, you seem to be a good one."

She snorted in a most unladylike fashion. "I'm thrilled to hear that."

"Surely we could work around that."

"I think not. Can you imagine how we'd disagree if I thought one of us or—" Her cheeks burned. She'd been about to say one of our children. Marriage and children went hand in hand but she couldn't say it aloud. "If I thought someone needed medical attention?"

"I'm desperate."

"Well, thanks. I guess." Just what she'd always dreamed of—the last pick of the crop to someone who was desperate. She edged along the pew until she came to the end and prepared to bolt.

"Wait. Listen to what I have to say." He pulled a battered envelope from his back pocket.

Nothing he said would change the fact they were as unsuited for each other as cat and mouse, yet she hesitated, wanting—hoping—for something to persuade her otherwise. She sucked in steadying air, sought in vain for reason knowing nothing he said would change the reality of her responsibilities.

He waved her toward a pew and she cautiously took a seat. He plopped down beside her. "This is a letter from a lawyer back in Lincoln informing me that my brother-in-law and his wife intend to adopt Jessie."

She gasped. "How can that be?"

He rattled the paper and looked bleak. "I needed help after Alyse died and Vera offered. Only then she wanted to keep Jessie. I thought she'd forget about it when we moved away." A shudder shivered up his neck.

Emma reached for him, pressed her palm to his shoulder. How did a man face the possibility of losing his son? "Surely they don't have a chance?"

He slowly brought his gaze toward her. At the look of despair in his eyes, her throat pinched closed and she scrubbed her lips together to stop the cry of pain begging to explode from her mouth.

"I went to see the lawyer in town, Ashby Milton, and he says the courts favor people who have money and their own home, but especially both a father and mother. He says my best chance is to get married."

She settled back, affronted to be no more than a means to an end, and yet, would her dreams and hopes never leave her alone? "And I was the only person you could think of?"

He snorted. "Do you see Betty or Sarah filling the role? Besides—" He shrugged. "You're fond of Jessie."

A burning mix of sympathy and annoyance shot through her. She withdrew her hand from his shoulder even though she ached to comfort him. She sat up straight, folded her hands together in her lap and forced reluctant words from her mouth. "Yes, I'm fond of Jessie but I can't marry—not you or anyone."

He narrowed his eyes. "Something wrong with you?"

She spared him a squinty-eyed look. "I have to help my family."

His breath released in a low whistle. "Whew. There for a minute… Never mind. I understand whatever you send your family each month is probably keeping them alive and fed right now, but the drought will end. Maybe we'll get lots of snow this winter and enough rain next spring—"

She cut him off. "They'll still need my help." She'd owe them for the rest of her life for what had happened.

"I don't understand. What about the farm? What about your brother?"

She leaned over as pain shot through her middle. She wanted him to stop asking questions. Each one drove a rusty spike of regret through her mind, reminding her—

"How old is your brother?"

"Sid is a year younger than I am." She thrust out the words before she had time to consider and instantly wished she could pull them back.

"Well. There you go. You're what—twenty-something?"

"Twenty-four," she mumbled. *Stop. Please stop. Don't make me think about it.*

"A good age. I'm twenty-nine myself. So your brother—Sid, right?" He waited for her slight nod. "He's twenty-three. He can help them until the drought ends. Then things will get better."

She burst to her feet and strode away then stopped, drew in a deep breath and slowly turned to face him. "It's not that simple. I'm sorry but I can't marry you."

He sank over his knees as if his spine had melted. "Then I'm going to lose Jessie."

She couldn't let that happen. But how could she prevent it? Not through marriage. She scrambled to think of an available woman. Two unmarried women sprang to mind but she quickly dismissed each. One was surely too mean-natured to be a mother to Jessie. The second—she tried to find some reason for discounting Marissa other than the fact she was far too pretty. Yes, she found it. Marissa was self-absorbed. Not a good match for Boothe and certainly not a good mother for Jessie.

She scrambled for other solutions as Boothe sat with his head in his hands. "What about God?"

"You think He'll help me?" Boothe's voice dripped bitter disbelief. "Does He care if I keep Jessie or not?" He gave a dispirited shrug.

"What I meant is I could never be unequally yoked with someone who doesn't believe."

He sat up and stared at her. "It isn't that I don't believe, only that my trust has been shattered of late. I'm trying to reconcile my belief in God's love and goodness with what's happening in my life."

They stared at each other as Emma considered his words, his offer of marriage, the consequence of refusing him, the impossibility of accepting. And yet...

To think of being Boothe's wife.

A chance to be loved and cherished. To have children. To have and to hold a man—

Heat burned up her limbs and pooled in her cheeks. Why was she allowing such errant thoughts? Why was she tormenting herself with impossible dreams? Even if she didn't have her family to consider, Boothe's proposal had nothing to do with love and mutual care. He only wanted a mother for Jessie.

Finally, Boothe looked away. He folded the letter and returned it to the envelope, stood and shoved it in his back pocket. "All I can do is hope and pray the judge will look favorably on me but I fear—" He stopped as his voice grew husky. "I fear I'm going to lose my son." His words came as a tortured whisper. He turned, his mouth drawn into a thin line, his eyes dark with despair. "I'm begging you, Emma, marry me. Help me keep my son."

She shook her head, as filled with misery as he. "I can't." Her eyes stung with tears. "I wish I could."

He nodded slowly. "I guess that's it then…unless… maybe we don't have to marry."

She gasped at the indecency of his suggestion.

He gave a snort as he realized how she'd interpreted his remarks. "I mean perhaps we can pretend to be engaged until after the court date. If the judge thinks I'm to marry, he might rule in my favor. And then we can go our separate ways."

Emma stared at him. "A *pretend* engagement?" Her initial shock gave way to another thought. It might be possible. A great hollow disappointment sucked at her thought. She wanted more. So much more. Impossibly more.

"Just until the court date."

"Which is when?" She couldn't believe she even considered it.

"Middle of February."

"Almost two months away."

"You think we could pretend to be in love for a few weeks?"

Oh, if only he guessed how easy it would be for her. She closed her eyes and despaired at how fickle her heart proved to be.

"For Jessie," Boothe added.

She opened her eyes. "I can't lie."

"We'll be engaged. You don't have to lie about anything. We won't be the first couple to change our minds before the wedding."

"I don't know what I'd say to my parents. They're counting on me."

"Assure them we won't marry until they no longer need your help."

It was all she could do not to sob. That time would never come, and she had no one to blame but herself.

She considered the idea as something warm and unfamiliar came from somewhere deep inside her. It would only be pretend but to allow herself to dream if even for a few weeks... "Very well. A pretend engagement until you go to court."

Before she realized what he meant to do, he swept her into a hug, lifting her off her feet as he swung her about, laughing. He put her down but kept his arms around her. "I could kiss you." He tipped his head, smiling as he studied her, letting his gaze linger on her hair, making her want to brush it into submission. He shifted his gaze down her cheeks and across her eyes with such intensity she bent her head and quickly, lest she miss any of this delightful exploration, again looked into his face. Before she could think what to do, he lowered his head and captured her mouth in a gentle kiss that slid past her defenses, exposing her dreams to the light of loving. She could love this man. She could and she did. Suddenly she wondered how she'd survive a pretend engagement. How she'd go back to being practical, focused Emma. How she'd accept what her life had to be.

Boothe lifted his head and holding Emma in the circle of his arms, laughed low in his throat. "I think I am a very fortunate man."

She slipped from his grasp. "How are we going to tell the others?"

He pulled her to his side and tucked her arm through his. "When they see you with stars in your eyes and me grinning like a gold mine landed in my lap, I don't think they'll have any trouble believing we've discovered we have enough in common to want to marry."

Emma swallowed back disappointment at his words. Even in pretense he couldn't bear to say the word *love*? And what did she expect? Love did not exist between them—only a fabrication. What possessed her to agree to such a thing? But as he helped her put away the boxes, held her coat as she slipped into it then dropped his arm across her shoulder and gave her a quick hug, she knew she would forever cherish the next few weeks and forever hold them close to her heart. She only hoped they would be enough to satisfy her dreams.

She let a curtain of contentment filter her thoughts as they made their way back to the boardinghouse. Boothe couldn't seem to stop laughing and squeezing her close. The gesture was only gratitude and relief that she'd given him a chance to keep Jessie but her brain ignored the facts; her heart pretended far more than their agreement included.

They burst into the house, laughing as they tried to jostle through the door at the same time. He took her coat and draped it over the banister before he hung his own.

"Let's go tell the others," he whispered.

She hung back. What had she done? How could she deal with this without lying?

He grabbed her hand and pulled her into the center of the front room. "Everyone, we have an announcement."

Six pairs of eyes focused on them and Emma squirmed. She hated deceiving her friends.

He held up their joined hands and laughed. "Emma and I are engaged." He shot her a look of reassurance as if to say he didn't have to lie.

Aunt Ada stared at them. "Well, I'll be."

Loretta nodded. "Good news."

Betty squealed. "I'm not surprised. I've seen the way you look at each other when you think no one is watching."

Emma ducked her head. She thought she'd hidden her interest in Boothe better.

The others offered their congratulations.

"When's the big day?" Betty demanded.

Boothe grinned. "We haven't had time to discuss details."

"I can make the dress," Sarah said.

"We can have the reception here." Ada glanced about the room as if already moving furniture and decorating. "Or if you wait until summer, out in the yard."

Emma lifted her palms to stop all the offers. "Thank you all, but we haven't made any plans yet. We haven't even told our families." She sent Boothe a panic-laced look. There were so many things to figure out. She grabbed his hand and pulled him into the kitchen.

"They'll think we've come to steal some kisses." He studied her mouth as if considering the idea.

She pressed a hand to his chest to hold him at bay. "What are we going to tell my family? What—" she leaned closer and demanded in a harsh whisper "—are we going to tell Jessie?"

He settled back on his heels. "He's going to expect us to get married."

"I don't want to hurt him, but I don't see how we can avoid it."

Boothe's expression hardened. "I can tell him the truth once he's safe with me. He'll understand."

"I hope so. What are you going to tell him in the meantime?"

"The same as I told the others. That we're engaged."

"What am I supposed to say when he asks me questions?"

"Surely you can tell him you care about him and want to help keep him safe. That's the truth, isn't it?"

Emma nodded, all the magic gone as she considered how this would affect Jessie. But she'd done this solely for his sake. To keep him safe, as Boothe said. She sent up a quick prayer for wisdom in handling the situation.

"What are you two doing?" Betty called. "We want to hear more about how this happened."

Emma shot Boothe an annoyed look. "I can hardly wait to see how you handle this." She marched back into the other room, Boothe at her heels.

"Well?" Betty said.

Boothe smiled with all the assurance of a cat licking down the last of the cream. "You could say I fell for her. I was putting the angel on top of the tree when the chair slid and dumped me at her feet. I looked into those beautiful dark eyes and well... I did more than fall off the chair." He grinned at Emma.

She couldn't fault him. Not once had he said anything that wasn't true except the part about her beautiful eyes. She only wished he meant it.

"I'm asking you all to keep it a secret until we've had a chance to tell Jessie. We want to do it together." He smiled at Emma with unfamiliar warmth. "But we'll have to wait until we're all home tomorrow afternoon."

He didn't have to wait for her, but the fact he'd thought to do so sneaked past her good intentions and landed in her heart like a dollop of honey.

* * *

She whispered a prayer of thanks as she hurried home the next day, certain only God's kindness and intervention kept her from making a mistake at work. Several times she emptied a bedpan or adjusted a bed with her mind elsewhere.

After a guilt-riddled sleep that left her restless and jumpy, she'd faced Boothe at the breakfast table, amid the watchful, curious glances of the others. He'd seemed quite relaxed and even made a point of slipping out to the hall to whisper goodbye as she headed out for work.

For a minute, as he stood close telling her they'd break the news to Jessie as soon as he got home from the garage, she feared he'd kiss her.

Feared he wouldn't.

When he stood back, holding the door as she stepped into the cold, she forcefully reminded herself this was all pretend.

Hours later, returning over the same path, she told herself the same thing. *It's just pretend.*

She stepped into the house. Jessie's voice and Ada's came from the kitchen. She tipped her head and listened. No other voice spoke. Her lungs released. An hour more or less before she'd have to deal with her errant emotions about this pretend engagement.

And before they had to face Jessie.

Time to prepare herself. She called hello into the kitchen then retreated to her bedroom intending to fortify herself with prayer before Boothe came home.

Her Bible lay on the table by her bed, and she sank to the mattress and let the pages fall open where they would. Her eyes fixed on a verse she'd marked for some reason, which now escaped her memory. *Pure religion and undefiled before God and the Father is this, to visit the fatherless and widows in their affliction, and to keep himself unspotted from the world.*

She groaned. Agreeing to this helped out a widower and a child who would otherwise lose his father. She assumed God would be pleased with her doing that. But "unspotted from the world"? Surely it was worldly desires making her ache for even a teasing taste of what she wanted—a husband and a child.

"Lord, God," she whispered, "I want to do this for the right reasons—to help Boothe keep Jessie. Forgive me for all the times my own desires get in the way. Help me keep my good reason firmly in the front of my mind."

When she heard Boothe downstairs, she closed her Bible and put it back in its spot. Her fingers lingered on the cover, and then she went to join Boothe.

He smiled as she entered the kitchen, and despite her promise and prayer from a few minutes ago, her heart lifted in joy at the way his eyes warmed. She drew in a deep breath and denied such feelings. Her lips felt wooden as she returned his smile.

Boothe turned to Jessie. "Come with us, son. We have something to tell you." They walked into the front room. He closed the door to ensure their privacy.

Jessie backed away, his eyes wide with wariness. "What's wrong?"

Boothe waved Emma to the sofa. As soon as she was seated, he sank down beside her and beckoned Jessie.

"You're going to send me away, aren't you?"

Boothe chuckled. "You couldn't be more wrong, son." He took Emma's hand and favored her with another grateful smile. "Miss Emma and I are engaged."

Jessie looked puzzled.

"That's what people do before they get married."

Jessie looked from Boothe to Emma. "You're going to marry my daddy?"

Emma considered her words carefully. She wouldn't lie. "We're engaged." Guilt made her squirm. She hadn't lied with her mouth, but they lived a lie with this pretense.

Jessie stepped closer and studied their faces in turn then gave Boothe an intense look. "Does that mean you love Miss Emma?"

Emma's heart set up an incessant ticking. How would Boothe handle this? She forced herself to look at him, met his suddenly sober gaze.

"That's—"

Jessie threw himself against Emma, wrapping his arms around her neck, burying his face against her shoulder and pinning her arms to her side. "I love you, too, Miss Emma. I prayed you would be my new mommy."

Emma couldn't speak. She loved this boy. She loved his father. And she sensed two out of the three in this room were going to end up paying a high emotional price for this little deception.

Her eyes stung. Her heart turned into a heavy lump of lifeless clay. A sob tore at her throat. She managed to choke it back.

Boothe rubbed Jessie's back. She forced herself to meet his gaze, saw a reflection of her aching regret. Seeing his misery only increased the choking sensation in her throat and she coughed.

Jessie released her from his neck hold, planted himself firmly between them and reached up to wrap his arms around their necks. "This is the best day of my life. The last day of school before Christmas vacation. The concert tonight. And now this. Yup. This is the best day ever."

Emma sniffed and swallowed hard. When he learned the truth, it would no doubt be the worst day of his life.

Jessie bounced to his feet, slammed open the door and raced back to the kitchen where he yelled, "Aunt Ada, did you know my daddy's going to marry Miss Emma?"

Emma twisted her hands in her lap. "I can't do this," she whispered.

Boothe squeezed her hands. "It's harder than I expected, but I don't know how else to make sure I keep Jessie. And we've gone this far—we can hardly undo things now."

She understood the truth of his words. Having given Jessie a promise, even if only by failing to be truthful, they might as well stick to their plan. He wouldn't be hurt any worse seven or eight weeks from now than he would if they told him the truth now and certainly far less than being taken from his father. "Seems we're stuck in our lie."

"We haven't lied."

"Not by word but we have by our deeds. Is there any difference?"

"I suppose not. I just don't see what else to do."

"I agreed to help you and I'll do so." She pushed to her feet and forced her rubbery limbs to hold her upright as she made her way to the door.

Boothe caught her before she made it out of the room. "No one is going to believe you if you run around with a long face."

She tried a smile, found it shaky.

He turned her to face him. "A newly engaged woman should have stars in her eyes." Before she could think what he meant, he planted a firm kiss on her mouth. He let his lips linger until she forgot the problems of being engaged to this man.

He broke away and studied her. "That's better."

Her cheeks flooded with fire. "Oh—"

He grabbed her hand and pulled her into the hall. "Doesn't feel so bad now, does it?" He led her into the kitchen without giving her a chance to answer.

She suffered through supper and the cleanup afterward without drawing any curious questions, even though she felt edgy and knew she jumped when someone spoke to her. Then she and Boothe accompanied Jessie to the school.

This school was not like the one-room, wooden-frame structure she and Sid had attended. This was an impressive two-story brick building, with a set of wide stairs going up and down from the entryway. There were two classrooms on the lower floor, another on the second plus an auditorium.

Jessie dragged them to a row of chairs. "You sit here. I'll be up there with my teacher." He pointed to the row of squirming little boys and dressed up little girls. "Do I look okay?"

Boothe squeezed his shoulder. "You look fine."

Jessie waited for Emma to say something. She bent over and whispered, "You are the best looking boy in the room."

His chest lifted several inches before he rushed off to join his class.

"What did you tell him?"

Emma told him, pleased when Boothe chuckled.

"You made his day."

"Well, he is. And he looks real fine in that little sweater and dark pants."

Boothe's expression darkened. "Vera insisted on buying the very best."

"Aah." That explained the fancy clothes Jessie wore.

"I won't be able to afford to dress him that well when he outgrows his current set of clothes." Boothe looked troubled as he watched his son.

She squeezed his arm. "I think what you have to give him is far more valuable than pretty clothes."

Slowly he turned toward her. "What do I have to offer him?"

"Your love. And your commitment."

His face relaxed. "Thank you for saying that. It's what counts, isn't it?"

She nodded, and then silence fell on the crowd as a teacher stood on the platform to welcome them.

Jessie's group was among the first to perform.

Emma's heart warmed as she watched the students line up. Jessie lifted his hand to his shoulder and waved. His teacher signaled him to stop. He lowered his hand but leaned forward to speak to the teacher and in a stage whisper that could be heard in every corner of the room, said, "That's Miss Emma with my daddy. She's going to be my new mommy." He smiled like a bright Christmas star and waved at them.

A sound of amusement rippled across the audience, and dozens of eyes turned to stare at her.

Emma's face felt as if it were about to ignite. She

wound her fingers together to keep from covering her cheeks.

Boothe squeezed her hands. His steadying touch sent calming strength to her shuddering mind.

Chapter Nine

Boothe felt her quaking. He squeezed her scrunched fists. She put on a good front, but this whole engagement thing put her in an awkward position. He wished there was another way, but he could think of none. He had to keep Vera and Luke from taking Jessie.

He owed Emma immensely for her cooperation with this idea. Right after the court date, he would thank her profusely and end this farce. He squeezed her hands tighter, telling himself they could both walk away unscathed by this whole business. He ignored the little twist in his heart. This slight shift in his feelings toward her was his own fault. Plain and simple, you couldn't kiss a woman without having some sort of reaction. And if his reaction surprised him—well, he would be careful not to kiss her again.

She strained forward, and he realized Jessie was about to speak his piece.

Jessie beamed enough to rival all the stars in heaven as he said his few words and smiled at them for approval. Boothe nodded, so proud of this scrap of humanity he'd produced he couldn't contain it. He grinned at Emma, saw an answering gleam in her eyes. She truly cared about his son. He turned away as a twinge intruded into his conscience. She wouldn't want to give up Jessie any more than Jessie would want to give her up.

His smile slipped sideways at the thought, but it was only for a short time. They'd all recover.

The other children did their parts, and then each received an orange and a small bundle of candy tied up in brown store paper.

Jessie raced to join them and held out his gifts. "An orange. Auntie Vera used to give me one."

Boothe's mouth watered at the forgotten pleasure. His heart twisted to think he could not provide such luxuries for his son. But he didn't have time to dwell on it, nor enjoy watching Jessie's pleasure at Emma's praise of his performance for well-wishers immediately swarmed them, pumping his hand and surrounding Emma. Some hugged her, others patted her like they all wanted to touch her. He reached for her hand, pulled her to his side, his arm around her shoulders to hold the eager fans at bay. He began to edge toward the door and escape.

A man blocked their path. He pushed his hat to his chest and darted a glance toward Emma. "Nurse Spencer." His voice was barely audible but the word *nurse* shouted through Boothe's mind. It shivered over his memories and scraped across his resentment. He'd vowed to avoid all contact with anyone in the medical profession. He promised himself they could practice on someone else's family. He could never bring himself to forgive the whole works of them for killing Alyse.

Yet he couldn't equate his feelings about medical

people with his feelings for Emma. *Which were?* he silently mocked. Gratitude, of course, for her help without which he'd surely lose his son.

The man's words brought Boothe's attention back to the scene before him. "My wife wanted me to say thank you for looking after her when she was so sick."

Emma touched the man's elbow and Boothe gritted his teeth to keep from pulling her arm back.

"How is she, Mr. Anders?"

"Almost good as new." He gave a quick smile. "You saved her life." In a flash of gratitude, the man grabbed Emma's hand. "You are a fine nurse."

Boothe stiffened and fought the desire to plant the heel of his hand in the man's face and shove him away.

Thankfully, the man ducked his head and hurried off.

Emma gave a short laugh and kept her face turned away. He guessed she sensed his disapproval. He hoped she put it down to talk of her being a nurse when the emotion that bit at his thoughts was far more elemental. He resented the freedom the man and so many others seemed to have about touching Emma. He snagged Jessie as he prepared to run after a friend. "Let's go home."

Emma restricted her conversation to comments on the concert as they walked toward the boardinghouse, which suited Boothe just fine. He was in no mood to talk. As soon as they got home, he insisted Jessie prepare for bed and followed him to their room.

"Is Miss Emma going to tuck me in tonight? Like a mommy does."

"She isn't your mother yet." Boothe struggled to keep his words soft, but he didn't want Jessie building too many dreams that were destined to be shattered. "She might not want to tuck you in even when she is."

"Yes, she will. She likes me a lot. I can tell."

Despite his own warring emotions, Boothe laughed. Oh to have the confidence of a six-year-old. He didn't leave the room after he smoothed the covers over Jessie. Instead, he lay on his bed, a lamp burning on the dresser. He wished he had something to read, but he normally spent only sleeping hours in this room.

"Daddy?"

"Yes?"

"Will we live here when we marry Emma?"

"I don't know. Aunt Ada will still need our help." He hadn't thought about it because it wasn't going to happen. Yet a picture flashed across his mind of Emma in the kitchen, children playing in the yard and—he closed his eyes and called himself every kind of stupid.

"I could stay here, and you can move upstairs with Mom—I mean, Miss Emma."

He wouldn't even allow his thoughts to take that journey. None of Jessie's wishes, nor any of Boothe's stupid dreams would be fulfilled. "I don't know if that would be a good idea."

"Why not?"

Boothe didn't want to discuss it. He didn't want to think what would happen after the court date. All that mattered was keeping Jessie. The rest he'd deal with on a need-to basis. "Go to sleep."

Jessie sighed and rolled over. In a few minutes he snored gently.

Boothe turned out the lamp. If only he could fall asleep as easily but he lay staring into the darkness for a long time.

This whole idea seemed reasonable in his frightened reaction to the lawyer's letter. But now he wondered how he would carry through without coming apart like a shoe with the stitching worn away. How would any of them?

The next morning, he hurried into the kitchen. He'd dismissed the troubling thoughts of last night. No reason he should concern himself with anything but his goal—to prove to the judge he intended to give Jessie a home equal to what Vera and Luke could provide. Perhaps not equal but adequate. It stuck in his craw to admit he couldn't give his son the best of everything, but he wasn't alone. The drought and Depression had reduced many families to meager existence.

He had coffee made and bacon frying when Emma hurried into the room. He poured a cup of the brew as she secured her watch on the bib of her apron.

"Thanks." She took the cup and downed a mouthful. She must have burned her tongue, but she didn't seem to notice. "I'm late." She glanced at the clock and swallowed more hot coffee. "I don't have time for breakfast."

"You have to eat something if you're going to be on your feet all day. No judge will look favorably on a woman who got ill because she wouldn't take care of herself."

She jerked back as if he'd insulted her.

He ignored her stinging look, pulled out a chair and edged her toward it.

She resisted. "I'm not your responsibility because I agreed to a pretend engagement."

"How long does it take to eat a couple pieces of bacon? And I'll slice some bread for you." He figured he'd have some eggs fried by the time she'd managed that and persuade her to eat them, too.

She hesitated then sat down—rather begrudgingly he figured. "I'm going to be late."

He scooped out three slices of crisp bacon and dropped them on her plate and quickly cracked two eggs into the hot fat, stirring them with a fork. He sliced two slabs of bread and slipped them to her plate. A minute later, he added the scrambled eggs.

She shot him a narrow-eyed look and ate hurriedly. She looked at the clock again, gasped and jerked to her feet. "I have to run. Thanks for the breakfast." She spared him an amused look. "And for making me really and truly late."

He grinned. "My pleasure."

And then she ran. Literally. He watched out the window as she trotted out of sight. Then humming, he turned back to breakfast. Most of the boarders had left for their respective homes to celebrate Christmas with their families, but Aunt Ada and Loretta would make an appearance any time now. A thought hit him hard enough that he gasped.

Christmas. Gifts. As Emma's fiancé, he would be expected to present her with a gift. What could he possibly get? He thought of the little bit of cash left from his first paycheck and the many incidentals he needed to buy. He could spare a bit for a present.

Jessie drifted into the room, rubbing his eyes.

"What are you doing up so early?"

"I want to see Miss Emma before she goes to work."

"You just missed her."

"Aww. Now I don't get to see her until this afternoon." Jessie gave a long, heart-wrenching sigh.

"She does have to work, you know."

"I know." He shot Boothe a quick look. "I bet she's the best nurse in the whole world."

"I wouldn't know." He didn't want to talk about that part of Emma's life. He didn't want to even think about it. There was no reason he should. After all, this was only temporary. "You can help me find a Christmas gift for her."

Jessie bounced up and down. "Goody, goody gumdrops. Can I buy something?"

"We'll choose something together." At Jessie's frown of disappointment, he added. "You can make her a card to go with it."

Jessie practically left skid marks on the floor as he raced back to their bedroom. He returned in a few minutes with a piece of paper and the package of crayons Vera had bought him. Another luxury Boothe could not afford. He clamped down hard on his teeth. Luxuries were nice, but the only thing Jessie truly needed was a warm and loving home and *that* he could provide.

"Maybe you should wait until you've had breakfast."

Jessie put his coloring things to one side and parked his hands on the table. "Okay. Where is it?"

Boothe laughed. He couldn't imagine life without his son. "You're quite the guy."

Jessie consumed his bacon and eggs so fast that Boothe blinked. "Might be a good idea to chew your food."

"I did." He shoved aside his plate. "I'm going to make a really pretty card with snowflakes and hearts." He shot Boothe a questioning look. "Can you draw kisses?"

How did you draw the way her lips felt cool beneath his? How did you describe the jolt of surprise at the sense of connection, the collision of something faintly dangerous? "I don't know."

Jessie kept busy with his card while Boothe took care of chores. They headed for the stores right after lunch.

"I want to get her a real pretty brooch to wear on her pink sweater. I think she's pretty in that sweater, don't you?" Jessie said.

"Uh-huh." He'd actually never noticed. He'd been too busy trying to ignore her.

"She likes pretty things."

Boothe laughed. "How do you know so much about her?"

Jessie ducked his head. "I like looking at her."

Sensing his son's embarrassment, Boothe restrained his amusement.

"I'm glad you like her, too," Jessie whispered.

Thankfully they arrived at the store so Boothe didn't have to respond. "Here we are. Let's see what we can find." He led the way inside.

Jessie hurried to the display case featuring jewelry, hair doodads and the kind of stuff Boothe hadn't looked at since Alyse's death. Fact is, even before that he hadn't spent more than a minute or two examining such stuff. Alyse always knew exactly what she wanted, saving him the need of making such choices. He stared at the display, overwhelmed by the selection.

In one corner was a brooch with pink stones set in the shape of a spray of flowers. "I like that one."

Jessie stood on tiptoes and leaned over the glass case. "I can't see good enough."

Boothe signaled the woman behind the counter. She pulled out the brooch, nestled against white satin in a blue velvet case.

"Ohh, pretty," Jessie said.

"How much?" Boothe feared it would cost more than he could afford.

The woman named a price that would require a good portion of what he had in his pocket.

"It's perfect, Daddy."

He couldn't disappoint his son and nodded. "We'll take it." He dug out the money and waited for the woman to wrap it in a piece of fancy paper.

Jessie skipped all the way home, so excited that he couldn't stop talking. "Do we have to wait until Christmas to give it to her?"

"It's only two more days. I think we should wait."

Back at the house, he allowed Jessie to hide the box under his bed.

"I can hardly wait. Every Christmas I am going to buy her something special."

Boothe wanted to warn Jessie not to build dreams around Emma, but he had to keep the truth to himself until Vera and Luke's adoption request no longer posed a threat.

Emma worked again Sunday.

Jessie managed to get up before she left. "I want you to stay home."

"I'll be back by supper time and we'll go to the church program together." She looked as eager for their outing as Jessie.

Boothe stilled the screams in the back of his head warning him people were going to be hurt by this deception, but none of them had a choice if he was to keep Jessie—and he intended to do whatever it took to ensure he didn't lose his son.

Emma waited until Jessie skipped away to whisper to Boothe, "I can hardly wait to see how excited the children will be at the gifts we made."

Boothe realized this brought the spark of excitement to her eyes, not the idea of spending time together, pretending to be engaged. He wasn't disappointed. Not a bit.

By the time they sat in the church watching the children act out the Christmas story, Boothe had quieted both his worries and his wantings. He sat beside Emma, his arm draped across the back of the bench, his fingers touching her far shoulder—for all intents and purposes, a happily engaged couple. They had to maintain that appearance and convince every observer of that fact.

And he had to remember this was pretend.

The program ended amidst loud clapping.

Emma edged forward as Pastor Douglas and his wife moved toward the tree where the gifts were piled. She squeezed his hand—a gesture he took to be as natural as the bright smile she sent him. And not in the least about him.

She perched on the edge of the pew as the children filed up to receive gifts.

A boy of about four or five sat ahead of them, clinging to his mother's hand as he watched the proceedings.

"Go ahead," the mother whispered, "I'm sure there'll be something for you."

The boy hesitated. "For me?"

Emma leaned over. "There's something special just for you. Go see."

The brown-eyed child ducked his head then glanced

toward the front where children eagerly took their gifts and hurried to their parents. Still the boy hesitated.

His mother urged him forward, and he made it as far as the aisle before he stopped. Boothe could smell his fear and uncertainty and half rose, intending to lead him forward.

His mother pushed gently at his back. "You want a present, don't you?"

Nodding, the boy stepped into the aisle and tiptoed to the front.

Mrs. Douglas placed a gift and a pair of mittens in his hands. The youngster raced back to his mother and sat with the package in his lap, staring in wide-eyed wonder.

"Open it, dear."

Slowly as if wanting the moment to last forever, he pulled off the wrappings to reveal one of the airplanes Boothe had made. Boothe knew a special bubble of happiness with the way the propeller spun on this particular one.

The boy flicked the propeller. "It really works," the boy whispered. "It really works."

Emma's eyes brimmed with pleasure as she hugged Boothe's arm and murmured in his ear, "You've made this child very happy."

Something wrenched inside him—a fragile sensation of hope that slipped past the barriers he'd erected and headed straight to a tender, eager spot in his heart. Anger followed quickly on its heels. This romantic setup was pretend. Temporary. She was a nurse. He had promised himself—

The eager light in her eyes faded. She pulled her hands to her lap and faced forward.

She'd taken his harsh expression as disapproval of her behavior. He didn't intend to tell her otherwise. They both needed to keep the boundaries firmly in place.

Jessie raced to join them. "Look at the great truck I got. I got to show Marvin." He took off as fast as he came.

People started to mill around, visiting neighbors, wishing each other a blessed Christmas. Pastor and Mrs. Douglas made their way to Boothe and Emma.

"I want to thank you both for taking care of the gifts. Your generous deed has made many children happy," Mr. Douglas said.

"What's this I hear about you two?" Mrs. Douglas didn't wait for an answer. "Congratulations. You're perfectly suited to each other." She hugged both of them.

Boothe resisted an urge to argue. The Douglases hardly knew him. They weren't aware of his doubts about God's love and faithfulness. Nor did they know he'd vowed to never forgive Alyse's death. His unforgivingness blanketed every nurse and doctor. He glanced at Emma's glowing face. Maybe she could switch to being a teacher. Or stop work altogether despite her insistence her family depended on her. Realizing his thoughts had gone to impossible territory, Boothe clamped his jaws into a locked position.

The Douglases moved away and another couple came to them—a pretty young woman and a man with Indian blood.

The young woman squealed and hugged Emma long and hard. "What did I tell you at my wedding? I said you'd be married before the year was out." She studied

Boothe. "So you're the lucky man who has convinced Emma to let a little love in her life?"

Her words stung his heart like icy water. He was not a lucky man. He was a fake, letting people think he'd won Emma's love. "Fortunate the man who wins Emma's love."

Emma shot him a red-faced scowl then turned her smile to the others. "Charlotte, Kody this is Boothe Wallace. Boothe, the Douglases—Kody and Charlotte. Kody is Pastor and Mrs. Douglas's son."

They shook hands all around.

Charlotte hugged Emma again. "I'm so happy for you. If you know half the joy I've known with Kody—"

Kody grinned at her. "Doesn't take much to make you happy, does it?"

Chuckling, Charlotte cupped his cheek with her hand and gave him a look of pure adoration. "Only you."

"Ahem," Emma said. "We're still here."

"I haven't forgotten." Charlotte turned back. "I'm going to give a party to celebrate your engagement. How about New Year's Eve? Can you come to the ranch?"

Emma glanced at Boothe, her eyes questioning, full of regret and warning.

He shrugged. It would seem unnatural if they refused. "We'll be there."

Jessie hurried to them. "That was the best church Christmas ever. A real baby in the manger." The girl who played Mary had been allowed to bring her baby brother. "I been thinking—" He tipped his head and studied his father as if measuring him for some task. "Can we have a Christmas baby next year? Just like the baby Jesus?"

Kody choked back a laugh.

Charlotte sputtered.

Emma looked ready to melt like hot butter and slip through the floorboards.

Boothe grabbed Jessie's shoulder and turned him to face the younger Douglases. "Folks, this is my son, Jessie. Jessie, say hello to Mr. and Mrs. Douglas."

"Hello." He squirmed around to look first at Emma then Boothe. "Well? Can we?"

Boothe groaned. "We'll be sure to let you know."

Jessie nodded, his face so eager it rivaled the overhead lights. "I think God will send us a baby just like he sent baby Jesus."

At that moment, the building shuddered under a blast of wind. The bell in the tower overhead began to peal.

"Merry Christmas," Mr. Douglas called. "Now excuse me while I go secure the bell rope."

The first people to leave the building called back, "It's snowing heavily." At their words, everyone gathered their things and headed for the door.

Boothe helped Emma with her coat and pulled a scarf around Jessie's neck. The wind attacked them as they stepped outside. Snow descended like a furry blanket. He grabbed Emma in one hand and Jessie in the other. "Hold tight." They'd have to face the wind for the walk home.

Away from the shelter of the church, the wind increased in fury. Emma stumbled. He held on and pulled her closer. She pressed to his side filling him with sweet delight at her unspoken trust. By the time they burst through the door into the warmth of the house, they puffed from the effort of facing the wind.

Jessie shed his coat and raced into the front room to

show Aunt Ada his gift. Boothe hoped he wouldn't add his request for a Christmas baby.

Boothe hung his coat then saw Emma struggled to undo the scarf at her neck. Ice held the knot. He helped her. His fingers brushed her cold chin sending spears of unfamiliar sharpness coursing along his nerves. He stilled his fingers. Tried to quiet the sensation.

She pulled off the scarf and draped it over a hook. She kept her back to him as she unbuttoned her coat.

He didn't move away but waited and held her coat as she pulled out her arms.

She turned. The word *thanks* froze to her lips as she met his eyes, correctly reading the wishing, the longing he couldn't deny.

He brushed moisture from her face where snow melted. Her skin flushed with exuberant color. Her eyes shone as if lit from within. Her mouth looked pink and kissable.

He bent his head and gently, tentatively brushed her lips. In the back of his mind, he remembered his decision to avoid kissing her again. But as her lips warmed to his, a great hand seemed to reach into his chest and squeeze his heart open, pouring in a warmth that healed wounds left by the loss of Alyse, smoothed lumps left by his anger toward the bungling nurse and doctor.

That memory served to set him back on his heels. He was only confusing gratitude at Emma's willingness to help him for something else—an emotion he wouldn't name.

He headed for the front room, murmured a greeting to Aunt Ada and Loretta as he crossed to the window and looked out at the snow. He felt, as much as heard, Emma follow him into the room. "This snow could be the break in the drought," he said in an attempt to put his thoughts back on practical things.

"It might have waited another day or two." Emma sound faintly amused. "Until I made my trip home and back safely."

He jerked around. "You're going home?"

She quirked one eyebrow. "For Christmas. I did mention it."

He vaguely remembered. But that was before—

Before they became engaged. Even if it was just pretend, he suddenly felt responsible for her safety. And how could he keep her safe if she went away?

"You're going to see your mommy and daddy?" Jessie's voice rounded with awe and surprise.

"Yes, I am. And my brother. I haven't been home in almost two months, and I miss my family."

"When you and Daddy get married, they'll be my grandma and grandpa, won't they? And my uncle?" Jessie quivered with anticipation.

Emma shot Boothe a desperate look. He read her silent challenge to extricate them from this.

"Daddy, can we go with Miss Emma?" Jessie practically glowed. "To see my new grandma and grandpa and uncle?"

"Jessie—" His son built such high hopes on this little deception.

"I have to leave very early tomorrow," Emma said softly. "You'll still be sleeping."

"I can wake up. You'll see."

Aunt Ada put down her knitting and considered them. "It sounds like an excellent plan. I would feel better if Emma didn't have to travel alone."

"Emma travels alone all the time." Emma's mouth pursed as she spoke.

Aunt Ada nodded. "And I don't like it one bit. In my day—" She sighed. "Never mind. But shouldn't you take this opportunity to introduce Boothe and Jessie to your parents? They'll be anxious to meet them after they learn of your engagement."

Boothe didn't have to be much brighter than a five-watt bulb to understand Emma didn't welcome the idea. Certainly she might be reluctant to take this little deception of theirs any further. But it seemed there was something about her family she didn't want him to know. Or was it a convenient excuse for refusing to marry him? Not that he hoped to convince her to turn this pretend engagement into a real one. He managed to ignore the way his heart kicked with hope. No. They both had their personal reasons why it wasn't possible.

He faced Emma, a challenge burning on his face. "There's no reason we can't go, unless you don't want us to."

Chapter Ten

Panic flooded through Emma like the torrents of water that normally—before the drought—followed a spring thaw. It cornered her like a feral animal.

She could refuse but if she did—she looked at Jessie, so innocent and eager and then shifted her gaze to Ada—people would have reason to doubt the truth of their so-called engagement.

Boothe watched with mocking eyes, knowing she was well and truly trapped. She would do what she must to help Boothe—for Jessie's sake—but the look she flung Boothe was loaded with fire. She hoped it burned his conscience. "Of course, you're welcome to come with me."

His unrepentant grin showed no trace of the guilty regret she hoped for.

She sent a desperate prayer heavenward. *Lord, tomorrow would be a real good time for Jessie to refuse to crawl from his bed.* Everyone in the house knew Jessie was not an eager riser.

But at five thirty the next morning, they waited for

her at the bottom of the stairs. Jessie yawned hugely but showed no sign of changing his mind.

"You should have stayed in bed." She spoke kindly to Jessie, but her eyes flashed her true feelings to Boothe. She didn't want him accompanying her and would not pretend otherwise.

He grinned. "I'm anxious to meet your parents."

"I'm sure." She had no idea what he really wanted, but seeing as their engagement was a mockery, and they would never marry, she couldn't imagine what perverse pleasure he got from this.

He took her bag, and they stepped out into cold so crisp that ice crystals stung her cheeks. She bent her head and was thankful the need to hurry to the station prevented her from facing what lay ahead.

They found seats in the train. Jessie insisted on sitting beside Emma, which left her little choice but to face Boothe for the duration of the trip. She shifted to stare out the window. The station agent pushed open a door to the platform. A square of light dropped to the wooden planks as he shoved the trolley inside. The conductor swung a lantern and hollered, "All aboard." The whistle blew and the train huffed from the station. Then her window became a mirror reflecting Boothe's face. He studied her. Something unfamiliar, frightening, yet teasingly warm, ticked behind her eyes. A nameless feeling she'd tried uselessly to deny since she'd first laid eyes on this annoying man.

She sent him a fierce look, but he'd already proved impervious to her annoyance. All he did was flash her another grin, which made her want to scream.

Jessie curled up beside her, his head on her knee. In minutes he snored softly.

Boothe chuckled. "The boy does not like giving up his sleep."

"You should have left him in bed." Now that Jessie wouldn't hear them, she intended to give Boothe the full brunt of her displeasure.

"He'd never forgive me if I went without him."

"You know that's not what I meant." She scrubbed her lips together. She felt a need to squirm but didn't care to disturb Jessie. Instead she rubbed her hands up and down her arms. She didn't want Boothe to meet her family.

He leaned forward. "What's bothering you? It seems perfectly normal for me to be introduced to your family. But you act like—" He shook his head. "Are they criminals or something?"

She gave him a long, hard stare. He would know the truth as soon as he met them. She might as well prepare him. "No, not criminals but—" The breath she drew in seemed to turn into a vacuum that left her struggling to fill her lungs. "It's my brother, Sid."

"He's a criminal?" He shot a look at Jessie. "He's not a risk to my son, is he?"

Emma blinked. She hadn't considered the idea but with Sid one could never quite predict. "I shouldn't think so."

He read the doubt in her voice. "You should have told me before we started. I'd never put Jessie in any sort of danger."

"I noticed how quick you were to hear my protests."

He let his shoulders relax. "You got me there."

"I have to tell you about Sid." Where to begin? How to tell him without revealing her deepest, darkest secret?

"Yes?" His voice indicated he wanted the truth.

She tried to create a condensed version of it. "Sid used to be a strong young man. You might even say daring and adventuresome. But he had an accident that—" She shuddered, felt her eyes go bleak. She'd never be able to remember that day without wanting to cry. She waited for the pain to pass, waited for it to suck out her insides, waited for the empty, dead feeling that would follow.

Boothe grabbed her hands as she scrubbed them up and down her arms. He curled them beneath his palm, calming their restlessness. "It's okay. I'm here. I'll walk with you through whatever it is."

She clung to his words as desperately as she clung to his gaze. "Sid has permanent damage from his accident." She breathed hard, couldn't go on. Her beautiful younger brother on whom her parents had pinned all their hopes—whom she loved like no other. "He hurt his head, and now he's like a child in his reasoning. He's fearful. Mother and Father have to watch him constantly. He can't be left alone." Her voice dropped to a whisper that caught on every word. "It's been very hard for everyone."

Boothe squeezed her hands. "Your parents expect you to look after them the rest of your life?"

She sat up straight. "No, I expect it of myself."

"Why?"

The look of pity on his face, as if she were only an overly emotional, silly-headed woman sent a bolt of anger through her. "Because I am to blame." She gasped and sat back. She had to make him believe she didn't mean it. "No, forget I said that."

He released her hands, leaving her floundering like a blind, frightened animal. She would not let him guess it and tucked in her chin and faced him with her best don't-mess-with-Nurse Spencer look.

"I have no intention of forgetting such a statement. Why should you blame yourself? Didn't you say it was an accident?"

Pliers would not open her mouth. Not even her best friend, Charlotte, knew her secret.

"Seems like an awful weight to carry around the rest of your life."

They stared at each other like adversaries in a box-ing ring.

"Accidents happen. A person should forgive and move forward. Without assigning blame."

She snorted. "This from a man who blames a doc-tor and nurse for an accident. Seems you should follow your own advice before you expect anyone else to."

His expression underwent a transformation from kind and pleading to an angry scowl drawing his eye-brows together and filling his eyes with darkness. "That was different."

"How?"

"They insisted on being right rather than admit their mistake."

"But it was accidental. One shouldn't assign blame. One should move on." Her voice held a mocking tone as she repeated his words.

His scowl intensified.

She lifted one shoulder in a half-hearted shrug. "Give me advice when you're ready to follow it yourself." She got no pleasure out of hurting him. She only did it to protect herself.

He crossed his arms over his chest and kept his gaze locked on something at the end of the car.

That suited her fine. She did not want to continue this conversation. She stared out the window, but glimpses of Boothe's reflection disturbed her efforts to ignore the man. She pulled a book from her bag and pretended to read even though the light was poor and she had no interest in the story.

An hour passed in silence. They would soon arrive in Banner. Before they did, she must extract a promise from him. "Please don't say anything about this to my parents."

"This? You mean our engagement?"

"No. I mean what I said about Sid."

"I'm sure they already know he had an accident." His voice was dry as toast.

Was he being purposely obtuse, or only trying to force her into saying more than she wanted? Which, she could tell him, would not happen. She'd kept her secret eight years. By now she was an expert at it. "About it being my fault."

She ducked her head to avoid seeing how his look overflowed with disbelief. She felt his silent waiting like a blast of overheated damp air sucking at her lungs.

"They don't know you blame yourself?" His words, though barely above a whisper to avoid disturbing Jessie, rang inside her head like the clanging of a bell. "Isn't this something you should discuss with them?"

A protest exploded through her thoughts. "They don't know I'm to blame." She could never confess the truth. She'd promised Sid. Although he didn't seem to remember, she did. She'd never be able to forget. Or forgive herself.

Carefully avoiding Boothe's eyes, she pressed her nose to the window, cupping her hands around her face to block out the light. In the distance, a faint glow indicated the Banner rail station. "We're almost there. You should probably wake Jessie."

Only then did she allow herself to face Boothe.

He studied her intently. "Fine. Pretend there isn't a problem." His gaze flashed mocking amusement. "But I would have never guessed the practical, efficient, organized Miss Spencer would avoid confronting something."

His attitude irked her. "Mr. Wallace, when you deal with your ghosts, I'll consider letting you give me advice about mine."

His eyes glowed with some sort of victory as if he'd won the argument.

She realized he'd succeeded in getting her to say she had ghosts in her past, though they were only dark shadows she preferred to avoid.

Not bothering to disguise his grin, he slid forward and shook Jessie. "Time to wake up, son."

Jessie burrowed against her leg.

Boothe leaned closer.

She could smell the soap he'd used, the warm wool of his coat and something more she couldn't identify but would recognize anywhere as uniquely Boothe. She wished—

She closed her eyes as warring emotions rattled her composure. She was angry with this man for prodding her. It was his fault she was forced to pretend a lie with her parents and Sid.

Jessie mumbled a protest and clutched the fabric of her coat, reluctant to leave his sleep.

"Come on, Jessie. Time to wake up." Boothe shook him gently, then when Jessie continued to resist, Boothe slipped his arm under his son's shoulders and lifted him. The warm brush of his arm against her side poured such a longing into Emma that she strangled back a sob.

If only this engagement wasn't pretend. If only—

She slammed her mind against such thoughts. No more "if onlys."

The conductor came through the car, announcing, "Banner, next stop."

Sleep left Jessie in a clap of noise. "We're there?" He squirmed from Boothe's arms and scrambled to the window. "I don't see anything."

Emma laughed, glad to be diverted from the direction her thoughts seemed determined to go. "It's still dark, but once we're at the station there will be lights."

"Will your father or brother meet us?" Jessie's words were muffled against the windowpane. His breath formed a frosty barrier that he scraped away.

"No. Mr. Boushee, the baggage man, will give us a ride to the farm." She leaned over, her shoulder against Jessie's, as eager as he for her first, familiar glimpse of Banner.

The train slowed. The shadowed platform came into sight and then a pool of light around Mr. Boushee as he waited for the train to stop.

"We're here." She struggled to get her gloves on and dropped her book as she tried to put it in her bag. What would Mother and Dad say about her guests? Her insides quaked. Was there any way to explain the situation without jeopardizing the very reason for the pretense?

Boothe caught her hands. "You're shaking."

She dismissed it with a tight laugh. "It's only the rattle from the train still going through me."

He raised his eyebrows. "Really?"

She nodded. "Don't you feel it?"

"No. What I feel is a young woman worried when she shouldn't be."

It was her turn to voice disbelief. "Really?" She could think of several very good reasons to worry about this meeting.

"Don't you think they'll understand when it's over and you explain?"

"I hope so." She sounded as unconvinced as she felt.

Jessie trotted down the aisle to wait at the door. Boothe and Emma followed more slowly. Boothe grabbed her arm to whisper, "This pretense is hard for me, too. But I'll do anything to make sure I keep Jessie. And you promised to help."

She met his hard look without flinching. "I haven't changed my mind." He'd cleared away all her confusion by reminding her neither of them had any special feelings toward the other.

She hated lying to herself because she'd had unwanted feelings from her first glimpse. She lifted her chin and faced the future.

Mr. Boushee eagerly agreed to give them a ride to the farm. "Just in time for Christmas. Your folks said you'd make it but when you didn't come in last night... Well, I supposed you might have been called to work." He turned to speak to Boothe and Jessie in the backseat. "We're mighty proud of our young Emma. A nurse in the big city and all."

Emma chuckled. Favor didn't qualify as a big city to many people.

Boothe grunted, a sound Emma took for annoyance or disbelief or both. She understood he didn't like being reminded she was a nurse.

Twenty minutes later, just as the sun flung pink rib-
bons in wild abandon across the eastern horizon and
the snow turned into blue-shadowed drifts, they pulled
up at the farm.

Dad flung open the door and waved.

Emma jerked from the car and raced toward him.
She stopped short of throwing herself into his arms.

He leaned heavily on his cane and smiled. "Welcome
home, daughter." She knew by the way he stood that
his arthritis had grown worse since she'd last visited. A
giant ache filled her. He'd counted on Sid's help from
the time her brother was old enough to carry a bucket or
wield a pitchfork. Now he struggled through the work
on his own, managing around his pain.

"Glad to be here." It had always been the same between them. This strain or awkwardness or whatever
it was. A one-sided longing on her part for more. But
more what? Her father wasn't a warm, affectionate man,
but she knew he cared for her.

Mother called from the kitchen. "Come inside before we freeze. I'll have breakfast ready in two shakes."

Mr. Boushee carried her bags to the step and suddenly she remembered Boothe and Jessie. "I brought
company."

Dad called over his shoulder. "Mother, she's brought
company."

Mother hurried to the door wiping her hands on her
apron.

Emma waved for Boothe and Jessie to join them.
"Mother, Dad, this is—" She'd thought of a hundred
different ways to introduce Boothe and explain their
relationship. None of them seemed right. "Boothe Wallace and his son, Jessie."

Boothe shook hands with them both. An awkward silence hung like a transparent curtain. She felt her parents' silent questions, Boothe's patient waiting. But she didn't know what to say.

"My dad and Miss Emma are 'gaged. You're going to be my new grandma and grandpa."

No one spoke. Jessie glanced back at Boothe. "Isn't that right, Daddy?"

Boothe cupped Jessie's shoulder with his big hand. "That's right." He draped an arm around Emma's shoulders and smiled down at her. "You have a lovely daughter."

Emma couldn't speak as her insides twisted with anger. This was carrying the deception a bit far in her opinion.

Emma's dad broke the strain first. He held out his hand to Boothe. "I hope you're a good man. Our Emma deserves no less."

"I'll always treat her the very best," Boothe assured the older man.

"Well, come in, come in." Mother shooed them inside.

Sid waited for her beside the stove, poised, ready to run if something frightened him.

Emma paused, signaling Boothe and Jessie to wait, and stepped forward so Sid saw no one but her. Her insides welled up. As handsome as ever, grown tall and filled out into a good-looking man, his thatch of blond hair shining, his blue eyes overly bright with things she couldn't understand, sometimes fear, other times excitement. This morning she hoped it was the latter. She held out her arms. "Hi, Sid. How about a hug?"

He flung himself into her embrace. She backed up

to keep from toppling. "Emma, Emma, Emma." He said her name over and over in an endless word. "Emmaemmaemma."

She eased out of his grasp. "I have some friends for you to meet." She took his hand and pulled him forward.

Sid started to roll his head from side to side. He clutched her hand so hard that she had to wriggle her fingers. A low moaning sound escaped his mouth.

"Sid. They're my friends. They won't hurt you."

Boothe waited for Sid to accept his presence, but Jessie raced forward and touched Sid's arm. "I'm Jessie and you're going to be my uncle, Sid."

Sid stiffened. Dad guarded the door. Mother made shushing noises that sometimes calmed Sid. Boothe reached for Jessie. "Son, take it easy. Give the man a chance—"

"Uncle Sid." Sid's words rounded with awe. "Me, Uncle Sid." He reached for Jessie's hand. "Me, Uncle Sid. You call me Uncle Sid. Okay?"

Jessie nodded, grinning from ear to ear.

The whole room seemed to sigh. Another crisis averted.

"I show you my rocks," Sid said to Jessie.

Emma touched Sid's shoulder. "Wait. I want you to say hello to Boothe Wallace, Jessie's father. He and I—"

Sid didn't let her finish, saved her the necessity of trying to explain the relationship. "Hi, Boothe Wallace, Jessie's father." He beamed at Jessie. "You see my rocks?"

"Sure."

Sid kept his box of treasures in the corner of the kitchen farthest from the windows, and he led Jessie there. Emma and her parents had never been able to understand Sid's fascination with rocks but he sat cross-legged on the floor, Jessie beside him, and they soon engaged in a nonstop conversation about his collection while Mother made breakfast.

In a few minutes, they gathered around the table. Sid consented to join them when Jessie led the way. He sat beside Mother and insisted Emma sit on the other side. He eyed Boothe but ducked away whenever Boothe looked in his direction.

Emma sent Boothe an apologetic glance. He gave her a warm, understanding smile.

Sid noticed. "You like my sister."

Boothe nodded.

Sid turned to Emma. "You gonna marry him? Like Mom and Dad?"

"That's what it would be like." *If we married*, she added silently.

"You like him a lot?"

She couldn't meet Boothe's eyes, couldn't look at her parents. How could she answer honestly? She didn't want to confess she liked him in front of all these witnesses. Finally, she found the right answer. "He's a good man."

Sid nodded his approval then turned to his food.

After breakfast while Emma and her mother cleaned up the kitchen, Father headed out to finish the chores. Boothe volunteered to help.

Seeing Sid playing on the floor with Jessie while Father limped out to cope with work Sid should have done, Emma struggled to keep her sorrow buried. If only Sid wasn't afraid to go outside, he could still help, but the moment he saw the open spaces he started to run. One time Emma chased him for an hour before she succeeded in turning him around.

"That's the happiest I've seen him in a long time," Mother said, watching Sid and Jessie play together.

Emma nodded and smiled. Yes, it was nice to see him enjoying himself, but he was playing with a six-year-old. How happy could she be about that? Her brother, who had been big and bold and beautiful. He was still big and beautiful. She'd trade them both for bold and normal.

Boothe and Dad returned with Boothe carrying the bucket of milk and three eggs. Emma hoped he'd found them before they froze.

"'Preciate your help," Dad said, deepening the ache in Emma that went on and on like the prairie sky.

As soon as the milk was strained and put to cool and the chicken was baking in the oven, Mother shooed them into the front room to open gifts.

Emma took things from her overnight bag before she joined them. She'd bought yard goods for Mother, warm mittens for Dad and a small wooden box with a lid for Sid. He opened it and saw the tiny glistening rocks she'd gathered for him on a trip into the hills to visit Charlotte and Kody.

"Ohh, this is nice." He pulled out each of the dozen stones and passed them around for inspection.

When he finished, Emma opened her gifts from Mother and Dad. Dad had built a small tray for her stationery and Mother had crocheted a lace doily. "Thank you so much."

She handed out the gifts she'd brought with her for Boothe and Jessie. She bought them Saturday and thought she'd leave them on the kitchen table for them to discover after she left. That was before she'd been hornswoggled into letting them accompany her.

"How—" Boothe asked, staring from her to the gift.

She laughed, pleased beyond belief that she'd surprised him.

Jessie opened his gift and showed a red rubber ball. "Thanks, Miss Emma."

"Can I play ball with you?" Sid asked, eyeing the ball with interest.

"Sure."

"Better wait until we finish." Boothe slowly, painstakingly untied his parcel. When he pulled out a pocket-sized whetstone, he grinned from ear to ear. "I couldn't have asked for anything better."

The look he gave filled her with a warmth that turned her insides into pudding.

Suddenly aware of how long they'd been staring at each other, she cleared her throat and jerked her unwilling gaze away.

He nudged Jessie, who vibrated with excitement. Jessie pulled a parcel from behind him and, his eyes glowing, handed her a prettily wrapped gift.

"How? When?"

He chuckled. "I love surprises, don't you?"

She nodded.

Jessie stood in front of her. "Open it. Hurry."

"Jessie," Boothe warned but Emma laughed.

"It's okay. I like his enthusiasm."

"It's good for us all to have a child around." Dad spoke with such weariness that Emma's pleasure in pleasing Boothe with her gift vanished like a snowflake on a hot stove. She knew how difficult it was for her parents to care for Sid, how their dreams had been shattered and all they had to look forward to was constant supervision.

She silently renewed her vow to help them the rest of her life.

She opened her gift. A little brooch like a spray of spring flowers. "It's lovely." She pinned it to the shoulder of her gray sweater. "Thank you."

Intending only to spare Boothe a quick glance, she found she couldn't look away from his dark gray gaze. She felt every beat of her heart against her ribs as she silently explored the fragile feelings between them.

"Jessie helped me choose it," Boothe said, breaking the spell.

Again she reminded herself of the reality of her situation—a pretend engagement, a never-ending responsibility.

"Well," Mother said, pushing to her feet. "I'll get busy on dinner."

"I'll help," Emma gratefully escaped into the kitchen leaving Boothe to visit her father while Sid and Jessie played with the red ball.

They ate a simple meal of roast chicken, mashed potatoes, turnips and pumpkin pie. Then it was time to play table games. They played simple games that both Jessie and Sid could enjoy.

Emma's heart filled with grateful admiration at the way Boothe amused them. She would be sure to thank him for his kindness to Sid as soon as they were alone, which with some forethought on her part and any amount of cooperation from others, wouldn't be any time in the near future. She found it harder and harder to deny her feelings for him. And she must. She would play this pretend engagement out until the court proceedings, and then maybe she'd find a job elsewhere. Maybe closer to home so she could relieve her parents on her days off.

Bedtime approached. "Mother, I'll make up the extra bed." She grabbed sheets and headed for the small, unused room. Boothe and Jessie would be comfortable here, and if Dad kept the stove going all night long, they'd be warm enough.

When she returned to the kitchen, only Boothe and Jessie remained. Jessie's sprawled arms on the table cradled his head.

"Where is everyone?"

"Gone to bed."

"I have your room ready."

Boothe nodded. "Jessie is more than ready." He scrubbed his hand across Jessie's head but his eyes remained locked with Emma's.

"Come. I'll show you." Her mouth said come but her heart said stay. Stay and talk. But what was there to talk about? They both knew this was only make-believe.

Jessie stirred. Boothe scooped him into his arms and Emma led the way to the bedroom. Jessie curled into a ball when Boothe put him down. A now familiar and unwelcome yearning churned up her throat like a squatter with the intention of staying.

"I need to get our bag." Boothe turned and bumped into Emma, who stood like a thoughtless statue in the doorway.

He narrowed his eyes as she stared at him.

Afraid he'd read things in her gaze she didn't want him to, she hastily backed away. He headed toward the kitchen where his bag sat under the coat hooks.

Chapter Eleven

"Daddy, look at the snowbanks. Can we go slide on them?" Jessie stared into the bright outdoors.

Boothe had helped Mr. Spencer with chores before breakfast and now sat at the table enjoying a second cup of coffee. "Sounds like fun."

Jessie raced to Sid's side where he sat playing with his rocks. "You want to come out and play, Uncle Sid?"

Sid shrank back. "Don't like outside."

Emma signaled Jessie to her side. "Sid's afraid of outside."

Jessie looked shocked. "Why? It's fun."

Aah, Boothe thought. *That explained why Sid didn't help with the chores. Despite his mental limitations, Sid was a big man. He ought to be able to do a hundred things Mr. Spencer struggled with.*

Jessie returned to Sid's side. "Won't you come and play with me?" He held out his hand.

Sid studied the extended hand, turned his gaze upward to Jessie's smiling face. He scrambled to his feet.

Beaming, he announced. "I'm going to play with Jessie. He's my friend."

Boothe felt a collective drawing in of breath as the pair headed for the door. Sid pulled on a heavy coat, overshoes, hat and mittens just as Jessie did.

Emma rushed for her own outerwear. "I'll watch him."

Mr. Spencer pushed to his feet. "I'll be right along."

Whatever they seemed to expect to happen, Boothe intended to be part of if only to make sure Jessie was safe so he grabbed his coat and boots.

The sun shone bright enough to hurt his eyes. He pulled his hat lower to provide shade.

Jessie spied the sleigh Mr. Spencer used to trundle things back and forth between the house and the barn and grabbed it. "Let's slide down the hills."

Sid nodded, his eyes locked on Jessie's movements.

Emma hovered like a mother bird.

Banks of soil drifted against fences and buildings created hills, now dusted with snow. It seemed symbolic of the whole place—Emma's parents, weary and worn, hiding it behind a dust of a smile. Even Emma looked older here.

Sid followed Jessie to the top of the first hill. He looked around him. An expression of pure, uncontrollable panic swathed his face.

"Sid," Emma called. "Sid, look at me." She raced after him so suddenly, Boothe could only stare.

Sid shuddered and started to run.

Emma scrambled up the hill. "Sid. Sid."

Boothe broke into a desperate run though he wasn't sure why. He only knew Emma sounded frantic.

Sid slipped on the snow and stumbled, gained his feet and continued on.

Emma reached him, grabbed his arm. "Sid. Stop. Come on. Let's go inside."

Sid dragged her after him. A sound like the sighing, crying wind, came from his throat.

"Emma, stop him," Mr. Spencer called from the door as he tried to make headway with his crippled gait, hindered by his need to lean on the cane.

Boothe didn't know what sent them all into such a panic, but Emma continued, unsuccessfully, to try and stop Sid. He reached the pair. "Sid, Emma's trying to tell you something." When he realized Sid wasn't about to slow down, Boothe grabbed his arm and wrenched him to a halt.

Emma flashed a look of gratitude. "Sid, let's go home. See. Dad's waiting for you."

Boothe turned Sid toward the house.

They got through the door and helped Sid to a chair. Emma bent to remove his overshoes.

Jessie, eyes wide, followed. He faced Sid. "What's wrong? Why did you run?"

Sid shielded his eyes. "I don't like the open."

"Then don't look."

Sid dropped his hand and stared at Jessie. "That's right. I shouldn't look."

Emma chuckled. "There you go, Sid. Just don't look."

But no one suggested Sid go outside again, and after a bit, they had lunch of stew made from the leftover chicken.

Sid let Jessie sort through his rocks but carefully arranged them into orderly rows after Jessie set them aside.

It was a shame. Sid was tidy, well-behaved, gentle and kind—traits that would serve him well if he had a job somewhere. A man didn't have to work outside. Boothe himself was evidence of that. He worked in a garage. Yeah, he walked back and forth, which might present a problem for Sid. But still. There had to be something he could do. How long would Mr. Spencer be able to keep up with the farm work? He could barely walk. Emma should not feel she had the sole responsibility of supporting the family. He couldn't imagine why she blamed herself for Sid's condition. Accidents happened. He refused to give Emma's comments about Alyse's death any credit. *Her* death wasn't simply an accident.

"Your turn," Emma said. They played a game of chicken foot with dominoes. To him it was a simple game but she seemed to figure strategy was involved and took her time assessing all options.

Mrs. Spencer had announced she intended to nap after lunch, and Mr. Spencer nodded in the rocking chair.

The game over, Emma jumped up. "I have a treat." She hurried into her bedroom and returned with a small sack she handed to Sid. "Share with everyone."

Sid opened the sack and looked in. "Ooh." He pulled out an orange and handed it to Jessie. He carefully placed one in front of Boothe. He thanked Emma as he placed one in her hands. "Two left. One for Mother. One for Father."

Mr. Spencer stirred and Boothe took him an orange.

Mother hustled into the room. "I must get supper ready." But she took the fruit Sid offered and sat at the table to peel it.

"I'll make tea," Emma offered and supper was momentarily forgotten as the four of them drank tea and visited. Boothe felt Emma's look of appreciation when he regaled them with stories of activities at the boardinghouse. They seemed especially eager to hear about Emma's part in planning the Christmas gifts for the children.

They hurried through supper. At seven, Mr. Boushee arrived, as arranged, to pick them up.

"Come on, Jessie," Boothe called. "It's time to go."

"I won't forget," Sid said, as Jessie turned to obey his father.

Boothe waited until they were in the train to ask Jessie about what he'd said.

Jessie studied his hands. "I told him I knew about being scared. I told him something I remember. 'The Lord is my shepherd.'" He fixed Boothe with a determined look. "I think it means God takes care of us and 'tects us."

Boothe's thoughts stung with remembrance. Alyse had taught Jessie the verse. He'd mocked her, saying the boy was too young and the words meant nothing to him. How wrong he'd been. He stared down the tunnel of his memory. How many other times had he been wrong and didn't know it?

At the gentle concern in Emma's eyes, he realized his expression revealed far more than he wanted. He turned back to Jessie. "I think you're right, and it was wise of you to tell Sid."

Jessie bounced to the edge of the worn leather seat. "I like Uncle Sid. When can we visit him again?"

"I don't know." Every day this plan of his gathered momentum, collecting bits and pieces of future sorrow. He couldn't meet Emma's eyes, fearing her silent accusation.

Jessie spoke. "Sid gave me this rock so I won't forget him. I told him I don't need a rock. I will always remember him. I didn't have anything to give him. Maybe I can send him something."

"That would be nice."

"I like the farm." Jessie continued to talk about his experience for the rest of the trip.

Emma seemed preoccupied. Boothe missed the fun she'd been on the trip to Banner—feisty and kissable. *Whoa. Kissing is over.* This relationship was business. Nothing more. As it was, far too many people stood to be hurt, but he didn't know what else he could do. Except keep things as businesslike as possible.

Only six more weeks and the court date would arrive. Until then all he had to do was go to work, come home and spend a couple of unbearably sweet hours in Emma's company.

But he'd forgotten the Douglas's invitation.

Emma pulled him aside the afternoon of the party. "I'll never convince Charlotte we're really engaged." She twisted her hands together and sounded thoroughly unhappy.

He wanted to still her hands, but since their trip to the farm, he'd found it increasingly hard to remember this was a pretend engagement and had done his best to avoid touching her or being alone with her.

She gave him a misery-filled look. "I can't stand the thought of Charlotte thinking I'm trying to pull the wool over her eyes."

He forgot all his reasons, all his warnings and

squeezed her shoulders. "Emma, what would we have to do to convince her?"

She clung to his gaze, searching for his meaning. Her shoulders relaxed as she found the kindness he offered. "I don't know. How can we prove something that isn't true? I hate not being totally honest."

If he allowed himself total honesty, he would have to confess his growing interest in Emma—his enjoyment of her sweet nature, her manner of accepting life and dealing with it. He liked the way she cared about his son. He admired her easy grace and ready smile.

He slammed the door on such thoughts. That wasn't the sort of honesty she sought. From the beginning, she'd made it clear she had no room in her life for love and marriage. She'd been sure to remind him more than once since their visit to the farm. "You saw for yourself how my parents need help providing for themselves and Sid. He'll never be able to contribute. That leaves me."

He wanted to argue that it wasn't her responsibility, but how could he even suggest she abandon her concern? It wasn't that he didn't think she should help. But he resented how it left him with no hope. "What would you suggest we do differently?"

Her expression grew thoughtful. A flash of a smile widened her mouth.

His breath caught in the back of his throat as he waited expectantly for her answer.

But her shoulders drooped and her expression flattened. "I don't know."

Disappointment dug into his chest. She'd been thinking something more. He hoped she'd been about to admit she held some feelings for him. Perhaps even liked him a bit. Was it possible? "Emma, I think you are worrying too much what people will think." He spoke slowly trying to sort his thoughts ahead of his words. "Is it so hard to pretend we like each other?" He rubbed his knuckles along her jawline. She quivered beneath his touch. He hoped it meant she wasn't indifferent to him. "I don't have to pretend." His voice dropped to a husky whisper.

Her eyes darkened. He hoped she'd say she didn't have to pretend, either. But she stepped out of reach and lowered her head so he couldn't see her face. "It's not a matter of whether or not I like you. We both know this can only be pretend. Just until the court date. After that we have to tell everyone the truth. And for me the truth is… I can never contemplate marriage."

Did he detect a tremor in her voice? "I took you for a woman of deep faith. Isn't saying anything is impossible equivalent to saying God can do nothing?"

She jerked back and stared at him. "'With God all things are possible.' I can't believe you're pointing me to faith. Have you allowed yourself to remember God's faithfulness?"

He gave a short laugh. "I long to believe as blindly as I once did. I don't suppose I ever will, though."

She smiled slowly. "'With God all things are possible.'"

He didn't let his thoughts follow the trail of possibilities. "We can be friends without pretending, can't we?" He intended to get that confession from her mouth.

She nodded.

"That's all we have to do. For tonight, why don't you relax and have fun?"

She studied him. A mixture of doubt, dread and—

dare he hope?—anticipation crossed her face and she smiled. "I suppose I could do that."

He felt as if he'd shed a heavy overcoat on a hot day.

And so they set out for the party in a car he borrowed from Mr. White. Jessie had been invited and bounced up and down in the backseat.

The stars shone brightly as they drove along the road. He wished they could keep driving until they reached a place where their troubles would disappear. Instead, Emma pointed out the turn to the Douglas's home.

The ranch house surprised him—a large two-story log structure with lights flooding from top-to-bottom windows.

Charlotte and Kody stood in the open door. Emma rushed into her friend's arms.

Kody reached for Boothe's hand and shook it. "Welcome to our humble dwelling."

Boothe laughed at the gentle humor in Kody's voice. "It looks like a lovely home."

"The former owner built it. But we get to reap the enjoyment."

Charlotte drew Emma inside. Boothe and Jessie followed into the huge front room.

"I think you've met Star at church," Kody said to Jessie as he drew his daughter to his side. "She's five."

"Hello," Jessie mumbled.

Kody turned to the couple in the background. "These are my good friends, John and Morning." Kody's voice held a hint of caution as he introduced an Indian couple.

Boothe admired John with his proud stance and the gentle-voiced Morning. He liked Star immensely when she suggested Jessie might like to play.

"Not dolls," he firmly informed her. "I'm not playing with dolls."

Kody laughed as they marched toward the stairway. "They'll have fun together. Let me introduce Michael Barnes and his wife, Caroline. Michael is the town banker."

Boothe shook hands with the man he'd glimpsed in town. He appeared to be in his mid-thirties, his wife somewhat younger. It felt strange to be at a party with a banker who gave you permission to call him by his given name.

"I only wish the children could come, but Annie's been sick so we left her at home with her brother Henry," Caroline explained.

Charlotte allowed everyone to visit for a bit before she organized them into games. The children joined them for Blind Man's Bluff and Earth, Sky, Water. Star laughed so hard she couldn't speak let alone name an object from one of the elements. She giggled so hard Kody rolled his eyes, which sent Charlotte into peals of laughter.

Emma shook her head and chuckled. "I'd almost forgotten how much fun it is to be around all of you."

A fingertip of warmth trailed down Boothe's spine as he watched Emma relax and enjoy herself. As the evening passed, the tightness around her eyes left. She practically bounced with pleasure. Boothe had difficulty keeping his eyes off her. And to sit across the room watching her provided a lesson in self-control he didn't care to learn. He only wanted to go to her side and enjoy her presence.

Charlotte drew his attention from his useless wishing. "The children can bed down anytime. We have lots of room."

Boothe dragged his gaze from Emma's glowing face and noticed Jessie slumped in his chair. He knew a flash of guilt for not paying more attention to his flesh and blood instead of letting his mind wander along paths of never-to-happen delights.

"Come on, Jessie." He scooped his son into his arms and followed Charlotte up the sweeping staircase to a bedroom. Star hurried to another room without protest.

Back downstairs, Charlotte rubbed her hands in glee. "Now that the children are gone, we are going to celebrate a very special occasion—the engagement of my dearest friend, Emma, to this fine, upstanding man, Boothe."

The others clapped except for Emma, who shot him a help-me look.

Boothe smiled encouragement before he addressed Charlotte. "I might be a scoundrel, for all you know."

"Not if Emma has approved you. She's not easily fooled. She's as practical as anyone I know. I mean, look at her. Have you ever seen her with her hair down?"

Boothe didn't turn his gaze to Emma. He didn't want to imagine anything about Emma above and beyond what he saw and dealt with every day. That was challenge enough.

"Have you?" Charlotte demanded.

He shook his head, still avoiding looking at the object of their discussion.

"She has waves of golden hair. If I had hair like hers, I would let it hang free. But not Emma." Charlotte gave her friend an affectionate smile. "She's careful about everything she does. She wouldn't fall in love with a man who is anything but good and fine and noble."

Emma made a choking sound, her face wreathed in merriment. "He's a regular saint all right."

Charlotte chuckled mockingly. "Well, maybe I overstate the facts but never mind. We want to celebrate with you."

Emma met Boothe's eyes and shrugged. He nodded. What could they do but go along with the whole thing? Not that he found it trying. Far from it. He ran his gaze over her hair and wondered what it would take to get her to free that golden glory from the combs.

Soon Charlotte stood before them, a piece of paper in her hands. "They haven't given us any particulars about how they met or when they fell in love. So I thought we'd fill in some of the details our way. I'm going to go around the circle and ask you each to give me words." She began with Caroline. "Name a day. It can be something special or memorable."

Caroline mused a moment. "The day it rained buckets."

Charlotte moved on, chuckling as she wrote down the words each supplied. "Now I am going to read to you the story of Emma and Boothe's romance." She cleared her throat and rattled her paper.

"Boothe, an *arrogant worm* from *Timbuktu* came to town *the day it rained buckets*. The first person he met was Emma, a kind but *bowlegged* young woman. Their first meeting occurred *long after midnight* while *the cat chased the birds*. He was impressed with her *purple* hair and *wooden* complexion."

By the time she finished, everyone laughed at the imaginary courtship of Emma and Boothe.

Emma wiped tears from her face. "That was great fun, Charlotte."

"I'll make a copy for you to keep."

Emma's expression turned wooden. "Thanks."

Boothe chuckled. "You can tell your grandchildren."

Charlotte waved a finger. "Whoops. Don't you mean *our* grandchildren?"

Boothe nodded. "Of course. A slip of the tongue."

Michael leaned over and whispered, "You'd better watch those slips of the tongue. Women are sensitive to those kinds of things." He squeezed his wife's hand and smiled at her. "Not that I mind."

Caroline widened her eyes and looked sufficiently surprised. "I don't recall you ever having such a problem."

Boothe watched the interplay between them, sweet with trust and familiarity. He missed having someone to share his thoughts with, who understood the things he didn't say. He and Alyse had shared something special, but he didn't ache for her as he once had. With a start, he realized it wasn't Alyse he wanted to fill the void. It was Emma.

Emma must have felt him twitch. "Are you okay?" she whispered.

He gathered up his thoughts and stuffed them into a strongbox, locked it and threw away the key. "I'm fine. I just have to be more careful about what I say."

Charlotte glanced at the clock. "It's almost midnight." She rushed from the room and returned with party hats and noisemakers to pass around. Kody went to her side as they all watched the clock.

"Ten, nine, eight—" They counted down together.

At midnight, they blew their noisemakers and shouted, "Happy New Year."

Kody and Charlotte turned and kissed.

Michael and Caroline turned and kissed.

Boothe turned and smiled down at Emma's cautious face. He knew he shouldn't kiss her again. But everyone would wonder if he didn't. He claimed her lips.

Kody hadn't lit fireworks. There were no flashing colored lights. Except inside Boothe's head.

Chapter Twelve

Three weeks later Emma and Jessie walked along the sidewalk in front of the stores in Favor.

"Sid will really like what I sent him, won't he?" Jessie said.

Emma squeezed his hand. "He'll love getting a ball like yours."

Since the visit to her home, Jessie had a goal—he wanted to buy Sid a ball like the one Emma gave him for Christmas. He'd managed to earn the money on his own by running errands for the Millers next door and by sweeping the sidewalk in front of the general store. He finally earned enough to buy the ball, and they'd mailed it to Sid a few minutes ago.

"Sid will be so excited to get a parcel in the mail. I'm proud of you. You worked hard to buy his gift."

Jessie shoved his shoulders back. "Daddy says a person can always find work if they try hard enough."

Emma murmured agreement though she wondered where Sid fit into Boothe's philosophy. She might ask him except for one thing—since the party at Kody and

Charlotte's three weeks ago, she'd done her best to avoid him. She'd taken extra hours at work. Said she had to visit former patients. Found a hundred reasons why she must rush over to Pastor and Mrs. Douglas's house to inquire about one thing or another.

She couldn't look at Boothe without remembering that New Year's kiss. It had not felt pretend. To her shame and embarrassment, she'd wrapped her arms around his waist, pressed her palms to his back and acted like she didn't ever want to let go. Only the laughter of the others forced her to back away. She hoped Boothe would take it as good playacting.

But she couldn't fool herself any longer.

She'd foolishly, hopelessly fallen in love. It wasn't something she was proud of.

It wasn't part of the bargain between them.

Only three more weeks until the court date and she'd put this whole awful, beautiful pretense behind her. She'd already started to look for jobs in North Dakota.

"When can we visit your farm again?" Jessie asked.

"I—" She faltered. This was the hardest part of the whole deception—finding ways to answer questions from others without lying. "I don't know. It depends."

They had to pass White's garage on the way back to the house. Hoping to avoid seeing Boothe, Emma headed down the alley rather than pass the front of the garage.

"Can we go see Daddy?"

Emma hesitated beside the storage shed at the edge of the property. "He'll be working."

"I want to say hello."

A thump came from the building beside them. "Maybe that's him in the shed."

"Daddy," Jessie called. "Daddy, is that you?"

The world exploded in an angry roar and a flash so bright it seared the back of Emma's eyeballs. Flames erupted from the shed. The wall flew toward them.

Her heart kicked so hard it hurt her chest. She put out her hands to protect them. "Run," she screamed as the side of the shed slammed into her. "Jessie, run!" Hot air scalded her lungs. Heat seared her feet. She went down, the weight of the wall suffocating her. She fought to get oil-soaked air into her lungs.

She pawed at the weight pressing her to the ground. Panic, like a rabid animal, clawed at her.

"Jessie, where are you? Jessie!"

The weight on her shifted. She turned her head, her shoulders. She had to get up. She had to find Jessie. "Jessie!" She couldn't hear her own voice, only a roar like being run over by a train. She couldn't feel her feet. She twisted but couldn't see them. Panic clawed at her throat. *Where are my feet?*

"Jessie!" Her throat felt as if she'd swallowed rusty nails. Still she heard nothing.

She twisted and reached out, encountered a familiar texture. Jessie's coat. "Jessie, say something." Not a sound. Was he dead? Or was she deaf? She edged her hand over him, found his chest, felt it rise and fall. "Are you hurt?"

She edged her torso closer. Jessie's eyes were wide, blurred with confusion. He gave no indication if he saw her or heard her. Was she really speaking? She visually checked his head and neck for injuries then lowered her gaze.

Only her experience as a nurse kept her from crying out as she saw Jessie's exposed leg. The femur protruded. Blood gushed from the wound. Two thoughts twined through her mind. She had to stop the bleeding. The pain must be excruciating. "Jessie, be brave. I have to touch your leg."

She pressed down above the wound. The bleeding slowed and stopped. "Thank You, God," she whispered. She glanced around. They lay beneath part of the wall. Broken and splintered boards surrounded her. Fire licked at the edges. Panic seared her lungs. "Help. Help," she screamed, the words tearing from her throat. But she heard not a sound.

They had to get away. She pulled. Her legs would not move. With her free arm, she pushed at the debris. "Help! We need help!"

"Emma," Jessie moaned. "Are we going to die?"

His words came through mounds of cotton wool. She realized the explosion had rendered her temporarily deaf.

"Not if I can help it." She screamed again, ignoring the rawness of her throat. She was tempted to claw away the boards pinning them with both hands but if she didn't stanch the bleeding, Jessie would die. She could only bat helplessly with one arm.

"You aren't going to die."

Jessie clung to her gaze.

"I'll pray." She ached to help God but she was powerless. At His mercy. His tender mercy. She prayed out loud knowing Jessie needed to cling to faith as much as she. "Our Father, who art in heaven. Hallowed be Thy name." She said the entire Lord's Prayer. Never before had the words been more meaningful, or more comforting.

"Someone will find us." But they'd better come soon.

She fell back as a black curtain crept toward the edges of her mind. *No. I can't pass out.* Jessie would bleed to death. She fought back the blackness and screamed again for help. She hoped it sounded louder to others than to her. *God, let someone hear me.* She glanced at the fire licking around the edges. They better hurry.

Boothe felt a shudder under his feet accompanied by a boom. He glanced up. They must be having trouble moving cars down at the rail yards. He bent over the engine he worked on.

"Boothe, fire." Mr. White grabbed buckets and headed for the back door.

A fire this close to the gasoline pumps...

Boothe dropped everything and ran. The storage shed at the back burned. One wall lay broken and shattered in the middle of the yard. Flames shot from the wall as well as the pile of debris that used to be the shed. Already half a dozen men organized a bucket brigade to tackle the fire. Others came on the run. Mr. Crukshank dug at the debris. What was wrong with the man? There was nothing worth saving. Putting out the fire was the first priority.

Boothe grabbed a bucket of water and threw it on the flames. "Where's the fire engine?" he demanded of the man next to him.

"On its way."

Mr. Crukshank yelled something. A ripple went up the line as they passed his message. One by one the men dropped their buckets and raced to Crukshank.

What was wrong with everyone? "Let's get this fire out," Boothe hollered.

"There's someone in there."

He dropped his bucket, soaking his trouser legs, and raced over. He grabbed a corner of the wall, along with five others.

"On the count of three," someone called. "And let's be careful. We don't know what—" He didn't finish as someone counted, "One, two, three."

Slowly the wall lifted. The far corner crumpled. They scrambled to prevent the wall from falling again.

Other men crawled over the debris. "Two of them," a disembodied voice called. "One of them's Nurse Spencer."

Another voice called, "The other's a kid and he's hurt bad."

The blood drained from Boothe's face, and his legs went numb. Black spots danced across his vision. Emma and Jessie. Buried in this mess. Jessie hurt. *God, forget all my doubts. Don't hold them against me at this time. Keep my son and Emma safe.*

The wall shuddered. Some instinctive voice warned him not to let go. If it fell—

"Take this," he hollered to a man racing to the scene. When the man steadied the wall, Boothe dropped to his hands and knees and headed into the mess.

Someone grabbed him. "Stay back, man."

"That's my son and my fiancée."

He saw Jessie. Saw the broken leg and the blood. He slithered closer. Fragments of broken wood grabbed at him, hindering his progress. Something sharp cut his palm. He ignored everything but his need to touch Jessie. Find Emma.

"He's alive," Crukshank said. "We have to get them out of here."

The heat of the encroaching fire brought beads of

sweat to Boothe's forehead. He could see Jessie's face now. Even the ashes and dust couldn't hide his pallor.

Boothe shifted his gaze and stared into Emma's frightened, determined eyes. Several scratches marred her face. Was she okay? He scanned her body, praying she had escaped serious injury.

Her hands—his heart sank like a dead weight. Every beat brought pain. Her hands looked like raw meat. One lay across Jessie's leg. Gently, he reached out to lift it away.

"No," she screamed. "He's bleeding." She batted at him with her other hand.

He winced away.

He didn't want to further upset her, but he had to get both of them out of this mess before the fire spread. "It's okay. I'll take care of him."

She rocked her head back and forth. "No. You can't take care of him yourself. He must go to a doctor. I'll take him. I don't care what you think."

Nausea rose in Boothe's throat. His son was dying before his eyes. If they didn't move soon, they would all be burned, but the last time he'd taken a loved one to the doctor…

Emma turned to Crukshank. "Can you get us out together? And take us to the hospital."

"We'll do our best, ma'am." He turned and hollered. "Give us more room and send in a couple more men."

Boothe swallowed the bitter taste in his mouth. "No need. I'll take Jessie." He tried to get his arms under his son, but Emma batted at him. He paid no attention. This was his son. He'd care for him.

Emma grabbed a shattered board and hit him across the side of his head. "I won't let you take him."

Boothe drew back. She'd surprised him more than hurt him.

He glowered at her. "He's my son."

"And you'd let him die before you'd go to the hospital."

Were her words slurred? He studied her more closely. Her eyes drifted shut. She jerked them open. She looked about ready to pass out any minute. But he didn't have time to wait for it.

"Boothe." Even his name dragged in slow tones. "Promise me you will take him to the doctor. If you don't, he'll die."

Boothe knew she was right. He'd seen the bone sticking out. He couldn't fix that.

Emma closed her eyes. "Boothe, it's time you let go of your blame and trusted someone." Her words were barely a whisper.

Could he trust anyone? Or maybe the question was, could others trust him to forget his anger and do what was right? What kind of man would put his son and fiancée at risk to prove himself right?

"Emma."

She cracked open one eye.

"I promise you I'll take you both to the hospital. You can trust me."

She looked deep into his gaze with barely focused eyes. Then she relaxed. "Thank you. See where my hand is? Slip yours under mine, and keep pressure there until you get to the doctor."

He followed her instructions. Felt the stickiness beneath his palm. "I've got it."

She fell back.

"She's passed out," Crukshank said. "Let's get out of here."

Someone helped Crukshank pull Emma from the debris. Hands reached out to guide Boothe from the rubble and into a car that whisked them away to the hospital.

Boothe never once let up the pressure on Jessie's leg.

God, help us. Please make both Jessie and Emma okay. Please, God. Please, God. He repeated the words nonstop.

"We're here," the man driving the car announced.

Dr. Phelps and a nurse raced for the car, pushing a stretcher.

Dr. Phelps opened the door and leaned in. "Good job. We'll take it from here." He put out his hand to replace Boothe's.

Boothe couldn't let go. He couldn't give his son over to this man.

Dr. Phelps turned his gaze to Boothe. "He'll be in good hands. I promise I'll care for him like he was my own son."

Boothe saw assurance in the doctor's eyes. Understood he could trust the man if he chose.

Boothe decided he would be the kind of man his loved ones could trust. He nodded and let the doctor put his hand over the bloody area. As soon as the nurse and doctor had Jessie on the stretcher, they raced inside and down the hall with Boothe on their heels. As he started to follow them through swinging doors, another nurse caught him.

"You can't go in there. That's the operating room."

Boothe swung around. "Where's Emma? I want to see her."

"She's having her burns looked at." She edged him

toward a small room. "You wait here, and we'll let you know when you can see them."

He sank to the chair and bowed his head into his hands. *God, I never really stopped believing in You. You know that, don't You? I blamed doctors and nurses for Alyse's death. I blamed You. I wanted You to stop bad things from happening to me. A little selfish I admit. Now I know I have no right to ask anything of You. I don't deserve Your favor, but God, if You see fit, please let Emma and Jessie be okay.*

Someone dropped a hand to his shoulder, and he looked up to see Pastor Douglas and his wife. "We've come to wait with you and pray."

"They can use all the prayers they can get. So can I."

The pair sat down beside him and bowed their heads. Betty slipped in. Then Aunt Ada. Slowly the room filled up with friends.

Boothe felt their care and support. Their spoken prayers sent encouragement to his fearful heart, but his ear was tuned for footsteps coming down the hall. Each time someone passed, his lungs forgot how to work.

He had no idea how long he waited. It seemed like eternity before the doctor stepped into the room. Boothe forced his rubbery body to stand and cross to the doctor.

Dr. Phelps smiled wearily.

Boothe's knees threatened to buckle. Did that smile mean bad news?

"Jessie is going to be okay. It's a miracle he didn't bleed out. You can thank Nurse Spencer for saving his life. He'll be in traction for several weeks, but he ought to be as good as new once he's up and about."

Boothe shook the doctor's hand. "Thank you. What about Emma?"

"She still hasn't regained consciousness. It's a matter of wait and see. Her hands are badly burned. I've cleaned them up as best I can. They'll be bandaged while they heal." He chuckled. "I can't quite picture Nurse Spencer as a patient. I don't think she's going to be happy about being dependent on others."

"Can I see them?"

"Come along."

They entered the children's ward. Dr. Phelps pulled aside a dividing curtain between beds and ushered Boothe in.

Jessie lay on his back, his leg suspended from an overhead bar to a series of pulleys.

Boothe paused. It looked so barbaric. Was the doctor experimenting?

Dr. Phelps touched Boothe's arm. "It looks worse than it is. The weights on the pulleys keep the bone in alignment while it heals. Otherwise spasms will pull the bone crooked and he'll never walk properly again."

Boothe nodded. "Will Jessie be in any pain?"

"We'll do everything we can to make sure he isn't."

"How long?" Boothe waved at the ropes and pulleys.

"Could be as long as six months. But probably less."

Boothe couldn't speak past the lump in his throat. Jessie, who bounced from one activity to another, who never walked when he could run—he'd be confined like a trussed turkey for months. Boothe would help him. He'd do whatever it took to see his son well and strong again.

"He's still asleep from the anesthetic," Dr. Phelps said.

Boothe leaned over and kissed Jessie's forehead. "I'll

be here for you, son. Whatever you need from me, I'll give." He straightened. "Where's Emma?"

Dr. Phelps signaled him to follow, and they crossed the hall into the women's ward. Again, the doctor parted a set of curtains.

Boothe hung back trying to prepare himself for the shock of seeing Emma helpless. He stepped forward.

She looked peaceful except for the huge bandages swaddling her hands.

"She won't be able to do a thing for herself."

Dr. Phelps nodded. "I suspect it will be harder for her than many. She values her independence. She's got some damage to her lungs and throat from the smoke. She's still unconscious. There's a lump on the back of her head. But she's young and strong and stubborn."

"Can I stay with them?"

Dr. Phelps nodded. "They'll both be needing lots of help." He found a chair and parked it beside the bed.

Boothe waited until the doctor left before he bent over Emma studying her restful features. Her hair fanned out on the pillow as beautiful as Charlotte had said despite the smoke and debris in it. He tenderly stroked it back from her face. He leaned over and kissed the cut on her cheek. He would take her pain if he could. All he could do was be available for her. He whispered the same promise to her that he had to Jessie. "I'll be here for you, sweet Emma. Whatever you need from me, I'll give."

He jerked upright and crossed back to Jessie's bedside.

Pastor Douglas came in. "Boothe, we're here to help. What can we do?"

He wanted to be with each one as they wakened.

He wanted them to see him when they opened their eyes and understand he would be there as long as they needed him. But he couldn't be in two places at once. "If you could take turns sitting with one of them and let me know as soon as they stir…"

He couldn't say how long he waited. Hours ceased to exist. Time was measured by the next heartbeat and gentle breath of his loved ones.

"Boothe." Pastor Douglas touched his shoulder. "Jessie is waking up."

Boothe gave Emma a last lingering look. He'd been enjoying studying her peaceful features, filling his senses with the sight of her. He spun on his heel and hurried across the hall to bend over Jessie's bed. "Jessie, are you awake?"

Jessie's eyelids fluttered. He searched for the source of the sound.

"I'm here, son. I'm right here." Boothe's voice sounded as thick as it felt.

His son swallowed hard and whispered. "Daddy, I'm thirsty." He tried to sit. "I can't move." Panic gave his voice strength.

Boothe gently pressed him back to the pillow then held a cup with a spout to Jessie's mouth and let him drink. "You have a broken leg."

Jessie stared into Boothe's gaze, his look of fear and confusion tightened Boothe's ribs like a giant vise.

"We got hit by the shed. Emma caught the wall to keep it from hitting us. But it was too heavy." His eyes widened and he tried again to sit. Groaning, he fell back, panting as if he'd run three miles. "Where's Miss Emma?"

Boothe stroked Jessie's forehead. "She's in a bed across the hall. She's got burns on her hands."

"I want to see her."

"Perhaps later after you've both rested. Now you relax. I'll be here. If you need anything, you only have to tell me."

The breath went from Jessie's tiny chest in a whoosh, and then he dragged in more air. He closed his eyes. The covers rose and fell in steady rhythm. The nurse said, "He's sleeping. Rest is the best medicine. That and love."

"He'll get plenty of both," Boothe said.

He didn't want to leave his son even though he slept, but he needed to check on Emma, make sure she was okay and pray for her to regain consciousness.

Pastor Douglas nodded as Boothe returned to Emma's bedside. "She's peaceful."

Even unconscious Emma's faith felt alive and vibrant. Sitting at her side filled him with hope. Boothe hung his head. He didn't deserve one single bit of mercy from God, not after the way he'd pushed Him aside, blaming Him for everything that went wrong from Alyse's death to the drought, when all the time he could have chosen to trust God, to let Him hold his life in His all-powerful hands. Now when he needed God the most, he feared he had no right to ask for anything.

"I'll go sit with Jessie." Pastor Douglas squeezed Boothe's shoulder. "Remember, God is here for whatever you need."

I will never leave thee nor forsake thee. Great peace poured into Boothe's soul. God's faithfulness did not depend on Boothe but on His unchanging word. *Lord, whatever happens, I choose to trust You. Please, heal these two precious people.*

He lifted his head and stared into Emma's open eyes. Never had he seen anything more beautiful. He bolted to his feet and leaned over the bed.

"Emma. Welcome back." His words ached across his tongue.

A nurse hurried forward and took her pulse. Emma's eyes drifted shut.

"She'll probably drift in and out for a few hours."

Boothe waited a few minutes then returned to Jessie's room.

"How is she?" Pastor Douglas asked.

"She woke up for a few minutes."

"Praise God. A miracle for both of them."

"I don't deserve a miracle."

Pastor patted his shoulder. "None of us do. It is only by His great mercy that any of us receive blessings."

"I don't know if Emma is going to see this as a blessing." He chuckled. "I expect as soon as she's fully awake she'll be trying to devise ways she can manage on her own." He sobered. "This will not be easy on her."

Pastor Douglas agreed. "It's a good thing she has you."

Silently Boothe vowed she'd never regret having him if only for the duration of her wounds. A thought seared across his mind. Their pretend engagement would soon be over. They could have nothing more. She would never abandon her responsibility to her family. He wished there was some other way, but he respected her commitment. It was part and parcel of the strong, vibrant woman he—

Loved.

How could he be so foolish as to let himself fall in love with her? Yet he had. Helplessly, completely, joyously.

He vowed he would never utter a word of his love to her. He would not make this more difficult for either of them than it had to be.

Chapter Thirteen

The air sucked at her lungs, seared her eyes.

Sid. She had to get him out. She fought back the weight against her chest. Her hands wouldn't respond.

They were trapped. Sid. She had to save Sid.

Panic laced through her. She screamed and screamed.

"Emma." A voice whispered her name.

She turned, listened.

"Emma, you're safe. Wake up."

She struggled against the hand on her shoulder. Sid. She wanted to scream his name. The word formed in her mind but not on her lips. She tried to reach for him. Her hands refused to move.

"Emma, it's me. Boothe."

"Sid." She managed to croak his name. Wondered if anyone could hear.

"Emma. I'm here."

Boothe. He'd come. Her nightmare fled. He'd help.

"Get Sid." Wait. It wasn't Sid; it was Jessie. Her panic shifted directions. Jessie had been trapped beside her. Bleeding. She struggled to reach him.

"Emma. Wake up. I'm right here."

The sound of Boothe's voice eased back her fear. Something cool swiped sweat from her heated brow.

The dream cleared. She opened her eyes and looked into gray calmness.

"Boothe?" she whispered.

"I'm here." He wiped her face with a damp cloth. "I'll be here as long as you need me."

She wanted to touch him, see if he was real or part of her dream. Her hands were so heavy. Pain scorched up her arms. She cried out.

"Oh, Emma. I wish I could take your pain for you."

She wished so, too. She closed her eyes and practiced the advice she so freely gave to patients. Deep breaths. Don't fight it. Ride the pain.

She wished someone had told her how futile such advice was. Then the pain eased marginally.

She met Boothe's gaze, sought the comfort he offered, and finding it, drew in a long steady breath that hurt all the way down. She moaned.

Boothe slipped his arm behind her shoulders and held a cup of water to her lips. "Drink."

She let each mouthful glide over her raw throat. Shouldn't it ease the parched feel? The fire. Of course. Her throat had been damaged.

She nodded to indicate she'd had enough to drink. Told herself she didn't want him to keep holding her, yet tears stung her eyes as he withdrew his arm.

Tenderly, he wiped them away. "I am so sorry."

She nodded. There was something she had to ask. She struggled to find the information in her mind. She closed her eyes, fought the bliss of sleep. It successfully claimed her.

Again, the terror of searching for someone and not finding him filled her sleep.

Boothe's voice wakened her. His touch on her forehead soothed her. His gray steady gaze and gentle smile calmed her.

"Jessie?"

"He's okay."

"Thank God." She swallowed hard. Tried to dismiss the torment dogging her thoughts. "It was so scary. I didn't want Jessie to die. Or end up like Sid." She shuddered. "It was so much like Sid."

Boothe stroked her forehead. "It's all right now. Both of you are safe."

"No. You don't understand. I didn't stop him. I didn't help him." Her throat felt like each word was laced with razor blades, but she had to tell him all of it. Maybe then it would stop haunting her sleep. "We liked to play at the Holliday's farm. There were so few rules." She paused remembering it all. "Mother and Dad heard of some of the stuff like running down the barn roof and across the rickety lean-to. They forbid us to do it. But Sid—" Her voice caught.

Boothe held her shoulders and helped her drink more water. "You don't need to talk about this now. Wait until you're better."

"I have to tell someone."

He nodded. "I'm here if you need me."

She clung to his steady gaze. "Sid begged me not to tell our parents, and he and the Holliday boys raced off the lean-to into a stack of straw. The roof shook as they ran across it." She closed her eyes. Wished she could stop the memory. Knew it would never leave her. "They laughed. Thought it was fun. I wanted to stop Sid, but I didn't. I didn't want to ruin his fun. The roof collapsed. The Holliday boys managed to reach the straw stack but Sid—he fell. The space below was blown full of snow."

She tried to grab Boothe's arm, but for some reason her hands refused to move.

"He just plumb disappeared. I wanted to help dig him out but someone held me back. He wasn't breathing when they got him out. I didn't know what to do." She'd vowed she'd never again feel so helpless. When she became a nurse she'd learn how to handle emergencies.

Boothe didn't look away in horror and disappointment. Nor did he waste his breath trying to say it wasn't her fault. Because it was. She could have stopped Sid. She should have.

"Lie back and rest. Jessie is okay. He's across the hall with his leg in traction. You saved his life. Thank you." He pressed a kiss to her forehead.

She closed her eyes. She'd done something right. If only it would wipe away her guilt over failing Sid.

Light blared across her eyelids. She cracked them open. Sunlight flooded the room.

Emma glanced around. She was alone. And so thirsty her mouth felt like an acre of drought-stricken prairie. She reached for the glass of water on the bed table. Pain wrapped around her hands. They were mounds of white bandages. She remembered. They were burned.

"Boothe," she whispered. He'd been at her bedside every time she opened her eyes, but now he was gone.

She lay back and stared at the ceiling.

He's with Jessie, of course. Jessie's alive. She remembered Boothe saying his leg was in traction.

Thanking her for saving him and kissing her forehead in gratitude.

She smiled a little in spite of her pain. Boothe had sought the necessary medical care. He'd also promised to be here to help. Where was he? She needed a drink.

She remembered something else. She'd told him about Sid. Or was it only something in her dreams? No. She was certain she'd told him.

How would she ever face him? Even if he hid his condemnation, she could never look him in the face again without wondering what he thought. Though he could not accuse her more than she did herself.

Boothe stepped into the room. "Good morning. Nice to see you awake."

"It's not the first time. I seem to recall being awake off and on." Although she could barely speak past the dryness of her voice, she managed to express her annoyance. It defied reason, but she blamed him for knowing her secret.

He had the nerve to laugh. "Would you like a drink?"

She glared at him. Yes, she wanted a drink, but it about killed her to have to ask.

Still chuckling, he slipped his arm under her shoulders and held the glass to her lips. "I see you're feeling better."

She spared him a look full of annoyance and disbelief as she drank. "Thank you for the water. What makes you think I'm feeling better?"

"You're acting ornery."

Ornery? Not her. "I figure I'm being extremely patient considering the circumstances."

He laughed. Again. The man had a strange sense of

humor. Something she hadn't noticed before. "Do you mind finding me a nurse?"

"What do you want? I can get it for you."

Her throat protested but her mocking laugh felt good. The dull redness that crept up his neck felt like justice.

"Oh. Of course." He rushed from the room.

Nurse Lang came in a few minutes later. "Needing some help?"

"I hate to bother you but with these—" She held up her club-like hands.

"It's no bother to me. You call out whenever you need something." Lang helped her with her morning needs. "Breakfast will be here in a minute."

"Goody." As if she could eat breakfast with two worthless hands. "How bad are they?" She asked Lang.

"They'll heal."

More good news. The day was full of such. "How long?"

Lang shrugged. "You know burns, but I wouldn't think more than three weeks. But you ask Dr. Phelps what he thinks."

She certainly would.

Lang left Emma sitting up in bed waiting for the breakfast she couldn't eat. How could she not work for three weeks or more? How would she manage looking after herself?

Boothe stepped into the room carrying the breakfast tray and set it on the table. He removed the lids. "Porridge and bread. Coffee." He breathed in the smell. "Mmm, good."

It took all her self-control to keep from kicking him.

"I expect you want coffee first." He poured in a little milk just the way she liked it and held it to her mouth.

She glared at him and clamped her lips together. She hated being dependent on him. Hated the way it made her feel vulnerable and cherished. Hated it enough to refuse to eat.

He waved the cup back and forth in front of her nose. "Coffee. Smell it?"

The aroma filled her nostrils, sent her taste buds into a frenzy.

"I know how much you like your morning coffee." He held the cup to her mouth.

Her brain demanded satisfaction. Her eyes informed him how much she hated this even as she slurped a long, delicious, satisfying mouthful. She closed her eyes and let that first taste slide down her tender throat. Without letting Boothe see how good it tasted, she took three more swallows.

He put down the cup. "Bread or porridge?"

She was starved. She wanted it all. Every mouthful. Every crumb. "Porridge," she said grudgingly.

He fed her a spoonful. Every time she swallowed, he had another ready. His timing was infallible. His smile never faltered despite her nastiest looks. It irked her he was so nice about this.

Couldn't she get a rise out of him at all?

He slathered strawberry jam on the bread. She took a huge bite not wanting this to take any longer than necessary.

She regretted it almost immediately as the bread scratched her throat.

"No more," she said when she finally choked down the wretched stuff. "How's Jessie?"

"Cranky."

She read his unspoken message in the quick quirk of

his brows that he almost managed to hide. *Like you.* She studied the unfinished bread. She was being unreasonable but seemed powerless to stop herself.

"I want to see him."

"He wants to see you, too. I'll go find a nurse and ask if it's possible."

"It's my hands that are useless. Not my feet."

The annoying man chuckled as he left the room.

Emma still scowled when Lang came back pushing a wheelchair. "Climb aboard."

"There's no reason I can't walk."

Lang laughed. What was the matter with everyone that they kept laughing for no reason whatsoever? "Not until the doctor gives his okay." She parked the chair beside the bed and planted her hands on her hips. "Do you want to see Jessie or not?"

Emma resisted a childish urge to say if she couldn't have her way and walk she wasn't going, but she had to see Jessie and she choked back her pugnacious spirit. She plopped herself in the chair. "Wheel me away."

They crossed the hall to the children's ward. Jessie lay on his back, his leg suspended over the bed. When he saw Emma, he started to cry.

Ignoring Nurse Lang's order to stay in the chair, Emma rose and leaned over the bed. She couldn't smooth his hair. She couldn't adjust his leg. She couldn't wash his face or help care for him. Her eyes flooded and she wanted to wail. But he was okay. His leg would heal. Ignoring the pain in her hands, keeping them from touching anything, she hugged him with her arms and pressed her face to his cheek. "Jessie." Her throat clogged with tears. "I'm so relieved to see you're okay." All the reassuring words from the nurse, the doctor, even Boothe meant nothing until she'd seen Jessie herself.

"Daddy brought me to the doctor." His voice rang with awe.

"He saved your life." And maybe hers, too.

"You burnt your hands." He rolled his head to look from one side to the other, staring at her bandages.

Emma lifted them like a trophy. "I don't remember doing it."

"You did it saving my son." Boothe's voice grated with emotion.

Emma didn't turn. She didn't want to see gratitude on his face. She'd acted out of love for this child. Her heart swelled with gratefulness that Boothe had taken the necessary steps to get medical help.

At Nurse Lang's urging, she sat down. Parked in a wheelchair with her hands two big useless mitts. As useless as a short bit of thread. She didn't like the feeling one bit.

"Do they hurt?" Jessie asked.

"Not much."

"My leg doesn't, either."

Emma guessed he would put on a brave face to convince them all.

She turned to Boothe. "He'll be okay."

"Thanks to you."

"And you." In that silent acknowledgment between them, something strong and solid forged.

She jerked her gaze away. Strong, solid? Hardly. Temporary and pretend.

"Will you stay with me?" Jessie asked.

"As long as I can." She'd stay forever if she could, but forever was not hers to give.

"I'll leave you fifteen minutes," Nurse Lang said. "Then I think both patients should rest."

Emma wanted so much to hold Jessie's hand, smooth his hair. She couldn't so she impotently listened to Jessie recite the horrors of the accident while Boothe leaned over his son and did the things Emma ached to do.

As if reading her frustration, he squeezed her shoulder, rubbing his thumb along her collarbone in a rhythm matching the way he stroked Jessie's head. Comforted, connected to the pair, she rested an arm along Jessie's side.

Nurse Lang returned, took her back to her room and settled her in bed. Emma fought the massive weariness that left her teary, but she lost the battle and fell into a deep sleep.

When she woke, she saw Boothe at her bedside, his head bowed. Sighed deeply and fell asleep again.

For three days she could do nothing but sleep and make quick visits to Jessie courtesy of one of the nurses or Boothe.

She endured having everything done for her. Ada and Sarah helped the nurses but more often than not, Boothe appeared at mealtime.

She tried being rude. Not that she had to try very hard. She was petty and cranky without trying. But nothing deterred his good humor. She wanted only to escape somewhere and be alone. Because, heaven help her, she counted the minutes to mealtime. Listened for his footsteps down the hall. She'd even sunk so low as to resent the time he spent with Jessie.

He never mentioned her confession about Sid, so maybe he thought it was only senseless ramblings. All the more reason for the growing resentment burning inside her chest.

How would she cope when this was over?

He would stop pretending he cared about her. She would have to go on with her life, pretending she didn't care about him. She couldn't imagine how she'd do it. Her impatience mounted until it ruled her world. Four days later, she spoke to the doctor on his morning visit.

"Dr. Phelps, I want to go home. I can manage with help from Ada and Loretta." She'd seen her hands. Knew it would take time for them to heal. She knew, too, that Jessie would be confined to bed for several weeks. Boothe would no doubt spend his time at the hospital with Jessie. At home, she could get peace.

Dr. Phelps considered her request for a long time. Finally he nodded. "Your restlessness isn't doing you any good. Perhaps you would do better at home. I'll speak to the ladies and make sure they're prepared for your care."

"Today?"

"The end of the week at the earliest."

Charlotte came to visit that afternoon. Emma lifted her hands out of the way as her friend hugged her. "I came as soon as I heard."

Emma held her close. "It's so good to see you."

Charlotte wiped tears from her eyes as she edged back. "What can I do to help?"

"Put my hair up."

Charlotte laughed. "You're asking the wrong person. I've always preferred it down. It's beautiful. Like woven gold." Her eyes sparkled. "I'll bet Boothe likes it this way."

Exactly why Emma wanted it up. Several times she'd caught Boothe staring at her hair, knew he stroked it on her pillow when he thought she was sleeping. And her fickle heart loved it.

She did not need anything more she'd have to forget when this was over.

Charlotte pulled a brush from the bedside table. "I'll brush it." Her touch soothed away tension that had crept up Emma's skin making her scalp taut.

"You're a real hero. Everyone is singing your praises. They say you wouldn't let Boothe take Jessie until he promised to take him to the doctor. You really are a spunky gal."

"I just did what had to be done."

"You risked your life." Charlotte's voice caught. She put away the brush and came around the bed to face Emma. "I am so grateful to our good Lord that you're going to be all right."

Emma's heart smote her. "I've forgotten to be grateful," she whispered. She'd been far too consumed with anger at her helpless state, fighting too hard to resist Boothe's help, disgusted with her weakness in telling him about Sid's accident. *Lord, forgive me.* "I've been grumpy and unbearable."

"It's understandable. You've been through a lot and you're in pain."

The pain in her hands was nothing compared to the pain in her heart. Which, without a doubt, would get worse when the pretense was over.

"I've allowed myself to dream of impossible things."

Charlotte looked amused. "I suppose Boothe is somewhat distracted by Jessie's needs right now, but it doesn't mean he cares any less for you."

If only it were so, but she couldn't stand to deceive her friend any longer. "Charlotte, there is something

I must tell you." *Our love is only a pretense.* But it was real on Emma's behalf. What was the truth? That Emma had bought herself a world full of sorrow in the days to come.

"Here he is now," Charlotte whispered.

Emma, her back to the door, stiffened as she heard his footsteps.

He strode around the bed to face her. He was furious. She couldn't imagine why.

"Is what I hear true?"

"Depends on what you heard."

Charlotte shifted back from the towering man.

"You're pressuring the doctor to let you leave?"

"Aren't you the one who thinks hospitals are unnecessary?"

He dismissed her question with a short grunt. "Who is going to care for you at home?"

Charlotte touched Emma's shoulder. "You can come home with me. I'd love to take care of you. It's what I do best—look after people."

Emma considered the offer. It was tempting. She could escape the necessity of seeing Boothe every day.

"You can't go way out there. I forbid it."

"You *forbid* it? What gives you the right to order me about?"

"We are to be married, in case you've forgotten."

She narrowed her eyes. Who was he trying to convince? They both knew their engagement wasn't real. And she didn't care to deceive Charlotte anymore. "I have forgotten nothing. Have you?"

He managed to look slightly uncomfortable.

"And if you think marriage would give you the right to order me about—"

Charlotte sighed. "If you'll excuse me. I have no desire to see you two fight." She paused at the door. "Remember, after the fighting comes the kissing."

Emma waited until Charlotte left. The two other women who shared the ward were gone, one for a bath and the other for an X ray so she didn't hesitate to turn the full blast of her fury on Boothe. "How dare you come in here and order me about acting like you have some right. Our pretend engagement gives you no such right or obligation."

She wished she could cross her arms to emphasize her point, but her bandages made it impossible.

He glowered at her. "This has nothing to do with our so-called engagement."

"Really. What does it have to do with, if I might be so bold as to ask?"

Boothe's expression faltered.

Emma's lungs felt as if she lay under the weight of another wall. Would he say it mattered? That it was more than pretend? But what difference would it make? She would never be free to marry and have a family. Truth was, she already had a family and would be caring for them the rest of her life.

Pain attacked her heart, raced through her body and settled in her hands. She groaned and lowered her gaze to her swaddled hands.

"Lie down," Boothe ordered, holding back the covers. She did so without hesitation. He grabbed two pillows and put them at her sides. "Now put your hands on these. Keep them elevated."

"When did you become a nurse?" She meant to sound annoyed but her voice came out weak and needy.

"I'm no nurse but I can manage to offer comfort.

Between you and Jessie, I'm getting quite good at it in fact."

"How is Jessie?" The pain eased and she managed to fill her lungs.

"He's got some pain. They gave him something for that." Boothe sucked in air. "I can't imagine him lying in that bed for weeks."

She looked at him closely, trying to see him without the filter of her own needs and desires. He looked weary and yet peaceful. He met her gaze steady and calm.

"You aren't really going out to Charlotte's, are you?"

Did he want her to stay? Did he need her? If only—

There was no room for such thoughts.

She shook her head. "I can't. The doctor wants to keep an eye on my hands."

"Good. I'll feel much better with you here. I'm counting on your help amusing Jessie."

For a whisper of time she'd imagined he would say something else. Something—

He only cared because of Jessie.

She turned away to stare at the door, wishing Charlotte to return and save her from useless, impossible, wonderful dreams.

"Tell Jessie I'll be over to visit him soon."

Boothe rose. "Thank you. For everything."

She closed her eyes as he left. She didn't want thanks. She wanted what she couldn't have.

Lord, God, You have assigned me my path. Only in obeying You and following Your direction can I find true happiness. She knew it, believed it with her whole heart, but never before had it felt so difficult. *I can't do this without Your help. My heart is being rebellious even though I want nothing more than to be cheerfully obedient.*

Chapter Fourteen

Boothe fled Emma's room. The hospital walls closed in. He grabbed his coat and hat and headed outside.

Why did life have to be so complicated? He wanted to quickly and quietly end this farce with Emma. Spare himself the agony of seeing her every day, wanting to hold her and comfort her, knowing their pretend engagement didn't give him the right.

Boothe's stride lengthened. He turned down Main Street and headed for the lawyer's office.

Ashby glanced up as Boothe barged through the door. He rose and held out his hand. "Sorry to hear about your problems. How are the invalids?"

"Mending." Boothe yanked his hat off and scrubbed a hand over his head. The lawyer didn't know the half of it. "Is everything ready for the judge?"

"I sent him the statements, and he's requested depositions from your employer, the pastor and several close friends to substantiate your claim that you are gainfully employed and planning marriage."

Boothe nodded. Good thing he and Emma had kept

their pretense to themselves. Several times she'd begged to be honest with Aunt Ada and Charlotte.

"Can you give me some names of people to contact?"

Boothe named Charlotte, Aunt Ada, Pastor Douglas and the residents of the boardinghouse.

"I'll take care of things. We should know in a couple weeks how the judge will rule."

Cold sweat trickled down Boothe's spine. He'd done everything he could. Yet he still felt like his hands were tied with cords of steel. "Is there a chance he'll rule in their favor?"

Ashby sighed. "I wish I could say no but I can't with certainty. If your brother-in-law hears of the accident and your son's injuries, he might use it against you."

Boothe jolted to his feet. "How could I be blamed for that?"

Ashby pulled on the cuffs of his suit coat. "I hope you won't be. Not even by insinuation. Now leave this to me, and I'll get the papers prepared and off. That's about all we can do."

Boothe strode from the office, his insides on fire. He couldn't lose Jessie. Yet what more could he do? He needed a miracle.

He slowed. Pastor Douglas said no one deserved a miracle yet God still sent them. Boothe turned in the direction of the church and slipped into the icy interior. He perched on a pew near the front ignoring how the cold wood bit into the back of his legs. For the first time in over two years, he poured out his needs to God.

A few minutes later, he left the building resolved to do his part and trust God to do His. Boothe's number one concern was Jessie. He would do whatever it took to keep his son and see him well and strong and happy.

Emma was necessary both for Jessie remaining with Boothe and for his healing and happiness.

Which meant he had to keep Emma in his life for however long it took. He would hide his love. He would not let her guess how he felt. After her confession about Sid's accident and how she blamed herself, he understood she would never abandon her family. He knew only a breath of regret before he acknowledged his admiration of her dedication. If things were different, he might have been the recipient of that same dedication.

For now he had to get her to promise not to tell anyone their engagement wasn't real.

He returned to the hospital and went directly to her room. Her face bore the ravages of pain. He guessed she'd had her bandages changed. He hurried over and cradled her in his arms.

Emma closed her eyes but not before he saw the way she searched his gaze for something. Whatever it was she wanted—strength, comfort, company—he vowed he would be there to provide it.

He made shushing noises. The same sound he used to comfort Jessie. A tear formed a perfect bead at the edge of her lashes. He stifled a moan and kissed away each drop.

She sniffed. "You don't have to pretend. There's no one here."

"I'm not pretending—" He stopped himself before he uttered forbidden words of love. "To care."

Her eyelids fluttered but she refused to look at him.

He should be grateful because he feared he would not have been successful in hiding his true feelings. He touched her forehead. "You look flushed. I hope you aren't getting a fever."

"I'm fine."

"I've spoken to Ashby. He has to get statements from our friends and Pastor Douglas, affirming we are really and truly engaged. You didn't tell Charlotte the truth, did you?"

He waited. If she had, it would all be for nothing.

She gave a crooked little smile. "I thought of it but no, I didn't say anything." She met his gaze openly. "I have not told anyone the truth."

He didn't want her to go home. It suited him to have her at the hospital so he could pop over from her bedside to Jessie's and back. So he and Emma could sit at Jessie's bedside together.

But she insisted. Dr. Phelps allowed her to return to the boardinghouse after eight days in the hospital. Eight days in which Boothe's opinion of medical personnel was totally and completely revised. He'd seen nothing but genuine care and concern.

Having Emma at home was not as bad as Boothe expected. She had to go to the hospital for daily dressing changes. He went every day and took her in the car Mr. White lent him. Mr. White had been glad to accommodate Boothe's need to spend part of the day with Jessie and let him put in six hours before lunch. Boothe would never have guessed how precious those few minutes together in the car were. Something about the small space created a feeling of intimacy. Emma must have experienced the same thing because she shared flashes of personal information.

"Did I really tell you about Sid?" she asked one day, her voice low, her gaze riveted to her hands.

"You told me about him falling and being hurt."

"He was buried alive."

At the tightness in her voice, he squeezed her shoulder. "No need to blame yourself." He couldn't understand her continuing guilt.

She shrugged away from his touch. "I could have stopped him. He always listened to me. But I didn't want to ruin his fun." She sucked in a whistle of air. "I don't know why I'm even talking about this. I've never told anyone. Not even my parents. I feel bound by my promise to Sid to not tell Mother and Father."

"He was old enough to know how foolish it was."

"I was older."

"Neither of you could have guessed what would happen."

"We'd been warned. I ignored the warnings."

Boothe rubbed the back of his neck. It did nothing to ease the frustration giving him a headache. "Emma, I understand your feeling of responsibility toward your family, but I simply don't buy this burden of guilt."

She gave him a squinty-eyed look. "How would you feel if Jessie had been buried under that building? And you had to stand by helpless to do anything. Stopped by hands stronger than yours?" She didn't give him a chance to answer. Not that he could speak past the pain of imagining such a terrible event. "Exactly. Would you ever be able to forgive yourself for not fighting harder? Not knowing what to do when they pulled him out?" She shuddered. "I will never forget that feeling of helplessness. I will spend the rest of my life making up for it."

He sighed, reached out to touch her but pulled back when she shied away. "I wish you could find healing."

Purposely misunderstanding him, she glanced at her hands. "They're doing well."

"I will pray for you." He laughed at the way she gaped at him. "I discovered how important and alive my faith was when you and Jessie were unconscious. When only God could help, I had no trouble turning to Him." He chuckled again, just because he felt so good and right inside. "I know I don't deserve all His blessings, but you do. I'll pray you'll find exactly what you need."

She harrumphed.

But something developed between them at that moment. A connection as strong as steel, as fragile as spiderwebs.

And after that it became easier to talk of their childhoods. She told hair-raising stories about life in the nurses' residence. They shared bits of their dreams and their frustrations. Yet always, there was a constraint between them. He couldn't be totally honest because he couldn't share the emotion overshadowing all others—his love for her. Several times he came close, but it would be unfair to mention it when she'd made it clear from the beginning there could never be anything between them but pretense.

He could only trust God to bear him through the pain when it came time to end this.

Three weeks after the accident Emma's bandages had come off except for a spot on her right hand. She could finally feed herself. But Dr. Phelps warned she wouldn't be able to go back to work for a few weeks yet. She hated being idle as much as she hated being dependent on others, but her biggest concern was her family. She would have no wages to send them this month.

She'd had Charlotte write them a letter explaining her accident.

Boothe brought the mail home and handed her a letter.

She opened it and read Mother's usual weather report. "Wind. More wind. Some snow." Then, "The government wants to buy our land and the surrounding farms to create a wildlife preserve. Father is anxious to sign the deal. We will get enough money to buy a house in town. Father thinks he will be able to find work once the Depression ends. We'll be able to manage without your wages. Now you can begin your own life with Boothe and Jessie. What a sweet boy.

"We have a little house picked out. The one behind the general store. It's much like our home. We figure if we move all our stuff, and arranged it the same way it will seem like home to Sid." Emma knew the house, tucked away behind businesses and between two bigger houses. It did have a familiar design to it. *Lord, help Sid adjust to this move.*

She folded the pages of the letter and returned it to the envelope. She was free. She could dream of a future. Her engagement didn't have to be pretend.

Boothe sat across from her reading a letter. Suddenly he whooped.

Emma jumped.

"The judge ruled in my favor. Vera and Luke cannot have Jessie. Yahoo!"

Emma was glad for Jessie and Boothe but didn't feel up to cheering. This meant the pretending was over.

He dropped the letter and pulled his chair to her side. He took her wrist and turned her hands over to examine them carefully. They were reddened and scarred, and she wanted to hide them. But she let them remain in his palms wondering what he saw, what he wanted.

Still clasping her hands gently, he looked into her eyes. "Emma, I know this is as far as our agreement goes. You've played along very well and I thank you. That's twice I owe my son to you."

She watched him without speaking. In his mind it was always about Jessie.

"I have one more request. It's a lot to ask but…" He paused then rushed on. "Can we still be engaged?"

Her breath stuck somewhere behind her heart as she waited, trying to think what he meant. Did he intend to tell her he wanted more real and less pretend?

"Jessie will be in the hospital a few more weeks. He looks forward to your visits so much. I fear how it would set him back if we told him the truth now. So can we continue as we are a while longer?"

She wanted so much more than pretense. From the first time she saw him across the street, she'd had this impossible dream. Impossible because of her family. Now perhaps—just perhaps—it was possible. Or maybe she was jumping to conclusions. She didn't know if the sale of the farm would net her parents enough to live on. And Sid was still Sid. He'd need care the rest of his life.

Yes, there were still a lot of uncertainties, but there was no reason she couldn't pretend a bit longer.

He mistook her hesitation for not wanting to continue their relationship. "Has it been so hard to be engaged to me?"

No. And that was the problem. It grew increasingly harder to remind herself it wasn't real. Since the accident, Boothe had changed. It was easy for her to think his care was sincere. But it was only about Jessie. "You'll have to tell him the truth at some point."

"I will. When he's stronger."

"All right. We can pretend a bit longer."

He rose slowly. "Good."

Well, she must say he didn't sound happy even though it was his idea.

But over the next days she didn't mind the pretense. They continued to visit Jessie at the hospital. Together they helped him with his lessons and did their best to amuse him. He chafed at being stuck in bed, but on the whole, he did well. She reminded herself over and over that the continued engagement was for Jessie's sake. But she didn't deceive herself. She wanted a few more days of this relationship, too. Even pretend was better than nothing.

Another letter came from home.

"Sid is very happy living in our new house. He's started to go out. I think the closeness of the other buildings makes him feel safe. Last week, he got a job working at the store. He stocks shelves and sweeps and cleans. He seems to be improving right before our eyes."

Emma folded away the letter. Thankfully Boothe was not home and could not see her happy smile and perhaps ask its cause. She hurried upstairs to her room and fell on her knees. *Lord, God, this is such wonderful news. More than I could ever think to ask or dream. Sid working and improving. Thank You a hundred times over.* She rested her forehead on her hands and sorted through the thoughts tickling at the edges of her mind.

For the first time in eight years, she had no one who

needed her, no one who depended on her. Sid was growing up, becoming independent. She should be happier.

She loved Jessie. Wanted to be part of his life for a long time, not just until his leg healed.

She loved Boothe. But he would no longer need her.

Boothe and Jessie belonged here. Perhaps Boothe would take over the boardinghouse. Pain shafted through her. It would have driven her to her knees if she wasn't already there. She couldn't imagine seeing him day after day, continually hiding her love. She had to move on. Somehow. Somewhere. She'd stopped looking for another job since her accident, but now it was time to proceed with that plan. Yes, that's what she'd do.

She buried her face in her hands. She didn't cry. Her sorrow went too deep for tears. It scalded a place all it's own deep in her heart. The wound would never heal. The pain would never die.

"Lord, only with Your help can I move on. Send Your strength and healing into my heart. And if it is Your will..." She could hardly bring herself to pray the words. "Let Boothe see me as more than someone to help Jessie. Help him see me as someone to love."

She remained on her knees for a long time, pouring out her heart to God, encouraged by Scripture verses that came to mind. Peace filled her heart. God was faithful even when His people did foolish things.

She rose, tidied her hair and went downstairs to help Ada finish supper.

A smile curved her lips as Betty and Sarah came in. It remained firmly in place when Ed and Don returned from work. It faltered only slightly when Boothe hurried in from his stay at the hospital. Emma had been there earlier and left him helping Jessie with homework.

"Jessie hoped you'd come back," Boothe said, his voice more curious than scolding.

"I needed to take care of a few things."

He nodded, waiting, his gaze inquiring.

She didn't provide any more details. Soon he would know nothing of what she did while she would wonder every minute what he and Jessie were doing; how they were feeling.

"I'll go in and read to him at bedtime."

She hoped to go by herself. She wanted to walk. She needed to start pulling back from this relationship, but when she went for her coat, Boothe hurried to join her. She could hardly tell him not to come, but he did agree to walk rather than drive.

The night was so still that she could hear the crack of cold. Acrid coal smoke drifted to her from the house they passed. Gold light poured out of the windows and patched the ground before them.

"You're different," Boothe said.

"Oh? Different than what?" Was it possible he sensed her withdrawal from him?

He paused in a spot of light and studied her. "Has something happened?"

Her heart gave a mighty kick. *Tell him. Tell him about the sale of the farm. About Sid getting a job. Tell him how you really and truly feel about him.*

But her pride forbade it. He'd been clear about what this engagement was. Never had he uttered so much as one word to indicate he'd changed his mind. She'd spare them both the embarrassment of pouring out her feelings.

"I suppose I'm anxious to get back to work." That part was completely true.

He didn't pressure her for more details. In fact, he seemed unusually quiet as they went up the steps into the hospital. Perhaps he wondered how he would tell Jessie the truth when this was over.

She stumbled.

Boothe grabbed her, steadied her. "You all right?"

"Just slipped." Her whole world tilted. How would she say goodbye to Jessie? How did you forget a child you'd grown to love?

Two bittersweet days later, Emma struggled to capture her emotions and lock them into carefully guarded drawers. It was proving a difficult task. She ached every minute she couldn't be with Boothe and Jessie and began to look forward to the end so she could move on. Surely it would be easier to deal with her feelings if she didn't have to face them every day.

Today she purposely arrived at the hospital while Boothe was still at work. She checked Jessie's arithmetic questions and tried to get him to concentrate on his reading.

"My leg is almost better."

"I know. You've done so well. Can you read this page to me?"

He glanced at the reader and as quickly looked back at her. "Miss Emma, when are we going to be a real family?"

Emma tapped the reader. "Schoolwork, young man." No way was she going to lie to this child, promise him things she couldn't deliver. But neither did she plan to be the one to tell him the truth. That would fall on Boothe's shoulders.

Jessie's glance darted past Emma. "Daddy."

Good. Let Boothe deal with these questions.

Boothe squeezed Emma's shoulder and smiled at her. She took that touch and that glance, unlocked the secret drawer and slid them inside. She would not throw away the key yet. She'd allow herself the pleasure of examining a few memories when things got too hard to bear.

Boothe held out a parcel. "For Mr. Jessie Wallace. Someone has sent you a present."

"First time I got real mail."

Emma recognized Mother's handwriting then Jessie tore open the package.

"A coloring book." He flipped through the pages. "Just what I always wanted."

"There's a letter, too." Boothe handed him the page that fell from the wrappings.

"It's from Sid." He showed the letter to them.

Emma's eyes stung. To her knowledge, Sid had never written a thing since his accident.

"Help me read it," Jessie said.

Emma waited for Boothe to do so but he nodded at her. Through the sheen of tears she read:

dr jse
I sen yu this bok. Hop yu lik it. I hav job at stor. I ern mony. I lik it. we sel frm and liv in nu hus in toun. I lik it vry muc. Whn I see yu gain?
Luv Sid

Emma faltered and swallowed hard.

Jessie took the letter. "I like Sid. When can we see him again?"

"They've moved?" Boothe sounded angry. "Sid is working?" His voice deepened.

He moved away, went to the other side of the bed. His gaze seared her skin. She couldn't, wouldn't look at him. He had no reason to be angry. Their agreement did not include promising to share every detail of their lives. Even as she thought it, her heart denied it. Not because of any promise but because every corner of her wayward heart wanted to belong to Boothe—her secrets, her fears, her dreams and most of all, each and every beat for the rest of her life.

Chapter Fifteen

Boothe's stomach boiled with acid. The one thing he'd admired in Emma, counted on, was she could be trusted. How wrong could he be? Her parents had sold the farm and moved to town and she didn't think it bore mentioning? And now Sid had a job? Why hadn't she told him?

Because hiding behind her parents' and Sid's needs had become her protection against feeling anything real.

She couldn't have made it any plainer that she didn't want anything but pretense between them. Well, no more of it. From here on out it was honesty.

Jessie was strong enough to deal with the truth.

His anger abated. Jessie would be hurt.

Boothe stiffened his spine. He had no one but himself to blame, but he'd do it all over again if that's what it took to keep his son.

He admired Jessie's coloring book. He hoped he responded correctly to questions and comments. Emma, gratefully, had sense enough to be quiet.

He could hardly wait to get her alone and confront her.

"I'll give you a ride," he said, when it came time to leave.

"I don't mind walking."

"The car is here." His tone must have conveyed he would stand no argument. She meekly put on her coat and accompanied him to the automobile.

He waited until she settled in the seat beside him then faced her. "When did you plan to tell me your news?"

"Exactly what news do you mean?" Her eyes warned him she wouldn't be bullied.

"Did your folks sell the farm?"

She nodded.

"And Sid has a job?"

Another nod but not a hint of regret for not relaying this news.

He softened his voice, hoping it would have more effect. "Why didn't you tell me?"

"What difference does it make? Jessie is about to be discharged. Our pretense is about to end. I am applying for a job in North Dakota. I doubt we'll see each other again."

She said it with such hard certainty that it made him want to grind his teeth and spit out fragments.

"You didn't say anything because you no longer have anything to hide behind."

She quirked an eyebrow.

"Sid has always been your protection against letting yourself care about anyone. Now what excuse will you use? To think I felt sympathy for your plight. I prayed God would provide a way out for you." His snort of laughter was self-mocking. "Don't look so surprised. Yes, I prayed."

"Then it seems God has answered your prayers."

The fury left him. He leaned over the steering wheel. "Somehow I thought it would feel better."

"Really. What did you expect would happen? Why did you pray?"

He'd prayed so he would be free to love Emma. She obviously didn't feel the same way or she wouldn't have hidden this news. The acid returned to his stomach and burned like wildfire. "I wanted you to be free of your guilt and responsibility. But I see you never will be. You'll just find something else to become your shining badge of 'ought.'"

She opened the door. "I think I prefer to walk home in the fresh air." She stepped out and shut the door quietly but firmly.

He let her go. He couldn't deal with his raging emotions. He drove away, heading the opposite direction of the boardinghouse. He needed time to think.

He'd been so noble. Honored her commitment to her family. Poured out his affection without once admitting his love. Surely she had seen how hard it was to keep back the words.

Cold seeped through his bones, cooled his marrow. His anger died. He turned the car around and headed back. As he passed the church, he pulled over and stopped.

When all else fails, turn to God.

Jesus never fails.

God, You answered my prayer to relieve Emma of her responsibilities. And here I am angry about it. You know that isn't the reason I'm so upset, though.

Why was he so angry?

Because his trust had been shattered.

But had it?

What reason did Emma have to share her news with him? They'd both agreed this engagement was only until Jessie was better.

God, I'm in a pickle here. I don't want to lose her. How do I show her I want to make this real?

He had to start over. They'd break off this farce, and then he would court her for real. He'd show her how much he cared.

Back at the boardinghouse, he took a deep breath and held it until he felt in control. For a few more days he had to keep his love hidden. Just until Jessie got home. There'd be no more need for pretending. Then he'd show Emma how much he loved her.

He went inside. Emma stood in front of the stove, helping Aunt Ada with supper. Aunt Ada looked tired. Boothe tried to do as much as he could to help, but with Jessie in the hospital…

He would start over on a number of levels as soon as Jessie was discharged. It would take all his self-control to keep his feelings hidden until then, but he was determined to do this right.

Today was the day. Jessie was getting out of traction. Boothe wanted to be present for it, but Dr. Phelps said he didn't want a parent hanging about. So he put in his short day at work, forcing himself to do each chore carefully while his insides curled and knotted and twisted. Today he would take Jessie home. Today he would tell the truth about his engagement to Emma— that he didn't want it to end. And then he could begin his honest, heartfelt courtship of Emma. He closed his eyes and allowed himself to think of the pleasure of taking her for long walks, telling her all the things he had stored in his heart.

He yanked on his coat and hat and hurried to the hospital. He rushed into the children's ward and jerked to a stop. Jessie seemed so small without his leg suspended, without pulleys. He barely made a bump under the covers.

Boothe wanted to scoop his son into his arms and hold him like he hadn't been able to since the accident. He moved closer, saw Jessie's face wet with tears and was at his side in three strides. "What's wrong? Did it hurt? What can I do?"

"Not my leg," Jessie choked out.

"Then what? Tell me and I'll fix it."

"You can't."

"I'll try."

Jessie rolled his head back and forth.

Boothe wondered what had upset him. Was it just a reaction to knowing he could go home? "I thought Emma would be here." Dr. Phelps had said she could come in as soon as the traction was removed.

"She was." Jessie's voice wobbled, and a fresh flood of tears slid down his cheeks.

Boothe grabbed a hankie and wiped away the moisture. "Did she have to go somewhere?"

Jessie nodded and sucked in a noisy gulp of air. "She's gone."

"She'll be back."

"No. She said she wouldn't."

Bony fingers clawed up Boothe's spine. "What do you mean? Where's she gone?"

"She went home. She said you would explain."

Home? She'd left? Without a word? How could he tell her how he felt now?

Jessie gave Boothe a look rife with accusation then let out a gusty wail. He choked out a hiccuped sentence. "I want Emma back."

So do I, son. So do I. Boothe glanced at the clock on the end wall. "She's going on the afternoon train?"

"Ye-es"

"I'll persuade her to stay. I'll have to leave you here while I go get her. Are you okay?"

Jessie's expression brightened. "You'll get her?"

"If I hurry."

"You tell her to come back. You tell her I want her to be my mommy." Suddenly he narrowed his eyes. "You tell her I love her."

Boothe chuckled. "I'll be sure to tell her." And he'd tell her for himself, too.

He hurried from the room. He had just enough time to catch the train before it left.

Dr. Phelps stopped him in the hall. "Jessie did very well. Like I said, he'll have to work up to full activity gradually. But as long as he's careful—"

"Doc, I gotta go. I'll talk to you when I get back."

Dr. Phelps's mouth dropped open as Boothe rushed out the door.

Boothe headed for the train station, his heart ticking away each departing second. He had to make it—

"No." He braked. A wagon had tipped over on the ice, blocking the road. Half a dozen men struggled to untangle the horse. Several more worked to right the wagon and reload the goods.

He couldn't wait. Even as he turned the automobile around, he heard the train whistle. Ignoring the surprised glances of people he almost ran down, he drove as fast as he could for the railway.

He rounded the corner. The caboose was several hundred yards down the tracks. He dismissed the need to go to the station, turned a sharp left and raced after the train. It pulled farther away with every puff of smoke. Boothe slowed for a man crossing the street with a loaded wheelbarrow. Then a woman waddled across, her arms overflowing with parcels. The train pulled farther and farther away. He would never catch it. Why had he not told Emma how he felt? Why had he thought it made sense to wait?

Lord, I am so dense sometimes. Please give me another chance with her, and I promise I will be completely honest. I love her. Suddenly, he laughed. God had sent this woman into his life. She was exactly what both Jessie and he needed. God help him, he only hoped he hadn't ruined his chances with her.

He returned to the hospital.

Jessie pushed up on his elbows and looked past Boothe. "Where is she?"

"I missed the train."

Jessie fell back. "You let her go. You're mad at her. That's why she was sad."

"She was?" His heart beat a little more smoothly thinking she might regret her decision to leave.

"She pretended she wasn't but I could tell."

He knew what he had to do. "I'm going to catch the next train. It isn't until morning." The early train he and Jessie had taken to accompany Emma home for Christmas. "It means you'll have to stay here for another day or two while I go to her."

Jessie grinned. "I don't mind so long as you bring her back."

Boothe nodded. He only hoped Emma would give him another chance. Somehow he would convince her how much he loved her. He'd beg on hands and knees if he had to.

It's over. It's over. Every clack of the tracks reverberated with the words.

Emma forced her attention to the passing scenery though she couldn't have reported one detail of what she saw. She'd known from the beginning that this day would come. But she could never have imagined the way her insides writhed with pain, the way her brain felt fragile and brittle, nor the way her limbs turned to wooden foreign objects.

Yet it was time to move on. No matter how difficult.

She'd visit her family. See their new home. Make sure they really and truly were doing well and didn't need her.

Her throat tightened so she couldn't even swallow the tears clogging it. Her family didn't need her. Boothe no longer needed her. Jessie would soon enough forget her. She didn't even have a job. She'd left a letter on her matron's desk informing her of her resignation effective immediately. She hoped an opening in North Dakota would work out. Until then...

God, I don't know where I belong. Nor what You want me to do. Show me. Guide me.

She settled her thoughts on God's faithfulness and let peace seep through her body, easing her mind and relaxing her limbs.

I love Boothe. I wish it were mutual.

The train pulled in to the Banner station and she climbed down, her bag in hand. The rest of her things remained back at Ada's boardinghouse. She'd send for them as soon as she had a job.

"Come to see how your folks is doing?" Mr. Boushee called when he saw her. "I was some surprised when they decided to move into town. Heard they got a nice price for that farm. And Sid. Well, who ever expected him to be so useful? Best thing ever happened to him was getting off that farm. You run along now and see for yourself." He waved her toward the street.

Emma hurried away glad the man hadn't asked questions. She had no answers to give anyone. Not even herself.

She crossed the street and went down a block then stopped before the house Dad had purchased. It felt strange to think this was home now.

She took a deep strengthening breath and headed for the door, eased it open and called, "Mother, Father?"

Mother hurried into the hallway. "Emma. What a surprise."

"You're the ones full of surprises. Not a hint that you might be wanting to sell."

Mother fluttered her hands. "It all happened so suddenly. We didn't have time to tell anyone. It was unexpected though we'd heard rumors about the wildlife preserve." She took Emma's coat and hung it in the closet.

"Show me the house."

It was a house very like the one on the farm—a big comfortable kitchen, a small orderly front room, a small room that served as a sewing room and storage. Upstairs, four bedrooms. One had her familiar things. Yet it didn't feel familiar. She stood in the doorway looking at the quilt that had been on her bed as long as she remembered and let an ache wrap around her heart and flood through her veins. Emma didn't belong here. She didn't know where she belonged.

"Come to the kitchen and I'll make tea," Mother said.

"Where's Dad?" Emma followed her down the stairs and into the kitchen, full of furniture from the farm that she'd known all her life. But it all felt different.

"Well, that's another piece of unexpected good news. You know how he's always been good with numbers?" Mother waited for Emma's nod. "The government agency needed someone to keep track of the transactions on behalf of the preserve. They practically begged your father to do it." Mother shook her head, her face wreathed in disbelief. "We never expected things to turn out this way. We thought we'd have to stay on the farm for Sid's sake. This is so much better." She took a long breath. "God is good."

Emma nodded. "I can't believe Sid has a job. Does he really go on his own? What does he do?"

"He'll be home soon, and he'll tell you all about it. In fact, he'll probably want to take you tomorrow and show you what he does. Mr. MacKenzie says he's a great help and always so pleasant."

Emma couldn't remember the last time she'd seen her mother so animated.

As soon as they'd finished tea, Mother took her to the sewing room. "I'm making a quilt from the old trousers and things I sorted out at the farm."

"Mother, you haven't made a quilt since…" Since Sid's accident.

"Seems like we're all finding ways to start over."

"I'm so glad." They looked through the stacks of old clothes, Mother all the time talking about the different quilt tops she could make. Then Emma helped Mother prepare supper.

"Here comes Sid."

Emma hurried to the window. Sid crossed the backyard, swinging his arms. His lips moved. She leaned closer to the pane. "Is he singing?"

Mother laughed softly, pleased. "He sings every day as he walks to and from his job."

"He isn't afraid?" Since his accident, Sid had been afraid of the outdoors.

"He says it's like being inside, the buildings are so close."

"Who'd have thought things would turn out like this?"

"It restores my faith in God."

"Me, too." If God provided for Sid and her parents in ways none of them had ever dreamed of, she could trust Him to do the same for her. *Lord, God, I don't know what You have in mind for me, but I thrust myself into Your care. Guide me into what's next in my life.*

Sid hurried in, still singing, hung his coat and hat. Emma waited and watched from the kitchen door. He saw her and rushed to give her a hug, swinging her off her feet. "Emma, I got a job." He put her down and grinned so wide his ears wiggled.

"I heard. Good for you."

"Yes, good for me. Mr. Mac says I'm his best helper ever."

"I'm sure you are." She blinked back tears at the change in Sid.

Her father returned. He walked more sprightly than

he had in years. She could only guess that the farmwork had taken its toll day after day, and now he no longer had that strain, his joints felt better.

Despite her sorrow at having left Boothe and Jessie, Emma rejoiced along with Sid and her parents that evening. "This is how I remember our family," she said later after they'd shared tea and cookies and Dad had read the Bible aloud.

"I remember, too," Sid said. He pushed to his feet. "I'm going to bed. Need my rest to work tomorrow." They heard him singing in his bedroom.

Emma's pleasure at his happiness was marred by the talk she planned to have with her parents.

She waited until Sid called good-night. "Mother, Dad, before you go to bed, there is something I must tell you. It's time I told you the truth." She intended to clear the slate tonight. From this day onward, she would live with no guilty secrets. "I deceived you about Boothe and I being engaged. I did it to make sure Boothe was able to keep Jessie." She explained the situation. "That's over now. The judge ruled in Boothe's favor."

"I'm sorry," Dad said. "He seemed like a good man. I thought he truly cared for you."

Emma nodded, unable to speak for a moment. She sent a prayer for help. "I haven't been honest about something else." She sucked in air that seemed to go no farther than her nose. "Sid's accident."

Mother shook her head. "That's in the past."

"No. I have to tell you the whole story. It's my fault." She told every awful, painful detail. "I'm sorry," she choked out. "I should have stopped him." She hung her head, unable to face the disappointment she knew would be in both her parents' eyes.

"Emma." Father's soft, gentle voice drove her sorrow deeper. They'd endured so many years of hardship because of her neglect. "Emma, we knew what happened."

Her head went up like someone had jerked on a set of reins. Mother nodded. "We've always known Sid disobeyed us."

"I should have stopped him."

Mother gave a short laugh. "Do you really think he would have listened to you? Have you forgotten what a headstrong boy he was?"

"That's why you instructed me to watch out for him." She'd failed miserably.

"No. No." Dad sounded sad. "We didn't expect you to feel responsible for the choices he made. We only meant for you to caution him and try to persuade him to tame that wild spirit of his. Emma, we never once blamed you for Sid's accident. It pains me to think you blamed yourself. You have been the most dutiful daughter one could ask for. We're just so happy that we no longer need your help. You can get on with your own life."

Her parents didn't feel comfortable with expressing their emotions, but tonight she needed healing that could be wrought from their touches and words. She rushed to them, knelt between them and laid her head in Mother's lap. Mother made hushing noises and stroked her hair. Dad patted her back.

"Child, it's time for us all to move on. Thank the good Lord for providing us a way."

A sob rolled up Emma's throat. She captured it on the back of her tongue and held it there even though it threatened to choke her. She would not cry. She would not take one bit of pleasure from this new beginning for her parents and Sid. If it felt like the end of the world to her, she wouldn't let anyone know. She would trust God.

"It's time to forget the past and look to the future."

Emma let her father's words sift through her thoughts. "Boothe and I had an agreement—our engagement was only pretend until the court date was over." She shuddered. "I guess I forgot to pretend." She sat back on her heels and lifted her twisted face to her parents. "I fell in love with him. Starting over is going to be difficult."

"Emma, I am sorry for your pain." Dad gripped her shoulder. "But even this is not beyond God's help. Perhaps Boothe feels the same way."

Emma shook her head. "He was very honest. This was only about Jessie." She pushed to her feet. "I'm so glad things have turned out well for you and Sid." She wanted to escape to her room. God would help and sustain her. She believed all the right things. If only it would erase the pain. "Good night." She managed to get the words out without any tears escaping.

The sun shone bright, mocking Emma's emotions. She'd spent a restless night struggling to come to grips with her feelings. In the end, she'd fallen asleep exhausted and wakened too weary to think past the next few minutes.

She'd gone with Sid to his job, amazed at his confidence in walking the distance from home to the store. It would seem an insignificant thing to most people but for him to cross the yard and the alley to the back entrance of the store was a major step. When she asked him how he did it, he said Jessie had told him how. "Just don't look." Her throat had clogged at his words.

At the store, he showed her his tasks, amazing her with his confidence and pride. Mr. MacKenzie seemed genuinely pleased with Sid's work. "Once I show him what I want done, he never misses. I like a man I can count on."

Sid stood taller at the praise. "I always do what you say." He grabbed the broom. "I go clean the steps now."

Emma left him to his work. Rather than return home immediately, she decided to wander the main street of Banner hoping the fresh air would clear her thoughts. Spring was ready to burst forth, but somehow she found no joy in the fact. No anticipation. Nothing but empty dread. She gave herself a mental shake. She needed to get another job. That would give her something to focus on.

She jerked to a stop and stared at the man striding out of the hotel dining room. Boothe? How could that be possible? Had her mind conjured up the very person she'd been thinking about?

She tore her gaze away, let her eyes adjust to the bright sunshine as she stared across the street and focused on the sign above the mercantile store. She slowly allowed her gaze to return to the man adjusting his hat in front of the hotel. "Boothe?"

He turned. His eyes widened. "Emma."

He closed the distance between them in long hurried strides. "I came on the early morning train."

"Why?"

"You didn't say goodbye."

"Was it necessary?" He'd come all this way just to say goodbye?

His eyes grew dark and shadowed as if her words had disappointed him. And then he seemed to find purpose and he smiled so gently, so softly, it brought a sudden glut of tears to the back of her throat.

"It's such a lovely day. Let's walk." He pulled her hand around his arm and pressed her fingers to his forearm. For a moment, his hand lingered on hers.

She allowed herself to enjoy the comfort of his closeness then lifted her chin. She could say goodbye if that's what he wanted. And she could then pick up the pieces of her life and move on—with God's help, His everlasting arms beneath her and the shelter of His wings above.

They walked past stores so familiar to Emma that she didn't need to glance at any sign to know what they sold. The street was short; the selection of businesses were limited, many of them boarded up. Banner was a town struggling for survival. They came to the end of the street and faced the empty prairie.

Emma's heart shriveled inside her chest. She couldn't face the emptiness of the landscape on top of the emptiness of her heart.

Boothe rested gentle hands on her shoulders and turned her to face him.

She couldn't meet his gaze knowing she would be unable to hide her feelings. He'd see. He'd guess.

But he caught her chin with a long, gentle finger and lifted her head.

She closed her eyes, felt moisture clinging to her lashes.

He brushed a fingertip across each closed eye. "You're crying. Why?"

A breath shivered into her lungs. She held it and prayed for strength to endure this final goodbye. "So many things have happened. Sid and Dad both have jobs." Her voice refused to work and she sniffed.

Boothe's finger lingered on her cheek and traveled to her chin. "I'm glad things are working out for them. And you, I suppose." He cleared his throat. "Emma, I think it's time for a little honesty between us."

She jerked open her eyes.

"I mean about our feelings for each other. Or at least my true feelings about you."

Her lungs, her heart, her mind all stopped functioning.

"Emma, I want a chance to start over. To court you like you deserve. To show you I love you."

A distant ticking in her ears warned her she needed to breathe soon or risk fainting. She sucked in air redolent with spring and ringing with the songs of larks and robins.

"Emma, tell me I haven't waited too long." His voice rang with urgency. "Tell me there's a chance you might learn to care for me."

She blinked, tried to find the words to say to express the joy that grew with each beat of her heart. She laughed for the sheer volume of it. "Boothe, if you only knew how hard it's been for me to keep up the pretense of our engagement."

Lines in his face deepened.

She couldn't stand to see him so uncertain, so ready to be hurt. "Boothe, I've loved you since I first saw you."

"I was quite rude. I'm sorry."

"I don't mean when we met in the boardinghouse. I saw you outside. When you bent over and touched Jessie with such tenderness, I knew you were the sort of man I'd dreamed about—tender, able to express your feelings."

He looked so relieved that she wanted to hug him. But as suddenly as his expression had softened, it grew hard again. "I blamed nurses and doctors for Alyse's death. All of them. I was angry and had to blame someone. But after seeing how efficient and caring most of them are, I realized I can't brand them all because of one error. I pray that pair has learned their lesson, but I've forgiven them." He trailed his gaze over her face until she knew she glowed from it. "And one special nurse proved to be so stubborn, so principled, so loving and giving—is it any wonder I asked you to marry me?"

"It was for Jessie."

"It was. But I didn't mind having an excuse."

"And now?"

He chuckled. "I need no excuse. I love you. From your lovely thick hair that you insist on hiding to your giving heart to your practical nature. Say it again."

She knew exactly what he meant. "I love you, Boothe Wallace. For today and all my tomorrows." At the look of sheer wonder on his face, she vowed she would tell him often.

"Emma, I love you so much I can't think there will be enough tomorrows to allow me to show it but I will try."

He lowered his head and kissed her.

She thought it was a good way to start showing his love.

Epilogue

Emma raced to pull the burning cookies from the oven. She scooped them off the cookie tray, decided they were too bad to salvage and tossed them in the garbage.

She had to pay closer attention to what she was doing instead of staring out the window watching for Boothe to come home.

She glanced at the clock. Had it stopped? She cocked her head. No. She could hear it ticking. She went into the front room to check the mantel clock. It said the same time.

She returned to the kitchen and dropped cookie dough onto another tray. This time she would stand in front of the oven until they were done.

She forced herself to think about all the good changes she'd been privy to rather than think of the future.

She and Boothe had married a year ago. She loved him more with each day. And he found delightful ways of showing his love for her. He found little gifts for her, brought her bunches of wildflowers, but what she enjoyed most was how he touched her so often. Brushing her hair off her shoulders was the touch she loved the most. She chuckled. She'd finally given in and let her hair hang loose. She'd cut it to mid length so it was more manageable. She loved how Boothe squeezed her shoulder in passing, pressed his hand to the small of her back as they went into a room, how he rested his hand over hers when he read the Bible at supper. She loved those little gestures that said so much more to her than the words.

She checked the cookies again—not quite done—and closed the oven door.

Aunt Ada had insisted Boothe and Emma take over the boardinghouse.

"Loretta and I have had our eyes on that little house next door. Now we can both sit back and enjoy our rocking chairs."

Emma chuckled. Didn't seem to her either of them spent much time in their rocking chairs. They'd made a trip east to visit Aunt Ada's childhood home. They'd spent a few weeks in Victoria, British Columbia, and returned full of praise for the genteel British way of life. And they'd organized a knitting group to make blankets and mittens for the less fortunate.

She pulled the cookies from the oven and filled the kettle with water to make tea. Boothe had promised to be home early today. Mr. White was so good about letting Boothe take time off when he needed to, and today he wanted to be home before Jessie.

She heard his step at the door and hurried to greet him.

He swung her into a long delicious hug then leaned back to look into her eyes. "You're glowing."

"I'm so happy. It's finally happened. We are going

to have a baby." It had been the one disappointment to their marriage—her inability to conceive. Until now.

He hugged her again. "I can hardly wait to share a child with you."

She wrinkled her nose. "What do you call Jessie? A pet dog?"

He laughed. "No. He's my pride and joy."

"Mine, too."

"I won't love him any less, but this baby will be the product of our love."

"I could never love Jessie more, but I know what you mean. Do you think he'll be pleased?"

They heard him calling to his friends as he returned from school.

"I think he'll be very happy."

Jessie gave them both a questioning look as he stepped inside. He must have wondered why his father was home and why they grinned like kids on Christmas morning. He'd grown so much. And he seemed content.

"Let's have tea and cookies," Emma said. She served them each a cup, making Jessie's mostly milk.

She sent Boothe a silent message. She couldn't wait.

Boothe held his cup between his hands. "Jessie, we have some news for you."

Jessie stiffened. Emma understood he was still a little fearful that things would change on him.

"We are going to have a baby."

His eyes widened. His mouth rounded. He looked from Boothe to Emma. "A baby?"

"A brother or sister for you," Emma said.

"He'll be your baby, right?"

Emma shook her head. "He'll be *our* baby." She

pulled Jessie to her. "Someone for us all to love. Just like we love you and always will."

He nodded. "When is he going to be born?"

"It might be a girl."

Jessie waited.

"About Christmastime."

Jessie whooped and laughed. "Just what I wanted."

Boothe and Emma exchanged puzzled looks and then Emma recalled the first Christmas concert when they'd been together, she and Boothe pretending to be engaged, both already in love with the other but afraid to admit it. Thankfully they'd eventually eliminated the pretense. "You asked for a Christmas baby."

Jessie nodded then Boothe wrapped his arms around Emma and Jessie.

"I have been blessed beyond measure," he said. "Thanks be to God."

Emma, her voice muffled by being squished between the other two, managed to say, "His blessings are beyond comprehension."

* * * * *

SPECIAL EXCERPT FROM

Love Inspired® **HISTORICAL**

*When Bethany Zook's childhood friend returns to Amish
country a widower, with an adorable little girl in tow,
she'll help him any way she can. But there's just one
thing Andrew Yoder needs—a mother for little Mari.
And he's convinced a marriage of convenience to
Bethany is the perfect solution.*

Read on for a sneak preview of
Convenient Amish Proposal *by Jan Drexler
available February 2019 from Love Inspired Historical!*

Andrew shifted Mari in his arms. She had laid her head on his
shoulder and her eyes were nearly closed. "I hope you weren't
embarrassed by the man thinking that the three of us are a
family."

Bethany felt her face heat, but with her bonnet on it was
easy to avoid Andrew's gaze. *Ja*, the man's comment had been
embarrassing, but only because she felt like they had misled
him. Being mistaken for Andrew's wife and Mari's mother
made her feel like she was finally where she belonged.

"Not embarrassed as much as ashamed that he thought
something that was untrue."

Andrew stepped closer to her. "It doesn't have to be untrue.
Have you thought about what I asked you?"

Bethany nodded. She had thought of nothing else since
yesterday afternoon. "Do you think we could have a good
marriage, even in these circumstances?" She looked into
Andrew's eyes. They were open and frank, with no shadows
in the depths.

"You and I have always made a good team." Andrew
glanced at the people walking past them, but no one was paying

attention to their conversation. "I'm asking you to give up a lot, though. If there's someone you've been wanting to marry, you'll lose your chance if you marry me."

"What makes you say that?"

"Dave Zimmer said that he had proposed to you, and so had a couple other fellows, but you turned them down. He thought you were waiting for someone else."

Bethany tilted her head down so that Andrew couldn't see her face. She couldn't explain what kept her from accepting Dave's proposal a few years ago, other than it just hadn't felt right. Being with any man other than Andrew hadn't felt right. No one else offered the easy camaraderie he did, and she had never felt any love for any other man.

She shook her head. "There is no one else."

"Then you'll do it?"

Bethany pressed her lips together to keep back the retort she wanted to make. He made their marriage sound like a business arrangement. She couldn't tie herself to a man who would never love her, could she?

Just then, Mari lifted her head, roused by her uncomfortable position and the noise around them. She turned in Andrew's arms and reached for Bethany. When Bethany took her, the little girl settled in her arms with a sigh and went back to sleep.

If Bethany didn't accept Andrew's proposal, Mari's grandmother would take her back to Iowa, and she would never see her again. She swallowed, her throat tight. And if she didn't accept Andrew's proposal, she would never know the joys of being a mother. Because if she didn't marry Andrew, she would never marry anyone.

"*Ja*, Andrew. I'll do it. I'll marry you."

Don't miss
Convenient Amish Proposal *by Jan Drexler,*
available February 2019 wherever
Love Inspired® Historical books and ebooks are sold.

www.LoveInspired.com

Copyright © 2019 by Jan Drexler

LIHEXP65280

Looking for inspiration in tales
of hope, faith and heartfelt romance?

Check out **Love Inspired®** and
Love Inspired® Suspense books!

New books available every month!

CONNECT WITH US AT:

Facebook.com/groups/HarlequinConnection

Facebook.com/HarlequinBooks

Twitter.com/HarlequinBooks

Instagram.com/HarlequinBooks

Pinterest.com/HarlequinBooks

ReaderService.com

LIGENRE2018R2

SPECIAL EXCERPT FROM

Love Inspired®

Pregnant and abandoned by her Englisher *boyfriend,
Dori Bontrager returns home—but she's determined it'll
be temporary. Can Eli Hochstetler convince her that
staying by his side in their Amish community is just what
she and her baby need?*

Read on for a sneak preview of
Courting Her Prodigal Heart *by Mary Davis,
available January 2019 from Love Inspired!*

Rainbow Girl stepped into his field of vision from the kitchen area. *"Hallo."*

Eli's insides did funny things at the sight of her.

"Did you need something?"

He cleared his throat. "I came for a drink of water."

"Come on in." She pulled a glass out of the cupboard, filled it at the sink and handed it to him.

"Danki."

She gifted him with a smile. *"Bitte.* How's it going out there?"

He smiled back. "Fine." He gulped half the glass, then slowed down to sips. No sense rushing.

After a minute, she folded her arms. "Go ahead. Ask your question."

"What?"

"You obviously want to ask me something. What is it? Why do I color my hair all different colors? Why do I dress like this? Why did I leave? What is it?"

She posed all *gut* questions, but not the one he needed an answer to. A question that was no business of his to ask.

"Go ahead. Ask. I don't mind." Very un-Amish, but she'd offered. *Ne,* insisted.

He cleared his throat. "Are you going to stay?"

She stared for a moment, then looked away. Obviously not the question she'd expected, nor one she wanted to answer.

He'd made her uncomfortable. He never should have asked. What if she said *ne*? Did he want her to say *ja*? "You don't have to tell me." He didn't want to know anymore.

She pinned him with her steady brown gaze. "I don't know. I don't want to, but I'm sort of in a bind at the moment."

Maybe for the reason she'd been so sad the other day, which had made him feel sympathy for her.

He appreciated her honesty. "Then why does our bishop think you are?"

"He's hoping I do."

His heart tightened. "Why are you giving him false hope?" Why was she giving Eli false hope?

"I'm not. I've told him this is temporary. He won't listen. Maybe you could convince him to stop this foolishness—" she waved her hand toward where the building activity was going on "—before it's too late."

He chuckled. "You don't tell the bishop what to do. *He* tells you."

He really should head back outside to help the others. Instead, he filled his glass again and leaned against the counter. He studied her over the rim of his glass. Did he want Rainbow Girl to stay? She'd certainly turned things upside down around here. Turned him upside down. Instead of working in his forge—where he most enjoyed spending time—he was here, and gladly so. He preferred working with iron rather than wood, but today, carpentry strangely held more appeal.

Time to get back to work. He guzzled the rest of his water and set the glass in the sink. *"Danki."* As he turned to leave, something on the table caught his attention. The door knocker he'd made years ago for Dorcas—Rainbow Girl—ne, Dorcas, but now Rainbow Girl had it. They were the same person, but not the same. He crossed to the table and picked up his handiwork. "You kept this?"

She came up next to him. *"Ja.* I liked having a reminder of…"

"Of what?" Dare he hope him?

She stared at him. "Of…my life growing up here."

That was probably a better answer. He didn't need to be thinking of her as anything more than a lost *Englisher*.

Don't miss Courting Her Prodigal Heart *by Mary Davis, available January 2019 wherever Love Inspired® books and ebooks are sold.*

www.LoveInspired.com

Copyright © 2018 by Mary Davis

LIEXP1218

Love Inspired®

**Inspirational Romance to
Warm Your Heart and Soul**

Join our social communities to connect
with other readers who share your love!

Sign up for the Love Inspired newsletter
at **www.LoveInspired.com** to be the
first to find out about upcoming titles,
special promotions and exclusive content.

CONNECT WITH US AT:

Facebook.com/groups/HarlequinConnection

 Facebook.com/LoveInspiredBooks

 Twitter.com/LoveInspiredBks

LISOCIAL2018

SPECIAL EXCERPT FROM

Love Inspired.
SUSPENSE

With a price on his witness's head,
US marshal Jonathan Mast can think of only
one place to hide Celeste Alexander—in the
Amish community he left behind. But will this trip
home save their lives…and convince them that a
Plain life together is worth fighting for?

Read on for a sneak preview of
Amish Hideout by Maggie K. Black,
the exciting beginning to the Amish Witness Protection
miniseries, available January 2019
from Love Inspired Suspense!

Time was running out for Celeste Alexander. Her fingers flew over the keyboard, knowing each keystroke could be her last before US marshal Jonathan Mast arrived to escort her to her new life in the witness protection program.

"You gave her a laptop?" US marshal Stacy Preston demanded. "Please tell me you didn't let her go online."

"Of course not! She had a basic tablet, with the internet capability disabled." US marshal Karl Adams shot back even before Stacy had finished her sentence.

The battery died. She groaned. Well, that was that.

"You guys mind if I go upstairs and get my charging cable?"

The room went black. Then she heard the distant sound of gunfire erupting outside.

"Get Celeste away from the windows!" Karl shouted. "I'll cover the front."

What was happening? She felt Stacy's strong hand on her arm pulling her out of her chair.

"Come on!" Stacy shouted. "We have to hurry—"

Her voice was swallowed up in the sound of an explosion, expanding and roaring around them, shattering the windows, tossing Celeste backward and engulfing the living room in smoke. Celeste hit the floor, rolled and hit a door frame. She crawled through it, trying to get away from the smoke billowing behind her.

Suddenly a strong hand grabbed her out of the darkness, taking her by the arm and pulling her up to her feet so sharply she stumbled backward into a small room. The door closed behind them. She opened her mouth to scream, but a second hand clamped over her mouth. A flashlight flickered on and she looked up through the smoky haze, past worn blue jeans and a leather jacket, to see the strong lines of a firm jaw trimmed with a black beard, a straight nose and serious eyes staring into hers.

"Celeste Alexander?" He flashed a badge. "I'm Marshal Jonathan Mast. Stay close. I'll keep you safe."

Don't miss
Amish Hideout *by Maggie K. Black,*
available January 2019 wherever
Love Inspired® Suspense *books and ebooks are sold.*

www.LoveInspired.com

Copyright © 2018 by Harlequin Books S.A.